BETWEEN
LIFE
&
DEATH

JACLYN KOT

Between Life and Death

Jaclyn Kot

Copyright ©2023 by Jaclyn Kot

Editing by Jessica McKelden

Proofreading by Norma Gambini

Cover design by Fantasy Cover Design

Formatting by Imagine Ink Designs

For those who dare to dream.

Oh, who am I kidding?

For those looking for their next book boyfriend.

EDENVALE

WHISPERING PINES FOREST

OLD NORTHOWAY

MOUNT BRIMSTONE

FISHERMAN'S
PARADISE

LAKE
AZURA

GRASSLANDS OF OLD
NORTHOWAY

BLACK ELK
FOREST

OLDMAN'S RIVER

OLD WESTLAND

GRASSLANDS OF
OLD WESTLAND

THE RIFT

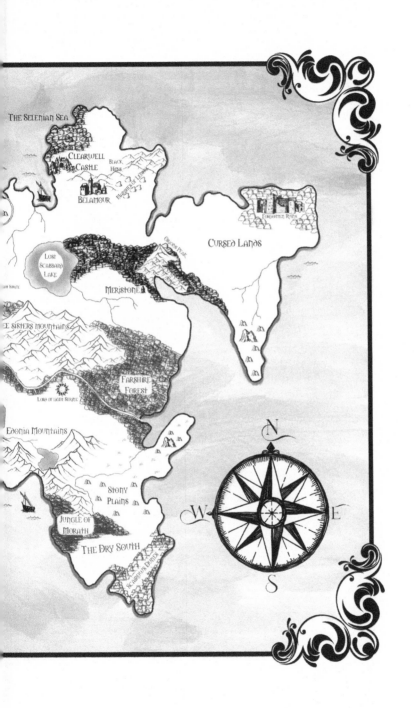

CHAPTER 1

Screams reverberated through dead village streets.

If it were any other day, the downtown core of Meristone would be bustling with the steady thrum of merchants and buyers. Bartering and trading. Exchanging goods for coin. But today was different. The azure sky was stained with crimson banners—waving and flickering, pronouncing the king's claim over these lands.

Not a soul, not one, walked the cobblestone roads of the little village. Most of the villagers had run home, locked themselves up and barricaded their doors. As for the ones who had not, they were standing in the village square—grouped together, frozen by fear, unable to look away. Me included.

Silence gripped at each one of us as we watched the fair-haired girl, not much older than fourteen, be dragged by two armor-clad soldiers towards the pyre. She wore the iron collar, the rusty nails on the underside sunk in like teeth into her pale, delicate flesh. A necklace of dried blood adorned her slender neck, disappearing under the ceremonial white garb they forced her to wear—a cheap piece of cloth—not that the king would spend good coin on something meant to burn.

The king. That is all I referred to him as. Because anyone willing to do this—willing to have such a blatant disregard for human life—they did not deserve to be called by their personal name. Because they were not a person at all. They were a thing. A bloodthirsty figurehead.

A woman, with the same honey-colored hair as the girl, pushed her way through the crowd. She clasped her hands together and fell to her knees, a frantic prayer for mercy falling from her cracked, pale lips. A soldier sporting the eagle crest of the king—talons stretched out, ready for the kill—stalked towards her, his bootheel the answer to her plea.

The girl wailed as she watched the woman crumble to the ground, the heavy blow rendering her unconscious—a merciful state to be in, considering the circumstances. The girl fought against the soldiers' unyielding grips as they strapped her to the wooden stake. She was a rabbit among wolves—the Cursed among the clean.

"Please! Please! I do not bear the Curse!" she cried out as tears raced down her bruised cheeks.

Her voice was immediately silenced as the taller soldier propped her mouth open, brandished his knife, and cut out her tongue. The soldier dangled the dripping, bloody slab in front of the girl's face before he threw it at her feet, taunting her. Horror painted her eyes as blood seeped down her chin—the butchered nub twisting grotesquely in her mouth as she attempted a gurgled, unnatural scream.

I turned away.

My stomach lurched, roiling like lava was in my gut, the

acidic contents stinging the back of my tongue. I suffocated the urge to vomit. Sunk my nails into my palms. Concentrating on the pain, I cemented myself in place as I watched them set fire to the platform, a stack of wood blanketed in dry, ready-to-catch kindling. Although my attention was on her, I felt someone's on me.

A tether pulled, an invisible string—the sensation strange, yet familiar.

I glanced over my shoulder, looking past the people standing behind me, landing directly on *him*.

A male, domineering in stature, towering in height, was fully cloaked in black. The loose garment did little to conceal the power brooding beneath, biding its time, waiting for release.

I could taste his magic. Feel it. The force of it was a sudden weight upon my chest.

His dark eyes fixed on mine, the color of them a bottomless black.

I nearly gasped. Nearly took a step back. But I held firm, reasoning that the shadows crafted by his hood played a role in the illusion of his otherworldly eyes.

Surely, they must be dark brown.

His black lashes were so thick, his eyes looked naturally rimmed with kohl. A heavy, yet neat stubble carved out his sharp jawline and angular cheekbones. Every one of his features dripped with untamed masculinity, the kind mothers warned their daughters about.

I couldn't avert my eyes. And as it would seem, neither could he.

Another unnatural, horrified scream came from the poor

girl, and it drove a dagger through our locked gaze, my attention darting back to her.

The flames started out small, slowly wiggling their way closer to her, as if cozying up to an old lover. Feral and wild, she thrashed about, her bindings biting deeply into her flesh.

A gentle breeze sifted through, coaxing the flames to reach higher until they lapped at her bare, ivory feet. A spontaneous burst, and the flames ramped up at an unusual speed. A tang of magic drifted on the air. I knew who it came from, but when I looked over my shoulder, the cloaked male was no longer there.

The gurgled, nightmarish screams were one thing, but the smell of burning flesh was entirely another. It was an assault of the senses, a horrific, sickening smell that burned away any desire to ever cook meat again, let alone eat it.

Flesh and bone fed the hungry flames as they lapped farther up her legs.

This was not the first Cleansing I had experienced, nor would it be my last, but that never made them easier. The smells and sounds haunted me, always replaying on the cusp of my mind, especially in the middle of the night.

The soldiers liked to put their own unique twists on the Cleansing—a cut-out tongue, severed ears, gouged-out eyes, or something else more sinister. They were always thinking of ways to create a memorable spectacle that would leave the villagers cowering in fear and it always worked. Despite the buildup, there was one factor that never changed—the Cleansing always ended in flames.

But the flames had not consumed her yet.

And maybe, just maybe, I could save a life.

The greenhorns, the new soldiers recognizable by their lack of armor, did not concern me. Half of them weren't even equipped with swords. But the one with the scar, etched like lightning down the side of his weathered face, his armor carefully tailored and forged from iron—that one would be a problem.

Another raw, horrible scream. I gritted my teeth. Something had to be done. My fingers twitched, itching to try. I widened my stance and locked my gaze on the scar-faced man.

A rough, calloused palm gently grasped my wrist.

I tilted my chin up, my eyes meeting a familiar gaze— Kaleb. Around six feet tall, blond-haired and blue-eyed and good-hearted. He wore an off-white tunic, black pants, and knee-high leather boots. A leather belt was cinched around his narrow waist, the excess fabric of his shirt falling over top of it in some places.

Although we did not share a drop of blood, he was my brother in every other sense of the word. Kaleb was older than me by two years, making him twenty-four.

"You shouldn't be here, Sage," he whispered, his eyes darting desperately between mine—a silent plea to leave. He gave my arm a gentle tug. "Come on, let's go."

"I'm staying." I planted my feet firmly, a tree rooted to the ground.

He squinted at me, his gray-blue eyes mirroring the fight within my own—two unyielding forces locked in a silent battle of wills. But this was one he had never won before. And he knew it. His shoulders dropped as he exhaled, and he offered an understanding, yet slightly annoyed nod and turned his attention to the pyre, his hand never retreating from mine.

Void of sanity, the girl started to laugh as the fire ravaged her. The flames snaked their way up her spine, burning away her curly blonde hair. When there was no more hair to burn, it gnawed at her scalp before laying claim to the rest of her face.

After the gods-awful laughter ceased, her body was chewed up and spit into ash.

I had never seen a body burn so quickly before—was it something to do with the male's magic I felt?

After the flames died out and the crowd began to disperse, the soldiers doused the heated pile with buckets of water taken from the village well, causing a billow of smoke and a hiss of steam. One of the soldiers unsheathed his sword and used it to sift through the embers and remaining bits of charred bone. He retrieved the barbaric collar made of iron and nail, swept it up with the tip of his sword, and dropped it into a metal bucket, an audible *tang* ringing in my ears long after the sound was gone.

The soldiers mounted their horses, and the clopping of hooves pounding against cobblestone sounded off into the hushed night. When the crowd was gone, all that remained were Kaleb, the unconscious woman, a pile of ash and charred bits of bone, and me.

A raven, sleek and small for its breed, stretched out its talons and landed gracefully on the ground. It walked over to the muddy ashes and began searching through the pile with its beak, occasionally using its talons. It reminded me of the soldier from before, searching through the ash with his sword, looking for the collar so he could take it back to his king. I wondered what the raven was searching for.

Perhaps it, too, is searching for something to take to its king.

The thought was an odd one, its origins foreign. Animals bowed to no king. It was probably hungry and looking for something to eat, but it wouldn't find anything there, not when the fire had already consumed everything.

Suddenly, it bobbed. And when it came back up, it had something shiny in its beak.

"Do you see that?" I squinted at the shiny thing—it looked like a marble but slightly larger. How could it be so clean when it had been birthed from a soggy pile of wet ash?

Kaleb followed my gaze. "The raven?"

I shook my head. "No. There is something in its beak."

"Sage . . ." Kaleb paused for added emphasis. "No, there isn't."

I blinked, watching as the raven flapped it wings and lifted from the ground with the glass orb locked in its beak.

Why couldn't he see it?

Then again, this was not the first time I had seen something that Kaleb could not—he had not been able see the feathers either.

The bird disappeared beyond the varied rooftops, their steep peaks reminding me of miniature mountains.

I nodded towards the unconscious woman. "We can't just leave her like that."

His gaze levelled mine, as he knew all too well what I was thinking. "What are we going to do with her?"

I shrugged.

He sighed. "We don't even know where she lives." He crossed his arms over his chest, his body language emphasizing his stance on the topic.

"Then we'll take her home," I offered as I walked over to the woman.

"Ezra is going to kill you." Kaleb said before he followed.

I grinned. "She can try."

I slung the woman's limp arm across my shoulders. I gave a heave and a ho, but it all added up to no avail and the woman slumped back to the ground, the back of her head whacking against the cobblestones . . . *Oops*.

"Out of the way, muscles," Kaleb teased as he gathered her with ease. His blue eyes settled on me, a shit-eating grin saddled proudly on his mouth as he drawled, "The things us men have to do for you women folk."

I rolled my eyes—knowing full well he was just teasing, trying to get a rise out of me. Kaleb was incredibly respectful of women; Ezra wouldn't have raised him any other way. Still, his words required a response. With the mighty strength of the Goddess of Storms, I powered up my flicker finger and unleashed its wrath against the tip of his turned-up nose.

"Ouch," he exclaimed, wiggling it from side to side.

"Come along, peasant," I instructed as I began to walk.

"Yes, your hein-*ass*," he replied, voice etched with sarcasm as he caught up to me, his long strides slowing a hair to match mine.

When we were out of the village and back in the comforting embrace of the woods, Kaleb cleared his throat. "Why do you watch them?"

I plucked at my bottom lip as I worked over his question, my stride slowing but not stopping. "To be honest? I don't know. Maybe I'm just like the others who stand there and watch. The Cleansings are horrible, yet I can't look away. And neither can they." It wasn't a lie. I *couldn't* look away. Time after time, I had proven I was as useless as everyone else—a bystander. No, worse—an accomplice because I did nothing to stop it. Nothing to stop the disgusting pillaging of innocent life.

I was just as bad as the soldiers I had come to hate.

"I don't think that's true. You're not like them, Sage."

He was not wrong.

I was *not* like them.

In fact, I had more in common with the girl they burned—that is, if she was indeed Cursed. I glanced at the middle-aged woman Kaleb carried bridal-style. He made it seem almost effortless, but the light sweat just above his brow hinted otherwise.

The mossy ground cushioned my knee-high leather boots as we walked silently among the whispering trees. A quartet of crickets played their rhythmic tune, and once in a while, an owl would chime in. In the far distance, the wolves howled, and although the sound was far enough away, it was still close enough to make the hair on the back of my neck raise—a standing ovation for the high-pitched, haunting notes.

Tucked safely underneath the woodland canopy of ancient oak trees, our humble log cottage stood. The stone chimney puffed out gray billows of smoke, scenting the air with the heavenly smell of burning birch.

"Kids? Is that you?" Ezra bustled out from the bushes, her spindly fingers plucking a twig from her unruly gray hair. Her cane tapped the ground, bobbing from side to side as she walked towards us. She wore her usual hand-patched garb—old, yet colorful, the tattered ends cut off at her thick, knobby knees, exposing her bony, bowed legs. A handmade satchel was slung across her wilting torso, most likely filled with various herbs, berries, or plants. And probably a few rocks.

She sniffed the air, her milky white eyes aimed at the sky. "You three smell of ash and despair. Three?" Her eyelids closed and she sniffed again. "Three," she confirmed with a satisfied nod. "Who is the third?"

"A lady from the village. She's unconscious—she has a lump on her head," I responded before Kaleb had a chance to rat on me. Despite the lack of details, it was the truth.

"Oh, I see," Ezra replied as she cracked a smile at her own overused joke, her prominent chin tipped to the sky. Moonlight filtered through the swaying branches, illuminating her laugh lines and crow's feet, handsewn by time. "Bring her in and I'll take a look."

She started to make her way to the cottage door, but before she entered, she turned and pointed the barren twig accusingly at me. "And you, child of half-truths, you are lucky I don't cut out *your* tongue."

I shivered. The vivid memory of that bloody knob twisting in the girl's mouth surfaced. I pressed my tongue between my teeth, reassuring myself it was still there.

Kaleb offered a halfhearted *I told you so* shrug.

I squinted at him.

He chuckled and followed Ezra inside, careful not to knock the woman's head against the doorframe as he passed through—not that I could say he provided the same care when it came to her foot. He gawked at me, looking to see if I had noticed. I had.

"Whoops," he mouthed before he continued inside.

Taking a moment, I inhaled, my lungs drinking their fill of burning birch mixed with woodland night air, before I followed them in. I ducked my head under the arched doorway, the familiar smells of cinnamon and peppermint and wood wafting towards me—the smells of home.

What the cottage lacked in size, it made up for by being cozy. The entry was small but open to the comfortable living room and humble, messy kitchen. On the far wall, a handcrafted ladder, more crooked than straight, slanted against the wall, leading up to the loft which sat overtop of two rooms. The first was Ezra's, and the second was a tiny bathing room—if you could even call a bucket of water and a porcelain basin that. As we did not have the luxuries of plumbing, the latrine was outside, and the bath was the lake.

This place—this small cottage with its arched doorways and foundation of wood—was the only home I had ever known.

Kaleb placed the woman carefully on the settee, his six-foot frame returning to its full height as he straightened. He crossed his arms and turned his head to the side, surveying the slumbering female. I glanced at her, pegging her to be in her early forties.

Ezra stood at the kitchen table. She hooked her cane over the back of the dining chair and slipped the strap of her satchel over her head. She turned it upside down. A handful of mushrooms and two rocks fell onto the weathered oak table. Her fingers glided overtop, her lips thinning.

"Ah, there you are," she exclaimed happily as she

plucked the rocks and cradled them in her palm. She bumbled towards the shelves, her arthritic knuckles unscrewing the top of an empty glass jar. She plopped them inside and placed it back on the shelf.

Inside the cottage, she had no need for her cane—what her eyes could not show her, muscle memory recalled. She dusted her hands against her worn tunic and walked over to the settee, her hands hovering an inch above the woman's face. Slowly, she moved them in rhythmic motions, covering the woman's body from head to toe, a low hum falling from the back of her throat.

I peeled potatoes while Kaleb tended the fire. He fed the glowing embers another two logs before the flame caught, gnawing away on the dry timber. A renewed warmth blossomed from the hearth, scenting the cottage in a wintergreen aroma with a slightly sweet twist. *Heavenly.*

Kaleb returned outside. Shortly after, the muffled sound of metal splitting wood could be heard.

As I worked, my stomach protested, vocalizing its hunger for the entire continent of Edenvale to hear. I dropped the cubed potatoes into a pot of water and hung it over the fire. I squatted by the hearth, wrapped my arms around my knees, and waited for the water to steam. This small distraction did very little to still my thoughts, which were still full of fire and screams. A lump bulged in my throat.

How many more would have to die?

Without a whisper of sound, Ezra squatted beside me. "It was not always like this."

I watched the water bubble, a sigh escaping my lips. "So you've said before."

"And so, I must say again." She gave me a gentle, playful nudge. She raised her hands, palm sides exposed to the crackling fire. Her bony, crooked fingers waggled back and forth, the fire emphasizing her thick, arthritic knuckles. "Many years ago, there was a time when the Cursed were looked upon with very different eyes." She waved her hand as if painting a picture. "Those born with the Curse of Air, they could bend the wind and bring the lost fishermen home, and when winter would stake her frozen claim, those who carried the Fire Curse would bring heat to every villager's hearth, keeping all families toasty and warm. Those who were given the Curse of Earth, they worked hand in hand with hunters—ensuring the forests were always full of game. Then there are those who bear the Water Curse." She tapped my nose. "They would aid the farmers—bringing rain to the soils that were dried out with thirst. And as for the fifth and final Curse, the Curse of the Mind, they would heal those with illnesses up here." She winked, two crooked fingers tapping the side of her head.

"I wish I could have seen it," I offered honestly, the heat from the fire brushing over my face.

"Maybe someday, you will," Ezra said as she wrapped a comforting arm around my lower back and gave a gentle squeeze. When I glanced at her, I could not describe the look on her face as anything but hopeful.

Warmth spread throughout my chest. Ezra was the closest thing I had to a mother, although she had never accepted the title, insisting we call her by her first name. She used to work in the village, operating her own apothecary. Through it, she met Kaleb's mom, a woman who did not want a child born out of wedlock. Ezra agreed to take Kaleb, to raise him as her own. Two years later, she found me in a bassinet by the lake not far from here—the where and how were details she had never divulged, so that was all I knew. Not that I cared to know more—a baby abandoned by a lake doesn't exactly scream wanted. And if I wasn't wanted then, my biological family probably did not want me now. After finding me, Ezra had closed her apothecary, gathered her things, and moved our potluck family to the cottage here in the woods.

Kaleb booted the door open, the loud *thunk* coaxing me from my thoughts. He carried the fresh-cut logs inside, the pile towering over his blond head. Making his way over to us, he dropped the seasoned wood onto the ground, the split logs smacking against one another as they tumbled to the floor. But with one sour look from Ezra, Kaleb quickly began to stack them neatly in place.

With a satisfied nod, Ezra scuttled off to the kitchen. I watched her carefully, wearily. She reached for a jar containing cabbage, or rather, whatever was left of it. This particular specimen had been festering on the shelf for nearly two months now, marinating in some sort of undisclosed yellow liquid. I stifled a groan—she was preparing one of her infamous recipes. The kind that was powerful enough to purge one's guts for a week.

And then some.

Kaleb made a worried face. I mirrored the expression.

When the potatoes were done, and the death dish was finished, the three of us sat around the table and ate. I stuffed a piece of bread into my mouth, eyeing the suspicious mix of greens on my plate, wondering what the fuzzy, blue-green stuff was. Mold, perhaps?

Probably not. Not even mold would try to eat this.

I glanced at Kaleb, who was also staring at the odd-colored greens, if they could be classified as green at all. We tried our best to refuse, but Ezra was persistent and would not take no for an answer as she dished a mighty helping onto our plates.

And so, there we were—one bite away from colon annihilation.

"The lady will make a full recovery," Ezra started.

I looked at my plate. *But will we?*

Ezra sucked in a breath before she continued, "I cannot speak on the state of her mind—it's fractured."

She's not the only one with a fractured mind . . .

Ezra whacked my hand with the back of her wooden spoon. My mouth popped open—her uncanny ability to see everything despite her lack of ability to see could be a real pain in the ass at times. Or in this case, I thought as I rubbed my hand, other places.

When our late supper was done and the house was quiet, I settled in on my twin mattress—no bed frame underneath as the slope of the loft roof wouldn't allow it. I turned on my side and watched Kaleb as he slept, his bed a few feet from mine, where it had always been since we were kids.

Many years ago, the individual mattresses we slept on seemed big, but now, looking at him, the reverse was true. Kaleb's bare feet hung well over the end, the mattress squished down, suffocated under his healthy, adult weight. Light muscle decorated his otherwise thin frame, and although he wasn't super broad-shouldered, his shoulders could bear a good amount of weight. He was handsome in his own way, with his sunshine hair and straight, slightly upturned nose. He had grown into himself these past few years—something the girls from the village had started to take notice of.

I rolled my eyes, recalling a particularly gods-awful title I overheard some girls at the market whispering amongst themselves the other day—Meristone's heartthrob.

Little did they know that Meristone's heartthrob drooled in his sleep. I stifled my chuckle, not wanting to wake him up from his peaceful sleep.

My nose crinkled as a yawn escaped my mouth, and before long, I lost myself to the realm of dreams.

But unlike Kaleb, when I slept, it was never a place of peace.

Chapter 2

The towering oaks were falling, their dead leaves like tears as they hit the ashen ground. As the ancient giants fell, puffs of black dust saturated the air. It clogged my nostrils and choked my breath, but when the smoke started to roll in, that was when my lungs pleaded—desperate for air. We needed to get out of there before the woods swallowed us whole.

Kaleb was to my left, swinging his axe as he tried to clear a path. I grabbed a fallen branch and dragged it to the side. I moved as many I could, my hands bloody and raw, needled with slivers.

A scream unlike any other I'd heard raked against my bones—I knew that voice.

"Ezra!" I cried out, my chest heaving as we clawed and fought our way towards her. Panicked, we searched for the direction from which her scream came.

She wailed again. Fear landed a destructive blow to my gut, its fingers clutching at my throat.

"There!" Kaleb grabbed my hand as we took off to the

edge of the woods, a wall of never-ending black mist swirling on the horizon, gobbling up the sky as if it didn't exist—as if that were the edge of the world.

Our grip broke as another tree came crashing down. We fell on opposite sides but were quick to get back on our feet as Ezra came into sight—there was no sound coming from her mouth.

They had dragged her to the pyre, her frail body crumpled, nearly lifeless in their hands, that bloody iron collar wrapped around her neck.

"No!" I screamed like some mighty, deranged beast as I willed my legs to move faster with every fiber of my being.

They lowered the torches. I cried out.

The fire began to lap up the wood. My mother.

It inched closer to her. My home.

I blinked away the tears as I let out a mighty roar and leapt into the sky. My jump carried me the last fifty yards, my body suspended in the air as time slowed.

I could hear Kaleb shouting my name, to come back, but it was drowned out by the roaring, consuming fire.

I reached out. So close. A second more and I—

Before I could blink, Ezra disappeared.

And instead of her body being strapped to the pyre, it was now mine.

I awoke in a puddle of sweat and fear, my heart galloping at an unsustainable speed. My knuckles groaned as I slowly released my death hold on my sheets. I tried to gain control over my frantic breath.

Inhale.

Exhale.

Wash.

Rinse.

Repeat.

As my breath began to slow, I glanced towards Kaleb. He was still asleep. At least I hadn't awoken him. For a moment, I wondered what he dreamed of. Hopefully, the opposite of my own.

Shucking off my covers, I crawled towards the round window nestled beneath the roof's peak and pulled the moth-chewed drapes to the side. I surveyed the position of the moon and pegged the time to be around four a.m. I shrugged off the loss of a full night's sleep, quietly gathered my day clothes, and made my way down the ladder, my bare feet padding silently against the wood-plank floor.

After I was dressed in a tight-fitting tunic and pants, I slipped out into the night.

The balmy autumn temperature made me wish I had put on an extra layer, but in a short amount of time, I wouldn't need it.

I walked through the trees on my self-made path, the starlight illuminating my way. The woods were so quiet—even the nocturnal animals had been lulled to sleep.

I peered up at the enchanting moon. I had always felt fond of her.

When I found my spot in the glades, I ensured my boots were tightly laced and plucked my chosen stick from the ground, something I'd acquired along the way. It was roughly four feet long and decently straight, other than the slight bow at the one end.

I rotated the stick, testing its weight, my hand quickly becoming accustomed to it. I began to move as I twirled it around my body, my warm-up more playful than my serious routine. I moved with ease, my muscles recalling each movement, each swing, each step—always ready for the next—a sacred dance. As I settled into the familiarity of training, my mind began to drift among the memories of this place.

"But I want to use the sword today," an eight-year-old version of myself protested as I plucked a blade of lush grass.

It had rained last night, rejuvenating the meadow—lush, rich greens and vividly colored wildflowers painting the enchanting glades. Even the red alder and quaking aspen looked thankful to see the rain.

"Swords are not always available," Ezra said as she balanced, her foot placed against the inside of the leg she stood on, prayer hands settled against her chest.

"But . . ." I motioned to the wooden sword. ". . . this one is."

Ezra opened one eye and peered at me—a hawk sizing up supper. But instead of whipping out her dinner fork, she simply replied, "A good warrior can use anything as a weapon."

"But a good warrior would probably choose a sword over a stick." I plucked out another blade of grass, as if it were to blame.

20

Now both of her eyes were propped open, and she was staring intently at me. She reached behind her head and tied up her gray-brown hair. "If you can knock me over while I use only one leg, I'll let you use the sword today."

I nodded with satisfaction, wrapped my hand around the hilt, and charged towards her. I aimed for her leg in an opportunistic move, but my confidence got the better of me as she leapt out of the way and flicked my forehead as I went sailing by. She landed gracefully on her other leg, not even a whisper of sound escaping her skillful movement.

"No fair!" I exclaimed in frustration as I scrubbed at my temple. "You said you'd only use one leg."

Ezra smirked and gestured to the right leg she now balanced on. "And so I am."

Gritting my teeth, I charged again, readying myself to move whatever direction she went. But instead of going right or left, she used my head as leverage. With her palm pressed against it, she catapulted over me. I swirled around and chased after her. My efforts were ridiculed with another flick. My brow lowered in frustration. I charged again.

Flick.
And again.
Flick.
And again.
Flick.

I crumbled onto the cool, dewy grass, my lungs itching for breath.

Ezra lay down beside me, her breath calm, not labored like my own. "After you've regained your stamina, we'll start practice."

I rolled onto my side and glared at her. "I'm too tired to practice."

She shot me a challenging look. "A good warrior always practices."

I let out an aggravated groan.

I bent over, my hands placed against my legs, huffing as I awoke from my meditative warrior state. Just under three hours had passed, and the sun was now rising, introducing the dawn of a new day. A light sweat trickled down my brow and neck, dampening my collar. Throwing my fingers through my hair, the color of fresh snow, my eyes teared as I inhaled an unsafe amount of the smell radiating from my armpits.

Damn—I stunk.

Deciding for the sake of humanity that I should take a wash, I headed towards the lake. A short walk led me to the edge of the woods—the slumbering, effervescent lake yawning before me, the same lake where Ezra had found me.

Directly across, a sky-scraping wall of black swirled with hunger.

The Endless Mist.

It swallowed the horizon, stretching from east to west, gobbling up the sky and anything in its path.

The Endless Mist surrounded all of Edenvale—a great barrier that allowed no one to leave—a dungeon, a cell, a prison that kept us locked away from the outside world. For years, people had tried to bring the Endless Mist down, but nothing worked, and any hope of doing so was now lost to the past.

According to Ezra, the Endless Mist did not always surround Edenvale. Hundreds of years ago, mystical beings with extraordinary abilities arrived in frightened droves on the continent. They seemed desperate, as if they were fleeing something. Some came with their families, utilizing ships called knars—large cargo vessels with square-rigged sails. Others flew here, carried by their own wings. They were given many different names—angels, demons, monsters, fae—but one stood out the most, especially when it came to the ones who had wings—Demi Gods, the children of the Old Gods.

Seconds after the very last of the Demi Gods arrived, the Endless Mist appeared. The stories passed down explained it as a deep groan from the earth that quaked the entire continent, birthing the black, endless beast—a black serpent curled around its nested egg—Edenvale.

Although some Edenvalians blamed the Demi Gods for the Endless Mist, most were quite struck by them. The Demi Gods were enchanting, after all. They were beautiful and powerful, the likes of which Edenvale, a land of mortals, had never seen. Spellbound, the men and women of Edenvale mated with them, their offspring birthing the Cursed—sons and daughters with elemental powers.

For a time, there was peace.

But people began to abandon the religion endorsed by the royal family ruling Edenvale during that time. The people turned to the religion of the Demi Gods, known as the Old Religion, filled with tales of the Old Gods.

Like wildfire, the Old Religion spread.

Threatened by this, the royal family proclaimed the Old

Religion illegal, and they started to push their endorsed religion on the people. The New Religion followed the New Gods. They demanded that all citizens of Edenvale worship the New Religion, that they be baptized under it. During this time, the Crown deemed the Demi Gods evil, utilizing the timing of the Demi Gods' arrival and the creation of the Endless Mist to further push their agenda.

The Demi Gods were hunted down, but their kind were not easy to kill. Some were dragged into dungeons, tortured, and tormented—until the Crown learned that the combination of fire and iron was what made them weak. That was how the Cleansing began, although originally, it was intended only for the Demi Gods—not their offspring.

The ironic part of it all was that both the Old Religion and the New Religion shared common beliefs. Both consisted of a variety of gods and goddesses, with one separate entity who reigned supreme. Both religions referred to this being as the Creator.

I believed in the Creator, even though I didn't really follow along with either of the religions. I knew more about the New Religion because information was easy to find—the king allowed it to be so.

As for the Endless Mist? I didn't think about it a whole lot. It was here long before my birth, and it would probably be here long after my death.

I slipped out of my clothes, my feet quickening in pace before I launched into the lake.

Despite the chill of the early morning, the body of water was not cold, but warm. The lake was fed by an underground heated stream, which meant it never froze or dried up. This meant two things: it was a great place to bathe and a terrible spot to fish—the heat made them extra slimy.

After a long day of training and chores, Ezra used to bring us here when we were young, dirty, little gremlins. Not much had changed since those days—I'd seen her haul Kaleb's grown ass down here more than once.

A smile touched my lips as I moved to the deepest part of the lake, my hands slowly swishing back and forth, feeling the smooth water glide between my fingers, over my skin. Inhaling a deep breath, I allowed my body to sink, my hair reaching towards the surface as I sank down into the dark abyss.

Sunlight held no dominion here.

The muddy bottom squished between my toes, coating them in lake floor essence, welcoming me home.

Here in this soundless world, I found peace.

Here in this soundless world, I could let my Curse be free.

I straightened my arms, my wrists touching as my left hand pointed upwards and my right hand faced down. I summoned my Curse, and like an old, faithful mare, it nudged against me, yearning to be let free—to play. I gave in and let my power out. A circle of water shot up around me, my power hurtling it upwards. I glanced up to the soft blue sky, my feet settled on the lake floor, as I inhaled a deep breath of air. With a flick of my wrist, the water twirled, creating a slow-motion hurricane that swirled playfully around me. I lowered my hands, untethered my will, and the water came crashing back down.

After I finished my morning dip, I stood on the shore,

wiggling into my pants, the fabric like glue against my wet legs. I slung on my cotton shirt and buckled the thin leather band to my thigh that holstered my knife.

Something spooked amongst the trees and a flock of blackbirds took to the sky. I watched as they glided on the wind, carefree and safe and out of reach. I wondered what it must feel like to be unshackled from gravity. Free. And although I would never know until I was a soul floating in the Spirit Realm, an answer appeared as it drifted in front of me.

I reached out, my palm open-faced as a sleek black feather fell into my hand.

I marveled at the silken plume colored the blackest of black. The feather was huge, three times the size of my hand. And for a feather that should be light, it had considerable weight. I picked it up by the quill and raised it to the sky, slowly turning it. The rays of the sun shone against it, catching on golden, glittering fragments embedded in the plume—like starlight amongst an onyx sky. Beautiful.

This was not the first time the sky had gifted me one of these unusual, exquisite feathers. I had a small chest full of them back home—a chest Kaleb frequently asked why I kept empty. But it was far from empty. He just couldn't see what was in it.

But Ezra could—I'd show her this one before I added it in with the rest of its kin.

Carefully, I tucked the feather into my back pocket and returned to the cottage, the trek taking close to an hour.

When I opened the front door, I paused midstep—the woman we brought home was sitting up, her mouth popped open, her horrified gaze locked on Ezra.

Chapter 3

Ezra, being Ezra, had chosen this morning, of all mornings, to sort through her collection of bones. Big bones. Little Bones. Bloody Bones. Fleshy Bones. Smelly Bones. Riddled with worms bones.

The entire collection.

By the looks of our petrified guest, Ezra was well on her way to the guillotine made of iron and flame.

"Your friend is awake," Ezra said as her fingers stripped the meat off a smaller bone. She dropped it into one of the piles and shoved her oily thumb in her mouth, sucking off the stray bits of meat. *Old, rotten meat.*

I nearly gagged.

She reached across the table and grabbed another bone, this time bringing it under her nose and inhaling deeply. Loudly.

I sucked in a breath as I scuttled behind Ezra. "Oh, don't mind her," I said as I offered up my fakest-pleasant smile. My hands dropped onto her shoulders, giving a gentle *cut-it-out* squeeze. "She's senile."

Smack.

A chicken wing slapped my forehead, the decaying, gooey meat like glue. Slowly, it slid down my face before it fell to the floor.

I blinked, brightened my smile, and offered sweetly, "Tea?"

Ten minutes later, Ezra, the woman, and I sat around the table, heaped with bones. Steam rolled from our clay cups, steeping a loose-leaf tea blend—herbs from the market, not Ezra's personal collection. Still, the woman plucked hers from the table and eyed it suspiciously before taking a small, hesitant sip. I couldn't blame her. I would have probably done the same.

"Where am I?" she asked, eyes nervously glancing around the cottage.

"A short walk from the village, in my family's cottage. I was there . . ." I paused, softening my tone as I fumbled for words. "We didn't want to leave you there. But we didn't know where you lived, so we brought you here." I swallowed. "I'm so sorry for your loss."

Her shoulders fell. "Anika was my daughter." Clouds of emotion pooled above her lower lash line. She placed her cup on the table and ran her finger along the imperfect handle. Her gaze rose, locking with mine. "She wasn't Cursed. I'd know if she had the disease. I'm her mother, for Lady Light's sake."

Ezra clicked her tongue.

The woman looked at Ezra, suspicion returning.

"She's religious," I piped up, trying to cover for her. "When we were kids, we'd get the ol' frying pan over the head any time we took the Goddess of Life's name in vain."

Smooth. My inner critic seethed at the lie.

"My apologies," the woman offered, teardrops tumbling down her rosy cheeks. "Anika adored Lady Light." A small sigh. "I remember her being just a wee thing, kneeling by the bed and praying to the goddess, asking her to keep us safe. To keep us healthy. And always together. She's all I had." Pain, visceral and raw, saturated every word. "And I wonder, when I return home, will she be there waiting on the doorstep for me?"

I did not know what to say to this stranger who bared her broken soul. And as I watched her drop her face into her hands and weep, guilt began to swell in me.

I had been there.

And I had done nothing.

Just as I had done nothing every other time.

Ezra's chair shifted against the wood floor as she stood, walked over to the woman, and wrapped her arms around her—stranger to stranger, mother to mother, heart to heart.

Later that afternoon, I accompanied the woman, whose name I learned was Mirabel, to the village, and when we arrived at her humble home with its empty doorstep, a tidal wave of guilt nearly dropped me to my knees.

I could have tried to save the girl.

But I hadn't.

I hadn't done anything.

Potter Street was the busiest street during the day. Down the middle, the market was made up of a string of pop-up vendors. The vendors called out, coaxing buyers to taste their produce or touch the fabrics or whatever else they had to sell. An occasional argument would break out when there was a disagreement over quality or price—something the soldiers would snicker over but never involve themselves in. On the east and west sides of the street, buildings constructed of stone masonry stood side to side, and a wide tapestry of shops filled them—smiths, merchants, traders, various craftsmen.

Unlike yesterday, Meristone was bursting with everyday life. Children of a variety of ages chased one another, their laughter filling the air. Not far away, a man with a voice soft as dew sang while he plucked at his lute, a small crowd gathered around him, clapping along as he sang a tale about a lover whose hair was spun from night and whose eyes burned like coal.

The cloaked male lingered on the apex of my thoughts and for a second, I could almost picture him standing there, his unnaturally dark gaze locked with mine, the taste of his magic filling my nose. The magic I sensed that day, it belonged to him. I believed he was Cursed with Air. That his magic fed the flames, causing them to quicken—to burn faster. But why would he do that?

Was he trying to end her misery?

Or was he the reason for it . . .

I nibbled at my bottom lip, waiting for my gut to kick in, but no answer came. Perhaps it was best I forgot the stranger.

Ezra had warned me about chasing ghosts more times than I cared to count.

Sighing, I glanced at my wicker basket before I stepped into the bakery, the bell hanging above the door announcing my arrival. The aroma of rising dough and a blast of heat occupied my senses as I took in the variety of freshly baked breads, buns, and desserts stockpiled on slanted shelves.

Behind the counter, Joseph, the owner of the shop, turned to greet me—a kind smile beneath his wiry, gray moustache. He brushed his hands on his apron, causing a waft of flour to dust the air. For someone who owned a bakery, Joe was slim and toned—not bad for a man in his early seventies. He walked towards the counter, a slight limp in his gait. "Good morning, dear. I was hoping you would stop by soon," he said, that signature twinkle in his eye, even as he palmed his aching hip.

"Mornin', Joe. Sorry about the wait on this one. Ezra finally got around to making it this morning." My fingers plucked a small, clear vial from my basket—an off-white, oily substance roiling inside. I hoped Joe didn't open it until he was at home because this batch smelled extra fishy. I set it on the counter for him to take.

"Oh, that's quite alright. I know she can be a busy girl," Joe said kindly as he took the vial and held it carefully, as if it were gold. I smiled at the *girl* bit. Joe and Ezra had been friends since their youth, and somehow, despite the years, that's still how he saw her—a young, wild girl. In their younger years, he had proposed to her on three separate occasions, and even though she'd turned him down, their friendship remained intact. Joe would have made a great addition to our odd little family.

I often wondered why Ezra never said yes. Then again, as someone who had no plans to get married—ever—I could not blame her. Whenever I thought of marriage, it made me feel . . . sickly. Even though I couldn't figure out exactly why that was, I had a feeling it was to do with my Curse. What would my husband do when he found out the truth about his blushing bride? Sign me up for a one-way trip to the guillotine made of iron and flame, no doubt.

No, thanks. I was perfectly content with my little life.

Joe gathered an assortment of breads, wrapped them in a white cloth, and slid them my way. "Here you are, dear. I added an extra onion loaf—I know it's her favorite."

I smiled warmly as I picked up the warm goods from the counter and placed them into my basket. "I think it's everyone's favorite, Joe."

It wasn't a lie. Joe's onion loaf usually had people lined up and down the street. And in a pinch, it could be a powerful bartering tool among the villagers, something I'd done before, although it pained me—the loaf was just that good.

"How much do I owe you?" I reached for my coin pouch.

He shook his head. "The tonic is more than enough." He tapped his hip softly. "Keeps these old bones in working order."

I smiled.

We made small talk as he began to work a mound of dough, and after a not so short but pleasant goodbye, I left the bakery and walked down the street, giving the merchants a wide *I'm not interested* berth.

Sitting to the side of a bush void of leaves, a woman who

looked not much older than I sat with a small child in her arms. The child nibbled on his sleeve. Both of their lips were pale and dry, the woman's hair thinning at the top. Her clothes were tattered and worn, like she had gotten into a nasty fight with the thorny bush beside her. She looked up at me, hunger etched into her faded eyes, that same look mirrored in her child's.

People glared as they walked by, hurtling names at her, labelling her, insulting her life choices—something I was certain they knew nothing about.

I crouched on bended knee, sifting my fingers through the knotted cloth, and pulled out an onion loaf—still warm. "Here," I offered the woman, motioning for her to take it.

All she did was stare up at me, questioning what my offer might cost her, no doubt.

"You can have it," I reassured her.

Cautiously, she took the loaf from me, uncertainty flagging her trembling fingers. "Thank you," she replied as she carefully ripped off a chunk and gave it to the boy.

"Of course." I glanced at the little boy, and he offered me a toothy grin before he looked to the bread and smacked his little lips. Slowly, he brought it to his mouth, and when he tasted it, his little body shivered with delight.

"Do you have a home, some place to go?" I asked.

She shook her head. "Not anymore."

"Do you have any family? Somewhere where you and your child can stay?"

"No, it's just us now. My husband was Cursed . . . and the king took him from us." There was no hate or anger in her words—just a great, open, festering void.

"I'm sorry," I offered, looking down. Not far from my shoe, an ant followed an invisible line, a small bit of leaf resting on his back as he dutifully marched back to his queen. The fable was not lost on me—by compliance or might, we all served the king—the executioner of fathers and little girls.

I looked to the woman. To the child. This was the result of our compliance.

"He had the element of Air," the woman offered, her hand reaching towards the sky. The child looked up, little eyes watching her every move.

I blinked, somewhat taken aback. People did not openly speak about the Curses, but this woman had, and I . . . I felt grateful for her honesty. Grateful to just hear someone talk about it. As if it were normal.

She looked at me—I mean, really looked at me—and asked, "Do you have a loved one who bares the Curse?"

My survival instincts screamed at me to lie, and so naturally, I replied, "Yes." And as stupid as it was to release this information to a stranger, I felt an overwhelming sense of peace. Of pride.

"Then I pray to the gods that you will never know what it is like to lose them at the pyre."

Her words coaxed a shiver to spider-walk down my spine, but not because of the warning she heeded—no, it felt . . . prophetic. Perhaps my recent nightmare had something to do with it as well.

"Aye! Peasant whore! No begging on the king's streets!" barked a soldier, his metal armor clinking as he stalked towards us—a *big* man exercising his authority over a helpless woman and a little child.

This was who the king chose to fight for him.

I stepped protectively in front of them, offering myself as a barrier from the king's meticulously bred, rabid dog.

Fingers gently squeezed my arm, her voice a cautious whisper. "Please, we don't want any more trouble. We'll leave."

I glanced over my shoulder as the woman took the little boy's hand and led him quickly down the street, speckled with the browns and yellows of freshly fallen leaves. As she left, the soldier turned and walked away, but not before he gave me a warning glance.

When his back was turned, I flipped my middle finger at him before I sauntered towards an old stone building on the corner of the street.

A wobbling wood sign squeaked above me, the gentle wind nudging it back and forth. *The Broken Mare* was painted in simple, black lettering, as if it might ward off the double vision of the heavy-drinking patrons that frequented here. The tavern wasn't exactly a humble establishment. It was well known for its horse-piss beer, not-so-sultry barmaids, and frequent crowd of pickpockets.

The sagging hinges provided some resistance as I shoved the rustic oak door open, the bottom groaning against the floor. I stepped through the threshold, the bottom of my shoes suctioning to the wide wood planks. I lifted one and peered at the guck stuck to my sole, the same sticky substance coating the rest of the main floor. The smell of day-old, aerated ale punched its way into my nose.

I made a face.

"Apparently, it was quite the crowd last night, but I guess

that's to be expected, considering there was a full moon," Kaleb said as he slapped the wet mop against the floor, a dishtowel slung over his shoulder. Apart from Kaleb, me, and a few mice, the tavern was empty. The hearth was void of flame, fanning the interior of the building with a cool breeze as it wafted down the chimney. But by the looks of Kaleb, he was probably enjoying the bursts of cool air. His brow was slick with sweat, cheeks heated red.

What he said made sense; Lady Light was the daughter of the moon, so when the moon was at its fullest, it was considered a good omen and the people tended to celebrate. During the summer months, when the sun was at its strongest, the celebrations surrounded the Lord of Light, who was the male heir of the sun.

"No kidding," I replied as I walked over to the bar area and placed the basket on the bar top, which had been freshly cleaned. The bar consisted of a wooden slab propped up by two barrels on either end. On the other side of the bar top, a pyramid of barrels three rows deep was stacked against the wall, containing the notoriously awful brew—some with spouts tapped in.

"Still happy you took the job?" I asked as I began my inspection for the cleanest dirty stool.

"Someone in the house has to pull in some coin," he said with a wink before he continued to scrub. He paused, eyeing me as I sat at the bar. "Do you want me to get you a drink?"

I snorted. "You'd have to pay me to drink *that* stuff."

Kaleb chuckled. "It's an acquired taste."

My brow shot up in challenge. "I don't believe one can acquire a taste for horse urine."

"You'd be surprised." He smirked as he plunked the scraggly mop back in the pail and wheeled it towards the back door, using the broom handle to steer. The muscles in his forearms contracted as he lifted the bucket, used his back side to heave the door open, and dumped the muddy water into the back alley.

The wheeled bucket was one of Kaleb's inventions, something he'd crafted to help the owner of the tavern, an elderly woman whose frail back no longer allowed her to lift the heavy bucket, even though her young heart wanted to. At the core of that was her desire to look after the tavern, and so, the wheels gave her the ability to do so.

Kaleb was like that—always trying to make life better for people.

When Kaleb returned with the empty bucket, I closed the distance with a few long strides and placed my hand over top, conjuring from the well inside.

Kaleb pushed my hand away. "No, Sage, not here." He lowered his voice. "What if someone *sees*?"

I surveyed the vacant tavern theatrically before I leaned in and feigned a serious tone. "I don't think the mice will tell anyone."

As if on cue, one went squealing by, its little claws prattling against the floorboards as it moved. It dove between two barrels, no doubt retreating to its self-chewed home in the wall.

Kaleb and I peered at the space where the mouse had disappeared, bursting into laughter.

Chapter 4

I stayed for the remainder of Kaleb's shift, helping him clean, and although he thanked me as we walked out the door, my intentions were not that pure—the cottage was the last place any living, breathing thing should be today, excluding Ezra, but she was a breed of her own.

Before I left this morning, I had spied the jar of fermented rabbit droppings sitting on the counter and instantly I knew—she was making Mrs. Stoddard's salve today. This particular concoction of Ezra's was so vile, so offensive to the nostrils, that I was surprised the woods had not plucked themselves up by the roots and left the cottage to stand on its own. And despite Ezra's solution to open a window and let it *air out*, there were not enough windows in Edenvale to let it *air out*.

How that poor woman, Mrs. Stoddard, applied it to her feet every night—the gods only knew. And how her poor husband remained at her side . . .

That must be true love.

"I would have stayed in Meristone for the night had I known Ezra was going to be making Mrs. Stoddard's salve today," Kaleb said with a sigh as we walked back to the cottage, the path riddled with sticks and fallen leaves that crunched under our shoes. He sighed again. "It took me a week to regain my sense of smell after the last time."

My eyes went wide. Oh yes, how could I have forgotten the last time? The death batch.

"You weren't even home when she made it," I seethed, sibling rivalry nipping at my heels for this round of *Who Had it Worse*. "It made my skin look purple. Purple, Kaleb."

He howled with laughter. "Oh, that's right!" He gulped down a breath of air in between snickers. "None of the vendors would have anything to do with you because they thought you had purple fever." His laughter reached hysterical proportions and he threw his hands over his stomach as if it were hurting him to laugh this hard.

I squinted at him. "Shut it, you hyena."

He offered a *can you blame me?* smirk and reigned himself in as he wiped away his tears, although every now and then, the memory would resurface, and a hiccup of a chuckle ripped out of him.

I rolled my eyes with added emphasis before I quickly turned away, hiding my smile.

"Do you remember when we were kids, we made up that secret language with our hands so we could talk without Ezra knowing?"

"Of course, I remember." I glanced up at him. "Which one do you remember the most?"

"Ironically, this one." He raised his hand, two fingers

tapping the spot over his heart twice. It was how we made up after one of our childhood spats. One tap to signal that we were sorry, and the second tap meant that we loved one another, more than anything else.

I couldn't help but smile. "That's the one I remember the most too." For the remainder of our walk back to the cottage, we joked with one another, riffing off one another, just as we always did. And although there was no blood between us, there never really needed to be for us to be siblings—family.

When we returned to our cottage home, it smelled . . . pleasant—of peppermint and wood. The hearth was unlit, and Ezra was gone.

Ezra leaving without a word was not uncommon. In fact, it was something she used to do rather frequently.

I found myself thrust into an old memory.

My uncertain, twelve-year-old eyes peered out the window, the single pane of glass chattering in fear at the wind's heavy blows. The blizzard had lasted for the past three days, forming mountains of fluffy, white snow—the kind you could play for hours in without noticing it chilled you to the bone.

Today marked one month and five days since Ezra was last home, and like our decreasing stack of wood, my hopes were starting to fade.

"Don't worry. She'll be back," Kaleb assured me as he placed the last four logs in the fireplace, the bed of embers glowing red hot, lapping at them hungrily. Despite his reassurance, I saw the way he looked at the empty firewood

rack—the uncertainty, the worry written on his face.

"What if she doesn't come back this time?" I asked, my little heart aching.

Kaleb gathered my hands in his, looked me square in the face, and said, "She will. She always comes home."

A fraction of me sighed with relief.

He frowned, his thumbs brushing my cold fingers. "Here, come sit. It will warm you up." He led me towards the fire. I nodded as I plopped down, my legs crisscrossed. A blanket fell over my shoulders.

"Okay, you watch the fire. I'll be right back," he said before trudging over to the door and beginning to bundle up.

I turned away from the fire, watching him. "You can't go outside in the storm. You won't be able to see."

He batted a hand at me. "I'll be fine."

Kaleb had hit a growth spurt recently, and his hands no longer fit in the gloves from last year, no matter how hard he tried to wedge them in. And so, he pulled down his sleeves, slung the axe over his shoulder, and walked out the door into the blizzard's mouth.

When the door closed, I scrambled to my lookout spot by the window and searched for him, but the blowing, swirling, raging snow had swallowed him whole. My nervous breath fogged up the glass. I pinched the fabric of my long-sleeve shirt, pulling it up so I could scrub the fog away, my eyes frantically searching for him.

Panic's nasty little fingers gripped at me—I couldn't see him.

I darted to the door.

While I pushed an arm through my coat sleeve, I shoved

my feet in my boots. I barely had my winter hat on my head as I charged outside into the embrace of the cold, wicked storm. It roared at me, laughing in my face. I could almost hear it say, This little girl is the reinforcement being sent in?

I ignored the doubt and the overwhelming fear as I wrapped my arms around my body and searched for his footprints. I couldn't find them. The storm had erased them, as if they'd never existed.

Panic trickled through my veins.

"Kaleb!" I screamed, my voice extinguished by the howl of the wind. I raised my hand in front of my face, as if that would help me see better. It didn't.

I screamed his name, again and again.

The storm answered, and it pushed me back, consuming my voice, pulling my hair, and shoving me around as if I were one of my sock dolls.

I stumbled through the snow, the feeling in my fingers and toes slowly beginning to retreat. A blast of ice and wind collided into me, pushing me to the ground.

I was cold. And scared. And alone.

Tears stained my vision, stinging my frozen cheeks.

"Get up, child," commanded a voice as strong as stone.

I looked up. "Ezra!" I cried out as I leapt to my feet and wrapped my arms around her waist.

She gripped me against her—my lighthouse, my saving grace. "Where is Kaleb?" she shouted above the deafening wind.

"He's out here, somewhere," I stammered as my tears continued to fall.

"I can't sense him," Ezra said as she kneeled, her fingers

drying my tears. "But you, dear child, you can save him."

"I-I-I can't. I don't know how." I sniffled.

"You may not know how. But this does." She tapped the spot over my heart.

I closed my eyes and searched for that well within, but when I got to it . . . it was frozen over. I looked to her and stammered through my chattering teeth. "It won't work."

"It will. You have too much to lose if it doesn't," she said, her fingers tightening on my shoulders. "Now fight for him, child, with everything you have."

I returned to the well in my mind, reaching my hand over the ice. I pressed against it, but it didn't heave. Kaleb's laughter filled my mind, memories of us climbing the swaying oak trees spinning in my mind. Those memories urged me on, and I pressed harder and harder and harder until—the ice began to crack.

I shoved with everything I could conjure—my might, my will, my heart. The crack shattered into a thousand jagged pieces and my water broke through. The liquid bubbled beneath my fingertips, moldable and tame—a good soldier, readying for battle.

Opening my eyes, I reached to the heavens and let my Curse break free.

Within seconds, I brought the blizzard crashing to its knees.

Without the snow coating the world in white, we could finally see. We shouted for Kaleb, my heart slamming against my frozen ribcage as we searched for him, my twelve-year-old hands holding the roaring snow beast at bay.

"There!" I exclaimed. Kaleb's black toque poked out

from the snow, the remainder of his body tucked under a coffin of white. Ezra and I tugged him free. His skin was an ashen gray. Our knees buckled as we trudged through the deep, endless snow, frantically dragging Kaleb as he faded in and out of this realm.

When we reached the safe embrace of the cottage, I stayed at Kaleb's side, watching as Ezra applied various salves, chasing the frostbite from his skin, the ice from his veins. When Ezra told me that Kaleb would survive, that small, remaining ember that kept me standing was snuffed out.

My knees caved and I bowed to gravity.

The dark abyss called sweetly as it dragged me down, down, down.

"What are you thinking about?" Kaleb asked, his fingers cracking an egg and pouring its contents into a bowl.

"Just about Ezra leaving again," I said as I moved to his side and began to cut up a red pepper, my fingers expertly dicing it.

He lightly ruffled my hair. "She'll be back."

I smiled warmly. "I know."

Chapter 5

"Wake up, child." A voice eased my frantic mind—a vivid, brilliant light among an endless void. I chased after the orb, and when I grabbed ahold, my body jerked awake, my mind still trapped in the aftershock of my nightmare.

"I couldn't save him," I panted, my cheeks wet. "I couldn't save Kaleb."

Ezra brushed my tears away, her voice a whisper. "All is well. Kaleb is right here."

I looked beside me. Kaleb was asleep, his chest rhythmic in its rise and fall. Peaceful. Safe. I looked to Ezra, my voice hushed. "You're back." It was strange for her to be back so soon; she hadn't even been gone for a full day.

She nodded, crawling her way over to the loft ladder. "Come downstairs and we can talk."

I peeled my sheets off my sticky, sweat-soaked legs. I rifled through my bag, plucked out the enchanting onyx feather, and followed her to the main floor.

When we were nestled on the settee, warm teas in our

hands and a heavy, patchwork blanket draped over our laps, I looked to her. "Yesterday, when we got home, I thought you would be gone for a while."

She took a loud swig from her cup, her shaky hand nearly spilling the steaming liquid. "I thought I would be too."

"What changed?" I asked, using a wee bit of my magic to command the tea to lie dormant—I didn't want her to spill it on herself. I couldn't determine if her shaking hand was caused by old age or something more.

"Things change." She gave a half shrug.

A cryptic answer. I didn't care. I pried some more. "Where do you go?"

The same question I had asked a thousand times before.

"To a place that fills me with hope," she said, her aged voice softening. And I swore, for a second, her milky eyes began to clear. I blinked. No, I'd just imagined it.

"Why must you always give such cryptic answers?" I pleaded, my frustration growing. I turned my head to the side, too annoyed to look at her blank stare. This déjà vu conversation never went anywhere.

Then Ezra said something she had never said before, and the shaking in her hands stopped. "I believed I could protect you."

"Protect me? From what?" I asked, my brow hooked on a lure of confusion.

She let out a withheld breath, her lips flattening as her blank orbs stared past me. "From this world and the next, and all that it will ask of you." Her shoulders sagged in relief, and although she'd unloaded a mighty burden, by the look of her face, it seemed tainted with defeat. I didn't like it. I had never seen such an expression written in the hollows of her face before.

"I don't need protecting anymore," I replied softly, warmly, my hands placing my cup of tea down on the side table and then clasping the one in her lap. "I'm no longer a little girl."

"No." She chuckled, and although it was warm, it tasted of sadness and longing. "I suppose you're not."

"If anything, I should be the one protecting you now." My fingers gently squeezed her hand, time stitched with age spots, wrinkles, and scars. "Oh, I almost forgot. I found another one." I dug into my pocket and revealed the shimmering black feather, radiant with starlight.

Gently, I set it in her palm.

She raised it, studying it for a second with her vacant gaze, as if her blindness couldn't stop her from seeing it. A soft smile touched her lips. "It is just as beautiful as the others," she said, returning it to my palm.

"What do you think they mean?"

"I don't know." She chuckled, her bony shoulders shrugging a bit too theatrically. The curious smile on her lips prescribed the opposite meaning to her statement. I might have bought her answer when I was younger, but not anymore.

"You know. Don't you?" I countered softly, not looking for a fight but still not quite willing to let this go.

Her smile grew wider. "I might have an idea or two."

"Will you tell me?"

"No," she said firmly, shaking her head.

"Why not?"

"Because it is not my story to tell."

"Whose story is it?"

She beamed, white eyes shining in the firelight. "Yours."

Later that morning, after training, I walked to town with a basket full of items Ezra had plopped inside and a list of things I was to barter for—most of them I could not pronounce. Half of them probably didn't even exist. I mumbled, tempted to chuck the list into the wind, but as soon as my bootheels hit the cobblestone streets, I came to an abrupt halt.

Soldiers filled the village, the king's crimson banners waving in the wind, a dreadful hello. With this many soldiers, I suspected a mass Cleansing.

A crowd, louder than normal, had formed in the village square, the group growing larger with each passing minute. I wedged my way to the front, itching to get a look, and when I made it, I nearly fell to my knees.

Three rows of men were lined up, fifteen in each row. I knew most of them. Standing at the end of the back row was Kaleb—his face ghastly white.

I screamed his name.

He jerked his head up and our eyes locked.

I shoved at the wall of soldiers that separated us. My Curse felt like lava, rolling through my veins, beckoning for release. I had to get to him—

"Hear ye. Hear ye," shouted a man wearing a finely tailored wool tunic and a voluminous wig. The leather belt wound around his waist emphasized his bulging gut. He stood on an upturned crate, a scroll stretched out before him. He cleared his throat twice. "His Majesty's army continues its just and righteous work, cleansing the lands of the Cursed and driving them farther into the Cursed Lands. As of this day, October sixteenth in the thirty-fifth year of the king, a royal proclamation has been bestowed. Any man over the age of eighteen and under of the age of twenty-four is to be conscripted, immediately, into His Majesty's Royal Army to help rid us of the Cursed filth."

"No!" I bellowed, my voice lost amongst a hundred others. Mothers, fathers, siblings, and lovers, all of us begged, pleading for our loved ones' lives. The angry crowd started to push, but the wall of soldiers held firm.

In the past, when the king had enacted conscription, the conscripted were sent to training camps and then to the Cursed Lands—the last stronghold of those who actively rebelled against the Crown. They were known as the Cursed rebels.

The men sent there never returned home.

The thought of Kaleb's body lying on a bloody battlefield, face void of life, surfaced in my mind.

There was no way in the Spirit Realm I was going to allow that to happen.

I clenched my fists, my gaze locking with Kaleb's. But where fear should have been, he had replaced it with something else—a plea.

Not to do anything.

I shook my head—my mind was already made up.

"Please," he mouthed, his shoulders sagging in defeat.

He raised a shaky hand, his long fingers spreading over his heart, tapping twice as he held my gaze firmly with his own.

Tears pricked my eyes. Blurry-eyed, I looked around. The defeated crowd was starting to disperse. I wanted to scream at them. Tell them to turn around. To fight. To make a stand. They did not realize the power they held.

And perhaps, neither did I.

Until now.

My gaze locked on the soldier about ten feet from me, the king's crest so proudly stamped on his armored chest plate—that would be the first thing I wiped off.

I gritted my teeth and tugged my arms to my sides as I conjured from that deep, eternal well within. It swelled. Filled to the brim. Eagerly lapping. Ready to explode. I dropped into a warrior's stance, my bridled Curse ready to be unleashed. Finally.

But before I could conjure a single drop . . . the air evaporated from my lungs.

I grasped at my throat as if it had been sewn shut, my mouth opening and closing like a fish out of water. My body quaked, starved of life-giving oxygen.

The world was fading.

No, no. No! Flashes of red carved out my sight as I dropped to my knees, the hard cobblestones chewing into my flesh.

Before my head hit the ground, I had one final thought.

If this was what dying felt like . . .

I only wanted to do it once.

Chapter 6

When I awoke, my body was bombarded with a variety of aches and pains. I groaned. The pressure in my head was the worst of them all. Gods and goddesses, why did everything have to throb?

I forced my unwilling, traitorous lids open.

Dull, flickering candlelight illuminated dark, unfamiliar surroundings. A medium-sized bed, which I was currently lying on, encumbered the small room. To my right was a tall dresser—a couple of black and silver rings carelessly scattered on top—and on the other side of it, a closed door. At the far end of the room was a closet, the bilateral doors with wood slats tightly closed. To my left, a window, the blackout drapes pulled shut. And although they were made of a thick navy fabric, where daylight should have trickled through the seams, it did not.

Realization hit me—it was some time after dark.

How long had I been out?

And where in the Spirit Realm was I?

My heartbeat quickened its trot. Although I was not under the bed's blankets, there was a light blanket thrown over top of me. I slid it off and scrambled to stand, but the room swirled, so I plopped back down and closed my eyes, willing my brain to restore control over my cumbersome body. After a minute or two, I determinedly licked my lips and tried again. Slowly, I tested gravity's pull before I stood up. Thankfully, the spinning stopped.

So far, so good.

I slunk towards the window and cascaded the drape to the side. A row of houses stood across the street, their cracked, sparse clay rooftops bathed in the light of the moon. The problem with clay rooftops? They were a far cry from the cedar shakes used in the village I knew. I swallowed, my bones riddled with unease . . . I was not in Meristone anymore.

I surveyed my surroundings, searching for anything I could use as a weapon. My search stopped when I got to the top of the dresser. There, I spied a heavy-bottomed brass candle holder.

That would do.

My fingers wrapped around the neck of the candlestick—the hefty bottom turned upwards as I cracked open the door and peered into the dark and empty hall. Maybe I was alone? My gut grumbled in doubt. Heeding its warning, I dared a step forward, and then another as I slowly made my way down the hall, my booted heel soundless against the carpeted floor. A door to my left was closed.

My fingers itched . . . What was inside?

I smothered that dangerous urge. Curiosity be damned—

I knew what happened to the cat.

The hallway led to a string of steep stairs going down, a set of seven runs, a small landing, and then eight more that jutted to the side. I sucked in a breath as I tested my weight on the first one—thankfully, no protest—not a squeak. When I made it to the step above the landing, I peeked around the wall.

I sucked in my breath.

A demon of a man—shirtless and dangerously built, with wild, long onyx hair—had his back turned to me. His back was chiseled in lean, steely muscle—built for lethal movements, the kind that only took one swing.

The tattoos that adorned his back were mostly black, but a select few contained a small dose of color. Some of the tattoos lapped lazily over the others, like they were an afterthought upon a canvas that was running out of room. But despite the chaos, it was a work of art. The ink did not taper at his narrow waist, but instead slipped underneath his pants, slung loosely at his hips. I wondered how far those tattoos went down.

I rolled my eyes at myself. *Stop ogling your abductor, idiot.*

Was that an apple tattooed on his forearm?

Focus.

Right.

The room slowly began to seep into my vision. The kitchen was nothing to boast about, although it was a step up from the cottage. Shoe-weathered wooden planks lined the floors, and reddish-brown cupboards with oval brass knobs hung on the walls. A rectangular table with worn edges sat in the middle. To the far left, an open doorway led to another room, which I presumed to be the living room, judging by the tasseled edges of a rug that I could just barely make out.

Chop. Chop. Chop.

He diced something on a cutting board, rhythmic strokes of pressure being applied before the knife slipped through and bit into the wood beneath. Now *this* was a sight—a male whose body was built like a war god was in the kitchen—cooking? How very . . . domestic. And so very strange—men typically didn't cook.

I . . . didn't mind the sight.

Yes, he has an impressive backside, but your abductor is currently holding a knife.

Right.

White-knuckled, I brandished the candlestick and prepared to launch my attack, checking on my Curse, which was still fast asleep, rendering it useless for the time being.

"Enjoying the view, love?" he asked, his deep voice playful. Sensual. Like a lover's caress. His fingers casually lifted a carrot and placed it on the wooden cutting board.

"Where am I?" I demanded, buying time as I formed a plan.

"Safe and sound," he purred, his knife skills making quick work of the carrot.

"That's not what I asked," I said through gritted teeth.

"You, Little Goddess—" He turned, and his dark, obsidian, lose-your-soul eyes drifted up to me. "—are in the not-so-grand city of Norwood."

My eyes widened . . . I had seen *those* eyes before. The distinctive color of them clawed in my memory. He was the cloaked male from the Cleansing. The one that had sped up the flames, ending the girl's life.

Although he had not strapped her to that pyre, he had still assisted in her death.

Screw a plan. My fight-or-flight reflex kicked in and I launched the candlestick at his head as I leapt down the stairs. A waft of magic tinged the air, and the brass holder was knocked off course, sliding to the floor before it came to a skidded stop.

"Try not to harm the goods." He motioned to himself and his wickedly stacked abs. He winked—the audacity of this man.

"You're deranged," I hissed, utilizing the table as a barrier between him and me.

"Only on Sundays." He brandished a wicked smile—the kind that ended a virgin's reign.

Lucky for me, I wasn't one.

"I'll be happy to baptize you," I said, reaching down for my Curse but finding the water beast still sound asleep. I growled, eyes searching for some other weapon.

"Has the kitten lost her claws?" he mused, watching me as I eyed a wooden bowl filled with apples. "Perhaps I can help her find them again." He placed the knife on the table, two fingers pressed against the handle as he slid it my way. A faint smirk toyed at his full mouth as he turned that sleek, muscular back towards me and continued his cooking.

I plucked the knife from the table. Oh, he was sick, thinking he could lure me into some false sense of security by giving me a weapon. I wasn't biting, but that didn't mean I wouldn't use it.

I tore around the table, my boots pounding against the floor as I launched at him.

Unfathomably quick, he swung around, his large hand shackling my wrist. I looked up, and then up some more . . . Gods, he was tall, like unreasonably tall. He peered down at me, those dark orbs raking me over. A shiver ran the length of my spine. Ignoring it, I sent my free hand sailing into his stomach, my knuckles groaning upon impact. It felt like I had punched a brick wall. He strengthened his grip on my wrist, forcing me to let go of the knife. It clamored against the ground. With his foot, he slid it to the side, his gaze never leaving mine.

"I'm growing bored of this. Are you done?" he asked—a cat playing with his food. I could practically see his invisible tail swishing from side to side in anticipation as he waited to devour me. Bored, my ass. He was enjoying this . . . the deranged bastard.

"Hardly." I brought my knee up, targeting his manhood, but his hand deflected the blow. He caught the back of my leg and tugged it upwards, pressing my thigh against the side of his leg—the position . . . intimate.

My inner goddess poked her head up—I shoved the traitor back down.

He leaned in closer, his breath drifting along my neck, his voice so deep I could feel it rumble all the way down to my core. "Are you done now?"

I answered him by ramming my skull into his, my teeth chattering in response. He let go of my leg, his hand massaging his head. My vision blurred and I stumbled back, but not before I threw a few more shots in his direction—they were sloppy, but I felt a sense of satisfaction when I landed one of the blows. He grabbed my hands, utilized his leg to take out the backs of my knees, and brought me crashing down. His massive body straddled mine, his hand cuffing my wrists above my head.

He peered at me through those thick, black lashes, his sinful voice in my ear. "I can think of a *dozen* other things I'd rather do with you on your back." He parted his lips, his tongue pressed against the bottom row of his teeth as his gaze slowly dropped—brushing over my lips, lingering on my neck. Suddenly, he released my captive wrists and raised to his feet, the mere height of him rendering me dumbfounded.

"Shall we start over?" He extended one tattooed forearm corded in thick veins and heavy muscle, offering his hand adorned with black and silver rings. "Von."

I glared at his oversized mitt, despised it . . . I took it.

But I didn't give him my name.

"As fun as that was, *Sage*, I would like to get back to supper," he said, a casual nod towards the cut-up vegetables.

My mouth popped open. "How do you know my name?"

"I know a great deal of things about you," he replied as he pulled a drawer open and took out a cast-iron skillet, muscles contracting with each movement.

His admission was far from comforting.

"Why did you bring me here?" I demanded.

"You were about to announce to a few hundred soldiers that you were Cursed, just to save your brother. Considering your power is in its infancy and you were heavily outnumbered, it was not the time or place to do so," he said nonchalantly as he tossed the vegetables into the pan.

"That wasn't your call to make," I said, frustrated that he had intervened. Because of him, I had lost my chance to save Kaleb, regardless of if it was a fool's plight. Rage bubbled and my Curse yawned awake.

"And it was yours? You were not capable of making a rational decision at the time. I stepped in. And I saved your ungrateful, *fine,* little ass. A mere thank you will suffice."

"*Thank you*?" I spat out the words as if they were poison. I locked my gaze on the back of his insufferable head, conjured from the well within, and hurtled a water spear, resembling ice in form but not temperature, at that damned tattooed back of his.

He jerked to the side, but his reaction was not fast enough. My water harpoon sliced the side of his arm before it obliterated the cupboard door, causing a firework of wood shards to rain down. He turned, looking to the wound in his arm, blood pooling at the torn flesh. He swept a finger over it, studying it—marveled at it, as if he had never seen blood before.

I fired another round at him, but not before I caught the look on his face.

I had once questioned if his eyes were brown or black, but now I knew. They were of night itself as they shifted to my throat and my supply of air was cut off.

My world went black and I returned to the land of nightmares.

Chapter 7

As I came to, a scream clawed up my throat, shredding its way out.

A muffled voice broke through, large hands wrapping around my trembling, sagging shoulders.

"Kaleb," I whispered in relief, my arms wrapping around him as I buried my face in his chest and wept. It had all felt so very real.

A moment passed before his warm hand began stroking my hair in rhythmic, comforting movements. I nestled in closer, but instead of citrus, notes of sandalwood and amber greeted me.

The illusion shattered.

I jerked away as I peered at the male with dark, endless eyes. He sat on the side of the bed, a cloth bandage wrapped around his bicep. As I looked at it, red started to soak through.

"Why have you not learned to control your dreams?" Von demanded, his tone clipped, as if he were angry with me. As if he had a right to be. I felt compelled to remind him that we were perfect strangers and therefore his anger was unwarranted.

I laughed. "That's absurd. People can't control their dreams."

"Those with the Curse of Dreams can."

"The Curse of Dreams?"

"You don't know? *She* didn't tell you?" he asked, a muscle feathering his freshly shaved jaw. His dark brows knitted, his handsome face stern-looking. Annoyed. He was overwhelming. From the expression he wore to the steely muscles that broadened his shoulders to his hair tied in a warrior's topknot—battle ready. He looked wild.

Focus.

"Okay, *abductor*, you are making very little sense right now."

I ignored that fatal attraction and reached down deep, stroking my slumbering Curse—waiting for it to wake. Biding my time once again.

"I did not abduct you. I saved you. And you are free to leave whenever you like." He crossed his arms, taut muscles flexing beneath that tattooed skin.

I quit petting the water beast—I was free to leave?

He leaned in closer. "And you, Little Goddess—" His voice returned to that smooth, firm leather tone. "—bear the Curse of Dreams."

"You are an idiot. I clearly have the Water Curse." I pointed at his arm, the bandage nearly soaked through—how strange. It was a small cut, and yet it was still bleeding. "Besides, there is no such thing as a Dream Curse," I responded, half tempted to fire up my quads and punt his beastly ass off the bed. Everything about him irked me.

He laughed, low and sensual and lazy. "I am amazed by how little you know. Perhaps I shall rename you from Little Goddess to Little Sprout."

I fired my foot at his face. Respectively.

He swatted it down. Respectively.

I hissed.

He laughed.

I flicked away my growing annoyance, curiosity taking the helm. "When you said *she* didn't tell me about dreams, who is *she*?"

"Ezra." A nonchalant reply. As if it meant nothing. As if it were that simple.

"Ezra?" I bellowed, confusion clawing at my mind, raking it over like coals.

Downstairs, a door opened, the exchange of air flow causing the old house to creak and groan.

Von smiled, those predator eyes shifting to mine. "Ah, here she is now."

I followed Von downstairs, my eyes boring holes in the back of his wild, raven-haired head.

Ezra's cane leaned against the wooden, lightly varnished chair. She hummed as she helped herself to a plate of food, plopping the stir-fry onto the stone-colored plate as if it were just another day.

My mind seethed. My eyes narrowed.

Ezra. Was. Helping. Herself. To a plate of food. In this

stranger's house.

Because . . . she was familiar with it.

All those times. All those times that she left us, was she coming here? Why keep it a secret from us? Was this her refuge from us?

To think, I had imagined her being off on some sort of great conquest, like some hero from one of my books. The notion felt laughable now. Bitter and ironic. I choked it down, wondering if my teeth had rattled loose in my head because it felt like they had just been kicked in.

What else had she hidden from us?

"Such scary-looking eyes for someone who wishes to save the lives of the Cursed," Von teased as he walked towards the counter. The carnage from my water harpoon was gone, the only remaining evidence being the doorless cupboard. He grabbed a cup and filled it with a dark amber-colored liquid—a drink in preparation, as if it were going to be a long night.

I scowled.

Ezra turned around, offering me a kind, warm smile as if we were back in the cottage, as if everything were normal. "I found an interesting rock on my way here. It's in my bag by the door if you want to see. But I warn you, don't peer too closely. I think it might trap souls."

I clenched my fists. "Rocks, Ezra? Rocks?" I stalked towards her and slammed my hands down on the smooth wooden top, the utensils on her plate clattering in response. "All of these years. Is this where you came when *you* needed a *break* from *us*?"

Ezra looked at me, her milky white eyes nearly as blank

as her face. She opened her mouth and then closed it.

Without a word, Von refilled his glass before he proceeded outside. The light pitter-patter of rain sounded briefly as he opened the door, the peaceful sound cut off when he closed it. The smell of wet earth and fresh rain sifted through the house, soothing my livid nerves momentarily.

"Will you sit down and give an old fool a chance to explain?" she asked, her untouched plate gently scraping against the wood as she pushed it to the side.

I sat. Not willingly. But I sat.

"I want to know everything."

"And so, you shall," she said, her hands reaching across the table, feeling, in search of mine. I withheld them in my lap, the betrayal of knowing someone and then realizing you don't know them at all burning up my insides.

She nodded, took a deep breath, and then she began. "You've always inquired about my travels, even when you were just a wee thing. I never gave a proper answer. But I suppose now, the time is right." She paused, her voice lowering, as if the walls were listening. "I am one of the Cursed rebels. Throughout the years, my travels have led me to the Cursed Lands, or sometimes on various quests."

I took a breath. Ezra was a Cursed rebel. It was a lot to take in, and yet, it made sense.

"I guess I'm not completely surprised to hear that," I replied, shoving my hand through my hair. It explained why a woman who hustled rocks and grew mold was so knowledgeable about fighting. It also explained why she never married Joe, never laid down any permanent roots. "All of these years . . ." I shook my head. "Why hide it from us?"

She paused, searching for an answer, before she said, "I wanted to give you a normal childhood. I planned to tell you when the time was right. That's why I trained you so much."

"What about Kaleb? You never trained him." Kaleb. A lump bulged in my throat. I wondered if she knew.

"Bah." She batted her hand at me as if that were a silly thing to ask. "That boy was not born to fight. That, my dear, has always been *your* path."

"Okay, but why are you choosing to tell me now?"

She grinned. "Because, child, the time is finally right."

I felt my frustration mounting.

Her smile faltered. "I sense your anger towards me, your confusion. But know this, I have poured the very essence of my soul into the Cursed rebels—it is why I cannot see so well anymore. But I would do it again without a second thought. And all of it, child, I did for you. So that you could have a future."

I thought about her words. I could almost see how much it had taken out of her throughout the years. Each time she returned, she always looked somehow older, her hair a bit grayer. Her gait less strong—less warrior-like.

I felt ashamed of my actions from a moment ago and questioned how I could grab my pitchfork so quickly and take aim at the only parental figure I had ever known. She had sacrificed so much, including her vision—all so I could have a future.

Her vision loss. The toll it had taken on her entire body . . .

It was my fault. I felt sick.

"No, you must never think that," she said, knowing my silence all too well.

Frustrated with myself, I opened my mouth, but she continued, "You are blameless in this. The Creator chose for you to be born now, during a time where those who are different are hunted. But being different is not a curse. It is a gift. *You* are a gift. A gift that deserves to be shared with the world, not hidden behind closed doors . . . hidden in a cottage in the woods." Slowly, she took a deep breath.

I focused on her aged hands. They had always been like a lifeline thrown out at sea—a sea preoccupied with pushing me down. But here she was, pulling me out.

Just as she always had.

Chapter 8

We talked late into the night.

As the rain droplets gave way to a heavy downpour, we moved to the living room, a knitted quilt draped over us both, just as we had done hundreds of times before. The living room was cozy, to say the least. Two large oval rugs, their colors faded yet still warm, were draped over the wooden-slat floor. A settee and a loveseat sat adjacent to each other, a low, rectangular table centered in front of them. A small fire crackled, the hearth producing a comfortable amount of heat, reminding me of home.

She told me everything—everything the Cursed rebels had done over the years. The good times—the victories, the friendships. And the bad—the blood, the tears, and the goodbyes that never got to be said. During those stories, my heart ached. Ezra could have very easily been one of the rebels who died on the battlefield. Just as she was my someone, those people were also somebody's someone. Fathers, mothers, sisters, and brothers—good people fighting for the same goal—a *future* for the Cursed.

We spoke about Kaleb, and of course, Ezra already knew. She assured me, in her uncanny way, that we would get him back. Something we would do with the aid of the rebels. Four of those rebels I would meet tomorrow, here, in this house. I learned that Von was a rebel as well, and that Ezra had known him for many years—since he was a young boy, I imagined. She said he was their best fighter, by far, and played a huge role in making sure the Cursed Lands stayed a step ahead of the Crown. She spoke rather highly of him. Hearing her do so softened my feelings towards him. Slightly.

As night began to yawn into the young hours of the morning, she patted my lap and suggested we go to bed. I didn't move as I felt one more question burning within me.

I cleared my throat and asked, "Do I have the Dream Curse?"

She looked at me, and even though her eyes were a blank canvas, an emotion flickered in them—one I had no label for. "Yes," she finally said, her head tilting down as if her blind eyes were studying her hands.

"How is that possible? I thought we could only carry one Curse?" I asked. My brow furrowed, tackled by confusion.

"Having more than one Curse is rare, but it happens," she offered with a nonchalant shrug.

I scanned her face. Why did it feel like she wasn't telling me something? I pressed on. "What *is* the Dream Curse?"

She cleared her throat. "The Dream Curse enables one to see the past, present, and future through their dreams, as well as the ability to see and talk to the ghosts of the dead." She bobbed her head. "The Dream Curse has made a lot of people go mad . . . It's not natural for the living to talk to the dead."

I pursed my lips. "So essentially, I have not one, but two Curses—one of which makes you see dead people and eventually you go insane."

Ezra nodded, her nonchalant response almost comical.

All of this was a bit comical. My head spun. My brain groaned. I gathered everything I had just been told about the damn Dream Curse, chucked it in the ol' fuck-it-bucket, and mentally wiped my hands of it.

Ezra was silent, no doubt searching my mind to see if the marbles were still there or if I had finally lost them.

"Still here," I assured her, tapping the side of my head.

In the quiet of the early morning, as I lay under the covers in this unfamiliar room, I was afraid to fall asleep—to dream. I did not particularly want to slip into that world of prophetic horror and decay, much less strike up a conversation with the dead.

I plucked at my bottom lip.

Had I done that before? Had I spoken to the dead?

Anxiety snaked a hand around my throat.

I hissed at it and turned onto my left side, peering at the blackout drapes, pushing my thoughts along, processing.

For as long as I could remember, my dreams had been riddled with nightmares. Ezra said that some might simply just be dreams, that not all of them were connected to the Dream Curse. Still, some had the potential to be prophetic.

The question was, which ones were real and which ones

were not?

All of it felt like shattered glass, the pieces broken apart, waiting for me to reassemble them, but when I touched them, they cut deep. How did one go about assembling shattered glass?

I let out a defeated sigh.

My body was tired. My brain was not.

I should try to sleep. I would have to be up soon, anyway, to meet four of the rebels and figure out a plan to get Kaleb back. My stomach churned as I thought of him, longing and sadness overwhelming me.

What if we failed?

No, I couldn't think like that.

I sighed for the tenth time, rolled onto my stomach, and shoved my arms under the too-flat pillow. I could hear Ezra's light snore through the paper-thin walls. Gods, this was going to be a long night.

Von had not returned.

He probably ended up in a brothel somewhere—he looked like the type, not that a male such as him would need to pay for sex. I didn't doubt that women constantly tossed themselves at him . . . I could only imagine what his body count must be. A number I probably didn't want to know.

Just to further torment myself, I pictured him lying on his back, those two large arms of his draped around curvaceous little brunettes, their bodies curled up on either side of his—a satisfied grin hanging on his full lips.

Great divine, he had nice lips.

Ugh. I grabbed the pillow and flung it at the wall, hissing at my laughing inner goddess, the traitorous snake.

I flopped onto my back and draped my forearm over my eyes, forcing my eyelids shut, and began the tedious process of counting sheep. By the time number twelve waddled his fluffy butt up to the imaginary fence, I gave up and headed downstairs.

Just as my foot touched the main floor, the door in the living room creaked open. Von, looking like a big, mischievous cat, peered at me as he strolled inside, his invisible tail flicking from side to side as he closed the distance between us.

It wasn't just his height; it was in the way he walked—Von didn't just take up room, he commanded it.

"Having trouble sleeping?" he purred, his body all too close to mine, his masculine scent bombarding my senses. It stirred something feral within me.

I shut it down. "I'm not in the mood." I turned away from him and fetched myself a glass of water.

"Pity. I do so love to play with you." He walked over to the counter and poured a glass of amber liquid into a short glass.

I didn't reply.

"Some things—" He slid the cup towards me, his head tipping to the side, watching, waiting. "—require more than water."

I eyed him suspiciously before I picked up the cup, brought it to my nose, and took a delicate sniff.

He chuckled, a deep, lazy sound. "Such a mistrusting little thing. If I were looking to poison you, I would utilize *other* means."

"That's comforting," I replied sarcastically. "Why did

you speed up the flame at the Cleansing?"

Onyx eyes flicked to mine. "I didn't want her to suffer."

"That's it?"

"That's it."

"Did you know her?" I asked as I took a careful sip. The liquid was heavier than whiskey, and it was filled with notes of vanilla, caramel, and something else, something that reminded me of the cottage—charred oak. I took another, my draw much deeper this time.

"No." He poured himself another.

"What's this stuff called?" I asked as I peered at the warm amber liquid. It was a far cry from the horse piss they served back at The Broken Mare.

"Bourbon." His deep, sensual tone made the word sound enchanting—like it was magic.

"I've never heard of it before," I stated flatly, drinking some more.

"Very few have."

"It reminds me of whiskey, but smoother." I glanced his way. "How did you come across it?"

"By accident," he started. "I make whiskey in my downtime. Sometimes I try out different ingredients, and one of the barrels I experimented with I forgot about for a *few* years and this ended up being the result." He gave me a devilish smirk. "Now, it's my drink of choice."

"Why do you call it bourbon?"

"It's a secret." He winked.

I rolled my eyes. "It's *not* bad," I goaded—the alcohol plying me, loosening me up.

"I thought you weren't in the mood tonight," he teased,

noting the shift in my mood as if it were written clearly on my forehead. Where some women might be charmed by this, I saw it for what it was. His species of male was a rare breed, the kind that used attentiveness, along with their arsenal of wickedly handsome good looks and dark, masculine charm, to gain an overnight pass. I doubted he was the kind that stuck around in the morning. Not that I planned on finding out.

"I'm not," I said flatly, any small morsel of fun drifting from my thoughts.

"Well then—" He reached for the bottle of bourbon. "—let me top you off." He raised the clear bottle to my glass and began to pour, his gaze lingering too long on mine before he pulled away and leaned against the cupboard beside me.

Those dark, incredible eyes unearthed my reserved state.

"Trying to ply me with alcohol?" I asked, daring a glance at him.

"Always," he said with a wicked grin as he clinked his glass against mine. He shot it back, the rose tattoo on the side of his neck making its debut. The detailing was impeccable, lifelike, and so unlike the simple tattoos I had seen before. I was tempted to touch it.

I tipped my cup back instead, the burn feeling good as the bourbon raced down my throat.

Warmth brushed over me, coating me in an armor of confidence.

I pushed off against the cupboard and moved so that I was facing him. Slowly, I lifted my gaze, putting on my best sultry, bedroom eyes. He kept his large hands against the countertop, his posture relaxed, that large torso of his inviting me in. I brought my mouth close to his, stopping an inch away.

Just when he was about to take the bait, I stepped back and sashayed my *ungrateful, fine, little ass* all the way to the staircase. I called over my shoulder, "Good night, Von."

Me – 1. Bastard – 0.

Like I said, I knew his type.

As I crawled into bed, it occurred to me that bourbon might just be my new drink of choice. Not that I could say the same for Von. Tall, dark, brooding males had never been my thing. I rolled my eyes at the obvious lie.

As if my thoughts had conjured him, the door opened and Von strolled in. He glanced at the pillow on the floor with amusement, knowing full well it hadn't walked there on its own. He tugged off his shirt, revealing his neatly stacked abs and plethora of tattoos. The bandage on his arm was gone— the wound now completely healed. That was odd. He unbuckled his belt and slowly tugged the leather strap free. All the while, his dark, onyx eyes were set on me. The muscles in his forearm flexed as he tossed it on the floor. Before I could protest and tell him to leave, he shucked off his pants.

Six-foot-too-many-inches-to-guess stood in front of me, ripped and corded in muscle and wearing nothing but a *too-tight* pair of underwear.

My mouth sprung open—gods, that better be a sock shoved in *there* because no man had any right being *that* well-endowed—I clamped it shut.

He snatched the pillow from the floor, threw it onto the bed, and collapsed on the mattress, his flipper of a foot stretching territorially across my side. Staking claim.

What an ass.

"What are you doing?" I seethed between clenched teeth.

He shot me a victorious, unlawful grin. "This is *my* room. *My* bed. And *you* are in it."

I huffed at him and rolled over, my back towards him. "Bastard," I muttered under my breath.

But the insult was drowned out by a windstorm of a snore emulating from his stupidly full lips.

I tugged the blanket over my head.

Chapter 9

Despite the peaceful nature of my dreams that night, four hours of sleep was not nearly enough. Now, I was tired—tired and groggy and heavily sleep-deprived.

I glared at Von, who sat across the table from me, his heavily toned arms folded over his chest. The black leather pants he wore today were sinfully tight, endorsing his muscular legs and strong, sturdy ass. Great divine, *that* ass—everything about it screamed *built for thrusting*. It repeatedly snagged my attention this morning as he made a brew of coffee.

As if there were a tether connected to my gaze, those incredibly dark eyes of his lifted and settled on me, sending a soft smolder my way.

I shoved my thoughts surrounding his great assets to the side, labeled him an idiot once more, and rolled my eyes with added emphasis.

He chuckled, lapping up the attention, regardless of if it was good or bad.

Ezra busied herself in the kitchen as she worked on whatever she was working on—I hadn't quite figured it out yet. It looked mushy, like something I would feed a pen of hogs. My stomach lurched—was *that* . . . lunch?

"Um, Ezra, can I help you?" I offered.

By help, I meant toss it in the trash—it was past redemption.

She shook her head. "No, no, I'm almost done." She sniffed the air, a smile touching her face. "They are here."

I swallowed.

I would be lying if I said I didn't feel a twinge of nerves. It had always just been Ezra, Kaleb, and me. Now, that was changing.

A brief knock came from the living room door before it swung open and birthed a hulk of a man.

There was no way around it, he packed one hell of a physique—the kind that required years of heavy training, not genetics. His skin was deeply tanned, a warm, luxurious brown that framed his striking eyes. They were 3:00 a.m. eyes—the kind you stared into as you danced at the tavern, the kind you knew you probably shouldn't go home with, but you did anyways, the kind that kept you up all night. His off-white tunic hugged his muscular arms and torso, the V-collar loosely strung, exposing a sneak peek of his rippling pectorals. He dropped the bags he was carrying on the floor with a loud *thunk* and began to stretch out his impressive physique as if it had been a long ride.

The female version of him strolled in after. Turning to him, she gestured to the bags dropped carelessly on the floor and hissed, "Why did you have to dump all of the bags right at the door? Take them downstairs."

"I was just stretching out my back. I'll do it in a bit," the male replied, leisurely taking his time as he continued to stretch, just to annoy her a bit more.

They had to be siblings.

"Do it *now*," the woman huffed at him.

He gave her a challenging look that suggested he was ready to throw down with her if need be.

Yup—definitely siblings.

And judging by their looks? It was even more likely they were twins. I guessed they were somewhere in their mid-to-late-twenties.

Like him, she was tall, but where his muscle was bulky, hers was lithe. Her features were strong on their own, but when you looked at the full canvas, she was strikingly beautiful. She wore riding clothes—tight pants and a cropped shirt, exposing her midriff. Her style was so unlike the layers of clothing most women wore. But she owned the look, just as she owned the room she just walked in to—confidence and certainty exuded from her in heavy, undiluted waves. The kind that might make other women balk if she glanced their way.

Shortly after, a smaller female walked through the door. She threaded her fingers with the taller female's. There was nothing kin-like about the way they held one another's hands, leaving me to presume that they were a couple.

The smaller female looked like a little doll with her wavy auburn hair and wandering doe-like eyes. Our gazes briefly connected and she immediately looked to the floor. She wore a lovely taupe-colored dress with long, flowy sleeves, the bodice adorned with delicately stitched flowers like icing on a tiny, little cake.

The last person to walk in was nothing but legs. Judging by the brown trousers, *it* was a *he*. He carried a heap of bags in his arms, the towering stack well over his head, making it hard for him to see. For a second, he reminded me of Kaleb, but before I could let any deeper feelings bubble up, I walked over to him.

"Can I give you a hand with those?" I asked, peering around the stack of bags, seeing his face for the first time. He looked young, boyish still. His dirty-blond hair hung over his brown eyes. He blew up a chunk of hair to the side so he could see and offered me a kind smile. "I think I'll be alright. If you could just get the basement door." He nodded in its direction and I peered over my shoulder, noticing it for the first time.

Oh yes, he reminded me of Kaleb—always biting off more than he could chew but pushing forward anyway.

"Of course." I walked towards the basement door tucked into the underside of the stairs and opened it for him. He used his foot to feel for the step before he slowly started his descent.

"Hello, kids," Ezra crooned behind me as she bustled over towards them. They exchanged hugs with her, making small talk about the weather before moving on to the headway being made with the rebels and so forth, filling Ezra in on anything she had missed.

Watching her interact with them, these people she clearly had an established relationship with, was—well . . . it was odd. But I supposed it was something I would get used to.

I offered my hand to the doe-eyed girl who just happened

to be the closest to me. "Hello," I said in greeting.

She peered at my hand, leaving it hanging there, as if she were unsure what to do with it.

The tall brunette stepped in between us, and although the movement seemed protective, she offered a warm smile. "I'm Harper, and this is Lyra," she said, gesturing to herself and then to the petite female at her side. Lyra stepped closer to Harper, the magnetic pull between them impossible not to notice.

Lyra offered me a timid smile, but her eyes did not meet my face.

"Nice to meet you both. I'm Sage," I replied, returning my name.

The brown-haired male slipped in, his hands in his pockets. He let out a low whistle. "Von didn't mention you were such a looker." He flashed a roguish smile, showcasing his perfect white teeth. "I'm Ryker."

The way he said his name, with such ownership—such confidence, I didn't doubt that he was. He could slap a copyright mark on it and I wouldn't think twice.

"Nice to meet you, Ryker," I said, banking on him having heard me say my name to Harper and Lyra a few seconds ago.

"Pleasure's all mine," Ryker replied, that handsome grin making another debut. With a smile like that, I wondered how many women chased him down, begging for an encore.

There was no doubt about it. Ryker was a stud.

Von silently maneuvered to my side, his feet having no business being that quiet.

Ryker looked at Von, his smile fading. In all seriousness, he said, "Did you drink all the bourbon without me?"

Von thumbed over his shoulder towards the kitchen. "Just restocked it yesterday."

"You two idiots better not be planning on screwing off to the taverns tonight," Harper scolded.

In that moment, I decided I liked her already.

"Sister, listen here." Ryker slung his arm over her shoulder, the weight of it causing her shoulder to drop. "The fact that you're fifteen minutes older than me means diddly fucking squat."

"I'll show you diddly fucking squat," she hissed as she shook off his arm, her hand emitting a ball of burning flame.

Ezra whacked them both over the heads with the back of her wooden spoon, an audible *thunk-thunk* sounding in the process. "That's enough, you two."

Harper's flame ball retreated into her palm as she reached up and rubbed the ache. Ryker performed the same action, his movements mirroring hers, their synchronicity comical.

Von and I chuckled, and judging by the humor in Lyra's eyes, she would have as well—if she could. I had yet to hear Lyra speak . . . I was beginning to wonder if she could.

Ezra shooed us to the table. "Alright, kids, take a seat. We have a few things to discuss. But first—" She plucked the giant bowl of mush off the counter and plopped it onto the table. "—let's eat."

We were all thinking it.

The big question.

Is it safe?

I shoved the mush around on my plate, my roiling stomach begging me not to. And by the looks of the others—minus Ezra who was busy chowing down—they were thinking the exact same thing. Apparently, Ezra's cooking was more notorious than I realized. How many others had fallen victim to her so-called meals? Perhaps we should have a moment of peace, pray for those poor, poor souls.

Harper pursed her lips, her eyes shifting to Lyra, who looked genuinely horrified. The young boy, whose name I learned was Soren, braved the first bite. We all looked at him, waiting to see what horrors awaited us.

He tipped his head to the side, his brow furrowing, and then . . . he flashed a smile. "Wow, Ezra, this is *actually* good."

I nearly fell out my chair. And by the looks of the others, they nearly did too.

I eyed Soren as he took another bite, and then another.

I was mystified. Somewhat intrigued. But mostly shocked.

Lyra caved next, testing a very, very, very small bite. We all watched her. Her face lit up and she offered the rest of us a thumbs-up.

The twins looked at each other, shrugged, and dove in, both tempting an impressively sized bite.

Von and I were the last man and woman standing. He gave me a *go on, dig in* nod.

I returned the nod, bidding him to go next. He shook his head.

My grumbling stomach goaded me into submission, so I took my first bite. The Spirit Realm must have frozen over because it was . . . good.

As we ate, the sound of clinking utensils and conversation filled the air, but despite the warmth and laughter, I felt a sense of longing—a sense of sadness. Kaleb would have enjoyed this. He would have slipped into the conversations with ease, talking to Soren in his big brotherly way and impressing Ryker and Von with his extensive liquor knowledge. But instead of being here, he was somewhere out there. I glanced out the kitchen window hanging over the sink, my own guilt weighing me down.

The sun had almost reached its highest point in the crisp blue sky, not a single cloud in sight today. Was the sun shining where Kaleb was? Or was it cloudy there? The fact that I didn't know bothered me enough that I excused myself from the table, put my plate in the sink, and slipped outside through the back door.

I inhaled a deep breath of fresh air as I leaned against an exposed timber. The mortar that used to surround it was cracked in places, bits and pieces on the weedy ground below. A layer of goosebumps dotted my skin as the cool October air brushed over my arms. I rubbed my hands together, but despite the chill, my mind was elsewhere.

My thoughts were with Kaleb and wherever he might be. Was he safe? Or was he . . . My thoughts stitched from worry to fear until one single question lingered—what if we failed?

My breath snagged in my throat.

A whisper of fluttering wings caught my attention and I looked to the sky. But in place of the bird I expected to see was a feather, as black as a starless night. I reached out, and although I couldn't explain it, I just knew it would come to me—they always came to me. And sure enough, a gentle breeze nudged it along, and the onyx feather drifted into my hands. It was identical to the other ones I had found—shimmering and huge and radiant. Ethereal.

A shadow draped over me and the cool breeze floated away, my bare arms no longer cold. I looked up from the onyx feather into the eyes of Von—his eyes the same perilous black as the feather in my hands.

You found me, whispered a breathless voice inside my mind.

My eyes widened in surprise, and I dropped the feather. It was snatched up by the wind.

I scrambled, trying to get it back, but Von caught it with one swift reach.

His fingertips pinched the quill, the tip of the feather pointed towards the sky. He extended his arm towards me, his eyes locking with mine. "I believe this belongs to you."

Slowly, I reached for it. Despite my carefulness, my fingertips brushed against his as I took the feather, and upon contact, a male's voice—*his* voice—sounded in my mind.

As I promised I would.

I jerked away from him, clutching the feather against my pounding chest. He looked like he wanted to reach for me, but his expression receded and his hand slipped into his pocket instead. Casually, he watched me, the rise of his broad shoulders set at a steady, controlled pace.

Mine was the exact opposite as I stumbled for breath. "We should go inside," I blurted out. The easiest answer to my current situation.

"As you wish," Von replied with an unprecedented

amount of dark swagger. His hand slipped around the brass handle and he opened the door, gesturing for me to go first, as if he were a gentleman. The notion was laughable.

As I passed the threshold, he turned and followed me inside, his body a breath behind mine. He dropped his head over my shoulder, whispering in my ear in his deep baritone, "Do you know what causes a predator to chase something that runs from it?"

I raised one lone brow, already skeptical of where this was going. "What?"

"A strong prey drive," he answered, his heat a caress upon my skin. "So please, continue to run, Kitten," he purred in his primal way. "I've always enjoyed the chase."

His words coaxed a shiver to stroll down the length of my back. I couldn't explain it, but part of me wanted to play—to run. Just to have him chase me down.

Goddess divine, help me . . . Where was this coming from?

Chapter 10

When we returned to the house, the dishes were cleared from the kitchen table and the group was in the living room. Lyra and Harper sat on the floor, while Ryker, Ezra, and Soren took up one of the settees, which meant that Von and I sat alone on the smaller one.

Ezra must have briefed them about Kaleb because we skipped that part and delved right into the meat of it—how we were going to get him back.

Lyra rifled through the vast stack of papers scattered on the coffee table, plucking a few out and handing them to Harper. Harper relayed what they were and why they might help us before she handed them out to us. Together, the two of them performed like a well-oiled carriage wheel.

Based on the information Lyra had compiled, I could tell she was incredibly knowledgeable about the king and his soldiers. One drawing—a map of Clearwell Castle, the king's favorite—was very detailed. I wondered if she had once lived there and if that had something to do with her not being able to speak.

By the time the sun dipped beneath the horizon and dyed the sky in soft pinks and light purples, we were not much further than when we began. The biggest problem? Figuring out which one of the king's twelve training camps, scattered across Edenvale, Kaleb had been taken to. I studied Lyra's hand-drawn map of Edenvale, marveling at the great expanse of land, while the others conversed.

"Are you nuts? We can't abduct the king's advisor," Harper said to Ryker, her arm draped over Lyra's shoulder, the two of them still on the floor.

He leaned forward. "I know it's drastic, but think of the bargaining power it would give us."

"I'll keep that in mind when I'm strapped to the pyre." Harper nodded in somber agreeance with herself, her ponytail bobbing. "Besides, a mission like that would take months to plan, let alone execute."

"Harper is right. The king is not one to associate with rebels," Ezra chimed in. "Fifteen years ago, we attempted something similar, and it resulted in many lives needlessly lost."

"The Battle for the Red Rose," Soren said, his gaze drifting to the floor. His fists clenched so tightly, the whites of his knuckles showed, the stretched skin chasing off blood flow.

The room fell silent—a brotherhood of sadness linking them all—one that I could not understand. But I wanted to.

"What was the Battle for the Red Rose?" I asked, extending a newborn branch to their deeply rooted tree.

Soren looked at me, his face solemn. "As I'm sure you

know, the king doubled down on the Cleansings fifteen years ago. During that time, our people tried to plead with the king for mercy, but he would not listen—his hatred for our kind was too strong."

Soren paused, searching for the right words.

Ezra patted his leg comfortingly and she continued for him. "Our people came up with a plan. If the king's ear remained closed to our voices, we would open it. We sent out a group to abduct the queen—we had no intentions of harming her; we only wished for the king to listen. When the group was successful and they returned with the queen, we sent our demands to the king. He agreed to meet with us, to discuss a peaceful outcome." Ezra tapped her chin thoughtfully. "Seems to me, I missed that meeting, as you and Kaleb were both sick at the time." She shook her head. "Anyway, the king agreed to the terms. We returned the queen, his Red Rose, to him, and he signed the contract that we all believed to be binding."

"But his word meant nothing," Ryker cut in, his large frame dwarfing Soren, who sat beside him. Ryker leaned forward, his face solemn as his eyes met mine. "That night, the coward sent an army to butcher all of us in our sleep."

Soren's voice cracked. "That battle was the one that cost my parents their lives." He glanced down at his hands. "I was two."

Empathy overwhelmed me. He had been two—*two years old*—when he lost his parents. "I'm so sorry," I offered, a small part of me wishing I had never asked at all.

"It's alright," Soren said with a soft shrug. "I'm not the only one who lost family members that night."

Lyra rubbed Harper's back—a comforting touch, Harper's shoulders lacking their usual straight structure. Ryker looked no better than his twin, those broad shoulders of his also pushed down.

How many orphans were created that night because of the king—because of his hatred?

Von's voice cut through the silence, his steel tone carving our attention. "The king's advisor is still our best bet for finding out where the new recruits are stationed. But we don't need to abduct him." Von cocked that proud, strong chin ever so slightly to the side. Perilous, dark eyes swept over me, lingering too long on my lips before they shifted to meet my eyes. "Because he's going to tell you."

The way he said it, it sounded absolute.

"How?" I asked, my brow crinkling.

"Patience, love. I will get to that. But first, you are going to need a horse," he answered, draping an arm over the back of the settee, just behind my head.

I glanced at Ezra for answers, but her blank eyes stared right on past me. I licked my lips, my brow shooting up. "A horse?"

"Yes, Little Goddess, a horse." Something wicked tugged at the corner of his lips. "Unless you would rather ride with *me*?"

I eyed the palomino mare as she plucked a broad-leaf thistle weed, small enough that it would still be tender. It was a jackpot of a find for her, considering the crowded, dirty corral she was in. Years of manure and rotting hay were piled so high, it was a wonder she didn't walk over the remaining few feet of fence. But she didn't—she was too invested in searching for a blade or two of grass among the heaping piles of horse dung and swarming black flies.

I didn't know much about horses, as I had only ridden them a handful of times, but judging by the looks of her sunken haunches and weary eyes, it had been a while since she'd left the confines of her corral—and a while since she'd had a proper meal.

"Good bloodlines this one. She's about sixteen hands high, a bit on the taller side for the breed," said the horse dealer—a short man with a sparse gray beard he frequently stroked. He patted her backside twice, a puff of dust coating the air.

She flicked her tail at him, swatting him away as if he were just another bothersome fly.

"What do you think?" Von asked, his tattooed arm draped over a wooden post, the paint worn off by the strokes of time.

I shrugged. "I don't know. Do you think she'll make the journey?"

Gray Beard cut in. "Don't let her old age fool you, she's still got a lot of miles left in her."

He misunderstood what I was asking. I wasn't talking about her age—more so her gaunt, malnourished state. I could hardly imagine her making it across town, let alone the three-day ride it was going to take for us to get to the city of Belamour.

But she was the only horse available, and as I watched

her as she searched for another nibble of grass, compassion overwhelmed me. No living thing deserved to be kept in such a tight, confined space.

"We'll take her. Does she—" The end of my sentence was clipped short as a black fly took a greedy bite out of my arm. I wacked at it, cursing the little beast as it flew away.

"Does she have a name?" I finished.

Gray Beard nodded, his fingers rhythmically stroking the wiry strands of his beard again. "Yes, milady. Full name's Lightning Breeze, but I call her Lightning."

The name did not suit her. Lightning implied speed, and nothing about her suggested that. She even chewed slow, like molasses being poured on the coldest of January days. I performed a mental shrug, my hands too busy defending myself from the black fly horde buzzing around me. Eager to get away from the swarm, I gestured to Gray Beard, my voice directed at Von. "Well, pay the man."

"So bossy," Von murmured amusedly, completely unbothered by the flies—even they knew he was rotten to the core. Von tossed a small cloth pouch towards Gray Beard, the coin clinking inside as it landed in his hand. "We will be needing a saddle as well."

Gray Beard hastily dumped the pouch out into his calloused, soil-blackened palm. He jiggled the coins, testing their weight. He offered us a wide, toothless smile and then stepped into his shop, the slab door groaning in protest as it closed behind him. Not long after, he returned, producing a worn brown saddle.

Later that day, I sat atop Lightning, my hands wrapped around the saddle horn. Von held the bridle, leading us through the dirty, sludge-filled streets of Norwood. People watched as we walked by, and some women even stopped their bustling to stare—at Von. I couldn't blame them—he was something to look at. No wonder the husbands quickly tugged their wives along, one even covering his wife's eyes, saying "Look away, woman," as if Von were the king of sin, sent here to corrupt her soul with his primal masculinity.

And those damn leather pants were not helping matters.

Despite the constant looks and blatant staring, Von didn't seem to notice, didn't seem to care.

As we made our way through the older part of town, I surveyed the poor, rundown condition of the homes. From the cracked, moss-covered foundations and the bowing timber walls to the sagging roofs, spotted with a few remnants of clay slats, everything here seemed worn, old, and tired. Given up on. It reminded me of the poor horse I was riding, the thought stirring my hand to pet her neck a couple of times.

To my left, a few houses ahead, a door flung open, the sound of a crying babe coming from inside. A red-cheeked woman rushed out, carrying a heavy-looking chamber pot. With a huff, she dumped it onto the streets before she hurried back inside. The sound of the baby's cry snuffed out as the door slammed behind her.

And then it hit me. *The smell.*

I made a face, clamping my mouth shut and fighting with the contents of my roiling stomach. One would think after living with Ezra for so many years, I'd be used to such putrid smells, and yet the opposite was true.

"Norwood uses the old sewage system," Von said nonchalantly, as if he were immune to the rotten, festering egg smell.

"I can see that." *And smell it.* I pinched my nose.

The old system relied on manual labor for sewage disposal and fresh water—this meant dumping chamber pots by hand and fetching water from the closest well.

The new system had been invented by a man named Horace Crete. He used underground clay pipes to move fresh water and sewage to and from homes—in separate pipes, of course. Originally, the Cursed had used their powers to pressure and heat the system, but after the ruling monarchy declared war on them, the system was forced to rely on heavy rainfall for pressure and fire to heat the water instead. It was considered a major step back as the system no longer ran as well as it had when the Cursed looked after it.

When it was discovered that Crete was Cursed, despite giving Edenvale the gift of indoor plumbing, he was captured, tortured, and Cleansed.

I owed my knowledge of Crete to Kaleb. As Kaleb was an aspiring inventor, naturally he looked up to Crete—learned everything he possibly could about the man.

I glanced at Von. "I didn't know the old system was still in use within the cities. I thought it was just some of the villages and towns that had yet to switch over." Meristone had made the switch many years ago—well before my birth.

"There are still many towns and cities that rely on the old system—some are just better than others at hiding it," he replied, knee-high leather boots sounding against the broken remnants of cobblestone, which had been chewed up by horses' hooves and pounded out by carriage wheels.

"Why don't they convert to the new system?" I inquired,

my hands gripping the saddle horn, the sway of the horse still somewhat unfamiliar.

"A system like that takes coin, and the people here don't have it. The majority of Norwood lives in poverty," he answered, his raven-colored hair appearing almost a dark blue under the orange gaze of the sun.

"Why is that?" I inquired, daring an inhale. The foul smell was starting to dissipate.

"It *was* predominantly a Cursed community, and one of the first places the Crown started Cleansing. In some cases, entire families were wiped out, whether a direct result of the Cleansing itself or by losing the provider of the family. The impact of those losses, the removal of parental figures, has rippled into what you see today."

"That's terrible." I surveyed the decrepit remains of the city as I mulled over his words. "You seem to know a great deal about Norwood. Did you grow up here?"

He tilted his head to the side, and it was just enough that I could see the slight upturn of those salacious lips. "No, Kitten, I did not. I grew up somewhere very far from here."

"Does this *very far from here* place have a name?"

"It does," he mused. But that's all he offered.

By the time we returned to the house, it was late afternoon, and the preparations for our departure were well under way.

Chapter 11

Just before the break of dawn, while Norwood slept and the twinkling stars still dotted the black sky, the seven of us stood outside, readying to leave.

"Are you sure you don't want to come?" I asked, Ezra's warm, boney hands in mine.

Her milky white orbs shifted to the sky, pausing before she spoke. "This is not a journey for me to make, and my old bones would only slow your young ones down. I will be in the Cursed Lands, waiting for word of when you and Kaleb return." Her hands slid from mine. Patting her pockets, she searched for something. I hoped it wasn't another rock—she had already given me one for the journey. Victory chartered her smile as she bore down on a pocket inside her deer-skin coat, withdrawing two vials. "The green one is for sleep. I tested it out last night. Worked rather well. The orange, citrusy-smelling one loosens the tongue." She placed them carefully in my hands. "The second one might have a few side effects," she muttered to herself.

"Like what?" I asked, peering down at the two glass vials, their liquid sloshing from side to side despite my hand being perfectly still.

"Who knows." She offered me a toothy grin, accompanied by a wink.

With her wooden cane in hand, the stain on the handle rubbed off from years of use, she bobbed it from side to side as she walked over to Ryker, following the sound of his voice as he spoke with Von.

Carefully, I wrapped the vials in a thin piece of linen. And even more carefully, I placed them in my saddle bag. My hand slid from the buttoned flap, moving on to stroke Lightning's flank. She nickered in response, her tail not bothering to swat me away like she had done with Gray Beard. So far, the two of us were off to a good start.

I took a step back, taking her in.

Even though we had just gotten her yesterday, I could already see an improvement—proper nutrition apparently did wonders for a horse, although she still had a long way to go. I just hoped this journey wouldn't be too much for her, but Ryker, who'd tended to her, claimed she was a strong-willed old girl and would be just fine.

A day into riding, and I was beginning to feel sorry for Lightning. Despite dropping the pace numerous times, she was having an increasingly hard time keeping up with the other horses.

Truth be told, I was struggling as well, although it killed

my ego to admit it.

A dull ache in my back had started a few hours ago. Now? I nearly writhed in pain. I gathered the cracked leather reins in my right hand and massaged the ache with my left. It helped. A little.

Von's white stallion sidled beside mine, instantly dwarfing my mare. He was a monstrous beast who had no business thinking he was a horse. Stacked with lean, powerful muscle, the horse, whose name I had yet to learn, matched his owner in stature and size.

I craned my neck, looking up at Von. His black hair was tied up in a tight topknot, a small braid forming at the base of his neck and falling over his shoulder. It was secured at the bottom by a thin strip of leather and a delicate white feather. Under the setting sun, it glistened like it had been sprinkled with flecks of shimmering gold.

Beautiful.

He caught my gaze and something inexplicable shifted between us. Something I had no words for. All I could do was feel. The force of it—a constant pull.

His obsidian eyes shifted, darting to my back.

Instinctively, I quit massaging and recoiled my hand into my lap—I didn't want him to think of me as weak. But when his eyes flickered back to mine, I realized he already knew.

He pulled on his reins and the horse reared back, its magnificent mane swaying with the movement. Turning to the others, he said, "We will set up camp for the night. The horses need to be fed and watered." His gaze slid back to mine, and he offered me a wink, extending his double meaning . . . *I* was the horses.

I scowled.

He chuckled in response.

"That works for me, I'm starving." Soren's voice sounded from the rear.

"I could eat the crotch of a dead cow," Harper proclaimed as her chestnut-colored mare trotted up beside us. Lyra rode with Harper, her arms wrapped tightly around Harper's gold-chained waist.

"I don't doubt that," Ryker quipped from the helm as he led us off the beaten trail and into the overgrown thicket of the woods painted in browns and oranges and yellows—the palette of autumn.

When the willows' dangling branches grew too thick, we dismounted our horses and led them the rest of the way. I was thankful to be walking, sensation slowly returning to my tingling legs.

I heard the sound of rushing water long before I saw it.

Choosing a flat spot beside the rocky, winding bank, we set up our temporary camp. I inspected the width of the river, pegging it around forty feet wide. Farther up, where the elevation was higher, the river channel steepened and the water fell over the edge, tumbling towards the river below. The turbulent flow caused by the waterfall created a light mist, illuminated by the moonlight.

While Ryker tended the horses, Harper and Lyra worked on gathering wood and building a fire, although judging by their giggles and constant touching, they weren't taking their jobs too seriously. Soren took to the woods to hunt, while Von just up and left without any explanation.

And I?

I was a useless sack.

Plopped on a stump, I massaged my back, willing the white-hot spear of pain to go away. I was thankful none of them seemed to mind. They simply let me be while they worked on their tasks. Besides Ryker and Harper's frequent spats, the group worked incredibly well together—an attribute brought on by years of comradery.

What would Kaleb think of it all?

A lump, unpalatable in size, welled in my throat. I shoved my feelings to the side and watched as Harper stacked the wood, creating a teepee shape. She waved her hand over it, the dry kindling catching instantly, the flickering of orange and yellow illuminating Lyra's soft features and wide, doe-like eyes as she sat down.

"When did you find out you were Cursed?" I asked Harper, reaching my hands out towards the warmth.

"When I was a young child," Harper replied as she sat beside Lyra, her arm draping over Lyra's petite shoulders.

"She lit our aunt's house on fire. Burned it right to the ground," Ryker cut in as he joined us, a wide grin spread across his handsome face.

"I was four. It's not like I knew what I was doing," Harper defended with a one-shoulder shrug. "Besides, I wasn't the dumbass who nearly killed himself because he wanted to get rid of his gods-given Curse." She pointed her gaze accusingly at him.

Ryker's jaw ticked, his twin's words skillfully plucking a nerve.

"Is that even possible? Getting rid of one's Curse?" I asked, curious.

"It is," Ryker answered, heavy muscles flexing as he reached over the fire. The flames turned a white-hot blue and the crackling increased as it mowed down the wood.

"How?" The question slipped out.

The twins exchanged a worried look with one another, and I was reminded how little they knew me. Kaleb would know that pure curiosity was my motive for asking—not because I wanted to get rid of my Curse, something I was proud of, more than anything.

"I'm just curious," I offered.

Harper's gaze shifted from Ryker to me. "There is a nightmarish device, a crown made of thorn-covered vines. When it is worn, it can unstitch the Curse from our cells. But it's a horrific process, and very few have been known to survive it—if any. It was rumored to be crafted by the God of Death as a gift for his bride."

I had heard of the God of Death before, but what I knew about him was limited, mostly because his stories belonged to the Old Religion, which had been banned many years ago.

"There are no words to explain what it's like." Ryker paused. "I've tried, but I can't even come close."

I swallowed—my mouth suddenly dry. "Like glass in your veins." I breathed out.

They stared at me, blinking.

"Yeah," Ryker drew the word out, one thick brow raising. "How did you know that?"

"I have no idea." I glanced down at my hand, but it held no answers. I looked to Ryker. "Where did you find it?"

"The Cursed Lands have miles and miles of catacombs beneath them—some of them still explorable. In an unmarked section, rumored to be the burial grounds of a forgotten queen, the device was found. Initially, no one knew what it was or what it was for, and it wasn't until it was tested that its purpose was discovered. Scared that it might fall into the wrong hands, the Elders tried to destroy it. They tried nearly everything they could think of. They even tried to throw it into the Endless Mist, but not even the mist would take it."

"It's called the Crown of Thorns," Soren added as he walked up to us, two bloody rabbits hanging by their feet by a rope he held in his hand. He stopped a few feet from the fire and offered me a huge smile, his eyes squeezing shut. "Hope you like rabbit."

"I do," I answered warmly before I turned back to Ryker. "How did you come to be in possession of it?"

"The person who originally found it was our father." Ryker's hand gestured to him and Harper, his bicep flexing with the motion. "After the Elders accepted that they couldn't destroy it, they entrusted it to him."

"He didn't tell any of us where he put it, not even Mom," Harper added, her fingers drawing light, rhythmic circles on Lyra's arm. Lyra performed the same rhythmic movement against Harper's leg.

"So then, how did you find it?" I asked, eager to hear more.

Ryker smirked, leaning back in his perch on the fallen tree. "I'm *very* resourceful when it comes to tracking things."

"It's true," Harper confirmed.

I was chock-full of questions, but there was one pressing harder than the rest. "Why did you want to get rid of your Curse?"

Silence passed. For a moment, I wondered if I'd pried too much.

Ryker's brown eyes firmly met mine. "Because I was in love."

"In love?" The word tasted foreign on my tongue.

He nodded. "I was sixteen at the time. Young, foolish—but still just as handsome." He winked before his playful tilt returned to his low, resonant tone. "Word reached the Elders that the king was preparing an army to attack us. It was rumored to be larger than one he used for the Battle for the Red Rose. Harper and I were tasked with tracking a group of soldiers camped on the cusp of Roganbush—a small village a day's ride from the Cursed Lands. I don't think I'll ever forget that night—the storm was like a rabid wolf. The rain was so thick, I could hardly see my hand in front of my face. There was so much lightning, I thought the gods were fighting in the clouds. But it was just what we needed. Under the cloak of it, we infiltrated their camp and kidnapped a soldier." A smile teased the corners of his broad mouth. "Fallon."

"One of the best female fighters I've ever gone hand to hand with. I still have the scar to prove it." Harper tilted her chin upwards, showcasing the thin white line on her otherwise flawless skin.

"We took her back to the Cursed Lands." Ryker leaned forward. "The Elders didn't treat her well. As soon as we returned, they threw her in a dark, cold cell. They interrogated her frequently, and sometimes they even used force." His right hand clenched—his tell. "And I let them do it." He didn't mince the self-loathing in his words.

"We didn't know, Ryker. We didn't know how far they

were going to take it," Harper offered, a rope thrown out to her twin who was drowning in an ocean of guilt.

He must have latched on because his gaze lifted and he continued, "I couldn't stay away from her, regardless of the contempt she held for me. I was to blame for her abduction—for the cell she was locked in. I felt compelled, almost like I owed it to her to make things better. I'd take her food, and for the longest time, she'd just shove it away. One time, she even threw it at me—I couldn't blame her." He chuckled to himself, shaking his head slightly. The smile drifted, his expression shifting. "Eventually, she started to accept the food. I'd watch her eat, and sometimes we'd just sit there in silence and stare at each other. And then, one day, she just started to talk." His eyebrows raised, almost as if he were still in disbelief. "She told me that she had lost her parents when she was young. Having lost my own mother and father, I understood that pain, and we bonded over it. As the nights stretched longer, and our talks became deeper, I realized I was falling in love with her—our first kiss was through those metal bars." He stopped, muscles tensing. "She was in that cell for a total of three months, but she never caved—never gave the Elders the information they wanted, no matter what they did to her." The fire cast a warm, honey glow on his face, but it did little to soften the firm setting of his clenched jaw and furrowed brow.

On bated breath, I waited for him to continue, but instead, he asked me a question. "Do you know what crossing the unconscious mind barrier does?"

"Yes, Ezra goes on frequent rants about it—she does not condone the act."

Ryker nodded. "The barrier protects the unconscious mind, but if someone with the Mind Curse crosses that barrier, a piece of them gets stuck, like a sliver wedged inside. This means that they are always privy to that person's thoughts, that they can loot through them and even distort them. It's like peering through someone's bathing room window and watching them undress, except the perpetrator can *make* them undress, make them think they are in a bathing room, when in reality, they are stripping their clothes in the downtown square. Crossing the unconscious mind barrier is rape of the mind, and its use is disgusting."

I swallowed, not liking where this was headed.

He continued. "The Elders ran out of options, and they were running out of time. They held a council meeting that lasted three days, and after a nine to eight vote, they decided to break Fallon's unconscious mind barrier." Ryker shook his head, his expression filled with disdain. "I couldn't stomach the thought of them doing that to her. That night, Fallon and I forged a plan. I would break her out and we would leave— together. But there was one problem—I was Cursed and she was not. You know how the outside world treats people like us, what they do to the people who are close to us—even if they aren't Cursed. I refused to be the reason she was shunned from society should the truth ever be found out about me."

He paused. I think we all did.

He supplied a single determined nod, and then he continued. "It took me three hours to find where the Crown of Thorns was hidden, and half of that was spent digging. But I was a fool. I had no idea what I was in for."

Harper stared at the dwindling flames, her voice shaky as

she spoke. "When I found him, his blood, it was . . . It was everywhere." She turned her hand over, staring at it as if the blood were still there. "His veins, it was like they had turned to glass and sliced through his skin."

I leaned in, my heart galloping.

"I thought he was going to die," she whispered. "It took all of my strength to rip that fucking crown off his head." She clenched her jaw, tension rolling off her in heavy waves. "After the healers had him stabilized, they told me how close he had come to losing his Curse—to losing his life. He was unconscious for six weeks."

Ryker cracked his knuckles, his shoulders set, tense. He looked lost in thought, her words returning him to some sort of private damnation.

The five of us sat in silence, each of us consumed with our private thoughts.

When the fire was just about to go out, Harper fed it four more logs. A flick of her wrist and it was stoked into another monstrous flame.

If we were somewhere private, there would be no need for the theatrics of logs, but considering we were not far from the traveling path, a fire without wood would lead to a lot of questions should someone come by. Those types of questions tended to create problems. And problems were not something we had time for.

Soren walked over to the river. Producing a jackknife from his pocket, he started the tedious process of cleaning the rabbits. Harper excused herself from the group before she got up and walked over to Soren. She held out her hand, and he placed the knife in it. From there, she took over cleaning the rabbits, explaining to Soren how to properly do it.

Lyra got up, dusted her backside off, and walked over to the food sack. She pulled out a tied cloth filled with different breads—I knew what was in it because I had packed it before we left.

I turned to Ryker, one last question on my mind. "If you were in a coma for six weeks . . . what happened to Fallon?"

He shot me a victorious smirk. "Von broke her out."

"So then, where is she now?"

He tilted his head, searching the night sky. "I have no idea."

"What about the Crown of Thorns? Where is it?"

His gaze drifted to mine. "That's just it. No one knows. It disappeared the same day as her."

I rolled onto my back, the thin bedroll offering limited protection against the jagged rocks and lumpy, cold ground. I stroked my full belly lazily, stocked full of fire-roasted rabbit and bread as I breathed in the crisp, midnight air. Everyone else was asleep—well, everyone except for Von, who still had yet to return.

There were two snorers in the group—Ryker and Harper. Their light snores tangled with the melody of the forest—frogs and crickets, dancing leaves, and constant rushing water.

Although my body felt tired from the journey, my mind was busy sorting through everything I had been told tonight, from the Crown of Thorns to the girl Ryker loved—Fallon.

My understanding of this world was continuously expanding more and more. I wasn't sure how I felt about it. At times, I wished I could close my eyes—close my eyes and return to the innocence of last month's life, where it was just Ezra and Kaleb and me. Our little family in our cozy, humble cottage.

I peered through the sighing canopy leaves, studying the twinkling, vivid stars dotting the onyx sky.

Could Kaleb see them tonight?

Wherever you are.

My heart panged.

I turned on my side, Soren's bedroll not far from mine.

As he slept, my mind adjusted his features—straightening the nose and deep setting the eyes—making him look like Kaleb. Pretending he was here, safe and sound, gave me enough peace that I closed my eyes and surrendered to the realm of dreams.

Or nightmares—whatever my Dream Curse had planned for me.

Chapter 12

I jerked awake, gasping for air. The muscles in my legs burned, as if the exertion of running in my dreams had transferred over to reality. I was tempted to look over my shoulder and make sure that the thing that was chasing me in my dreams wasn't actually standing behind me, ready to lunge.

In my nightmare, pounding rain, the color of blood, had beat down on me. I was running for my life as something dark, something menacing, chased after me—but I was too frightened to turn around and face what it was. Just when it was about to reach me, I woke up.

As my heaving lungs slowly returned to normal, I took in my surroundings.

In the wake of my nightmare, the woods loomed ominously, my mind forging shadows into monsters. I blinked, reminding myself that I was awake and safe.

Everyone else was still peacefully asleep—except for Von, who was nowhere to be seen. I glanced towards the slumbering horses. His massive beast was sleeping beside the others. Part of me felt the faintest bit of relief seeing it there— a feeling I didn't bother to unpack.

Deciding the land of nightmares was the last place I wanted to return to, I left my bedroll and headed into the privacy of the woods to relieve myself.

Gods, I hadn't realized I had to pee *that* bad. I tipped my head back, my eyes closed as my stream cut out, the unburdening of my bladder feeling blissfully good. Standing, I wiggled my pants over my hips and did the buttons up before wandering over to the river.

Reaching the edge of the grassy bank, I knelt down and dipped my hands into the racing waters. The current was strong, but I breathed my will into it, and it stilled peacefully around my hands. Raising my cupped hands to my lips, I drank the cold, crisp water before it could trickle out through my fingers. I wiped my mouth with the back of my sleeve, listening to the sounds flowing around me.

The switchgrass chattered, their swaying directed by the gentle breeze. Every once in a while, it sounded as if something small were moving through them, like a young child running barefoot—a sound from my childhood, one I knew well.

But the sound suddenly changed. The chattering became forced, as if an adult was barreling through the switchgrass— straight for me.

I jerked upright, twirling in place.

A mouth with two curved fangs, stretched unnaturally wide, was headed straight for me.

I swung my forearm upwards, and the mouth attached to

a snake clamped around my arm. The snake was massive, its girth well over the size of the widest part of my upper leg. But its size was the least of my concern, considering its needle-like teeth were plunged into my arm. An inferno of pain burst through my nerves, starting at the bite before splintering off and traveling throughout the rest of my body.

Frantic, I conjured a dagger, its structure packed so tightly, it resembled more ice than water. I yelled as I drove it into the side of the snake's head before pulling it back out and driving it in again and again. The snake's inky blood saturated my hand, my dagger, staining it a blackish red.

Unclamping its iron bite, the snake released my arm, recoiling into itself. It slammed its head against the ground repeatedly.

I threw my dagger to the ground, clamped my free hand over the bite, and turned to run, but my legs would not move. The white-hot, branding pain was being smothered out, leaving a great numbness in its wake. My knees wobbled once before they gave out. I tried to curse as I fell into the billowy switchgrass, but my tongue felt like a lump of coal, weighted down and impossible to lift.

Although I had never been around a snake of this size before, I had been around enough of them to know that some possessed venom that could cause paralysis . . . which explained my current state.

I lay like a broken doll tossed carelessly on my side, waiting for a child to pick me up and give me life. Even though my eyes were the only thing I could move, they stayed locked on the snake. It continued to thrash its head against the ground, causing bits of rocks and dirt to fly up with each strike. It let out a sound, a blood-curdling scream that sounded . . . human.

My pupils narrowed.

"You stupid wench," it cried out, its tongue slithering over the *s*, the words dragged together.

. . . The snake was talking to me.

That *or* the venom was making me delirious—which was also a possibility.

It shook its head to the side one last time, as if it had finally knocked the pain loose. It slithered towards me, its powerful body crushing the ground beneath it. Utilizing its tail, it wrenched me off my side and flipped me onto my back. My head lolled uselessly to the side. A quick swipe of the snake's tail straightened my head so I had no choice but to look at it.

Its slit pupils stared into mine, the side of its head still oozing with blood. It was a wonder the creature was still alive. It leaned forward, its forked tongue slithering in and out of its mouth, flickering over my face. "All I was going to do was eat you."

I wanted to recoil, to get away, but my body was a useless husk with a fully functioning brain—it was horrifying. I had to do something, anything. I turned to my Curse, but that, too, was rendered immobile.

"You see, young human females are my favorite treat. They are a tender meat and so easy to digest. They are so soft and supple," the snake hissed in a male voice. "I was so looking forward to swallowing you whole, but then you stabbed my beautiful face." It wobbled its triangular head woefully from side to side before it stiffened its neck and flashed its venomous fangs at me again, spitting saliva and words in my face. "Again! And again!" It paused. "But if I eat you now, you will never feel the pain that I felt . . . I think I will drag you back to my den and keep you as my human pet," it said, the words strung together like a haunting melody.

A sickness, born from panic and fear, washed over me. I wanted to vomit, I wanted to scream, but I could do nothing. That was terrifying in itself.

The snake chuckled. "Now, now, don't worry. I can turn into a man, you know. A handsome one, at that. If you prove to be a good pet . . . I could pleasure you as well." Its tongue flickered over my face, over my lips—furthering its meaning.

In that moment, I was thankful I couldn't feel.

"Of course, you wouldn't feel any pleasure per se, as I would have to keep injecting you with my venom. I wouldn't want you to try to hurt me again." The snake wrapped the end of its tail around my ankle, slowly sliding it upwards. "Perhaps you would prefer me in this form. Afterall, my species has two cocks and—"

In a flash of metal and moonlight, the snake's voice was cut off as a sword glided through the air and chopped its head clean off, revealing a much larger predator that stood behind the snake's convulsing body.

Obsidian eyes stared down at me, blacker than the Endless Mist itself.

The snake's body did not fall to the ground. Instead, it recoiled like it was still alive. It slithered maniacally, its sporadic movement causing it to roll around as if it were fighting itself. I heard a giant-sized splash, indicating it had fallen into the river—leaving its twitching, snapping head behind.

Von returned his sword to its leather sheath, his dark gaze never lifting from mine. He cocked a black brow, the one with the slit through it. "How did you manage to get yourself tangled up in this situation, Kitten?"

I glared at him, or at least pretended to.

He smirked. "You know, I think I might prefer you like this . . . less mouthy."

Bastard.

My reply must have transferred to my eyes because he tipped his head back and laughed, knowing full well what I had called him inside my head.

If it were not for his unreasonably high arrogance, I might find him attractive right now.

Powerful arms wrapped around me as Von plucked me from the ground and carried me farther down the river, away from the snake's bloody head. After a short walk, he lowered us both to the ground, my useless body stretched across his lap with my torso propped against his chest.

He inspected the bite marks. My head was angled just enough that I could see them. There were two cylindrical markings, the area around the holes bumpy and swollen, like a handful of pebbles had been shoved under my purplish-red skin.

"I detest seeing another's marks on you," Von murmured, his eyes lifting from the wound, meeting mine. He growled softly. "They should be *mine,* Kitten." His head dipped as he pulled my arm to his lips. His mouth wrapped over the bite, and he began to suck. The powerful muscles in his jaw worked as he drew out the venom mixed with my blood.

But he did not spit it out. Instead, he drank it straight down.

Slowly, the feeling in my body began to return, starting with the area he sucked. To my dismay, I was locked in a body where the only thing I could feel was Von's hot, wet mouth against my arm.

And damn it, it was rapturous.

No mouth in any of the three realms had any business feeling *that* good.

If I had been able to throw my head back and cry out in pleasure, surely I would have. Instead, my defrosting lips just barely parted, and the strangest mumbled moan fell from them. It was equal parts embarrassing and horrifying.

Von's mouth lifted and I could feel his laughter against my waking, feverish skin.

Great.

His carnal lips twisted into a grin, noting the telltale redness in my cheeks. "Yes, Little Goddess," he purred, his eyes shackling mine. "My mouth feels *that* good. Just imagine how good it will feel between your thighs."

"Bastard," I hissed, but it came out more like *ba-her*.

"What was that?" he teased, enjoying this far too much.

I rolled my eyes, my gaze darting to my arm, telling him that I wanted him to continue. Especially so I could say the word *bastard* again. Properly.

"So very bossy." He grinned wickedly, but he did not budge. Instead, he stayed there, watching me in my half-frozen state.

"Hurry up," I demanded, the words sounding like *Urry*

uh.

"Only if you mumble pretty please for me with that half-lead tongue, darling," he mused coyly, his fingers drifting to my chin, tilting my face towards his.

Pretty please? I'd rather claw his eyes out.

But I needed the feeling in my hands to do so.

"Pretty please," I mumbled out, the words hardly audible.

"Good girl," Von praised in his smooth bourbon tone. It rumbled all the way down south, conjuring a liquid heat in my lower belly. He returned his lips to the bite and began to suck some more.

As feeling returned to my body, I writhed beneath him, not realizing how strong the draw of his mouth was—until now. What had felt intensely pleasurable before was now starting to hurt. I wiggled again, but he held me in place, refusing to let me go until he had sucked out every last drop.

The venom had to be mixed with my blood—how could he swallow either of them and not be sick?

"Why doesn't it effect you?" I slurred, my tongue still clumsy in its execution, but better than before.

He lifted his mouth from my arm, licking his lips like a cat that had just feasted on a plump mouse. "I'm immune to venom."

I thought I saw something green flicker in the depths of his obsidian eyes. I blinked, looking again. No, it was just my imagination.

"How can you be immune to venom?" I asked with less of a slur.

"I've built up a tolerance to it as I have been exposed to

114

it countless times."

I had heard of that before, especially with the people located on the far south side of the continent, where venomous snakes were said to be more common. Was that the *far*-away place Von had referred to when I asked him where he was from? It made sense.

I nodded to myself as I slowly moved upwards and off his lap. His broad hand supported my back, aiding my movement. When I was sitting, I shifted towards Von. "I have never seen a snake that size before. Have you?"

Von smirked. "Yes, I've seen ones even bigger than that."

"Bigger than *that*?"

"Yes, Little Goddess, bigger than that."

"Gross."

Von chuckled.

"I, uh—" I paused, fumbling with the words. "I heard the snake talk."

Obsidian eyes met mine. "Is this your first time hearing an animal speak to you?"

"Yes." I nodded. My thoughts skittered to a halt. "Wait, can you hear them too?"

"I can," he said nonchalantly—as if it were normal.

"Von, animals don't talk."

"Don't they?" he challenged.

I nibbled on my bottom lip, weighing and dissecting. "I have gone twenty-two years without hearing an animal speak. Why now?"

He shrugged. "The gods work in mysterious ways."

"I guess," I said, his reply about as helpful as a hungover

Kaleb on a Sunday.

"What did it say to you?" Von asked, his tone plated with cool iron, the muscle feathering his jaw suggesting otherwise.

"A number of things I'd rather not go over again," I replied, wrapping my arms around my bent knees.

Von didn't press, but I wasn't entirely done with the topic. "It said it could turn into a man."

Von's expression didn't change; he just waited for me to continue. But I did not have anything to continue with—that was it. I wanted him to reply, to tell me if it was possible or not.

I sighed. "Well, is it possible?"

"It is," he said, his body unnaturally still in that predatorial way of his.

Me? I nearly convulsed. "What?!" I exclaimed. I could hardly believe it—so I stated as much.

"Why is it so hard to believe?" Von asked. "You wield water and I wind. Magic exists in our world. Just because you have not experienced it before does not mean it isn't possible."

I suppose that made sense. Sort of. "It's a lot," I said, gently shaking my head.

"And it's going to continue to be that way. Your world is about to get a lot bigger, Sage." He held my gaze. "Are you prepared for that?"

"I have to be," I replied honestly. I had no other option but to forge on, to walk the path I currently found myself on. I had to—for Kaleb. After a moment of silence, I said, "Thanks for, uh, saving me." I struggled with the words even though my tongue was back to normal.

"It was *my* pleasure," he purred in that smooth, deep baritone, the kind of voice that could make a girl undress without realizing it.

I looked away, fighting the heat in my cheeks. "We should probably get back to camp."

Von raised a black brow. "Is that what you really want to do, love? Or would you rather . . ." He shifted his weight onto his hand, leaning farther into me. ". . . stay here, with me?"

I swallowed, half inclined to take him up on his offer. But the other half of me won out and I pulled away from his intoxicating male pheromones. "Morning is well on the way and we have a long day of riding ahead of us. I'm already tired just thinking about it."

Von chuckled. "Your excuses will only hold out for so long against me, and when they do run out, which they will, I will be sitting at the end of an exceptionally long table. And do you know what will be spread out in offering on the table before me?"

An indecent blush rose on my cheeks. *Don't ask. Don't ask.* "What?" Gods, my traitorous tongue.

A wicked, wicked grin. "You."

My heart fluttered, but it was no longer in my chest—it had headed south.

"But until then, until *you* are ready—" He stood, extending a tattooed hand to me. "—we will continue this little game of cat and mouse."

Cautiously slow, I placed my hand in his. There was a great contrast between the two—unmarred and moonlit framed by tanned, heavily inked skin.

"I've been meaning to ask," I said, wobbling my way to

a standing position, no better than a freshly born fawn. "Why do you have *king* tattooed across your fingers?"

A letter on each one, from pinky to pointer. A crown on his thumb.

Midnight eyes met mine as he spoke in that rich, bourbon tone. "For the same reason I'm going to ink yours with *queen* someday." His broad hand covered the small of my back, strengthening my unsteady frame. "It is what fate demands."

Chapter 13

According to Harper, we would be in the city of Cent, the "c" pronounced as a "k," within the hour. As it turned out, Harper was right.

When we arrived, the welcome sign read, "If you *CAN'T* find it anywhere else, you'll find it in *CENT*." Once we hit the main part of the city, I could see why they choose that slogan. The number of traders, merchants, and vendors was overwhelming. They reminded me of the swarm of baby mice Kaleb and I found that time we moved the log shed, all scrambling over one another, darting every which way.

Due to the densely packed streets, the group was forced to break apart, although Von prowled close behind me.

Last night's conversation hadn't gone much further, especially after his musings about my knuckles being inked with the word *queen*. Although part of his proclamation made me feel weak in the knees, it also made me roll my eyes. I had no desire to be a queen—none whatsoever. The notion itself was laughable.

Surprisingly, the bite mark had almost healed, which was odd, but considering that a snake had spoken to me *and* it could turn into a man, a quick-healing wound wasn't nearly as insane sounding as the rest.

"Pelts for sale! Pelts for sale! Come and get your pelts," shouted a merchant, a young girl, pretty, even with her pockmarked skin. She set her ocean-blue eyes on me. "Oy! Miss! You look like you are in need of a nice mink pelt." She wrapped a brown one around her petite shoulders, modelling it for me. "Not only are they the latest trend in fashion, but with winter on the way, it'll keep you warm. Better than a lover's arms!"

"Sorry, I'm not interested," I said as I walked by. Lightning followed dutifully behind me, her slack reins in my hand.

An older woman, shoulders bent like a hawk's talon, stepped into my path. Her gray hair was streaked with deep purples and vibrant reds, the colors globby in some places and crusty in others. What was the medium she used to color her hair? I looked closer, noting the tiny seeds.

Berries—*freaking berries*.

"What does your heart desire, my dear?" she asked, her colorful skirts rustling as she waddled towards me. "Tell me and I can make it come true. Restored health? No, you are too young to be worried about that. You must be after what all the women your age want: true love. Or perhaps, just *great* sex!"

The last option didn't sound half bad—goddess divine, it had been months now.

Her hand, stained purple, clasped my forearm. She leaned in. "And after that great sex, if his jelly is not for your toast . . ." She dropped her voice to a whisper. "If his seed is not something you want sowed—well, dear girl, I have something for that too."

I stifled a laugh at the strange use of jelly. Then again, judging by the looks of her hair, she probably had all kinds of uses for it—some I probably didn't want to know.

Shaking my head, I gestured I was not interested.

Suddenly, her expression changed, her eyes darting behind me. "Oh my." Like a cat in heat, she yowled out the rest: "You won't be needing that last one!"

I tracked her gaze to Von.

And damn it, she was right.

The God of Sin, who was rumored to be devastatingly handsome, had nothing—absolutely nothing—on Von. The wind mussed the rich black fur that was draped over his broad shoulders, emphasizing their powerful breadth. And those tight leather pants—well, they had no right to look that good on a man. He wore his thick, raven-colored mane in a messy, voluminous topknot. Two braids, barely visible, ran down the left side, the white feather peeking through. His hairstyle was so unlike what other men wore. Where their hair was trimmed, neat and proper, his suggested the exact opposite—unleashed, wild, warrior.

As if he sensed my gaze, his onyx eyes met mine. Yet one more thing that was un-nerving about him—those dark, perilous eyes. Before they could swallow me whole, I looked away.

"*That* won't be happening," I stated dismissively.

"Are you blind?" she asked, waving her hand in front of my face.

I batted it away. "No."

"Darlin', life is short, and they sure don't make them like *that*. In fact, I've never seen one like *that* before!" She howled loud enough for all of Cent to hear.

She wasn't wrong. Von was a breed of his own. Heat bloomed on my cheeks.

"Ah-ha! There it is." She smiled victoriously at me then patted my arm before she let me go. "Would you grant an old woman a boon?"

I eyed her suspiciously, not sure where this was going.

She clasped her hands together, tucking them just beneath her chin. "When your belly is swollen with his pup, come back and visit me. I do enjoy a good love story. And with the current state of things, the Creator knows we all need one."

I blinked, dumbfounded by her brashness. Quickly, I walked away from her, my long legs too fast for her to keep up.

She was nuts—the Ezra kind, probably a relative. I could find out by asking her stance on rocks, although I had a feeling I already knew. I patted my cloak's pocket, Ezra's rock still there—miraculously. I was surprised it had not fallen out by now, especially with all the jostling from riding.

A shadow fell over me, blotting out the light of the moon. Von peered down at me, a hawk surveying its prey.

"Why do you do that?" I asked, our horses falling into step with one another.

Something akin to a smile tugged at his mouth. "Do what?" He knew full well what I meant.

"Look at me like you are sizing up your next meal."

The words sounded even worse once they escaped my mouth.

He tilted his head in that superior-than-thou way, the glint of his sharp canines flashing as he spoke. "Perhaps, Little Goddess, I am."

"You are insufferable," I huffed.

"And you are divine," he purred.

As we reached the east side of the city, the tents and vendors faded, leaving streets bordered with taverns and inns and the odd brothel house. Even this side of town was packed with people, a continuation of that slightly chaotic thrum. The only difference? The scrambling mice were drunk on this side.

Ryker led us to an inn in an older building consisting of three floors. But despite its age, it was well cared for and still possessed a particular charm.

I grinned as I tethered Lightning's reins to the hitching post, imagining the hot meal that awaited me inside and the soft bed, void of a foundation of sharp, pokey rocks.

There was one more ingredient to my smile—we would reach our destination tomorrow.

Chapter 14

Belamour hooked my breath the second I saw it—a city of color nestled in the gentle embrace of rolling hills. Stores with large, stained-glass windows bordered wide, brick roads. The people here wore finely tailored clothes, the fabrics dyed in lush, rich colors—colors I had never seen before. It was like opening a velvet sack and finding handfuls of sparkling gemstones inside—emeralds and rubies and sapphires.

The Jewel of Edenvale—that's what they called it.

I could see why.

It took a while for us to get through the downtown core of Belamour. I may have dawdled a bit, my eyes wide as I breathed all of it in.

Soren's voice caught me off guard. "Well, here is our home for the next little while."

I took in the gothic manor that stood ever so proudly before me. It dwarfed the rich homes leading up to it. It looked like it had come from an entirely different era—the architecture boasting in grandeur.

We led our horses through the towering black-iron gates, up the winding path.

"Who owns this?" I asked Soren, gawking at the grand entrance—specifically the door. It was stupidly large. I wondered what type of tree they used to make such a massive slab—a century-old oak, perhaps?

"The Cursed rebels own it. The title is buried under a dead commoner's name, so the Crown has no idea it actually belongs to us," Soren answered as he, too, surveyed the large door.

Von looked like he was tempted to roll his eyes, but he stroked his beast's silken mane instead.

"The Cursed rebels own a variety of properties throughout Edenvale," Harper added as she and Lyra started to unstrap their traveling bags from the chestnut mare.

I felt a sense of satisfaction knowing that the properties were owned by the Cursed rebels and the king had no idea. In a way, I was beginning to understand that hope Ezra had referred to—could understand why she had devoted her life to this cause.

In some moments, I could see myself doing the same—anything to fuck with the king.

An hour later, after I unpacked, I stood by the arched window in my private chamber, surveying the picturesque landscape surrounding Belamour. Rolling hills sprawled, sloped, and churned, their curves bathed in oranges and yellows, soaking in the last rays of sun before it gave way to night.

I scuttled across the hall to Harper and Lyra's bedroom. It was like my own, a colossal-sized room decorated in rich, bulky furniture, all of it a bit masculine in taste.

Harper rifled through her traveling sack. She was still working on unpacking, and judging by her packed versus unpacked bags, she had a long way to go. She pulled a small bag out and plopped it onto the bed before she gestured for me to sit. "I call this my little bag of tricks," she said, all smiles.

Lyra watched as Harper began painting my face. She stroked a precise black line on my upper lash, with a drastic, sharp wing shooting to the side. She sank a goat bristle brush into a glass vial and coated my lashes, not once, not twice, but three times with it. As a finishing touch, she painted my lips red before she took a step back to admire her work. Satisfied, she offered me a mirror.

I glanced at the girl turned woman staring back at me. The kohl made my blue eyes bigger, brighter—almost glowing, if not a bit feline. And the liner she had used on my lips—lips I had thought of as thin—made them now look pouty, plump. I smiled at the face in the mirror before I gave her an approving nod. "You are good at this."

She batted her hand. "When you have a good canvas to work with, it makes things a lot easier." She turned to the dresser mirror and began to do her own.

Lyra settled on top of the dresser, watching Harper, her expression almost dreamy.

"What are you going to wear?" Harper asked as she smacked her freshly painted lips together.

"Um, probably just this?" I gestured to the plain tunic and riding leathers I currently wore.

She shook her head. "No offense, doll, but you are dressed like a beggar—you'll blow our mission. Go to the room across the hall. The armoires are stockpiled with ladies' clothes."

I sighed and did what I was told.

The room across the hall was a closet, large enough I could fit the cottage inside it. Sconces along the walls were lit, casting the room in a warm, honey glow. I opened a set of mahogany doors and a small gasp escaped my lips—I had never seen so much tiny lingerie before. The colors, the fabrics . . . I reached out. My fingers danced over one that caught my eye—onyx-colored silk, the dye so dark it reminded me of a night sky without stars, without a moon— the purest form of black.

Seeing you wear my colors . . . It makes me feral, said a distorted male voice—impossible to place. It was gone as fast as it had come.

My hand fell to my side. I blinked. What in the Spirit Realm was that?

"How's it going? Did you find anything?" Harper asked as she began rifling through another armoire, the hangers clattering in protest as she shoved them to the side.

"Nothing yet," I replied, still somewhat mystified. Gods, I needed to get some sleep.

She pulled a nearly see-through dress out and chucked it my way, the action forcing me out of my trance-like state. I caught it, surveyed it. I sputtered, "My underwear offers more coverage than this."

"That's the point," she said with a grin before shooing me to the bathing room. "Try it on."

I let out a sigh before I began to undress. If Kaleb only knew what I was about to do for him.

I was right. My underwear *did* provide more coverage than this sheer bit of fabric.

I, the cottage shrew, had never worn anything like this. Ever. To say I was out of my comfort zone did not even scratch the surface. It felt like I had been plucked from my cozy little home and now I was being dangled over a lion's den, hungry mouths snapping at me.

I couldn't wear this.

I stuck my head out the door and told Harper to find me something else. She sighed before she picked out a different one and handed it to me.

This outfit was better, still far out of my comfort zone, but better. The icy-blue silk was thin, but not sheer like the last outfit. It had a plunging neckline and high slits that went all the way up to my waist. A pinch of tightly sewn fabric offered just enough coverage to block out the peaks of my breasts, but not enough to cover the roundness. Although this was a slight improvement from the last string of cloth, I still could hardly believe I was wearing this.

Harper's outfit was a vibrant red, nearly identical to the first one I had tried on, although it tapered at the bottom. At least she possessed the confidence to wear it.

I, the woodland peasant, did not.

"Do we need to go over the plan again?" Harper asked as she picked at her freshly manicured nails, painted in a fiery red.

"I think I'm good," I lied, while my mind seethed, *What have I gotten myself into?*

"Okay, good." Harper nodded briskly.

We put on the fur coats we found in the one armoire and headed downstairs to the main floor, to the sitting room, a grand room just off the side of the main foyer. The room was adorned with bulky, leather furniture, a bar area, and a massive stone fireplace that produced a continuous blast of dry heat. Tall, slender windows loomed on either side of the fireplace, their glass tinted so no one could see inside. The far wall was lined with shelves and books from ceiling to floor, two double doors propped open in the middle—leading to the library, something I planned to explore later.

The guys sat around the sitting room, their conversation clipped short as we walked in.

Von's eyes immediately met mine. My breath hitched, but it wasn't because of the tight, black shirt that hugged his steel-built frame. It was the way he looked at me now, with that intense, predator gaze. I could only imagine what he might do if he saw what I'd stowed away beneath the fur coat. A small part of me wanted to take it off, just so I could find out.

Only to tease him, of course.

Ryker plopped his big, muscular arm on top of Harper's head as he looked at me. "Damn, Sage, you look so good you made me forget my pickup line."

Harper shoved him away, her hand quickly shooting up to fix her hair. "Why are men such pigs." It wasn't a question.

Ryker burst out laughing.

Von prowled towards me.

I stepped back, tightened my coat.

When his body was but a breath from mine, he studied

my face, his gaze lingering too long on my painted lips. I could almost feel his thumb brushing over them. But his hand was in his pocket, the other at his side, his touch a figment of my imagination. "Are you ready?" he asked, his voice holding no softness, just all hard edges and dark, heavy smoke. Something was bothering him.

"As ready as I'll ever be," I replied, my inhale longer than intended, tattling on me.

Visually, he gave me one final sweep before he nodded, and the four of us headed out into the embrace of the cool night.

Chapter 15

Just from looking at the bathhouse from the outside, I could tell it boasted luxury in every sense of the word, and as much as I was dreading seeing the inside of it, curiosity was starting to take hold.

Von took care of the arrangements. He spoke privately with a woman who looked happy to see him—happy enough she threw her arms around his neck.

I sucked in a breath at that.

Her strawberry-blonde hair was piled on top of her head, a few ringlets falling loosely by her face, bouncing as she spoke with him. Her clothes looked expensive, but it was the chunky emeralds hanging around her neck that screamed wealth. She was beginning to show her age, especially when she smiled, but the fine lines did little to distract from her beauty—and she was beautiful.

They walked towards us. The woman gave Harper and me a once over before she swung the arched door open and ushered us up the single step and inside. I turned around, my gaze locking with Von's just before that thick, wooden door slammed behind us.

But not before I saw the way the muscle ticked in his jaw.

The woman led us through a dark stone hallway, the only light provided by the brass candle holder hooked on her finger. We walked for some time, and just when I was certain she may very well be leading us in circles, we came to a brighter, wider hallway. Sconces, meticulously carved and dipped in gold, hung on the marble-slabbed walls. They were spaced evenly, about every five feet, their burning candles illuminating our surroundings.

The bathhouse was scented with jasmine, but it wreaked of old, tainted coin and sex.

She took us into a room filled with twelve stunning women who lounged on comfortable, plush chaises and sofas, their laughter and conversation amplified by the stone walls and mosaic floors.

"Alright, ladies, let us have a look," she said, her arm outstretched in preparation for our coats.

Harper and I glanced at one another before we slipped them off and gave them to her. She chucked them on a burgundy velvet chaise and then began her assessment of us. She tilted her head back and forth, her gaze raking over us like we were nearly burnt-out embers.

"I suppose you'll have to do," she huffed, as if slightly unsatisfied. "Shift change will be in about fifteen minutes, and then your group will work the floor. Thermes de Luxe caters to nobility and people of great wealth. They expect nothing but the best from us, and we make sure we give it to them. Let me make myself clear—I hear one complaint, just one, and you are out. There are no second chances here and plenty of girls lining up and down the street to work at the number one bathhouse in Belamour. Am I understood?"

We both nodded.

"Very good. The other girls will show you what to do when it is your turn to work the floor. Also, the king's advisor is known to frequent here quite often." She glanced at Harper. "He has a thing for brunettes." She gave us a curt nod and left the room, her heels chewing up the mosaic tile as she walked down the hallway, emphasizing her departure.

"She seems fun," Harper said sarcastically before she strolled over to the other women. Their conversation stalled as their heads shifted towards us.

A blonde with curled hair patted the empty seat beside her. "We're up in fifteen. Might as well take a seat in the meantime."

Harper and I plopped down beside her.

The girls were welcoming, friendly, almost like a sisterhood, accepting us immediately as one of their own. They told us what our duties were when we worked the floor and what our duties might consist of should we be required for a private bath. When the other group returned, Harper and I fell to the rear as we walked to the public bathing area. A pool of clear water yawned before me, dusty pink rose petals floating on top. Steam sifted from the surface, coating the air in a dense haze, adding to the allure of the bathhouse. Under the water, I could faintly make out a raised ledge that wound its way around the pool walls—a place to sit.

Men of various ages and body types relaxed in the pool. Some were here to bathe, and some were here to appease their desire—*their need.*

Those men were easy to spot.

Their eyes raked over the women who tended to them with carnal lust. Some dismissed the girls that didn't pique their interests, quickly moving on to ones who did, as if they were selecting a piece of fruit to gnaw on.

Surrounding the pool, giant stone columns were carved with nude, curvaceous females, their arms stretched towards the ceiling. It was not lost on me, the symbolic nature of the statues. Even though they were naked and meant to add to the erotic nature of the bathhouse, these carvings were holding the roof up, effectively keeping it all from crashing down. Just as women so often did when it came to their own homes, their own families.

Pillars of strength.

Pillars of divine femininity.

I felt a sense of warmth towards the architects and wondered if their message of female strength was intentional or not. I leaned towards the former.

Harper studied the statues. I could tell the message had reached her too, judging by the look written on her face. Her brown eyes glanced my way. "Ready?"

"Not really," I replied honestly as we headed into battle.

Chapter 16

"If I have to scrub a moly, hairy back ever again . . ." I shivered, resisting the urge to upchuck my supper. This place made every inch of my skin feel like it had been doused in ants—red ones, the kind that bite.

"At least you didn't get called into a private bath," Harper huffed, flicking her ponytail over her shoulder.

"Did you use Ezra's tonic?" I asked as we walked down the long, never-ending corridor, the candlelight glinting off the marbled walls. I wrapped my arms around myself, relieved to have my coat back on, to be covered again.

"Yup, and it worked like a goddess-blessed charm. He's probably still sawing timber in there. Hopefully he doesn't drown." She gave a half shrug, suggesting she couldn't care less if he did as she shoved the heavy door open and stepped out into the stark moonlight. How she managed to retrace our path and lead us to the back door, I'd never know. Then again, directions weren't my forte.

Ryker leaned against a knotty pine tree, his arms crossed

over his torso. A tattoo peeked out from beneath his rolled sleeve, his bicep bulging. "How did it go?"

"It didn't. The king's advisor wasn't there," Harper exclaimed, her hip cocked.

"I guess we just keep trying then," Ryker offered, his tone optimistic.

Harper shot up a brow, "*We?*"

"Where's Von?" I interjected before they started their sixteenth fight of the day.

Ryker thumbed over his broad shoulder.

I looked down the back alley. Beneath the whispering, pale moonlight, two figures stood, their bodies close enough to share breath. There was no mistaking that one was Von, and the other silhouette belonged to a tall, slender woman.

Something deeply planted within me began to surface—it was an ugly feeling.

They were talking—or rather, she was talking. He was, surprisingly, listening.

I didn't dare take a step towards them, but I leaned forward, trying to decipher what she was saying. But the mere inches I'd gained were of little help. They were too far away.

Suddenly, her voice grew louder. I had never heard anger ring out with such clarity before. "Liar!" she screamed. The word echoed into the night. The wind which had been dormant before began to pick up.

Von said nothing.

She raised her hand with incredible speed, but before she could strike, his hand shot out, cuffing her wrist, rendering it immovable. When she tugged, he let her go. He watched—we all watched—as she turned and disappeared between two overgrown bushes, their branches nearly barren.

If I had not heard the door slam shut, I would have thought her disappearing act some sort of magic trick.

I mentally retraced the bathhouse, noting that the hidden door she went through was part of it. My mind whirled, questions abound. Who was she? And why did she go into the bathhouse?

We gave him a moment before the three of us walked towards him, his silence washing over us all in undiluted, powerful waves.

"What did you say to that poor woman?" I remarked. Half of my comment was meant to get a rise out of him—the other half was due to my own selfish reasons.

He ignored me. It irritated me worse.

Harper shot me a look, but I had no idea what it meant.

"Oh, knowing you, I'm sure you deserved it," I goaded playfully, even though that peculiar green-eyed beast raised her head just above the water. Watching. Waiting. *Mine,* she said.

I drowned her obnoxious ass out.

"I do," he stated, his voice cloaked. It was always smoke and mirrors with this one.

Ryker slung his arm over Von's shoulders. "Don't worry about it, Von. There's a bottle of bourbon with your name on it back at the manor."

As we walked back, that ugly feeling returned, stitching itself to my insides.

Who was that woman?

And what did she mean to Von?

Soren tended the crackling fire, yet another attribute that reminded me of Kaleb. He loaded it up with logs, the flames lapping at the wood eagerly, producing a continuous roll of dry heat—the kind that chased away the bitter cold, warming you to the bone.

Harper draped an arm over Lyra, the two cozied up on the settee, their legs tangled together over a round stool with three wooden legs, a fur slung over them both. Lyra traced invisible circles on the back of Harper's hand. A light smile adorned Harper's lips as she watched Lyra perform the small, endearing action.

I wondered what it must feel like to have *that* with someone.

Von had said very little since we returned. He was all hard edges, tattoos, and bourbon tonight. I knew I should probably say something to him. I just didn't know where to even start. He was infuriatingly unreadable, as usual.

Sorry you had a spat with that woman?

Sorry I gave you a tough time after?

Is she your lover, you bastard?

I shoved the green-eyed monster down, smothering her under the water. Where was this even coming from?

I *did not* like Von. He was unbearable. Full of himself.

And built like a god—a dark, brooding, emotionally unavailable one.

I sighed and shifted my weight further into the embrace of the settee. At least it would hold me.

Oh, for Lady Light's sake! Get ahold of yourself.

Ryker returned from the kitchen carrying a large cutting board stockpiled with nuts, fruits, crackers, cheese, and various meats. He placed it on the oversized coffee table. And like the rabid beasts we all were, we closed in on the tray—everyone except for Von.

I snagged a piece of cheese, a cracker, and some meat to make a little sandwich.

Ryker looked at it and nodded his head in approval. "Nice, but I'll let you in on a little secret. The key—" He slapped two pieces of cheese and two pieces of meat on his. "—is to make it a double stacker."

Harper shook her head. "Your cracker ratio is way off. Sage, you are my cracker sandwich soulmate. Two crackers, one slice of cheese, and one slice of meat." She made one for herself before she stuffed it into her mouth. Lyra beamed, the simple action of watching Harper eat coaxing a smile to her lips, like she found this simple task so incredibly endearing.

Soren jumped in, explaining we all were wrong, and that a cracker sandwich did not require a top cracker, only a bottom.

Ryker's giant hand patted Soren on the back, the strength of his tap nearly causing Soren to double over. "Are you telling us you are a bottom?"

Soren stuttered. "I am not! I like girls—women!"

Ryker quirked a disbelieving brow.

Harper dove in, joining in the banter. Before long, we were all laughing.

Before the tray was empty, I placed a few bits of cheese, some crackers, and meat on a napkin and took it over to Von. "Sorry for what I said earlier. It was really bad timing." I raised my humble offering to him. "Peace offering?"

He brought those dark eyes to mine, fingers brushing against my palm as he took the napkin. "You don't need to apologize."

A light shiver dusted my spine. "Yet here I am," I said as I sat beside him, one leg tucked underneath me, my body facing his. "And I'm apologizing."

"Then I accept your unnecessary apology," he said as he tipped his head back against the settee, eyes closed. A skull encased with dark red roses was tattooed on his neck, green vines wrapping like fingers snaking their way over that thick, purely male throat—a blueprint of where to touch, where to caress, where to kiss.

I blinked and reeled myself up from the gutter. "Do you want to talk about it?" I asked, not really caring if I was overstepping.

"No." He didn't look at me. "This is not something that concerns you, Little Goddess."

It bothered me more than I wanted to admit that he was not looking at me—that he was shutting me out. And damn it all, I wanted to know who the woman was.

But I didn't bother to pry.

When I got up and walked away, he didn't seem to notice.

Later on, sprawled out on the end of Harper and Lyra's bed, my gaze traced the intricate clove pattern etched in the copper ceiling tiles. Lyra sat near the headboard, a glass jar sitting on the table beside her, a thin brush in her hand as she painted her toes. Tonight, she chose an emerald color, reminding me of the jealous beast that kept spontaneously appearing in my head.

I realized that as much as I hated to admit it, I was attracted to Von. But I barely knew him and I had no right to interject myself between him and that woman. He'd had a life before we met. And whatever I had witnessed was clearly part of that life. I sighed.

"Okay, what's up, Sage? You've been stuck in your head for the past half hour," Harper said as she strolled out of the bathing room, a crisp white towel piled on top of her head and a clay mask smeared all over her face.

Lyra stopped painting, her eyes looking my way, like she, too, had been wondering the same thing.

I rolled onto my stomach, my hand propping up my head. "The woman outside the bathhouse. Do you know who she is?"

Harper unwrapped the towel from her hair. Balling it up, she chucked it into the wicker hamper sitting to the left of the door. "Not really. I don't know much about her."

"Not knowing much and knowing nothing are two different things. Come on, Harps, tell me what you know," I drawled, waiting for her to continue. I didn't know if that made me feel worse or better—that Harper knew something about the woman.

Worse, I finally decided.

She glanced at me, her shoulders performing an apologetic shrug. "All I know is that Von sees her every time we come to Belamour and it never goes well. I don't know anything other than that." She paused. "Did you try asking him about it?"

"I tried. He was not in a talking mood." I picked at a thread on the blanket, pulling it until it wouldn't pull anymore. I wound it around my finger, trying to snap it off. It wouldn't budge.

"He's always been like that," Harper said after a moment of silence.

"Not in a talking mood?" I glared at the black thread and then I yanked on it some more.

"No, I mean that he just never really divulges much when it comes to personal things. He's been like that for as long as I have known him." She walked towards the mirror, her fingers plucking a brush from the makeup vanity. Her reflection offered me a half-smile. "I dunno, maybe just give him some time and then see if he will open up." She shrugged. "Men are odd creatures, especially *that* one."

I gave up on the thread—*the stubborn bastard.*

And as much I didn't want to, I decided to take Harper's advice and give him time.

He could have one week.

Chapter 17

Before I knew it, one week gave way to two.

I stared up at the ceiling in my room, glaring at it as if it were its fault that I couldn't sleep tonight. Frustration was beginning to overwhelm me.

Over the past two weeks, we had not seen the king's advisor once. Worse, we had not even heard so much as a whisper about him. We had nothing to go on—when or even if he would attend the bathhouse—which meant we were no closer to finding out where Kaleb was than when we had arrived.

For all we knew, the king's advisor had found a new favorite bathhouse, or maybe he'd found new satisfaction with his wife—if he had one.

We knew nothing.

I groaned and rolled onto my side. I was beginning to wonder if this plan, Von's plan, was pointless.

The gemstone allure of Belamour was losing its luster. I was tired of the loud, constantly thrumming city life, the lack of chirping birds and tall, swaying oak trees.

I missed home. I missed Ezra. And I missed Kaleb.

All of it was beginning to feel so incredibly far away—almost as if it were out of reach.

My spirit felt like an old, hand-me-down coat stuffed away in the back of a closet, worn and forgotten.

To make matters worse, I still had no idea who the woman was or what role she played in Von's life. Or where he disappeared to during the late, late hours of the night, his silent footsteps echoing loudly on the cusp of my mind.

Was he with her?

Despite the mantra I repeated to myself—that I barely knew him, that it was none of my business—something deep within me wanted to know, *demanded* to know. As if I had some gods-given right.

Riding a wave of pent-up frustration, when the house was quiet, I shifted from my covers and walked down the hall towards his room.

My knuckles rasped against the door lightly so I didn't wake the others.

On bated breath, I waited to hear his voice.

There was no reply.

I told myself to walk away, to go back to my room and stare up at that damned ceiling until I fell asleep. But something else inside me prevailed, and before I knew what I was doing, my hand fell to the handle, and I opened the door.

I peered into the silent darkness.

The bed was made, and he was gone.

In the morning, I sat at the sprawling obsidian island in the kitchen. Like the rest of the estate, the kitchen boasted high-quality materials, from the marble floor to the custom cabinets to the polished, onyx ceiling. Everything was sparkling, shiny, and clean. To my left, a butler's pantry, large enough it could fit the cottage kitchen and living room inside of it, was chock-full of foods and spices, some I had never even heard of before.

I dropped my elbow onto the cool countertop, plopping my head in my hand. I stared at the bowl of porridge dusted with a sprinkle of cinnamon, more focused on shifting it around with my spoon than eating it. Last night, I had warred with myself—my thoughts. On the positive side, I was thankful we weren't working at the bathhouse tonight—Lady Light knew I needed a day to rest my weary soul—not that my body needed any rest.

To my right, the view of the outdoors from the expansive window summoned me, whispering in my ear—they had been doing so since I woke up.

Answering its call, I shoved a spoonful of porridge in my mouth, trashed the rest, and headed outside. The sun was the first thing to greet me, the sounds of my training roommates the next. Today felt more like a summer day than an autumn one. I breathed it in. With my shoes in my right hand, I stepped off the brick patio and onto the browning grass, my toes wiggling happily. I rooted myself in place, my body filling with peace.

Built on the top of a hill, the manor had a height advantage when it came to the remainder of the estate. From this vantage point, I could survey the entire backyard—well over eight acres. Towering, fireclay brick walls outlined the perimeter of the estate grounds, providing a great deal of privacy from any prying eyes. Carved statues, figures with wings, sat on top of the walls, surveying the domain they protected. Vines snaked from the ground, their long tendrils wrapping themselves around the statues, some almost fully encased.

For the past week, Harper had focused on teaching Lyra how to use a sword. She'd started her off with a wooden one, and today, Lyra graduated to metal.

I offered her a thumbs-up and she smiled at me.

Harper utilized the distraction to her advantage as she took a swipe at Lyra, stopping a hair from her neck, the action speaking volumes of her swordsmanship. Harper pulled her blade away, telling Lyra that she must always keep her eyes on her opponent. Lyra nodded dutifully, returning her attention back to Harper.

Lyra did not possess much in the way of fighting skills, and although she bore the Earth Curse, I had never seen her use it. It was almost like she was scared to. For the most part, Lyra remained a mystery to me. I had never heard her speak, nor did I know if she could. I didn't have it in me to ask Harper why that was. I figured she would tell me when the time was right.

A bit farther down, Soren and Ryker sparred with one another. Soren was on the ground. Ryker gripped Soren's hand as he helped him back to his feet. "Let's run through that combo again."

Soren nodded and he swung, swords clashing as they went at it again.

Shirtless Ryker was a sight to behold, the fire twin chiseled in all the right places. A slick gleam of sweat highlighted his heavily carved muscles, carefully honed from years of battle. His body moved with speed, precision. Watching him spar was like watching a carefully tuned instrument of destruction. I could only imagine what he must be like on the battlefield.

Could only imagine what he would be like in the bedroom.

A shadow cast over me.

"See something you like?" Von whispered in my ear, his head lowered over my shoulder.

Like this, I could feel the heat of him wash over me in heavy, demanding waves.

"Maybe I do," I replied, not bothering to remove my eyes from Ryker. Those three words felt better than I expected them to.

Von didn't say anything, but I caught that smile slip away, and I felt a sense of satisfaction—of smugness. Two could play this game. But what game was this exactly? My mood darkened.

"Train with me," he commanded, his tone almost playful.

"Fine," I said flatly as I trotted down the cement stairs into an open area, not bothering to wait for him. I plopped down on a black metal chair and hastily shoved my feet into my training shoes, all too eager to battle.

His scent, amber and sandalwood, barreled into me a second before his tunic hit my face. I jerked my head up from my laces, my hand shoving his shirt away, his scent lingering too long on my skin.

I bared my teeth at him.

He grinned wickedly.

How dare he stand there like that without a shirt. Those rippling pectorals and trademark abs—they were criminal. I stole a glance at his tattoos, that messy canvas that somehow resembled art, that resembled him and all that he was.

A windstorm of a male. The kind that sucked you in, fucked you hard, and then left you in the dust—messy-haired and wide-eyed and never the same.

Was that what he was doing with *her*?

Jealousy rode me hard.

Growling, I shot to my feet and charged towards him, firing a fist his way. He chuckled and deflected it with ease, but I was quick to return another. I dropped into a combo of jabs, muscle memory moving my arms on their own. Pent-up frustration made my movement sloppier than normal. Ezra would have strung me up for it—but Von was already on it.

"Keep your arms tucked in. You are leaving yourself exposed," he directed, his hand blocking mine with inhuman speed.

I swung again, concentrating on his stupidly perfect nose.

Another block.

I feigned to the right and brought up my fist, but his hand deflected it like he was swatting down a fly.

"Concentrate," he scolded. As if it were *that* easy. The bastard grinned, his gaze connecting with mine. "Do you need me to put my shirt back on?"

"Fuck you!" I seethed.

An infuriating smirk. "Is that what you would like to do, Little Goddess?"

I glared at him before I fired another one, and another one, until I was quickly soaring through punches. My speed picked up, my movements quicker than before, as my body had warmed up.

Hand to hand, Von was untouchable. I knew I would tire out long before he did, but I refused to lose this time.

I raced towards the weapons rack, my shoes kicking up the dead grass in my wake. Von was behind me, an arm's reach away. I grabbed a round wooden shield, shoved it onto my arm, and twirled around as I rammed it into his chest, the force so great, he stumbled a few steps back.

His head jerked upright as he regained his footing. "Seeing you with a shield, it nearly brings me to my knees, Kitten."

"Do not call me that," I hissed as we circled one another like vultures about to square off over the last slab of meat.

"Ask me why it nearly brings me to my knees" he ordered me, stepping one foot over the other, continuing our rotating stand-off.

"I couldn't give two shits," I growled.

"You have such a dirty, dirty little mouth." His eyes shifted to my lips, a toying grin on his.

It dawned on me—he was playing.

But I wasn't.

I made the first move, flipping the shield onto its side and taking aim for his neck.

With feline speed, he ducked down and my arm soared right over his head.

I twirled, chest heaving, attacking again. This time, I landed the shield against his chest. With a mighty yell, I shoved with all my might.

Von didn't budge this time.

In one swift, degrading move, he tugged it from my arm and threw it to the side like I was a child and he was the adult taking the annoying toy away. His predator gaze locked with mine. "Now what will you do, *Kitten*?"

He did not get to call me a pet name—not when he was probably calling *her* that as well.

A feral growl came out as my reply. I raced for the shield, my heart pounding. It felt like the hounds of the Spirit Realm were snapping at my heels.

Von's arm cinched around my waist, pulling me against him. I reared my leg back, hoping to connect with his shin, but my leg sailed right between his. Like a bear trap, his legs sprung closed, locking mine between his.

Despite the difference in our heights, like this, our bodies fit rather nicely. Where my soft curves ended, his hard edges began, as if they were meant to be like this.

That was when it hit me. Dead center.

Whether I liked it or not, I was attracted to him.

Worse—I had feelings for the bastard.

And the thought of him and that woman?

"I'm done."

He let me go, his retracted warmth leaving me cold.

I didn't bother to look back as I walked towards the back door and let myself inside. When I reached the hallway, bootheels thundered behind me, his long, powerful legs chewing up the distance between us.

He caught my arm and twirled me towards him, his face inches over mine. "You have barely spoken to me the past two weeks," he growled.

"When have I been given the chance to speak with you? You brood during the day and are nowhere to be found during the night," I fired back like an overheated teapot, my frustration well beyond its boiling point.

"I have been busy," he grated.

That was it? No explanation. Nothing?

"You are unbelievable," I seethed, tugging my arm out of his grasp. I took a much-needed step back. I gargled a thought before I spat it out. "Is *that* woman what is keeping you so busy?"

Something akin to amusement flickered in his eyes. "She is part of it, yes."

There it was—the truth. And I had no idea what to do with it. I took another self-protecting step back. I didn't need to know the details about them. I didn't want to.

"Oh, I see." My voice failed me—I hated the crack in it. Despised it.

"Don't do that." He stepped towards me.

"Do what?"

"Assume you know," he replied as if it were some horrible crime I committed repeatedly.

"I'll tell you what I know. While you have been shamelessly flirting with me, you spend your nights with her. Do you call her kitten too?"

I was venomous. Goddess divine, *where* was this coming from?

"Oh, my territorial, little creature. As much as I enjoy

seeing you like this, you have it so very wrong," he purred, the flicker across those midnight eyes suggesting he was tempted to laugh.

I crossed my arms. "Then explain it to me."

"Very well. She is my sister."

Oh.

. . . I'm the idiot.

The assuming idiot.

Damn it, he was right.

Even though my body lay in bed, mentally, I was somewhere else, lost among stacks of paper, sorting my private thoughts.

Our conversation didn't go much further than the admission that the woman was his sister. I felt too dumbfounded to ask anything else. And I needed some time to lick my wounded ego, so Harper, Lyra, and I went downtown for the day to shop.

It helped to take my mind off things, but now that I was alone again, I felt like an idiot.

I realized he was right. I *was* bad at assuming things. I had done it with Ezra more times than I cared to count.

So before I fell asleep, I decided it was something I would work on.

A little personal growth never hurt anyone.

Right?

Right.

Chapter 18

It was good to have a day off from the bathhouse, but now Harper and I were back at it.

I sat on the floor in front of the lush settee, nestled in the extravagant room with the other girls. Their seemingly carefree laughter and soft, feminine voices filled the air as we awaited our turn on the floor. The youngest of the group, Vera, sat cross-legged behind me, her slender fingers braiding my hair.

"I've never seen someone so young with white hair before," she mused as she worked away. "Has it always been like this?"

I fingered a loose strand of my hair. "Yes, for as long as I can remember."

"It's quite unusual." She paused. "But it is lovely, and it does suit you. There." She clapped my shoulders gently. "All done."

"Thank you," I said with a soft smile as I moved to sit on the settee beside her.

"Do you like it?" Vera asked as she held up a mirror for me to see.

I nodded. "Yes, it's beautiful."

As Vera returned the mirror to one of the many makeup vanities, my thoughts drifted to Von's sister. That night, she'd disappeared behind a door attached to the bathhouse. Why was she here? Thinking about it now, she had been wearing a courtesan's robe . . . Did she work here?

During the past few weeks, I had not seen her on the floor, but that didn't mean she didn't work here.

I licked my lips. "Can I ask you a question?"

"Sure," Vera said as she began to pick at a lone hangnail, which marred her otherwise perfect manicure.

"Are there women that work here that don't work the floor?"

She nodded, her freshly curled hair bouncing in reply. "There are. The women who bring in high volumes of clientele are given room and board—private chambers with fresh bed linens and all the clothes they could ever want. I heard they get three meals a day, and the food, apparently, is spectacular."

I nodded, noting how her eyes lit up at the mention of food. Come to think of it—she was impossibly thin. "Do you know any of them?" I inquired.

"Nope," she said, popping the "p." "Because they already have a list of regulars, they don't attend pool side or converse with us commoners." She giggled. "Seeing one of them is like seeing a magical creature—a unicorn." She giggled some more before she let out a dreamy sigh. "I would love to be one of those women."

"Why would you want that?" The question slipped out before I could close my big quest-blowing mouth.

Her face went blank, like she couldn't possibly understand why I would ask such a thing, but she shrugged her shoulders and replied, "Because life is hard on the outside. Some of us are overdue on rent and are a week away from being homeless. There are a few girls in this room that don't even have homes. To live here means a full stomach and a roof over your head. The clothes and clean linens are just a bonus."

I didn't know what to say.

Vera leaned forward, her gaze shifting to the ground. "Regardless of the price we pay, we all sell our bodies in one way or another—whether it be for sport, or labor, or sex." Her gaze met mine, a fire lit within in her eyes. "As women in a man's world, we do what we must to keep ourselves afloat."

I nodded, my tongue at a loss for words.

Although Vera did not carry one of the traditional six Curses, she carried another—not one, but two: the curse of poverty and the curse of being born as a "lesser" gender.

And although the curses were out of our control, we both were fighting our way through this unforgiving world, just as she said—just trying to stay afloat.

A bustle of voices came from the doorway, birthing fifteen girls who looked tired, as if they had just poured their souls into their performances.

But now, I understood.

These women were warriors, fighting for their survival.

The smell of jasmine and lavender wafted into my nose as we entered the warm, steamy atmosphere of the bathhouse. Harper shot me a good-luck nod before she headed to the far end, a basket of rose petals nestled in her arms.

I plucked a wash rag from the nearby shelf and began my dreaded tour.

Four hairy backs later, I rubbed my throbbing wrist as I listened to the balding male complain about his wife. The way he spoke about her, I wondered why they bothered to stay married at all. Apart from his marriage woes, I had learned that he was the commander of the second platoon and that he *personally* knew the king's advisor.

I schooled my features in girly delight and inquired more about the *oh so famous* advisor. The man boasted on about him, clearly enjoying how I lapped everything up.

With a bit of gentle pressure, he divulged that the king's advisor had been away on official court business for the past three weeks but was expected back for an important meeting tomorrow evening, and after, he would most likely attend the bathhouse to "blow off some much-needed steam."

I choked back a gag at the choice of words he used. Instead, I smiled softly, like a little doll—pliant, moldable . . . everything he wished his wife would be.

Inside, I was bursting. This was it—we were so close to finding out where Kaleb was.

But my internal victory was quickly squashed. He leaned in, his putrid breath sweeping towards me as he inquired if I would escort him to the private baths.

I poked his hairy shoulder.

He didn't move.

I eyed the small vial—did I overdo do it? I poked him again.

His mouth popped open and he let out a gallant snore.

Okay, good—so not dead then.

I raised from my squatted position, dusting my hands off and mentally congratulating myself on a job well done.

The private bathing chambers were small, intimate, and extremely hot due to the steam produced by the water thrown over the flame-heated rocks. I dabbed my brow as I walked out the door and into the hallway, the change in temperature hitting me instantly.

One of the guards leaned against the shiny, slick marble wall, his eyes shifting towards me, a bushy brow shooting up. "Done so soon?"

"I think he might have had one too many of these." I pretended to throw a drink back.

The man chuckled. "They always do. Have a good rest of your night, miss."

"You too," I replied pleasantly as I walked down the corridor, the irony of our small talk dawning on me—was I growing used to this place?

I paused mid step when I reached the hallway that led to the room we waited in. I glanced to my left, looking down the unexplored hallway, wondering where the private chambers were.

Several minutes later and after a good deal of wandering,

I realized I was most definitely lost. I took a right when I probably should have taken a left, and I had done that more times than I could count. Even the echoing voices in the main bath had long since died out. I sighed loudly. I was starting to feel like a mouse trapped in a maze.

"Maria, I can hear you. You are terribly late. Now quit dawdling and bring me my meal," a woman called out—she sounded annoyed.

I didn't move. I should sneak back into the shadows and slip down the other end of the cold, quiet hallway. But what I *should* do held little dominion over curiosity.

I slipped just outside of the woman's door, daring to take one little, harmless peek around the corner. The room consisted of four windowless walls and one closed door to the right. Light flickered from the wall sconces, and although the room boasted rich, expensive things, it felt cold. Isolated. And lonely.

A woman, raven-haired and incredibly stunning, stared back at me. Her eyes glowed a lush, deep green, like an emerald leaf illuminated by the rays of the sun. She was ethereal. Her features carved by angels.

And gods, she looked like him. The female version of him—Von.

She *was* his sister.

"You're not Maria," she sighed, sharp red fingernails pinching the bridge of her nose. "Are you her replacement? Never mind. Go over there and sit on the bed. I'll feed after I'm finished brushing my hair," she said as she gathered her silk skirts to the side and gracefully sat down on the red-velvet-covered stool. She plucked a shiny silver brush from the table and began to brush her hair.

. . . *feed*? That did not sit well with me.

I studied her. She wore an exquisite silk gown rimmed with silver sequins. It was low cut in the back, revealing the tips of two vertical scars, jagged and thick, that scoured her shoulder blades. The farther down the scars went, the closer they ran towards one another.

"So you're his sister," I blurted out, my eyes still studying those wicked-looking scars. How did she get them?

The brushing stopped, followed by a thud as she set it down, not harshly, but not softly either. She swung a long, toned leg out from underneath her gown and peered at me. "Unbelievable. I told him I would not help him, and so he sent one of his—" She glanced at me, trying to decide what to call me. I could practically see the wheels churning within her mind. "One of his side pieces."

The title hit me like a potato sack full of bricks. I knew their relationship wasn't great, but she must have some inkling about what Von was like. The side piece label made me feel even more insecure about what I felt for him.

But I was working on not assuming things, so I shoved her words to the side and asked, "What does he want help with?"

"Get out," she hissed, ignoring my question as she turned towards her mirror and grabbed the brush. What she had brushed with such care and gentleness before, turned into quick, forceful thrusts as she ripped the bristles through her sleek, blue-black hair.

"Answer my question and I'll leave," I said, my voice stringing together words my brain had yet to approve.

But she didn't reply with words—instead, she turned and hurled the brush.

I deflected it with the back of my hand, the wood clacking against the ground. Before the brush came to a skidding stop, she charged. Her speed was incredible. Her hand snaked around my throat as she shoved me against the wall.

"I have no interest in talking with him *or you*," she seethed, the words toxic and poisonous as they seeped from her tongue—the way she spat them with such venom, I wondered if it might be like a serpent's, long and slithery.

Goddess divine, I really needed to stop having run-ins with serpents.

"Is it because he is Cursed?" I bit back at her as we stood toe-to-toe. Eye-to-eye.

"Cursed—how idiotic. A testament of small, simple minds." She tipped her head back and loosed a birdlike cackle, as if it were the funniest thing she had ever heard. Her eyes sharpened to daggers and she threw them back at my face. "If only he were just *Cursed*. He is a means to an end. And if you are not careful, he'll suck your soul dry." She leaned in close, whispering in my ear, "I see the look in your eyes, filled with hope that you might mean something to him. But you, little mouse, are a fool. Snakes do not mate with mice. We eat them."

I felt the scrape of something hard against my ear, escorted by the heat of her breath. "A final word of advice, hmm?" she said as she took a step back. She licked her poisonous lips. "Stay away from him." She turned, snatched the brush from the ground, and returned to her stool. "Now leave me be," she hissed.

I didn't bother to say goodbye.

As my bare feet padded down the stretch of the corridor, I decided that I could not blame Von's sister for what she had become.

She was a product of this cold, dark place, of a world without sun.

Chapter 19

Back at the manor, I dropped the sheer lilac fabric on the bathing room floor and slipped into the warm tub of water, praising Crete for the gift of indoor plumbing. Gods rest his soul.

I scrubbed myself vigorously, a ritual to clean more than my body, but also my soul—something that was necessary after working at the bathhouse.

With a crisp, white towel wrapped around my torso, I stood in front of the mirror, my freshly scrubbed, rosy-red reflection staring back at me. My fingertips gently slid over the light bruising on my neck, her spiteful words echoing in my mind . . .

Clearly, she despised Von, but how could she hate her own flesh and blood that much?

What was I missing?

The answer felt as far away as Kaleb.

I sighed.

A knock came at the door, loud but patient. I knew who

it was.

Von's onyx eyes peered down at me as I opened the door. His arm draped over the arched doorway, his large frame consuming it completely. He wore his hair loose, the long black strands trailing over his shoulders. He dressed in casual clothes—a fitted, black tunic that hugged his muscled torso with a wide, tattoo-exposing neckline.

He offered me that unparalleled grin, full of swagger and charm and something primal—something dangerous.

"Yes?" I asked. It came out softer, more inviting than I had intended. I cursed my traitorous tongue, cursed the wildness he wore and how it called to me.

His smile slipped. His fingers, warm and gentle, tipped my chin upwards, his eyes narrowing. "Who did this to you?" His voice was calm, but the flash in his midnight eyes reflected something else entirely. I wondered if something dark did indeed lurk inside.

He is a means to an end. Her words chattered in my mind.

I hugged my arms around myself, caging the fabric to my frame. "I think we need to talk, Von."

He did not disagree.

"One moment." I closed the door and traded my towel for the white cotton robe that hung on the back of the door. After, I joined him in the small seating area by the large bay window that overlooked Belamour. Two tufted chairs, ivory in color, sat on either side of the window, looking towards it. A round end table between them.

A few of the books I picked out from the mansion's library were stacked together, sitting on top of the end table, just waiting to be read. The one titled *The Six Curses* was of particular interest as I needed to learn more about my Dream Curse. The other two were for my own gluttonous needs—hopefully filled with smut and morally gray males.

I sat in one of the chairs, and although it fit me just fine, Von's body dwarfed his. As if his personality didn't take up enough space, his size ensured it. His arm draped over the arm of the chair, those ringed, tattooed fingers ticking rhythmically like a big cat's tail swishing from side to side. He looked at me, all dark and handsome and broody, his question still standing.

I had nothing to gain with a lie, so I served him the truth. "I took a stroll around the bathhouse today. I met your sister." I gestured to the bruises on my neck. "She was so happy to meet me that she gave me this gorgeous necklace. She seems *lovely.*"

His fingers quit ticking.

I shifted uncomfortably in my seat. The way he looked right now—there was nothing human about it, and that scared me. But it wasn't fear for my life. Its roots were deeper than that but no matter how hard I tried, I could not figure out what it was.

As if he noted the shift in my mood, his expression changed, a carefully honed mask slipping back into place. He inclined his head. "What did she say to you?"

"She warned me to stay away from you." I paused, debating if I should continue or if I should hold some of my cards. I decided to wait, to see what he would say.

"She's not wrong."

Well then . . .

I swallowed his confirmation down, licked my lipstick-stained lips, and continued, "She said she refused to help you with something. What did you ask her for help with?"

"I asked for her help in locating an item," he replied, his answer given without hesitation, and yet something about it still felt calculated—I could tell by the way he leisurely surveyed me. Regardless of the lazy, rolling gaze, there was an intensity written in the depths of those onyx eyes.

"What item?" I pressed on, my leg crossing over the other one. My robe fell to the side, exposing a healthy peek of my thigh. I left it like that—just to toy with him.

Von noticed—I could tell by the direction of his gaze and the tick in his jaw. He tilted his head and returned his eyes to mine. He held me there. Steady. "The Crown of Thorns."

"The Crown of Thorns?" I did a poor job of hiding my surprise at this, the wide setting of my eyes stating as much. I sloughed it off. "Why do you want it?"

His large hand rubbed his jaw, metal rings catching the dim firelight. "Because it is dangerous and needs to be disposed of. It nearly claimed Ryker's life."

"I thought it couldn't be destroyed—that not even the Endless Mist would take it?" At least, that's what Ryker had told me.

"For it to be destroyed, it must be returned to the place where it was created."

"Where was it created?" I asked, leaning forward.

"Such a curious little kitten," Von's bourbon tone teased. "It was forged in the Spirit Realm."

"By the God of Death," I tacked on.

Von simply nodded.

I supposed that made sense. The God of Death ruled over the Spirit Realm. Since he made the crown there, it was fitting that was where it could be destroyed. The God of Death was said to be wicked and cruel, that he picked his teeth with the bones of the dead. Considering he created something as horrible as the Crown of Thorns as a gift for his bride, wicked and cruel seemed like vanilla descriptions.

"Why do you think he made the Crown of Thorns for his bride?"

"Most people believe it was because the Goddess of War was in his ear. That she persuaded him to create it. But no one held a knife to his throat. No, he did it all on his own." His lips flattened, almost tugged back at the corners, as if he felt disgust for the God of Death. The look subsided and he added, "He was a fool." His dark eyes retracted from the starry night sky, shifting to meet mine. "How much do you know about the Old Gods?"

"I don't know a whole lot," I replied honestly. "I know that the Old Gods were given life by the Creator, and before the New Gods were made, they used to preside over all three realms—the Spirit Realm, the Living Realm, and the Immortal Realm. The God of Death was the King of the Old Gods, but under his control, the Living Realm was caught in a state of decay, so the Creator gave life to the New Gods and asked them to take care of the Living Realm and Immortal Realm."

I paused, smoothing my robe against my leg.

"The Creator banished the Old Gods to the Spirit Realm. The God of Death was not happy about losing the two realms, so he declared war and tried to take it back. Ultimately, he lost. They say he will try again someday . . . That's why it is imperative not to worship the Old Gods, because prayers in his favor will increase his power." I paused, my thoughts skipping ahead. "I always thought it would be interesting to learn about the battles—how legendary a war between gods must have been—but any books that would have gone into detail about them are impossible to find thanks to the royal family."

Von spoke in his deep baritone, "Despite the Crown's attempt to erase information about the Old Gods, there are books that still exist—if one knows where to look. The battles lasted for many years and there were many casualties. Eventually, it became so bad, the Living Realm was nearly destroyed. But contrary to what you learned, the God of Death did not lose the war. In fact, he was seconds away from winning it, but he found something he never planned to find and he withdrew his armies. Later, an agreement was made. The two warring sides would be linked together through marriage—the marriage taking place between the King of the Old Gods and the Princess of the New Gods. But the marriage never took place because the Princess of the New Gods, the Goddess of Life, died."

My mouth popped open. "I had no idea Lady Light was the God of Death's bride."

Now *that* was juicy.

Lady Light was known to be a pure and just goddess, a champion of life. Linking her to the God of Death would certainly be a dark stain on her impeccable, saintly self. I found the thought oddly satisfying. I also found it a bit confusing as we were taught that Lady light was wedded to the Lord of Light and their marriage was sacred . . . eternal. But the more I thought about it, the less confusing it became. The gods and goddesses were immortal, so it was not entirely uncommon for them to change spouses over the decades. If giving her hand to her enemy resulted in peace, then I could understand why she would have agreed to it.

I turned to Von. "The New Religion makes her death seem like she was a martyr—that her death was crucial for the continuation of the Living Realm. But there is one thing I never understood about her death—I thought the divine were immortal, so how could she die?"

Von shifted, the too-small chair groaning in response. "That is a lie—her death was not necessary. And yes, they are immortal, but each god and goddess has a singular weakness. For the Princess of the New Gods, the woman you call Lady Light, it is the roots of a tree filled with white leaves. The roots feather into long veins, covered in thorns. That is her weakness." He paused. "The roots are what the God of Death used to forge the Crown of Thorns."

I pursed my lips, thinking for a moment. "The books on the New Gods skimmed over that. They romanticized her death, making it sound like she had passed peacefully in the embrace of the tree, a tree said to never lose its leaves—not even in winter."

"Another lie. Her death was anything but peaceful."

A lot of this was new to me. I wondered how much of the information written in the Crown-approved books was a lie, or rather, how much of the truth had been left out.

"Do you believe they exist? Both Old Gods and New Gods?" I asked.

"I do," he replied without an ounce of hesitation.

"You don't really seem like the religious type," I countered.

"On the contrary, darling." He grinned. "I am a pious man."

I scoffed at that. Pivoting from the topic of the gods back to his sister—a blatant shift—I asked, "Your sister . . . the scars on her back. What are they from?"

I didn't care that I was prying into something I had no right to stick my nose into. Curiosity had gotten the better of me.

"That is not my story to tell," Von said, proving he had more than just physical similarities with his sister. Just as she would not reveal what Von asked for help with, he would not talk about the reason for her scars.

I licked my lips, fumbling with this next one. "She said something about you sucking my soul dry."

He laughed, the sound throaty, masculine.

I squinted. "You find that funny?"

"I do," he said, a smile on his full lips.

I felt an insatiable need to swipe it off. "She also said I was *one* of your *side pieces*. Do you find that funny as well?"

"I don't do side pieces," he stated firmly.

I sat for a moment, processing. I wasn't sure if I believed him or not. "Why does she dislike you so much?"

"She has a number of reasons, but mostly because of our brother."

"I didn't know you had a brother. Where is he now?"

Von held my gaze. "He is with the dead, in the Spirit Realm."

My heart sank. I couldn't imagine what that loss felt like. Kaleb had been taken, and I had nearly lost my mind. As if it were instinctual, I moved towards him and crouched between his legs, my hands falling on his knees. "I am so sorry."

He leaned forward, his face inches from mine, his voice softer than usual. "You do not need to give me anymore unnecessary apologies."

"Yet here I am," I answered, my lashes flickering as I raised my gaze to his.

"Yet here you are," he repeated as he leaned back in his chair, his thumb and forefinger rolling thin air. His onyx orbs studied me intently, purposefully. I realized that Von did not lean back to distance himself—no, it was so he could take all of me in, as if I were a painting and he had not made up his mind about some perplexing question I imposed. When he parted his lips and rolled his tongue, I realized it was sexual, too, like he was debating *where* he wanted me.

I had a feeling it wasn't hung up on a wall but, rather, facedown with my fists in the sheets.

He leaned forward, his mouth beside my ear. "Would you like me to show you just how devout I can be?"

His proximity elicited a shiver to roll down the length of my spine. I licked my lips, knowing full well I was dipping into dangerous, dangerous waters. "Yes."

A wicked grin.

"I will start by getting down on my knees," he purred, his voice a sinister thing.

This proud warrior kneeling before me? The thought made me weak.

"Then?" I whispered, my throat bound in thistles.

He pulled back, just enough so I could see his face. His gaze, a scalding black flame, met mine. "I will spread these glorious thighs."

Slowly, his fingertips slid up my legs. My skin tingled in the wake of his featherlight touch.

I swallowed. "And then?"

He brought his mouth close to mine, close enough I could taste each word. "I will worship you with my tongue."

My breath caught in my throat.

. . . Was I ready for this?

I took one look at that sinfully built male looking down at me and . . .

I balked. Gods-damnit.

Awkwardly, I shot to my feet. "It's late," I stammered, backing up.

"Excuses, excuses." Von chuckled softly as he stood, a dark king rising from his throne, a predator emerging from the shadows and he was coming straight for me.

Ringed, tattooed fingers grabbed my chin, a hand clutching my hip as he backed me against the wall with a *thud*. My heart echoed the sound.

His lips feathered mine. "I want nothing more than to taste, to fill, to claim every inch of you. To sink myself into you so deeply that you will never get me out. I want to mar you so badly, you will be ruined from ever wanting to kiss another, fuck another, *love* another. I will devour you, Kitten. And when I'm finished, I will do it all over again."

I let out a shaky, shaky breath, words escaping me.

Von handed me a soul-damning smile. "So you best pray to the Creator, Little Goddess, because the next time we have a moment like this, I *will* collect what is mine. When I do, there will be no redemption for either of us."

He pulled away, the shadows parting as he strode towards the door, leaving without saying another word.

I slid down from the wall, into a puddle on the floor, both hands fanning my feverish cheeks. The fire beneath my skin was scalding me alive—and he was the one who had lit the match.

Chapter 20

"Tell me more," Harper preened as we got ready in my room.

"There's nothing else to tell. Everything was going good and then when things started getting . . . heated, I panicked. He left and I went to bed," I said, studying my neck in the reflection of the mirror.

The bruises were . . . gone. I thought they would be around for a week or two. But no, they were gone, the evidence of my run-in with Von's sister completely erased.

I turned my attention away and plucked the glass tube from the dresser. I pumped the goat bristle wand before applying it to my lashes. Three coats—Harper would not let me leave the manor without it. Although, I was beginning to understand why—who knew I had eyelashes? The girl from the cottage hadn't.

"I mean, I get it. He is not like other men," she said as she shucked off her top and shimmied into a flowy yellow bit of silk. The color suited her bronze skin tone. I could never pull that color off, not like she did.

"No, he definitely is not," I said honestly. "Are you nervous about tonight?"

"Not really." She shrugged, "You?"

I paused, thought about it, and shook my head. "No. I'm just looking forward to getting it over with. After tonight, hopefully, I'll be one step closer to Kaleb."

"One way or another, we'll get the information we need." She flashed a confident smile, her manicured fingers pulling her hair into a high ponytail—her tell when things were about to get serious.

My bare feet padded against the slippery, wet tiles, my toes working a bit harder to keep me upright. A light gold chain decorated in tiny, shimmering, dark crystals snaked its way over my ankle and up my leg, ending just above my calf. Earlier, Harper had found the small black box, adorned with a gold ribbon, by my door—no name attached. Although, when she handed it to me, I didn't need a written name to know who it was from. When we went downstairs and Von's gaze had drifted to my ankle, that was confirmation enough.

Tonight, I wore white—the color of a virgin bride. Lace hugged every curve, leaving my stomach and back exposed—the outfit of a harlot. And it was not lost on me that both bride and harlot had two vital things in common—both were woman, and both had sold themselves. The currency for their transactions was nestled in either coin or love.

The giant nude columns, carved with a manmade

hammer and chisel but crafted from the divine feminine, greeted me. I offered them a wink, feeling every bit of my confidence tonight. I looked the part—a fantasy, a dream. I prowled the bathhouse like a sex goddess, a far cry from the woodland shrew I started out as.

I caught my reflection in the crystal-clear water—where was the girl from the cottage?

That girl was gone now. Reborn a woman.

A woman who would do anything for the people she loved.

My fingers wrapped around the clay jug as I sauntered towards a group of boisterous men gathered on the west side of the pool. They were no better than a flock of hens as they clucked away, more interested in the tales streaming from the mouth of one man than the beautiful women who hung off them—women who would have enchanted their attention if it were any other night.

I wondered, for a moment, what was it about this man that seduced them in such a way?

"More wine, my lord?" I offered an elderly male, my voice sensual.

But my offer was declined as the elderly man waved me away, dismissing me as if I were interrupting the grown-ups.

Mentally, I hissed.

Physically, I wanted to do a whole lot worse.

It took every fiber of my being, but I refrained from drowning him and his patriarchal ways and glanced to Harper.

She was already in the pool, her toned arm draped over a shorter man with a wily beard, but he was completely uninterested in her.

She flicked her eyes to the man who sat in the middle of the group—the man who they all listened to. He was an eloquent speaker, his stories captivating, but still, I could not possibly understand why the other men were so ensnared by him.

That is when it hit me. It wasn't his stories—it was his power. His position. They all wanted to bask in the light of it, of him, in hopes that the sun would shine upon them too.

He was the king's advisor—the second-in-command of the kingdom of Edenvale.

He was a far cry from the old man I imagined him to be.

He was tall, toned, and roguishly good-looking. His hair was trimmed short at the sides and left long on the top. The red strands deepened in color as he combed his wet fingers through. A dusting of freckles was sprinkled across his tanned skin, lightly scattered over his nose, cheeks, and chest. Warm, honey-brown eyes glittered responsively as he weaved his tale, his hands emphasizing the story just so. There was an art to the way he spoke, the way he moved.

And as he maneuvered his muscular arms, his tight torso contracting in response, I realized that his body was built for the battlefield, not politics. Yet here he was, raptured in politics.

His gaze briefly landed on me before it shifted away, uninterested, as he finished his extravagant tale. The men around him applauded, a chorus of approval echoing amongst them, almost as if it were a game of who could throw themselves at his feet the fastest.

I glanced at Harper. She was our best bet. When we first arrived, the madame had told us that the king's advisor had a thing for brunettes. I willed her to look at me.

She didn't.

I willed harder, screaming her name in my head.

Nothing.

Okay . . . that was something we were going to have to work on.

I raked my mind, trying to figure out another way to gain his attention. I glanced at the wine jug . . . *That will do.*

With a silent prayer to the pale-stoned carved giants, I walked closer to him, his back turned to me, and that was when I feigned tripping.

My knees barked in protest as I fell on the hard tile, the wine jug shattering into oblivion, pelting his back in wine, the droplets of red dissipating in the pool.

"Oh my, I'm so sorry," I cried out as I crawled towards him, my hands trying to wipe the wine off.

He raised a hand, but not to strike, instead to still my frantic hands. He flashed a dashing smile. "It's quite alright, young miss. I was going to order more wine anyway."

The men around him burst into yet another round of applause for their shining star and his dazzling performance. They started cheering for more wine as they clinked their cups together—a droplet of a thought carried out into waves. The power he must have had.

The girls quickly scattered like a jar of upturned ants, scrambling to fulfill their orders. I had never seen so many wine jugs being plucked from the shelves.

The king's advisor winked at me, turned around, and started his next story.

Well, I had not expected that anti-climactic response, and

yet, there we were.

Huffing to myself, I glanced at my ruined outfit and bruised knees—this was a mess, both figuratively and literally. I raised to my feet and walked over to get the broom, my hand snatching it from the wall. After I finished cleaning up the broken bits of clay and wine and unfruitful schemes, I discarded it all in the trash. I crossed my arms and leaned against the wall, my mind whirring with thoughts of what I should do next.

Harper stepped beside me, her dark skin glimmering with beads of water, a wine jug in her hands. "That could have gone a lot worse."

"I know." I let out a frustrated sigh. "How are we going to get him separated from them? They cling to him like leeches."

"I could always torch the water and send them scrambling like little piggies. We could snag him then," she said, her fingers twitching as if she would do it right now.

I chuckled. "As much as I would pay to see that, that might create more problems than solutions."

She huffed. "Okay, fine, we'll hold off on that . . . for now."

"More wine!" a young man, barely a lick over sixteen, bellowed at us.

"Good to see they are starting his training early." Harper rolled her eyes. A hopeless sigh fell from her crimson-painted lips as she said, "That, right there, is why I have no interest in men."

We both snickered, and then she left to refill their cups.

Vera walked up to me, her eyes so wide I could see the surrounding whites. "You've been requested for a private bath."

"What? Who?" I asked, my tone more annoyed than I should have let on. Things could not get much worse at that point—I did not have the time to waste on some random man.

She popped her glossy, petal-pink lips. "The king's advisor."

My body was stripped of its clothes and the anklet Von had given me. Then it was scrubbed vigorously with a wad of something that felt like steel wool until my skin glowed red, red, red.

Aged hands painted my face before they moved on to style my hair—loose with a slight curl, just how *he* liked it, or so the woman muttered under her breath as she took out a pronged hair pin from her mouth and loosely tucked back a single wisp of curled hair.

A young girl helped the woman as she worked, handing her whatever items she needed—I guessed she was her apprentice. When the woman didn't require her help, the girl did other things, like mist my skin with a bottle of perfume—the scent a mixture of roses and gardenia.

Noting a pattern, I guessed it was *his* favorite scent.

The madame's prying eyes watched the entire process, and when the woman and the girl took a step back, she swirled her finger in the air, gesturing for me to turn.

I did it unwillingly, despising every single second of it. I had never felt so objectified. For the most part, I had been an actress playing a role. I was always in control with the aid of

Ezra's knock-out tonic, should I need it. In a way, that kept me an arm's length away because I was never working here for real. But this, what was happening right now, felt real—and it made me want to vomit. I was being stripped of myself. Saturated in *his* packaging. To be delivered to *him*. A *thing* to fulfill *his* needs.

It was too much.

I bent over and dry heaved.

The ladies jumped back out of projectile range.

The madame grabbed my shoulders and jerked me upright. "You have been chosen to serve our most distinguished guest. Now, pull yourself together."

I dry heaved again.

She slapped me—not hard enough to leave a mark, but still hard enough to hurt. The stinging flogged my attention and the uncontrollable ratcheting in my gut snuffed itself out. I felt half inclined to wrap a water bubble around her head and drown her where she stood, but I pushed away the thought because I knew why she did it. It was to redirect my thoughts, to give them something else to latch on to. And it worked. My nerves vanished. My mind fixated on the dull throb in my cheek.

I wondered how many girls had been subject to the same thing.

I could have sat with that thought for hours, but those hands were touching my skin again, forcing my arms up before a sheer bit of black fabric draped over my body, stopping at the widest part of my thighs. The worst part? It was completely see-through.

"I think I should wear something else," I insisted as I gaped at my essentially naked frame. Like this, I had nowhere to hide Ezra's vial—nowhere to hide the tonic that I needed him to take.

"Nonsense. You won't be wearing this for very long anyway," the madame said as she picked at her almond-shaped nails.

I was panicking inside. I needed to think of something, and quick.

"Ladies, please escort our *shining starlet* to the private chambers," the madame said with a clap of her hands.

"Wait!" I screeched, my hand reaching out to the dresser for stability. "Can I . . . Can I have a moment to myself?"

The madame looked at me like an owl watching a mouse, and when I was certain she would say no, she let out a breath and said, "Fine. Two minutes."

When the double doors closed behind the madame and the two ladies, I scrambled over to the locker I stored my things in, my heartbeat pounding in my ears. Frantically, my hands searched my coat pockets until I felt two glass vials. I grabbed one—a tonic to loosen the lips and cloud the mind. Neither Harper nor I had used it before.

My legs felt like rubber as I ran towards the wall of mirrors. I plopped the vial on the counter and stared at it—nibbling at my bottom lip feverishly.

How was I going to smuggle it in?

Where could I put it in this sheer bit of fabric?

Think. Think. Think.

My gaze fell south. No, that would be highly impractical, but it gave me another idea . . .

I looked up, to my freshly painted lips.

Bingo.

Chapter 21

One kiss.

That was it.

Just one.

I could do it. I could. I cou—

The thick door slammed with the ferocity of a crack of thunder, shattering my pep talk and locking me in the private chambers, which, to my horror, was not like the other private rooms. This one had a bed adorned in plush, expensive-looking furs and a floor covered in candles, their flickering flames providing a dim, sultry light. To my right, a doorway with drapes gathered on each side created a narrow passage to another room. Steam sifted between the drapes, slowly seeping in, a wandering hand claiming new territory.

Gag.

"You can come in," said a male voice—a voice belonging to the advisor of the king.

I sucked in my lips but quickly released them, remembering the venom they were coated in. Slowly, I walked towards the door, my fingers gently brushing aside the fabric as I ducked inside.

His muscular, tanned arms draped over the sides of the tub, his gaze briefly drifting over the curves of my body before he settled those wandering eyes on mine.

Part of me wanted to recoil, to regroup, to leave. But the stronger part of me, the warrior, the woman, stood my ground. I would play the part. Get the information and leave.

"Do you want me to join you?" said a sensual voice—my voice. Where it came from, I didn't know.

Without moving his arm, his finger raised, pointing to the private bar that was positioned behind me. "I'd prefer a drink."

"What would you like?" I asked, my tone honey sweet.

"Surprise me," he said, that charismatic charm long gone, although his voice was not unpleasant or unkind.

I nodded softly, turned, and moved to the private bar. Various crystal decanters of all shapes and sizes were placed neatly on the wood top, two crystal glasses placed in front of them.

I thought I heard him suck in a breath when I turned. I rolled my eyes, not appreciating his inspection of my rear assets.

"Your hair color is quite unusual for someone your age," he remarked.

I reached for the decanter with the dark amber liquid and poured a knuckle's worth inside. "I was born with it," I said as I returned the topper to the crystal decanter.

"You can have something, if you'd like," he offered, his pleasantry catching me off guard.

"I don't drink," I lied, not wanting to sample my own poison.

"Water or tea, perhaps?"

I shook my head. "No, thank you. I wouldn't want to ruin my lip gloss."

Wasn't that the truth.

I walked to the side of the steaming tub and offered him the glass.

His long fingers wrapped around it as he peered at its contents. A low chuckle left his lips. "I've never cared for whiskey."

"My apologies. I can get you something else," I offered, my hands reaching for the cup, but he retracted it out of reach.

An amused grin slid onto his face as he said, "It's alright. I live by one rule."

"What's that?" I asked, my arms wrapping around my torso.

"I finish what I start." He downed the glass. His muscles flexed as he lowered his arm outside the tub and placed the cup on the wood floor. "How old are you?" he asked, his brow furrowing as he examined my face, searching.

"Twenty-two," I replied. By reflex, I asked, "How old are you?"

"I have a few years on you," he responded with a wink.

"I do not mean to offend, my lord, but you look rather young to be the king's advisor."

"No offense taken," he replied, his tone nonchalant. "I have been judged by my youthful looks on more than one occasion."

I nodded, gesturing to his empty cup. "Would you like

me to get you something else?"

"Trying to ply me with alcohol?"

No, just poison.

To my horror, I nearly said it out loud. *Shit.*

"No, I just thought you might like another," I just barely slipped in.

"Where were you born?" His brow dipped inquisitively. The question was random, but I presumed this was his attempt at small talk.

Lie, a voice coaxed in my mind.

"I don't know the place of my birth," I replied honestly—too honestly.

"Do you not have living parents to tell you?"

Lie, the voice demanded this time.

"I never met them." I had no control over my tongue. I was starting to feel light-headed, a bit drunk even, like I was the one who had shot back that glass of whiskey, not him.

"Then who raised you?" he inquired further, his gaze piercing.

"A woman who took me in." I nearly clamped my hands over my traitorous mouth—I'd clearly poisoned myself with Ezra's truth tonic. I needed to direct the questions to him before he delved any further. "I don't mean to sound rude, but is my history what you brought me here for?"

"I would rather your history than to sit here alone with my thoughts," he replied as he leaned back against the tub, relaxing in the steaming waters.

"I don't understand. I presumed you would want to do other *things*." I dared to lift my gaze to his, allowing just the right amount of lust to saturate my eyes.

He ran his fingers through his wild, red hair. "I come here because it is the only place I can get some peace from the steady workings of the castle."

"Then you don't—"

He cut me off. "No. I come here to these private rooms for peace. And in exchange, I play the part, select one of you, but then I do not ask for any services. Ever. Most of the girls sleep while I sit alone with my thoughts."

"But the madame, she thinks you—how doesn't she know?"

"My coffers run a lot deeper than hers. I offer the girls a good deal of coin for their silence and they play along. Over time, their stories have spun the belief that I like a certain scent, a specific hair color—that I have a type." He looked like he might roll his eyes.

I was almost starting to feel bad about what I was going to do to him, although with this new admission, kissing him was becoming a bigger obstacle than I originally thought it would be.

"So when they doused me in the scent of roses and gardenia, that was for nothing?" I asked as I sat on the edge of the tub.

He chuckled. "I find the white gardenia flower quite pleasant, but I'm not a fan of the scent of roses."

"And the preference for brunettes?"

"I find blondes and brunettes equally attractive, but . . ." He leaned forward, the water sloshing to the sides. Thick, calloused fingers gently grasped one of my curls. "This unique color, I hold a particular fondness for."

"Oh?" I asked.

He nodded, letting the curl slip from his fingers, and leaned back against the metal tub. "It reminds me of someone I once knew."

"Where is this person now?" I asked, unable to stop myself.

"She is no longer of this world, her memory a ghost, always haunting me," he said, his chest expanding as he inhaled a deep, steady breath.

I could sense the yearning in him—for this woman who I thought might be a past lover of his. And if I wore her hair, perhaps I could use this power over him.

My vision was becoming cloudy, although my purpose was clear. With my gaze on him, I slowly dipped my foot into the water, testing to see what he would do.

He watched.

He didn't say no.

Slowly, I lowered myself into the grand tub. The girth of it easily accommodated two people.

"What are you doing?" he asked, his gaze meeting mine.

"I'm freeing you from your ghost—if only for a moment." I crawled towards him, the water overflowing, splashing on the floor.

"You don't have to," he said, although his wandering eyes said otherwise.

I placed a gentle finger on his lips before I removed it and brought my face to his. And for a moment, we looked into one another's eyes—two desperate souls yearning to bring a lost loved one home.

I closed my eyes and brought my mouth to his. I pretended I was kissing Von—that it was his steely, tattooed body underneath mine.

And dear gods, it was hot.

I lost myself in it, convinced it was him.

"What's your name anyway?" I asked a short while later, a giggle bubbling up on my swollen lips.

"Arkyn," the king's advisor replied as he studied his pruned fingers, water dripping down the length of his forearm. He brought his fingers closer to his face, as if it would allow him to get a better look.

"Ar-kyn," I tested the two syllables, smacking my lips at the end for added emphasis. I felt giddy, blissful, and increasingly drunk—holy dancing bananas, did Ezra's tonic pack a punch.

My mood instantly changed. I felt frustrated. Especially with myself. I was supposed to be doing something. I was supposed to be—

"You are quite easy on the eyes," I cooed as I looked at him, not caring that I'd blurted another secret out.

He dropped his hand in the tub, and we both laughed as if it were the funniest thing we had ever seen. He did it again and we laughed some more.

"You look so much like her, and yet, something is off," he slurred. "Like a veil has been conjured overtop. Your features are distorted, like I can't see the real you."

"What?" I hiccupped. His words made as much sense as my fragmented thoughts.

Footsteps came thundering into the room. It hurt my

ears—it was too loud.

Hands gripped my shoulders as a voice—Harper's voice—filled my mind. "Are you okay? I've been looking everywhere for you."

"I'm fine." I tried to tap her nose but failed, and my hand fell back into the water.

My head swiveled towards Arkyn, our gazes meeting, and we both started to laugh.

"We have to get you out of here," Harper said as she wrapped her arm around my torso and hoisted me up. My legs felt like two limp noodles—incredibly floppy, soggy, overcooked noodles, the thin, long kind. An older couple sold them at the market—what did they call it again? I thought about it hard, pushing my brain to its limits. I grinned. Ah yes, that was it! "Spaghetti," I cried out triumphantly, nodding in satisfaction.

"Come on, Sage, work with me," Harper said as she continued to heave.

"You there, brown-haired girl. Tell me, do you see a veil on her?" Arkyn asked, shaking his head as if he were seeing double.

I didn't catch Harper's reply because my body felt heavy and my head was—oh, my poor noodle legs. I jerked my head up, an important thought occurring. "Wait. Did anyone bring the sauce? Apparently, it is best served with sauce."

"Ooo-kay then," Harper said as she dragged me away from the tub.

"What about Arky-boy?" I protested.

"I'm fine. You can haunt me tomorrow, but only if you take off the veil," he slurred, a splash of water sounding behind me.

"I'll deal with him," Harper said as she half led, half dragged me to the bed.

I fell into a cloud of warm, furry sheets, so soft they felt like heaven, even though they were sticking to my wet skin. My body shivered, although I did not feel cold—or at least, I did not think I was cold. How could spaghetti be cold?

I could faintly hear Harper and Arkyn's voices, but they were little more than a buzz within my whirring mind. I blocked out the swirling ceiling by closing my eyes. I wanted to sleep, to float carefree among the land of dreams, away from my nightmares, weightless and free.

Like a feather floating on the breath of the wind. Up and up and up.

A strong, sturdy gust lifted me higher.

I knew it was him.

My windstorm, carrying me away.

Chapter 22

Bits of red and black static danced in my vision long before I had a chance to open my eyes. I nestled down, my body overburdened with the heavy layers of too much rest. I could stay here in this place, stuck in between awake and asleep, for the rest of my life. But the thoughts of my conscience were beginning to swell—a tidal wave of responsibility. It shattered my peace and jarred me awake.

I swallowed. My throat felt like a bag of nails had been rammed down it. Repeatedly.

My room was dark, but I was not alone. Soren slept in the chair next to me, his mouth slightly gaped open, a tiny river of drool marring his chin.

Why was Soren sleeping in a chair beside my bed?

Better yet—why was I in bed?

I stretched into my memories, a closed chest in need of dusting.

The last thing I remembered . . .

My lips entangled with those of the king's advisor.

My fingertips fell over my mouth. I'd thought of Von, pretended it was him . . . wanted it to be him.

Von and I were far from being a couple, far from being anything with a label, but I still felt betrayal clawing at my heart, its hold bewildering and strange. I had not just kissed the king's advisor . . . I'd made out with him.

And after that? The events were out of my grasp.

"You're awake!" Soren exclaimed, his nose crinkling as he emitted a lion-sized yawn.

"I guess so," I said, my voice as present as my thoughts. I shook my head, my hands still riffling through foggy memories. "What happened?"

"You've been sleeping for the past forty-eight hours," Soren said as he yawned again. His face appeared sallow, bags under his eyes making him look a shade older—just like Ezra did whenever she returned after a week of being away. As both possessed the Mind Curse, I was starting to wonder if that was part of it.

"Two days?" I stammered. What, for the love of Lady Light, had Ezra put in that tonic that it knocked me out for two days?

"Umm, Sage, I need to tell you something. I sort of . . . I had to . . ." Soren paused, hesitant.

"Had to what?" I asked.

"You wouldn't stop screaming. We couldn't wake you up. I just wanted to help you. So I . . ."

"Yes?" I shook my head, not quite sure where he was going with this.

"I crossed the unconscious barrier and silenced your mind so you could sleep. Peacefully," he said, his hands clasped tightly together, his shoulders slumping.

A heavy weight landed in my stomach, like a boulder made of lead.

Suddenly, I could feel him, on the cusp, lingering in the depths—a shadow that would never leave. My private, intimate thoughts were no longer mine. The intrusive nature, the loss of consent—all of it hit me like a tidal wave.

Get out, I screamed at his silhouette.

I can't. I'm so sorry. You were screaming. And crying. The blackened version of Soren turned towards me.

Reverse it.

His shadow proceeded on slow, careful feet. *I can't. But I can disappear into a crevice. I won't come out.* He did as he said, his phantom turning into a mouse and backing into a hole—out of sight, but not out of mind. He would always be there from now on... until one of us died. Unless there was a way for it to be reversed.

"I'm sorry." He looked at me, his eyes pleading, his face saturated in anguish.

"It's just a lot to take in." I stumbled over my words, still battling the thick of it.

"I know. I felt horrible while I was doing it," he said, tears brimming in his eyes. "Your screams—your night terrors—it sounded like the hounds of the Spirit Realm were chasing you down."

"I have fought with those nightmares ever since I was a child. They are a part of my Dream Curse. You really didn't have to—" I sighed again. There was no changing what had been done now. "It's alright. Ezra might have an idea how we can fix it. Until then, I guess you'll just be privy to *every* thought I have."

Saying it out loud did not make me feel any better.

"Where is everyone else?" I asked, my hands fisted in the lilac sheets.

"Preparing to leave," he replied.

Leave?

How could we? I'd bombed the mission with the king's advisor. But I would try again until we had the information we came for. We could not leave now—not when we had no idea where Kaleb was stationed.

The bottom of my cotton nightgown dusted the lip of the wooden stairs as I scrambled towards the main floor. Soren followed me, protesting me moving, suggesting I should still be in bed resting.

I shot him a fierce look. He clamped his mouth shut.

The front entrance door teetered back and forth as the wind pushed against it, a large, burlap bag placed in front of it, effectively keeping it from closing.

Outside, Ryker slung a bag over the back of his horse, his hands expertly buckling it in place. Harper was checking her mare's hooves, her bags still on the ground.

"We can't leave," I declared, my voice saturated in authority.

Ryker shook his head, his fingers gently stroking the backside of his gelding. "Sorry, darlin', the other night was a bust. We need to go home, regroup, and come up with a different plan."

"There has to be something else we can do." I refused to admit this was defeat.

"Like what? We blew our one and only option," Harper

said as she let go of the horse's leg. She jerked upright, the cool autumn breeze tugging at the tips of her swaying ponytail. I caught the superiority in her voice—the blame.

"Are you implying it was my fault we didn't get the information?"

She looked at me pointedly.

"Are you serious?" I seethed.

"You should have come to me. If you'd let me know you were chosen, instead of just leaving without saying a single word, I would have made it there in time to question him, but instead, you decided to work alone." Harper crossed her arms. Oh, she was pissed.

Good. I was looking for a fight.

"When do you think I had the time to come to you? When the madame was stripping me naked or when they shoved me in that room with him?" I shot back, my rage echoing the fire twin's temper.

Her fierce expression—the anger, the rage, the fire—was suddenly snuffed out.

She strode over to me and took me in her arms, squeezing me tightly. Her voice softened. "I'm sorry. Sorry we didn't get the information we need to find Kaleb."

It hit me like a bag of bricks. The loss I felt. The failure. All of it had been for nothing. I wanted to sob, but I bit the tears back. Those feelings slowly caved to something else—a new plan began to form.

"I want to go back," I said, determination setting my jaw.

Harper pulled away from me, sharing a confused look with her twin. "Back?"

I nodded. "To the bathhouse."

Steel cuffed my wrist, twirling me towards *him*. Even the shadows that often clutched to his side seemed to cower in fear. "That—" Von snarled as he brought his face inches from mine. "—is the *last* place *you* will be going."

But unlike the shadows, I would not hide from him. I glared right on back, focused on those unbound, wrathful eyes as dark as a starless night and in return, I showed him the oncoming storm in mine.

"Maybe we should hear her out." Soren's voice scissored Von's gaze from mine.

At the same time, we both turned our heads to look at him, our bodies still facing one another, dangerously close.

"You, *of all people,* will stay out of this." Von's voice hit a predatory low. It was a warning.

"What's going on?" Ryker cut in, demanding to know.

"Tell them," Von demanded, his tone resolute, gilded in the unyielding power of a god, his judgement inescapable.

"I . . ." Soren choked on his words. "She was in so much pain. So I . . . I crossed it."

"What did you cross?" Harper said, taking a step forward.

Soren stepped back. "The unconscious barrier."

Ryker clenched his fists, expression murderous. Through gritted teeth, he said, "You did *what?*" As if he needed him to say it one more time before he pommeled him.

Harper mirrored her twin's actions. "You can't be serious."

Lyra walked through the doorway, struggling with a sack that rivaled her petite size. Confused, she looked at us, surveying our faces for answers.

"I thought I was helping," Soren squeaked, the color draining from his face, painting him a ghastly white.

"Helping? Fuck you, Soren!" Ryker clenched his jaw, his broad shoulders rising on an inhale, disgust written all over his face.

When he charged for Soren, it was Von who held him back, to my shock. Before Harper had a chance to do the same, Lyra was there, wrapping her slender arms around Harper's waist.

"This… will not help," Von said to Ryker, the two goliaths butting head-to-head, a fearsome duo.

I felt like I was hypnotized, stuck in a cage of white noise, watching the entire scene play out. Unable to do anything. Say anything. I understood Ryker's rage because of what happened to Fallon. I could also understand why Harper would feel the same way—she'd almost lost her brother because of what had transpired from just the intent of breaking the unconscious barrier.

But this wasn't about them.

It was between Soren and me. It was a mistake, and I was a masterpiece of mistakes, so who was I to judge? Besides, he had already apologized profusely. And I was working on accepting it.

Mainly because there were more important things at stake—like Kaleb's life.

"Enough!" I yelled, the command in my voice surprising even me. Heads swiveled my way. I shook mine. "It doesn't matter."

"How can you say that?" Ryker and Harper seethed at the exact same time.

"Because. I'm here. Alive and safe. And Kaleb is out there." I threw my hand to the side, gesturing to the outside world. My heart hammered fiercely, pumping an intoxicating mixture of adrenaline, fear, and determination through my veins.

Kaleb was out there.

I didn't care to hear anymore from them or waste any more time, so I turned and strode to the door. Before I stepped through, I made a pledge for them all to hear, for the entire world to hear. "I'm going back to that fucking bathhouse."

I could feel her, my warrior, waking and stretching within.

I would not fail this time.

Chapter 23

I opened the little black box, my fingers drifting over the black diamond anklet Von had given me—it was beautiful. I had never owned something so exquisite, been *gifted* something so exquisite. After I'd bombed our mission at the bathhouse, Harper had grabbed it, as well as the rest of our stuff, and brought everything back to the mansion. I was thankful she did—we did not need them going through our coats and finding two glass vials.

Closing the lid, I set it back down on the makeup vanity and began the task of brushing my hair. Despite my two-day slumber, it wasn't that bad. I stared at the cluttered top of my dresser, looking at nothing as I brushed. My thoughts were adrift, flowing with determination and ebbing with doubt.

I had no other choice.

I had to return to the bathhouse. It was the only lead I had, and I would be damned if I let it go. But what would I do when I returned? Beg for forgiveness? Whose wrath would be worse—the madame's or the king's advisor's? But I didn't care. I would face them both, if that was what it took to get Kaleb back.

A constant, pulsing whisper beckoned me from my thoughts.

I knew it was *him*.

Wood clicked upon wood as I set the brush down on the oak top.

I lifted my gaze, meeting his in the reflection of the mirror. Goddess divine, *those* eyes.

Tonight, I had chosen black silk, the same piece of cloth that I'd felt drawn to on the first night Harper and I worked at the bathhouse. Now that I had it on, it felt like it was tailored especially for me. The neckline plunged deceptively low between my breasts. Thin straps reached like arms, winding delicately around my neck. The fabric ended at the curvature of my hips, dipping in front, just enough to cover my core and peachy backside. The back fell open, revealing my slender, feminine muscles.

Von's black lashes slowly drifted down, coaxing a shiver to stroll the length of my spine. I could feel the soft, intimate brush of his knuckles roaming down my skin. The sensation of his touch—it stirred something, a hunger, a need, and I found myself yearning for more.

But when I looked up, he was still standing by the door.

I hated how real it felt—I *wanted* it to be real. Wanted to feel him touch me like that.

Normally, I covered myself up, but tonight, I would let him look.

Tonight, I would not run from him.

I gathered my hair and swept the wintery strands back,

the length of it cascading in soft, sultry waves. Sifting through my makeup bag—something Harper had encouraged me to get during our adventures downtown—I moved on to my makeup.

I applied a dark, moody, red paint to my lips—the whole time feeling him, every bit of him, watching me. After, I searched for the brush with the fine tip. When I found it, I dipped the end in an inky glass pot and began to slowly outline the top of my lashes with kohl, winging it at the sides.

When I was finished, I heard his unspoken command . . .

Come to me, Little Goddess.

Slowly, I turned, the velvet fabric of the stool snagging against the silk, pulling it up, exposing my upper thigh, the caress of it eliciting another shiver. My nerves felt like embers ready to ignite. I stood, my heels clicking as I walked towards him. I looked up, caught on the hook of the one predicted to suck my soul dry.

In this moment, the *way* he looked at me . . . I would let him.

His knuckles drifted lightly over my shoulder, a spark left in their wake, threatening to catch. "I think you finally found your color," he murmured, his tone a dark decadence. "But this strap . . ." His finger slipped under the thin strap, gently stretching it upwards, testing its strength. With one snap of his finger, easily, it would break. "It is so *very* thin. And right now . . ." He leaned in, whispering in my ear, "It is all that keeps *you* from me."

The intent behind his words elicited the same feeling as if his ringed fingers were between my thighs, working that sensitive bundle of nerves. *Goddess divine.*

"Then snap it off." I didn't offer—I demanded.

He pulled away, a wicked gleam catching the sharp tips of his canines. "I do not think the owner would be too happy with me if I were to do that." His eyes looked pointedly at me, implying I was the owner.

"It's not mine," I replied honestly.

"Oh?" he countered, a teasing smile touching the corners of his devastating lips.

"Kiss me," I said, my fingers drifting to the lapel of the black jacket he wore. It looked painfully expensive and so unlike the fashion worn here. It matched his otherworldly eyes. Both didn't belong.

He tipped his head to the side in that predatorial way—painting him as the wolf and I the rabbit. "What will you give me in return?"

"Anything . . . Everything," I whispered breathlessly, lured by his gaze—by him. Intoxicating, consuming him.

The constant push and pull between us had finally reached a precipice.

Now, I was at its mercy.

His fingers caressed my cheek. "Are you so sure this is what you want to bargain with?"

I nodded, desperate. I'd tell him just about anything right now, say just about anything if it meant he would just kiss me, touch me.

"Consider it a deal, Little Goddess." Something sinister flashed victoriously across his eyes, like he had just watched me stroke my signature across the bottom line of a contract. In that second, I wondered what in the Spirit Realm I had just agreed to.

I took a step back, driven by a moment of uncertainty.

He tipped his head in the predatorial way. "Oh no, little one, there will be no retreating from me now."

He moved so fast, there was no time for me to react.

Roughly, he cupped my ass, using it as leverage to pull me into him. He squeezed it just enough that it teetered between pleasure and pain, just enough to bring me up on the tips of my toes. His hand weaved in my hair at the back of my head, angling my face up to his. He took one look at me before he brought his lips down on mine, setting me aflame.

Von was not gentle. He was demanding. And goddess divine, I craved every bit of it.

His mouth *claimed* mine.

I wrapped my arms around his neck as my mouth moved against his, yearning to claim his right on back.

When I felt his tongue sweep over my lips, they parted willfully for him, as if they knew what he wanted. He growled at my body's responsiveness to his, the sound of it rumbling through me, all the way to my core, to my curled toes. His tongue slipped inside. He dragged it across the roof of my mouth in one dominant sweep, pulling it back until the tip of his tongue reached my teeth. But instead of exiting, his tongue flattened and drove back in, continuing his exploration, all the while tasting and teasing, chasing away every unexplored inch before he tangled it with mine.

With ease, he swept me from my feet like I was no more than a trembling leaf caught on the wind. He walked us over to the bed, his lips still moving against mine, tethering me to him.

All of his hard edges pressed into my soft curves. Smoke

and water. Leather and silk. Obsidian and snow. It was him and it was me—his divine masculine summoning my divine femininity to break free from her reservations.

Eagerly, she did.

I tore off his jacket and chucked it to the side, removing his shirt next as he lowered me down onto the bed. The softness of the bed contradicted the steel pressed against my front. My fingers roamed over his broad, tattooed shoulders, down his thick pectorals to his stacked abs.

Great divine, every part of this man was *hard*.

An addictive mixture of anticipation and nerves coursed through my veins as I wrapped my legs around his waist. He rolled his hips into mine, pressing himself against my throbbing core. I groaned at the sudden friction, desperate to feel more. My hands shot to his waist, aiming for his belt buckle. But he captured my wrists and hauled them over my head, pinning them there with his one hand.

Von tore his lips from mine, setting my mouth free.

But I didn't want to be free. I wanted his mouth back on mine. I was feverish, aching, riddled with need. I looked up at him, my expression conveying as much. I unwrapped my legs and dug my feet against the bed, using the leverage to better grind myself against the bulge tucked beneath his pants, my body blatantly telling him what I wanted. Telling? It was outright screaming.

I wasn't embarrassed by my bluntness—that dominant side of him axed me from my shame, leaving me in a wake of carnal, animalistic lust.

A slow, steady exhale fell from his mouth as he studied me like he was trying to decide what to do with me. He parted his lips, his tongue rolling over his perfectly white bottom row of teeth, his sharp canines poking out from his top lip.

I suppressed a whimper, wondering what it would feel like to have them at my throat, in my throat.

Fuck. Where was this coming from?

"I must confess, Little Goddess," he started, his voice husky, dangerously low. "I'm angry with you. Angry enough I'm tempted to tie you to this bed and leave you here for the rest of the night, until I can return later and *finally* taste what is *mine.*"

A shiver ratcheted through me, straight to my desperate, throbbing core. I nibbled on my bottom lip, the thought of him tying me to the bed only serving to turn me on more.

"Dirty girl," he mused before he hauled his mouth against mine, his kiss punishing this time. Branding.

I took everything he gave greedily, happily, and when he pulled back again, I nearly cried out in frustration. I tried to pull my wrists free, desperate to touch him, to force his lips back to mine, but his grasp was unbreakable.

I glared at him, my brows knitting. This was torture, and judging by that coy smirk, he damn well knew it.

"You are so incredibly beautiful, even when you scowl," he praised as his fingertips slid up my leg, a whisper of a touch.

He watched my reaction the higher his hand roamed. Watched my lips part as he cupped my breast, his large hand easily enveloping it.

A breath, painted with pleasure, fell from my lips.

His rings glinted in the candlelight as he played with my breast, massaging and squeezing and teasing. I arched into his touch and pressed my head back, wiggling my hips beneath his in circular motions. He increased the weight of his hips atop mine and I moaned, welcoming the added friction.

His hand released my breast, moving higher, his hips pulling back from mine.

I let out a growl, increasingly frustrated with his teasing. I wanted him. Everywhere.

"As lovely as you are, you don't get to be angry right now because that honor is all mine." His rings bit into my neck as he glided his hand over it, applying just enough pressure to make it uncomfortable in all the right ways. Roaming higher, he slid his hand over my jaw, stopping when he reached my mouth. He brought the rough pad of his finger against my bottom lip, swirling it, dipping the tip of his thumb inside, making it wet.

Unyielding, claiming eyes met mine. "The next time you think of kissing another?" Von leaned forward, bringing his lips a breath away from mine, just enough so I could taste his words. "Come to me first. So I can remind you who these lips belong to."

Breathing became difficult.

I met his firm gaze, pushing this one step further, needing to hear him say it. "Who do they belong to?"

"These pretty, pretty lips—" He smeared my bottom lip to the side, tugging it forcefully as he ground himself roughly against my core, teasing that part of me, extending his claim. "—are mine."

Proving his point, he smothered my lips under his kiss, kissing me in such a sinful way, I knew from this point forward, I'd forever be ruined.

My lungs rasped as I kept up with his mouth, our bodies moving against one another. His hand gently lay against my throat, and even though he wasn't squeezing, my oxygen felt controlled by him. Each time his lips parted, I breathed his oxygen in. Deeply.

He nipped at my bottom lip, locking it between his teeth, before he let it slip free. "Whose are they?"

"Yours," I breathed against his lips.

"Good girl," he purred darkly, the combination of his praise and his voice making me melt beneath him, my bones turning to jelly.

He pulled back, his weight instantly gone.

My eyelids sprung open.

Von was gone. Like gone, gone.

I blinked, confused, dazed. And damn well straight out of my mind.

"Von?" I asked the silence.

No answer came.

I rubbed my eyes, as if that would help. It didn't.

Had I imagined him?

I propped myself onto my elbows, all too aware of the liquid heat pooling at my core, soaking the tiny string of fabric deemed underwear. I touched my lips. They felt tender and raw.

No, I hadn't imagined it then.

I got up from the bed, taking in the hot mess staring back at me through the oval mirror. My makeup was ruined, the lipstick smeared, the kohl liner smudged. My hair—my gods . . . What was once soft silk now resembled a rat's nest.

I definitely had not imagined it.

Sighing, I walked over to the makeup vanity. I picked up the brush and repeated the process of getting ready, ignoring the female equivalent of blue balls currently happening in my nether regions—my mouth wasn't the only thing throbbing.

I growled—that male was *insufferable*.

And yet . . .

Come to me first. So that I can remind you who these lips belong to. His bourbon voice replayed in my mind.

Fuck. I wanted him.

When I was satisfied with my restoration, I left the ghosts in my room and headed over to Harper's and Lyra's chambers, knocking first.

"Come in," Harper called out, her voice muffled through the door.

When I entered, I found Harper stretched out on the bed, lying on her stomach. Lyra sat cross-legged on the other side, a set of cards in her hands. She waved at me, offering a kind smile.

I smiled back. "Hi, Lyra."

Harper plucked a card from the stack sitting in front of them before she turned and looked at me. "I didn't think you were actually going to go back." She gestured to my outfit with her free hand. "But apparently you are."

"He might come back. I have to try again." I sat on the edge of the bed.

"It's foolish, Sage. What if he figured out you drugged him? Can you imagine what the king's advisor, of all people, will do to you? He'll have you thrown in jail and hung before noon!" she exclaimed as she threw down two cards, the game they played foreign to me.

"It's a risk I'm willing to take," I said, watching as Lyra played her hand.

Harper sighed in defeat, chucking her cards onto the bed. "Fine, but you aren't doing this alone. Give me five to get ready."

"You don't have to. I'm the one who created this mess."

She looked me dead in the eye. "Yeah, you kinda did. But I'm not going to make you clean it up alone." She leapt from the bed and headed towards the bathing room.

I helped Lyra clean up the cards, and before long, Harper stepped out from the bathing room wearing a little orange number that set her dark skin aglow. With her hair braided and pulled up into a ponytail, she shot me a thumbs-up. "Alright, I'm ready to go."

I nodded, grabbed our fur coats, and the three of us headed downstairs.

Ryker sighed when he saw us. "Not you too."

Harper and I exchanged confused glances. "What do you mean?" I asked him.

"Von just headed to the bathhouse." He gestured to us. "Judging by the official *we're going to the bathhouse* coats, you two are as well."

"Wait, what?" I blurted out. "Why is Von going to the bathhouse?"

"He's going to try to track down the whereabouts of the king's advisor," Ryker said, rubbing the stubble on his jaw, rough finger pads sounding against the short bristles.

I highly doubted Von was going to dress up in a skimpy little outfit and entertain the men. Which meant he was going to use another tactic.

I had a feeling it involved force.

"We gotta go." I looked down, reaching for Harper's hand.

That was when I noticed it—the tattoo. A delicate, thorny vine started at my wrist and slithered up and around my forearm.

What in the Spirit Realm was that?

Chapter 24

The errant breeze plucked at my hair, mussing it as we ran down the soaked stone streets towards the bathhouse. The smell of fresh rain, decomposing leaves, and wet soil painted the air with heavy brush strokes. The droplets swirled and twirled as they gently rained down, and although they did not pound with ferocity, it was the constant, steady trickle that left us soaked and cold—the temperature low enough that it felt like winter was stirring awake.

Ducking inside, I shook off the water droplets that had yet to soak into my clothes, my teeth chattering.

Harper's painted lips quivered, her makeup smeared, her hair clinging to her head. I imagined I looked no better. I groaned, realizing I would have to do my hair and makeup for the third time today.

"Where have you two been?" screeched a woman's voice with the tenacity of a vulture. The madame stepped out from the shadowy claim of the stark hallway. She jerked the bronze candlestick upright, casting the deep planes in her face in a harsh glow, illuminating her age. Her hair, which was typically neatly piled on top of her head, looked a bit more sporadic tonight, some forgotten wisps falling loosely by her neck.

Two hulking men stood behind her—that could not be good.

"We were sick," Harper lied, her hands rubbing her arms, chasing away the bitter cold.

"You two better have been deathly ill. I received word from neither of you explaining that you would be away. Do you know that I had to ask some of the girls to work double shifts? Do you think that is fair?" she scolded us like she had just found us with our hands in the cookie jar. In some strange way, it almost came across as . . . motherly.

"We were *really* sick," I chirped. *Smooth*—not.

Her cheeks, tinted with frustration, matched the red in her velvet gown. She turned to me, eyes shooting daggers. I was lucky she wasn't Cursed. "And *you*! Do you have any idea what trouble you caused for me?"

Shit. She knows. Harper and I exchanged worried looks, both of us ignoring the warning in our guts—shrieking to cut and run.

"The king's advisor refuses—he *refuses*—to see any of my girls," the madame spat at me, her tone acidic. She clenched the candlestick holder, her knuckles bone white, the dancing firelight illuminating the lines of the angry, bulging veins threatening to explode out of her hand. I noticed a matching vein protruding from the middle of her forehead. I thought she was going to launch the candlestick at my head, but instead, she let out an aggravated groan and pinched the bridge of her nose, as if she felt a nosebleed coming on, induced by stress. "He says he will only see you."

What?

My stomach flipped and then it flopped. Or perhaps, it was the other way around.

"He has returned every night, demanding to see you. His men traipse around, barge into private rooms, and leave them a terrible mess in their search for you. It is as if the assholes think they own the place," she scoffed under breath. "I don't know what you did, but he has threatened to close Thermes de Luxe down should I not produce you by this Thursday."

The king's advisor was threatening to shut the bathhouse down? Clearly, I had not just poked the so-called bear—I had harpooned a grizzly.

I swallowed.

"She isn't well enough," Harper exclaimed, trying to cover for me, trying to bucket our way out of my sinking plan.

"Well, that's a shame, isn't it? The king's advisor is here tonight, and I will be *damned* if I let years of hard work be for nothing," the madame hissed at Harper. She turned to me. "You have two choices, Sage dear. You can come with me on your own, or—" She gestured to the bare-chested brutes standing behind her. "—Maximus and Enricho can drag you there."

Harper took a protective step in front of me, but I caught her clenched fist and squeezed it gently. "It's okay. I'll go with them."

She turned to me, concern weighing her brow.

"I'll be fine," I offered, nodding reassuringly. I squeezed her hand one more time before I followed them down the long, quiet corridor.

Exaggerated moans and breathy laughter echoed around me, the sounds changing ever so slightly with each closed door we walked by, but the crescendo was always the same—overdone and fake.

The madame had me stripped, scrubbed, and decorated—a repeat of before. They adorned my curves in sheer fabric, painted my lips a soft, virginal pink, and scented my skin with rose and gardenia.

After, they paraded me through the halls like some prize, unbred mare en route to the mating stalls.

The madame offered me a withering glare before she slammed the door behind me.

I jumped, startled by the abruptness of it. "Hello?" I asked the all-too-quiet room dipped in the essence of sex, jasmine, and must.

No answer came.

My attention shifted to the doorless frame draped in strings of crystals and beads, wondering what waited for me through there. Candles dotted the floor, their light casting the room in a honey, soft glow, their flickering flame mirroring the sensation in my churning gut.

The air shifted. It cracked. And out from the shadows stepped . . .

"Von?" I asked, not understanding how he could suddenly just appear. Perhaps he had been here all along, my logical side reasoned.

Tonight, he wore all black. And when I say he wore it, I mean he fucking *wore* it. His tight leather pants showed off his toned, powerful thighs. His hair, an obsidian mane thrown into a messy topknot, a few strands left out, fell around his face, framing his masculine features which were currently set in stone. Cloaked in darkness, he stalked towards me. "I meant what I said. You were not to come back here."

"It's not like I have a lot of choices," I countered as I stepped back towards the door, my movement driven by the carnal way he looked at me.

"I'm not accustomed to being disobeyed, Kitten." He raised his arm over my head and pressed it against the door, locking me between two exceptionally hard things—one made of oak and the other of steel. "But as infuriating as I find it—it is your most attractive quality." He whispered, his breath hot against my ear, "It makes me want to fuck you against this door—make you praise my name so loud that all three realms hear you."

His words, primal and unadulterated, were like a summoning, coaxing my inner self to embrace her sexuality.

I sunk my teeth into my glossy bottom lip, tugged at it, and then I said, without an ounce of shame, "Then do it."

Then everything was moving.

His demanding mouth delved to my neck, the tip of his sharp canines grazing against it as he kissed the sensitive skin. I tipped my head back, exposing my neck to him—whatever he wanted, I would let him take. His fingers bunched and gathered my hair as he moved his lips up, over my jaw, and then brought them down to my mouth.

With strong, skillful arms, he lifted me from the floor.

Free from gravity, I wrapped my legs around his torso, my core pressing into his hardness, his pants, which I had admired mere seconds ago, now something I cursed. My hands shot to his waist. I fumbled with his belt, my touch too frantic, too heated, too desperate.

When I heard bootheels coming from the other side of the wall, I pulled my mouth from Von's.

He growled at me—a big, sleek panther who had just lost his supper.

"Someone's coming," I said, panicked.

He lowered me to the floor, but he didn't let me go. "The king's advisor, I presume."

"What?!" My eyes went wide. Lust withered, and reality bloomed—*what was I doing*? I was going to blow it again. I pushed against his solid chest. "You have to go. Now."

As I pushed against his torso, my gaze fell to the random tattoo that had suddenly appeared on my arm after my last encounter with him. The bastard had a lot of explaining to do, but this wasn't the time or the place.

"We will finish this later," he stated, following my gaze.

"Oh, we definitely will," I gritted, glaring holes into him.

He spared a glance at my sheer outfit before he vanished.

I blinked at the empty space.

People didn't just evaporate . . . *but something that wasn't human might.*

I shook my head, shoving the thought out. My hands moved to straighten the ridiculous fabric the madame had forced me to wear, but when my fingers touched it, it felt of silk, not lace. I glanced down and gasped. Ribboned around my frame was the black, silk lingerie I had chosen earlier tonight. Unlike the thin, flimsy fabric that filled me with discomfort, that showed too much of my body—this one was opaque, yet still sexy.

But I did not have time to mull over how my outfit had spontaneously changed or, more importantly, what kind of strange magic Von was using because the door swung open and in walked the advisor of the king.

Chapter 25

Arkyn strode in, fully clothed, a sword sheathed on his left side, indicating he was righthanded. His tall, lithe body was saturated in the colors of the king—crimson and gold. His pleated jacket looked perfectly tailored, clutching his broad shoulders and cinching in at his narrow waist. A livery collar, a thick, gold chain, draped over his shoulders, dark gemstones evenly embedded throughout. They shimmered dutifully— rubies, I presumed. I could not fathom what something like that must cost, although I had a feeling it could fetch enough coin to bring indoor plumbing to every city, town, village, *and* lonesome hovel in Edenvale.

"My men are stationed outside the doors. I have instructed them not to allow anyone in or out," Arkyn stated flatly, his lips pressed into a firm line. His fingers drifted over the pommel of his sword, massaging it as if it were his Curse—waiting, biding for release. "It would be in your best interest to cooperate with me. Am I understood?"

I nodded, feigning my best doe-eyed look. Meanwhile, I

reached within, stroking my slumbering water beast—two could play this game.

"Good." He gestured to the wicker chair beside me. "Please. Sit."

The way he said it implied he was not asking, so I turned around and plopped in the chair, my shoulders slumping against the scratchy, worn wicker. He stood there in silence, studying me—my hair, my face. His eyes sharpened, and it felt like he was peering in, beyond the layers of my skin, like he was stripping them away to see what lurked beneath. I hated the feel of it. I wanted to slap it away, but I held my tongue as he conducted his search.

Curiosity flickered briefly across his face. The expression changed, shifted to satisfaction, as if he had just fished something out. He broke the silence. "What did you drug me with?"

My eyes narrowed. *Shit.*

I licked my lips. "I don't know what you are talking about."

"Is that really how you want to play things tonight?" he asked, cocking his head to the side, arms crossing over his chest.

I didn't know what to say, so I held firm in my silence.

"Fine. If you won't tell me what you used, then you will tell me why," he stated, his tone growing increasingly annoyed.

"Why what?" I asked, knowing full well what he meant but sticking to my dumbfounded role.

He looked at me pointedly, his expression saying I knew what he meant. He verbalized it anyway. "Why you drugged me."

"Why do you think you were drugged? You spent a lot of time in the pool, and you drank that night. Are you sure you weren't just drunk?" I deflected.

He looked like he wanted to laugh. "It is a shame such a pretty thing bears a serpent's tongue." He moved closer to me, propping his hands on either side of the wicker chair. "Are you aware what the punishment is for drugging the advisor of the king? Something that could be seen as an attempt on my life?"

I pursed my lips. "Not particularly."

"You are a smart girl." His eyes fell pointedly to my neck. "I'm sure you can figure it out."

I bristled, imagining an axe being swung back before it was brought down on my—*nope*. Didn't like that idea.

His brown eyes looked into mine. "If you answer my questions with honesty, I will ensure you leave this place without a silky, white hair out of place." His fingers captured a ribbon of hair before he tossed it to the side. "If you continue to lie, then I will be forced to take you back to the castle, where I will utilize *other* means to loosen your tongue. So you see, I have given you a choice. Which of the two will it be?"

Some choice.

As much as I wanted to pay a long, overdue visit to the king, I was running low on time, and so I answered with a sigh. "Okay, fine. I drugged you with a truth serum. But it was not my intention to hurt you. I was not aware what the other side effects would be. I know now because, in the process, I accidentally drugged myself."

"A truth serum?" he repeated, processing. Then he—he

chuckled.

Well, I certainly was not expecting that response.

"That is rather ironic," he muttered under his breath. His gaze shifted back to me. "You gave me a truth serum, which implies you are looking for information . . . What do you want to know?"

"I need to know where the conscripted are being sent," I said, hoping he didn't pry any further.

"Why? Do you have a *suitor* that was conscripted?" he asked curiously.

The question felt out of place, like he was fishing for relationship status more than anything. I didn't like the intrusion into my personal life, no more than I liked the sheer cloth they made me wear earlier. I felt a slight thankfulness for Von and his departure gift.

I shook my head. "No."

"Another lie," he hissed as if I had scalded him with hot water. He pulled his hands from the chair and started to walk to the door. I knew what waited on the other side.

"Wait. I wasn't lying. It's my brother," I disclosed swiftly, amazed at how fast he was at detecting my half-truths.

He came to a quick stop. "A *blood* brother?"

I did not understand why it mattered, but I answered anyway, "No, but a brother, nonetheless."

"What do you intend to do with the information should you have it?"

I ripped the bandage off and the truth came oozing out. "I'm going to break him out."

"And you intend to do this on your own?" he said, although it felt like he already knew the answer.

"Yes."

"*Tsk, tsk*, another lie," he replied in an almost teasing tone. There was a brief exchange of silence before he looked at me and said, "I would like to make you a deal."

"A deal?" I asked. This sounded vaguely familiar.

He nodded. "Yes, a deal. You give me the name of your brother, the place where he was conscripted, and I will find where he has been stationed. It may take me a few days." He waved his hand, dismissing the last detail. "Semantics. I will find the information you seek."

Hearing compared to believing was as stark a contrast as day and night. Everything I had done since I left Meristone, although it had not always gone as planned, all of it had led up to this exact moment. He was going to find where Kaleb was, and although I should feel happy, relieved, or something in between, I was far from it. Because one question clouded my victory—why would the king's advisor, of all people, help me?

I swallowed hard, ignoring the rising nausea. "What do you want in exchange?"

He flashed his perfect white teeth. "I would like to court you."

Chapter 26

The mansion was quiet tonight. Soren, Lyra, and Ryker had gone to bed hours ago, and, as per usual, Von was nowhere to be seen.

Harper and I sat at the kitchen island, fork deep in a strawberry cake.

I inhaled the smell of sweet cream butter, smooth vanilla, and humble notes of strawberry. Lyra had made it this morning and it was nearly gone. Three quarters of it were left—before Harper and I found it tonight, which meant we were the reason for its quick departure from this world.

Despite my distended belly, I wasn't sad about it.

"This whole courtship deal with the king's advisor—I don't like it," Harper said as she carved out a piece of the velvety-smooth cake. Apparently, I wasn't the only one thinking about tomorrow.

I swallowed before I replied, "I don't either."

We exchanged worried glances and delved back into the cake as if it held the solution to our problems.

"By the way," Harper said with a mouthful. She motioned to my forearm with the pronged end of her fork. "I've been meaning to ask, where did you get the time to get a tattoo?"

I glanced down at the tattoo on my left arm. The vine and its thorns looked delicate, yet strong—the ornate detail of it made it almost lifelike. It started at my wrist and circled up and around my arm, the fine, detailed vine more spread out as it got to the end. It was beautiful, enchanting even, yet it felt like it was missing something. I didn't know what . . . *I didn't know what?* I could hardly believe myself—what was I saying? Some mysterious tattoo showed up on my arm shortly after I kissed Von and now I was admiring it? I needed to get it together, figure out where it came from, and how I could get rid of it. And I had a feeling all the answers I needed could be given by the male who just strolled in on unnaturally silent feet.

I pointed my fork at him accusingly. "Ask him."

Harper's brow shot up before she looked at Von, waiting for an answer.

Von took his irritatingly sweet time as he plucked a sizable red apple from a heaping bowl of fruit. His large hand dwarfed it instantly. We waited while he leisurely inspected it as if he had nothing better to do. I realized he wasn't even listening. That, or he was just toying with me.

I squinted at him, deciding it was the former. "Go on, explain to her why I have a tattoo because I am eager to find out as well." My fingers wrapped tightly around my fork, strangling the handle as if it were his irritatingly divine, purely male, kissable fucking neck.

His eyes, black as coal, didn't bother to shift from the apple. "She made a deal with me."

That was it. That was all he offered.

This male was infuriating.

Harper nodded like she now understood. *Like she now understood?*

My eyes flared and I hissed, "I did not."

"Oh yes, Little Goddess." Those endlessly black eyes lifted to mine. "You did."

I grumbled. I wasn't making any headway. I switched tactics. If he put it there, he could damn well remove it. "I want it removed. Now."

"No." He bit into the apple.

Unreasonable, insufferable, stupid male.

I looked at Harper for help, but judging by the awkward look on her face, it seemed like she had other places she would rather be. Still, I dragged her in, kicking and screaming, no less. "Harper, please reason with this demented male and tell him to remove the tattoo," I gritted between clenched teeth.

"I can't," she stated, giving me a half apologetic shrug.

I shook my head. Clearly, they had both lost their minds. "And why can't you?"

"Because you made a deal," she said, as if that explained everything.

It didn't.

I caught the amused look on Von's face. I couldn't tell what he was enjoying more—Harper's unwillingness to defend me or that damned apple. I was half inclined to water arrow it right out of his hands.

"Regardless of if I made a deal or not, that doesn't give him the right to tattoo me." I dropped my fork onto the empty cake plate before I impaled one of them with it.

"Sorry, Sage, but it sort of does. It's not exactly practical, but laws drafted by the Old Gods so rarely are," Harper stated as if it were a matter of fact. She got up from the wood stool and went to the sink where she began to wash our forks.

"What does a tattoo have to do with the Old Gods?" I asked. I could feel Von's eyes on me, that familiar tug pulling at me like a string. I ignored it.

Harper dried the forks, put them away in the drawer, and then turned, hands spreading out on the counter behind her. "As you know, our ancestors, the ones that came here all those years ago, brought the Old Religion to Edenvale. Tattooed bargains were part of the religion created by the Old Gods. A tattooed bargain, although a bit barbaric, is one that is set in stone. A tattoo is given to both parties involved in the deal. Unlike a flimsy piece of paper, it is not something you can just tear up—the grounds of the deal must be met before the tattoo is removed. It's binding." She paused before she added, "Although, we don't see it happen very often anymore. Those who possess the magic for it, well, there aren't very many of them left. Actually, Von is the only one I know who has the ability."

I fumbled over what I was told. The tattoo was binding, something that would not be removed until the deal was complete. The deal I had promised Von . . . My breathlessly soft voice hummed in my ears. *Anything . . . Everything.*

I glared at Von. "It's an impossible thing to give."

He smirked, a brow raising in challenge. "Is it?"

I threw my hands up in anger. "You unsufferable males and your deals. It wasn't enough that I had to make one deal tonight, now you tell me I've made two? At least *he* didn't tattoo me after."

Von's smugness abruptly shifted to something much more sinister. The shadows even seemed to peel away from him. "What do you mean by *two deals*?"

I looked at Harper for backup, feeling every bit of the foot I had just crammed in my own mouth.

Harper feigned a quick stretch and an obnoxiously loud yawn. "I think I'm going to go to bed. Good night, you two. Play nice." She scuttled away faster than I could ask her to stay. I shot a withering glance at her as she dodged around the corner and out of sight. *Traitor.*

Suddenly, Von was beside me, the apple gone. His finger swept under my chin, guiding me to look up at him. "What other deal did you make?"

I swallowed. Hard. "The king's advisor said he will find Kaleb's location and give it to me."

"What has *he* asked for in return?" Von demanded. Even though his touch was soft, I could feel the heavy tension clinging to him. It was strange seeing him like this—he was always so controlled all the time.

"He wants to court me, or rather, one outing."

Von scowled. "And you agreed."

"Of course," I replied defensively. "I didn't have any other option."

Snarling, he said, "*You* always have options."

"Do I?" I raised my arm for him to see. "Then why is this on my arm?"

227

His hand gently captured mine, softly guiding it towards him. His fingers swirled around my wrist, gently turning it over, studying the sprawling tattoo. "If I explain it now, I will sound like a jackass," he said, his fingers drifting over the vine, his touch so featherlight, so intimate, it made me shiver. His eyes met mine. "But there will come a time you will understand why this was necessary."

I let his words sit with me as my gaze drifted up his long, ringed fingers to his wrist, to his forearm. There, over top of the other tattoos, in fresh, black ink was the twin to my own— although they were not identical.

Like yang was to yin, his was the masculine version to my feminine one. Where mine was all elegant, dainty details, his was more vicious looking with its thick, claiming vines and sharp, menacing thorns.

Seeing it there filled me with an inexplicable satisfaction. Something that had started as a push and pull between us had quickly teetered to a constant pull faster than I could fathom. What was the magnetic force that was bringing us together at such an intense, impossible speed? And why did it feel like Von knew?

I watched as he repeated the same gentle brushing strokes, but my attention drifted to the remainder of his tattoos. I had once thought of them as a messy canvas that somehow resembled art, but now they seemed more like a map, charting his dealings throughout his life—gods, there were *so* many.

My fingers slid just above the one that twinned mine to a woman's hand holding a lush, red apple, a snake wrapped tightly around her arm, its mouth stretched open, revealing its fangs. "Is this one from a deal you made?"

"Yes," he replied, his voice a smooth, dark bourbon.

I sat with that for a moment before I asked, "How many of your tattoos are from deals?"

"All of them."

I swallowed. "You have to fulfill every one of these?"

Looking into my eyes, he replied, his tone dropping an octave with each spoken word. "Every last one."

Silence fell between us. The weight of his words, the way he said them, the way he looked at me—it reminded me of the way a groom spoke to his bride, stating his vows just before they were deemed man and wife.

Why did it sound like he was making a promise?

I looked down, eyes roaming over the various tattoos, searching them for answers, but there were so many of them, I didn't know where to start. "Isn't that overwhelming?" I asked, curious how he could walk around with so many reminders of the deals he had made stamped all over his body.

"Never." His hand cupped my cheek, and he looked at me in such a way that I believed every word that followed. "When I'm lost and out of my mind and waiting for *my* light to return, they are the very thing that guides me through the darkness."

Like a curtain pulled back, the mask he wore lifted, revealing the truth beneath. There, in the gaze of those starless eyes, I understood where the stars had gone—they had fallen.

It was both beautiful and heartbreaking, to the point that tears filled my eyes. Standing, I raised to the tips of my toes. He dipped his head, a strand of black hair tumbling forward as our lips found each other. His fingers drifted into my hair as he deepened the kiss, and for a moment, I felt like I was his oxygen—like I was the only thing tethering him to this world.

To be kissed like that, there was no coming back from it. Ever.

Chapter 27

After I washed and crawled into bed, my thoughts were scattered.

There were so many things about my life that felt unchartered and unknown, like something was missing. Like there was a bigger picture, but it was out of my grasp. I was tired of feeling that way, and I had ignored my Dream Curse long enough. It was a part of me, and if I wanted to understand whatever it was that I was missing, I needed to learn more about the Curse.

Flipping my quilt off, I strolled over to the stack of books on the end table. I sifted through the towering pile of smut and filthy dark romance books, looking for *The Six Curses*. The honey glow of the fireplace gave off just enough light that I could make out the titles. I found *The Six Curses* at the very bottom of the pile. I had ignored it for far too long.

Snagging it, as well as a brass finger candle holder, I returned to the comforts of my bed. Careful not to spill the wax, I placed the lit candle holder on my nightstand. Leaning on my side, I propped the book up on a pillow, angling it so that the light from the candle made the words visible. I flipped through the pages, scouring for anything that mentioned the Dream Curse. About a quarter of the way in, I found what I was searching for, and that was where I started to read.

Word for dreaded word.

Gods . . . smut was so much better.

After an hour or so of reading, I was no closer to finding any answers. I didn't need the candlelight to clearly see that the author's prejudice towards the Cursed shone through vividly. They wrote about their experience with someone who had a Dream Curse, and they made them sound like a complete lunatic.

Sighing, I closed the book, tossed it onto the table, and blew out my candle.

I nestled into my covers, Von the very last thing on my mind before I drifted off to sleep.

"Just one bite," a male's voice commanded. It echoed in my mind, building and churning, caressing and obliging. I wanted to obey.

I blinked, looking around, trying to see where the voice had come from, but I could not see—not when the darkness was peering so intently at me.

"Who are you?" I asked the darkness.

"Your Curse," it said in a rich, deep tone. So purely male. So ethereal.

"And who am I?"

"My blessing," he purred, fingers drifting along my cheek. *The darkness swirled behind me. I wanted to look, but . . .*

A beam of light flickered from up above, shining on a golden, shimmering apple suspended in the air, hovering before me, just an arm's reach away.

"One bite," he said, *his voice enchanting. Spellbinding. Impossible to resist.*

I reached for it, my fingers curling around the apple as I brought it to my lips and sank my teeth deeply into its flesh.

It was divine. Impossibly nourishing. When I felt its juice trickle down my throat, my body sighed with relief. I had never felt so full, so satisfied. And I . . . I wanted more.

But when I opened my eyes, the apple was gone.

In its place—a tattooed wrist.

I tried to shove it away, but the darkness wouldn't budge.

I choked on the metallic taste.

It was poison, corroding my insides.

His hand snaked around my throat, his sinful praise in my ear. *"That's it. Drink up, Little Goddess."*

Chapter 28

I had never ridden in a carriage before—until now, that was.

Early that morning, Soren had popped his head inside my room, explaining that a carriage awaited me outside. Having just woken up, my skin slick with sweat—no thanks to my nightmare—I'd hastily gotten dressed while brushing my hair. On my way out, I grabbed an orange from the kitchen, staying clear of apples and tall, dark, wickedly handsome, confusing males.

At the end of the winding lane, four black horses with perfect white stockings led a sizable carriage, vines and leaves hand carved into the sides. Crimson banners waved from the top, proudly displaying the Edenvale emblem—the emblem of the king. I fought the sudden urge to obliterate the flags with my water harpoons.

Muttering a few curse words directed at the king, I ducked inside.

"Did you say something?" Arkyn asked, peering up at me over the top of a crisp newssheet.

"I was just saying what a lovely day it is outside," I covered as I sat on the opposite side from him.

The coachmen clicked his tongue, and the carriage began to move.

"Indeed," he replied skeptically, his gaze returning to the paper.

I leaned against the wall of the carriage, listening to the horses' hooves clack against the brick-paved road. The wheels of the carriage created a constant, steady hum. Occasionally, they would groan in protest before they kicked a stray rock to the side.

"I think it is rather odd that a girl who works at a bathhouse would be living in one of the wealthiest neighborhoods in Belamour," Arkyn remarked as he folded the paper and tucked it beside him. "Either you do your job exceptionally well, you are living in the back alley, or you have someone wealthy helping you. So, which one is it?"

I had a feeling this question was going to come up. "I'm staying with some friends," I replied honestly, remembering his unnatural ability to detect my lies. My hands smoothed my lilac skirts. I hardly wore dresses—most of the time I found them impractical and cumbersome—but this one, when I found it, I couldn't resist.

"Does the property belong to one of your friends?" he asked, crossing his legs, hands folding neatly in his lap.

"Tell me, my lord—" I smiled sweetly. "—do you conduct interrogations with all the women you court?"

He chuckled, a wink of a dimple appearing in the corner of his cheek. "I only do it with women I find particularly intriguing."

"How flattering," I said ambiguously, choking back the sarcasm. The clacking of horses' hooves sounded different than before. Now, it sounded softer, more forgiving. I tugged the merlot curtain open and peered out the window. Panic gripped me—we were no longer in Belamour.

An expanse of tumbling, rolling hills spanned the horizon ahead, the gentle rolls blanketed in long, brown grass that had long gone to seed.

"Where are we going?" I demanded to know.

"We are going to the Temple of Light," Arkyn replied. He gestured to the seat. "You might want to brace yourself; it is going to be a bit of a bumpy ride from here on out."

By the time the carriage came to a rolling stop, I was eager to get out. I had never felt such a vast appreciation for land.

A bit of a bumpy ride?

It was a gods-given miracle that the wheels had not fallen off. The soft, rolling hills had quickly turned into a steep, jagged incline, the trail full of big rocks and lumpy, frost bumps that made the carriage jump with each strike.

I hoped we did not have to take that same trail to get back, but I suspected we probably did.

Arkyn spoke briefly with the coachmen before he turned and walked towards me. The pin he'd worn earlier, a status symbol of the king, was no longer pinned over his heart. I wondered if he was trying to downplay who he was. I could think of a few reasons why he might do that.

He extended his arm. "The carriage won't be able to

make it any farther. We must walk the rest of the way."

"That's fine. I don't mind stretching my legs anyway," I replied.

If things weren't so whatever they were with Von, then I might have felt something when I settled my hand on Arkyn's arm. Afterall, Arkyn was handsome, with his wild red hair and glowing honey-brown eyes. He was tall and tan, and under the bright afternoon sun, he seemed almost . . . radiant.

But he wasn't Von.

And worse? He was the king's advisor—the *same* king who had overseen the deaths of countless innocents. The same king whose actions led to people living in poverty. The same king that had taken my brother for his selfish, useless war. I wondered, as we walked down the slender, bricked path, how big of a role Arkyn had played in all those needless deaths.

As we walked, people of a variety of ages and ethnicities joined us. Some were on the same path as us, and others joined from smaller trails that joined with ours. I imagined the trails were like the veins in a leaf, ours being the main one that fed the rest.

We walked on a steady incline, my view of what lay ahead blotted out by the tall trees that surrounded us. Their branches, almost finished shedding their leaves, swayed leisurely over top. There was something comforting in those slumbering giants, probably because they reminded me of home.

People by the dozens descended onto the path until we were shoulder to shoulder with them. It felt constricted, the pace dropping to a crawl. What started as a faint melody in the distance trickled towards us, carried on the tongue of each man, woman, and child.

> *Praise the Lady of Light,*
> *Our savior who paid the ultimate price.*
> *Praise the daughter of the Moon,*
> *Our barren angel in need of a child.*
> *Praise the Goddess of Life,*
> *Our mother who delivered us all.*
> *Praise her. Praise her. Praise her love.*

The trees parted, revealing an opening, revealing the Temple of Light.

Proudly, dominantly, it stood on a stepped dais—three steps in total that spanned around its base, allowing access on each side. Bathed in white, glittering stone, the temple looked like it was from an entirely different era, or perhaps a different realm.

I marveled at its unique architecture. Rectangular in structure and mountainous in size, it swallowed the horizon. Columns were used in place of walls, allowing the sunlight access to every part of the building. The fluted shafts of the columns were wider than the trunks of ancient oak trees, and their "Y" tops spread out like wings, hoisting the roof into the clouds. There was a feeling of depth and balance, and something else I couldn't quite place.

I turned to Arkyn, whose gaze was locked on me. "What do you think?" he asked, curiosity quirking an auburn brow.

"It is unlike anything I have ever seen," I expressed as we maneuvered around the people who sat on their knees, hands clasped over their chests. Some bent forward, their arms stretched out in front of them as they prayed. Their voices circled around me like white noise, but occasionally, the static would part—

"My mother is unable to work because of her poor health. I have three little brothers and two little sisters whom I must look after. I work all day and all night, and yet, I don't have enough money to feed all of us. Please, I pray to you, help me, somehow."

"Dearest Lady Light, my husband has decided that our daughter is old enough to be wed. I pray for your aid. Please help him find a proper match so that the marriage may be successful and gifted with children."

But it was the last one that caused a lump to bulge in my throat.

"I'm praying for my brother, who was conscripted for the war . . . We never got to say goodbye. I pray you will be with him. Please, Goddess, let him survive."

I traced the voice to a girl with long brown hair. She looked to be no older than fifteen. Emotions overwhelming me, I dropped beside her, my hand falling onto her arm. "I am sorry about your brother. Mine was taken as well."

Wide blue eyes peered up at me. Her hands fell over mine. "Have you come to pray for him?"

I nodded. "I will pray for yours too."

She smiled, tears clouding her gaze. "Then when I make my offering, I will offer it for your brother as well."

"Thank you," I replied, clasping her hands one last time before I straightened and returned to Arkyn's held-out arm.

We walked to the base of the dais, its three steps seeming so much larger than before. As we ascended, Arkyn mused,

"You must love your brother very much."

"I would do anything for him," I replied, every fiber of my being standing firmly behind the words.

Inside, gold bowls, large enough to bathe in, checkered the sparkling floors. Even though they had no wood inside, flames danced from their bellies. Even more peculiar was the color of the flame—a light purply-blue, like bottled moonlight.

Directly in the middle of the temple, a massive golden statue demanded my attention. A woman stood with a crown placed upon her head. The crown had eight points spiking out the top, each point displaying a phase of the moon. Massive wings flared out on either side of her. Her mighty face was a blank slate, frozen forward, hollow eyes forever set on the space in front of her. Her elbows were bent, her palms flat, facing upwards in offering. In each hand, a smaller golden statue stood. Both appeared to be women around my size. The one in her right hand cradled a baby in her arms, a halo suspended just above her head. And the one in her left hand was empty-armed. The statue hung her head in shame, a collar placed around her neck.

Arkyn led me closer, our footsteps lost among the praying voices outside. We stopped at the base of the statue, and I stared at it, surveying its grandeur for a moment, before I whispered, not wishing to wake the slumbering, gold giant, "I think a man designed this statue."

Arkyn bit back a laugh. "Why do you think that?"

"They gave her ridiculously large breasts." I rolled my eyes.

Arkyn tilted his head, his eyes going right to the

goddess's chest. "You are not wrong. They are rather cumbersome-looking, aren't they?"

My brow quirked. "Are we really discussing the size of her breasts?"

Arkyn leaned in closer to me. "I believe you started it."

I smirked. "Touché."

"Do you follow the New Religion?" Arkyn asked, honey-brown eyes meeting mine. He crossed his arms over his chest, the crimson jacket he wore crinkled, stiff, signaling it was probably new.

I didn't answer right away, as I needed time to consider my options. I knew the Crown's stance on the New Religion—that they were willing to do anything to ensure it succeeded, even slaughter people by the thousands. I didn't doubt Arkyn possessed a similar belief—he was the advisor of the king, after all. He also had an uncanny ability to detect my lies.

I decided to proceed with the truth. "I know the basics about it, what is taught to us in the books. I believe in the New Gods, I just don't know my stance on the New Religion itself. To be honest, sometimes it seems like it was written by a man—utilized as a means of controlling women and what they do with their bodies. These statues are a fine example of that. It appears that the goddess is offering women two choices. The first is the woman holding the babe. She is a good wife, producing heirs for her husband. And the second is empty-armed, which means she did not do her 'wifely duties.'" I couldn't help but pour a little cyanide in with the last two words.

"You are not far off, but there is quite a bit more to the

story than that," he said, pausing momentarily. "Despite being the Goddess of Life, Lady Light could not produce children for her husband." His gaze lifted to the goddess before he asked inquisitively, "What do you think the collar implies?"

A trip to the pyre.

I ignored the impulse to blurt that thought out and shrugged, studying the way it gripped her neck, a dreadful feeling building in my gut. I ignored that too. Quickly, I replied, "That she was a slave to her own desires and wants, and that kept her from being a good, little wife?" I couldn't help but roll my eyes. I didn't know much about the goddess's fertility woes, nor did I really care to find out more.

He turned to me, his voice rough. "Tell me, Sage, when you are faced with the same decision, will you be a *good little wife?*"

The question felt out of place, his intense gaze even more so—like he was boring into me, testing me. I took a step away, needing some distance between the two of us. Me? A good little wife who swept the floors, pregnant and bare foot, cleaning up after a man who sat on his ass, barking at me to bring him a tankard of ale?

Shaking my head, I said firmly, "I have no plans to get married."

Especially after working at the bathhouse. *No thanks.*

He stepped closer to me, his fingers capturing a ribbon of my white hair. "And yet—" His fingers drifted down the length, gently tossing it to the side when he got to the end. "I have a feeling you will."

I rolled my eyes.

The sound of trickling water sifted towards me, the smell

of something sweet tinging the air. I followed the sound. Behind the gilded statue, a wall-like structure towered. From the top, glistening waters fell, coating the wall made of white rock. But there was something off about the water, like it was heavy and thick and had a will of its own—harder for gravity to bend to its will.

People gathered around the expansive fountain, joy spreading over their faces as they cupped their hands under the water, filling them and drinking.

Arkyn led me through the crowd. "The fountain was discovered thousands of years ago. It is why the temple was built here in the first place. It is rumored to bring blessings upon those who drink from it in good faith."

Now close enough, he reached out and allowed it to flow into his large hands. He brought it to his mouth and slowly drank it down. For a second, I thought his eyes almost seemed to glow. He gestured to the water. "Go on, have a taste."

I cupped my hands together and watched as the heavy liquid filled them. I was surprised by the weight of it—like molasses, not water. Bringing it before my lips, I breathed in its vibrant, sweet scent before I drank the divine nectar down. Like a beating drum, the fibers of my being started to thrum, pulsing with life, like something sleeping had been awoken in me. The taste of rich honey coated my tongue. My Water Curse thrummed with veracity. I felt powerful. Divine.

"What do you taste?" Arkyn asked as he wiped his hands against a white cloth—where he got it from, I didn't see. He offered it to me.

I took it, drying my hands on the soft cotton. "It tastes sweet—like the richest, purest honey," I exclaimed, my hands slowing, the question striking me odd. "*Why*? Does it taste different to you?"

"No." He shook his head and smiled brightly. "I taste the exact same thing."

Arkyn left me under the shade of a swaying tree—apparently, *he had to go speak with someone briefly, but he wouldn't be long*. Or so he'd said. That was a good twenty minutes ago.

I occupied myself by studying the trees, racking my brain, trying to figure out what kind of trees they were. They possessed the same color as a birch tree, but their bark was like ash, covered in prominent furrows. I turned to one and ran my finger over a furrow, tracing the diamond pattern.

"You're still here," said a young voice, coming from my left.

I turned. The girl who came to pray for her brother gave me a kind smile, her eyes puffy and red. She no longer wore her long brown hair loose—her head now covered with a bandana.

"Yes, still here," I replied warmly. "I'm just waiting for someone."

"Oh, I see." Swishing her lips to the side, she paused in thought. Her eyes lifted to mine. "I made the offering for your brother and mine." She pointed to her head.

I eyed the bandana suspiciously. "I don't understand."

She untied the knot, slipped off the cloth, and revealed her hair was no longer there. Pieces of her scalp looked dry, irritated, like the hair had been plucked out by a dull, overused blade.

"The goddess does not care for false egos or material beauty. By removing our hair, we are paying tribute to her. I hope that she will grant her blessing upon me—that she will bring my brother home." She returned the bandana to its new home and tied it tightly at the back of her head.

I couldn't believe what I was hearing . . . what I was seeing.

I highly doubted the goddess wanted this young girl's hair—I blamed the Crown, yet another spun tale to control the masses, to control women. I wanted to tell her as much, but what good would that do? I could see the hope in her bloodshot eyes. And hope was better than nothing.

"Did you drink from the fountain?" she asked, curiously looking up at me.

I nodded. "I did. Did you drink from it?"

"Yup, every time I visit. I always drink from it," she replied with pride.

I didn't know why, but I felt compelled to ask, "What did it taste like to you?"

She looked at me as if I had just asked a very odd thing. "It tasted like water."

"Just *water*?" I repeated more to myself. "Not thick, decadent honey?" I asked, something odd churning in my gut.

"Honey? Gosh, no. I've never heard of such a thing," she stated with a shake of her head.

That struck me as odd.

"Does it taste different to everyone?" I asked.

"What? No. You can ask anyone here and they'll tell you it tastes just like water," she declared with the unwavering certainty of a teenaged girl.

Arkyn appeared beside me, cutting the conversation off. He gave the girl a kind smile before he looked at me. "Are you ready to leave?"

The caw of a raven came like a summoning from above. I looked up as the sleek black bird soared above. The glint of its vivid, black feathers gave off a purple shimmer as they reflected the sun, its beautiful tail feathers spread out like a fan, claws stretched out as it landed on a branch just above us. Neatly, it tucked its wings in and peered down at us, head cocked to the side. Watching. Waiting.

"That's not a good omen," the girl stammered as she took a step back.

"No." Arkyn gritted his teeth. "It certainly is not." He turned to me, offering his arm. "Come, Sage, it is time for us to leave."

Pulling my tethered gaze from the raven, I exchanged goodbyes with the girl before I took Arkyn's arm.

The raven's caw, unnervingly loud, haunted me all the way back to the carriage.

Chapter 29

The carriage groaned as it struck something hard, protesting, rocking from side to side. I pressed my hand against the wall, stabilizing myself. When the ripple effect of the strike faded, I nodded towards the cloth sack tossed carelessly on the seat beside Arkyn. "What's in the bag?"

Arkyn shifted a bored glance to it. "It's for the queen."

The mention of the queen sent an uncomfortable chill down my back—a reminder of how close I was to enemy hands.

"What's in it?" I inquired further, not expecting him to reply. Why would he divulge such information to me?

"It's hair," he said blatantly, his honesty nearly just as shocking as his reply.

"*Hair*?" I asked, my thoughts slowly drifting back to the girl. An image of her removing her bandana played in my mind.

"Yes, hair," Arkyn replied dully.

"Was it from that girl?" I crossed my arms, annoyance

hitting me as I connected the girl to the sack full of hair destined for the queen.

"The one you spoke with before we left?" He paused, his gaze falling to my arms, noting my defensive posture, no doubt. "Hundreds of girls and women visit the Temple of Light weekly to offer their hair. The chances are slim that it was hers. Besides, it takes a while to process them all."

The information sat as well with me as Ezra's cooking. "Where does all the hair go?"

"It goes to the wealthy upper class." He crossed his legs, his suspended black boot bobbing from the movement of the horse-drawn carriage.

"What do they do with it?"

"A lot of them suffer from the Great Pox—including the queen herself. It causes hair loss. So, they have the hair made into wigs."

The Great Pox—Ezra had treated a few people with it before. It was a disease that caused an inferno of a rash, as well as other symptoms—hair loss included. It was spread predominantly through sex.

I shook my head in disbelief. "All of these young girls and women believe that by having their hair plucked out, they are denouncing their beauty to the goddess and in return, she will bless them for their offering. But in all actuality, their hair is going to the rich nobles who can't stop fucking?" I scoffed, painting this hoax for what it was. "Just so they can cater to their own ego and cover their bald heads?"

"You are correct," Arkyn replied, a slight smirk touching the corner of his lips.

"That is disgusting," I hissed, furious at the corruption

and all of those who dwelled within in it. I looked at Arkyn accusingly, who sat quietly in his chair, expression blank.

For the remainder of the ride, I seethed in silence, processing what I had been told. For a moment, I wished I were born with the Fire Curse because I would gladly burn the corrupt monarchy to the ground, and anyone who stood for it.

The carriage came to a rolling stop, the abruptness of it returning me to the present. I slid the curtain to the side, looking out the window.

"We have arrived at your address," Arkyn stated, not bothering to look.

I jerked my head back to Arkyn but didn't move from my seat. My brow quirked expectantly. "The information you agreed to give me?"

"I've run into a few issues with gathering your brother's whereabouts."

"And you didn't think to tell me this earlier?" I argued, a mountain of frustration weighing on me.

Amusement touched his lips. "It didn't seem important."

"Important?" I fired the word back with all my might.

"Patience, Sage. I will find the information you seek," he said, a confident lilt to his voice.

It did little to reassure me. "When?" I demanded.

"Tomorrow," Arkyn replied, flicking an invisible speck off his pants. "I will pick you up for another outing, and then let you know at the end of it."

I scoffed. "That wasn't part of the deal."

"No, I suppose it wasn't," Arkyn answered with a slight careless shrug. "Regardless, you will agree to it."

I hated the way he said it. Hated that he was right. I

would agree to it because he was the only lead I had.

"Fine," I grated. "When should I expect you next?"

"Early tomorrow morning," he said, his honey-brown eyes dancing like liquid fire.

Annoyed at the situation, I offered him no goodbye. I gave him a curt nod, gathered my skirts, and left. If the coachmen had not been holding the door open, I would have slammed it behind me.

"And Sage," he called out as I walked away. "Make sure you pack an overnight bag."

The door swung closed, and the carriage pulled away.

Mumbling a few unladylike words under my tongue, I stormed up the path. I had higher expectations for today, had hoped the king's advisor would produce the information I needed, but all I'd learned was something I already knew—the system was corrupt.

The wealthy would always take from the poor—like leeches latched on, feeding until they were fat and plump and ready to fall off. I despised leeches. I despised the ruling system. I despised all of it. Anger scourged my veins.

Von loomed beside the front entrance, his back pressed against the wall, a knee casually bent. His face was cloaked in darkness, but when he tilted his chin, it was just enough to part the shadows, just enough for our eyes to meet. One black brow raised. "How did it go?" It was a question it felt like he already had the answer to.

I replied anyway. "It didn't. The king's advisor says it is going to take more time to find out where Kaleb is. He says he wants to meet again tomorrow."

Von's gaze flicked to the side as if he were blotting out a

roll of tobacco he no longer wanted.

I felt compelled to reach out, to touch him, but I stilled my hand at my side, fighting the urge that swelled within. Why was it always like this with him? Even when I was riddled with frustration and annoyance, I felt compelled to be in his arms.

My dream flashed to the forefront of my mind, the taste of copper riding my tongue. I took a step back as if I had been pushed.

"I dreamt of you last night."

"And what was I doing, Little Goddess?" he asked, his masculine features chiseled out by the light of the moon.

"You coaxed me to bite an apple that tasted of blood," I answered, my hand instinctually drifting to my throat. "You said that I was your blessing . . . That you were my Curse." My voice fell just above a whisper as I looked up at him and gestured to us both. "What is this? Between us?"

"Fate."

And it sounded like the most logical thing I had ever been told.

Chapter 30

I was losing my mind. Clearly.

I didn't really believe in fate, so how could I find logic in it?

How could I feel so tethered to someone I had known for such little time?

The only feasible explanation was that I was losing my mind, that my marbles were finally rolling loose. I cursed Ezra under my tongue—her insanity had finally worn off on me.

Or maybe this was a long-lasting side effect from her truth tonic.

I sighed. I would ask her about it when we were reunited—the three of us.

"Is something wrong?" Arkyn asked from across the carriage, amber eyes locked on the document he had spent the last four hours reading over. A satchel sat at the base of his feet, the button flap thrown open, showcasing the stacks of paper rolls tucked inside.

"No, nothing," I lied, peering out the window at the vast marshland dominated by waterlogged soil and billowy, swaying reeds. Not wanting the carriage to get stuck, the coachman had kept to higher ground. Unfortunately, that meant instead of cutting right through the marsh, we were forced to go around it. And from where I sat, I saw no end to the treeless landscape.

"How much longer?" I asked, my head rolling back as I looked at him.

"Another five hours or so. We won't arrive at Thornhill until nightfall," Arkyn replied, his tone clipped, occupied. He leaned forward, his gloved fingers walking through the papers in his satchel.

"What are you reading?" I inquired, tired of the silence, of my private thoughts.

He tilted his head up and smirked, "Oh, you know, advisor of the king things." The way he said it was like it was some private joke that I was not privy too.

"Such as?" I asked.

"Reviewing taxes. Drafting laws. Managing the day-to-day running of the kingdom," Arkyn replied as he plucked a stack of paper from the satchel.

"Sounds riveting," I replied sarcastically.

Arkyn didn't reply.

I wasn't letting him off the hook that easily. "And what of Kaleb? Do you know where he is?"

He spared a glance my way, although he did not look pleased. "Yes, I found him."

My heart began to race, my mind whirling. "And?"

"I will tell you later." He reached for another roll.

"Why not tell me now?" I interjected before he could delve back into his work—forging more laws to rip off the poor could wait.

"Because if I tell you now, you have no reason to stay." He sighed.

"Wouldn't that be better for you? Then you could return to your work." I gestured to his never-ending papers. "It's not like you are getting anything out of this deal anyway."

"On the contrary, Sage. I'm getting everything." He stated it as if it were a matter of fact. Dismissing any more conversation, he returned to his papers.

I sighed obnoxiously loud, just to irk him, and went back to my private thoughts.

The creaking of a wheel that was in desperate need of oil and the rhythmic clacking of horses' shoes against the grassy, compacted ground provided the only sound for miles. Occasionally, a horse would nicker, coaxing the others to reply. At least *they* were conversing. Not that I could say the same for my traveling companion and me.

Arkyn was still fully invested in his papers, even though the daylight was nearly gone. I marveled at how he managed to read in the dark. The wind outside started to pick up, gently pushing the carriage from side to side. I flicked aside the curtain, the moonlight tracing the silhouettes of the dark bottomed clouds looming up above.

"It's going to storm," Arkyn said as he tucked his papers away in his brown leather satchel that, too, supported the official emblem of the king. He flipped the flap over and buttoned it in place.

Another gust of wind slammed against the side of the carriage, causing it to teeter back and forth. I braced myself against the wall, waiting for the carriage to even out. Suddenly, a cracking noise sounded, followed by my side of the carriage dropping to the ground.

I fell into the corner, something hard walloping the back of my head. My fingers weaved into my hair, momentarily rubbing the hurt before I surveyed my hand. Despite the intensity of the ache, there was no blood.

Arkyn was by me faster than I could comprehend. He offered a hand. "Are you alright?"

I nodded in reply, taking his hand as I returned to my feet.

The door swung open, the wind nearly ripping it off. The ruddy face of the coachman looked frantic as he shouted above the roar of the wind, "Are you both okay?"

Arkyn looked at him, his face seemingly calm, considering the circumstances. "What happened?"

"The terrain, combined with these ungodly winds, is too rough on the carriage—must have caused the hub to bust off," the coachmen replied, his hand on top of his cap, trying to keep it in place.

"Can you fix it?" Arkyn asked, brown eyes fixated on the coachman.

"No, my lord, I'll need to take the wheel in for repairs," he replied honestly.

"We cannot stay here for the night," Arkyn said more to himself than us. "Unhook the horses. We will ride them the rest of the way."

"In this wind?" I exclaimed, shaking my head.

"Would you prefer to stay here?" Arkyn asked, a red brow raising in challenge.

Another blast of wind slammed into the carriage, this one far worse than the others. He was right—we couldn't stay here—but I couldn't imagine riding out there either.

A glint of steel flashed in the darkness, and before I could react, a sword cleaved its way through the coachman's chest. His head dropped down before it jerked back up, his eyes rounded at the corners, wide and filled with horror as blood sprayed from his mouth, speckling my seafoam dress red, red, red.

The sword was pulled out, leaving a gaping wound oozing with blood. He dropped to the ground, his eyes rolling to the back of his head.

My mouth gaped . . . He was dead.

Arkyn grabbed me, shoving me behind him. He withdrew his sword from its sheath, revealing a sleek, thin blade. The elegant details painstakingly etched into the blade did not distract from how lethal it looked.

"Come out of the carriage. Nice and slow," a gruff voice hollered from outside. Male.

"What's going on?" I asked Arkyn.

He looked over his shoulder and placed his finger over his mouth, signaling me to be quiet.

"Oy, you got a woman in there! Bring her out for the boys to see," the male voice said, his words accompanied by a few snickers. "You aren't afraid of my little hounds, are you?" As if on cue, the wind began to die down. "There, you see, I can be a nice guy."

"What do you want?" Arkyn called out, his voice firm, unyielding.

"Why don't you come out and we'll talk?" the man replied.

Arkyn turned to look at me. "Stay in here."

"You can't go out there alone. Who knows what you'll be walking into," I argued.

He grinned. "As much as I appreciate your concern, you are not to come out until I retrieve you. Do you understand?"

I rolled my eyes. If only he knew what lurked in my veins. I grabbed his sleeve, leveling my gaze. "You are the only thing linking me to Kaleb right now—I'll be damned if I let you die. I'm coming with you."

"This is not up for debate," he hissed before he tugged his arm free and walked out.

The male whistled low. "Oy, look what we have ourselves here, boys. Why, are my eyes deceiving me, or is that the advisor of the bloody king?"

I gathered my skirts and marched out.

Arkyn huffed at me under his breath. "As predictable as always."

I didn't bother to look at him, instead focusing on the men circled around us. They looked like a rough group, consisting of a variety of ages and sizes. A scar in the shape of a claw branded their foreheads, some of the scars fresher than others, separating the old members from the new recruits.

I counted fifteen in total.

A male, mid-fifties, stepped forward. He smirked at me, revealing a silver front tooth and a sparse smile. "Didn't know the advisor of the king was married." He cocked his head to the side, scrutinizing what I wore. "Or are you his whore?"

His men burst into laughter, some chanting the word.

"A whore, my men thinks you!" Theatrically, he jiggled his silver belt buckle. "Tell me, how much for a rub and a tug and a swallow?"

My Curse roared, brimming just beneath the surface. I would happily drown the fucker where he stood.

Above, the clouds groaned, and rain came sputtering down. It wasn't from me. Still, the air tasted of magic, different from what I sensed from the leader of the raiders, who had clearly been born of the Wind Curse. I couldn't pinpoint where the magic came from but I knew this storm was not natural.

"What is it you want, raider?" Arkyn asked flatly, bored.

"I want coin, gold coin. Lots of it. And—" He pointed at me with the bloody end of his sword. "—her mouth on my cock."

"Then you have wasted your time, as well as mine. You will have neither." Arkyn charged, his sword slung behind him, ready to strike.

I marveled at his speed, but my attention was clipped short as a man ran towards me. I darted around the carriage, searching for something to use. My gaze locked on the broken wheel, a few spindles sheared off. I grabbed one with a jagged end.

I twirled, using the spindle as a sword as my pursuer brought his down. His blade sliced through the wood, leaving me with half the spindle. I tossed it upwards and caught it in the middle, the spikey end pointed at him, and hurled it with all my might.

It met my target and embedded itself just above his heart. His mouth popped open as he looked down, his hands shooting to the wood spindle. He forgot his battle with me and worked on pulling the spindle out, his screams muffled by the sound of heavy rain.

Hands grabbed hold of my waist, and an unwanted nose pressed against my neck, breathing in my scent. My assailant pulled his head back and let out an audible breath as he pulled on my waist, dragging me towards the thicket. "Come, bitch." He snickered. Bad breath, smelling of rot and decay, seeped into my nostrils.

"You might want to see a healer about that," I choked out before I rammed the back of my skull into his face.

He stumbled backwards, his hand shooting to his forehead. I wound up my quadriceps and punted his hand, knocking his sword into the air. We raced towards it, but I was faster, catching it before it hit the ground.

I whirled, pointed the blade at him, and smiled ever so sweetly. "Come, bitch."

He gritted his sparse teeth and then charged. Like a matador, I jumped out of his path, my new sword biting into his flesh as he sailed past me. He fell to the ground, hands clasping his stomach.

Arkyn yelled, the sound so loud, it cracked like thunder.

I ran to the other side of the carriage, adrenaline filling my veins. And that was when I saw him, bent and on his knees, crawling in the mud.

Suddenly, the wind howled around me, pushing me every which way. I held on to the sword, but the wind was too strong, and it tugged it away—right into the hand of the male with the silver tooth.

"These rich folks never learn." He smirked as he brought the boot of his heel down on Arkyn's back, pressing his stomach into the mud. He raised the sword, preparing to bring it down on Arkyn's neck. "Deal's off."

Deal's off? What did that mean? I didn't have time to contemplate it.

"No!" I screamed, my Curse breaking free.

I hurled a throwing star made of water directly at the man's wrist. His Wind Curse pushed hard, and it was just enough to knock my star off course. It flew right on by, a hair's width away.

He cocked his head to the side, eyeing where the throwing star had nearly hit. He jerked his gaze back to me before he shouted, "Get the water bitch!"

Arkyn's gaze met mine, a look of triumph written on his muddy face.

Shit. He'd seen. He'd seen my Water Curse.

Suddenly, Arkyn shot to his feet, the man's weight no longer able to hold him down. Where had this sudden strength come from?

I jerked back as a blade went sailing but a few inches from my face.

My hand shot to the side, producing a water chain—thin and elegant, the molecules forced together, packing it like ice. I wrapped it around the neck of my assailant. I tugged, bringing the large oaf to his knees. His stubby fingers gripped at the chain, trying to remove it. I pulled it tighter until he turned blue. As he slipped into unconsciousness, I let it fall loose.

Cool steel chewed into my arm. I grimaced, my hand shooting to the gaping, blood-pooling wound that now occupied my right forearm.

Four men circled me, their bloodthirsty blades tipped, at the ready. I spread my feet apart and cinched up my chain, waiting to see which one would charge. I bet on the lanky, younger-looking one. What he lacked in age, he made up for with long limbs and sizable feet. Judging by the sneer topped with a dusting of peach fuzz, he looked like he had something to prove.

Sure enough, he charged, his feet slapping like flippers against the ground.

Bingo. We have a winner.

Before I could react, Arkyn was there.

He rammed his shoulder into the younger one, the force of it like a landslide taking out an unsuspecting, grass-nibbling hare.

I had never seen someone fly before, that was, until now. The boy was airborne, his body sailing until he came to a skidding stop on the ground, the back of his head ramming against a time-worn boulder.

I tore my gaze from the boy, looking at Arkyn, who was already working on the other three robbers. He moved so fast, it was hard to track him. In a blur of movements, lethal and precise, he brought them to their knees. They cried out, begged, a plea for mercy, their weapons thrown in defeat on the rocky ground.

But with his face painted in the colors of war—blood and mud and gore—Arkyn did not concede. One by one, he cleaved their heads straight off their necks.

I gasped, stepping back, tension tightening my shoulders. Headless bodies slunk to the ground, blood shooting and spraying from severed arteries, pooling out. The sight of it was gruesome.

"You are bleeding," Arkyn said as he walked towards me, eyes on my wound, cleaning the weapon of decapitation on his sleeve.

I ignored the blood, the gore, the brutality, the lack of empathy—it was something I would visit later. When I had time to think. Instead, I focused on the torn fabric at his waist. "You are too."

"You *are* Cursed." His brown eyes met mine. He emphasized the middle word, as if it confirmed something he had already suspected.

There was no denying it. No lie I could try to pass. There was only the truth.

I tilted my head, armoring my tongue with pride. "I am."

Silence drifted between us, hanging on the quiet night air, the wind but a whisper now. I waited. Waited to see if he would try to strike my head clean from my neck, just as he had done to the men mere seconds ago. Waited to see if he would drag me to the pyre and set my body aflame.

But instead of all that, he offered his hand. "Come. We will take the horses the rest of the way and find an inn to stay at."

I eyed it suspiciously. "Rooms apart, right?"

He gave me a funny look, like he had no intention of sleeping in the same room as I. "Yes, apart."

I took his offered hand. "Fine."

The truth?

Nothing about this was fine.

Chapter 31

I dabbed at the dried, crusted blood with a wet cloth. A porcelain basin with dainty flowers painted around its lip sat on the dresser. The water inside was clean and crisp.

I eyed my reflection in the mirror. My hair was a tangled mess, courtesy of robbers and riding horseback. In the low lighting of the small room, my eyes appeared less sky blue and more moon gray. It was fitting, I supposed, as I was feeling a whole buffet of emotions—up and down and all over the place.

I winced.

My gaze darted from my reflection back to the deep cut in my arm. The corner of the cloth had fallen into it. Carefully, I pulled it out. Not wanting to repeat the mistake, I took extra care as I cleaned the rest of it.

After I was done, I dipped the cloth in the water, my blood tingeing it red.

It took about an hour for us to get to the city. Weary-boned and wide-eyed—decapitation first-timer here—I turned in for the night as soon as Arkyn had paid for our rooms at the inn.

The quarters were small but cozy. A single bed pressed against the wall, a chest at the end full of extra quilts—all of them hand stitched. A hearth, matching the size of the room, crackled, the fire inside well stoked. It scented the room in the sweet smells of burning birch and bathed the walls in a flickering, honey glow.

I closed my eyes.

For a moment, it was almost like I was back at the cottage. I waited to hear the shuffle of feet in the kitchen, waited to hear the chopping of wood outside, but no such sounds came. Only the muffled thrum of laughter and music drifted from below, through the thick, wooden floorboards.

The laughter reminded me of my new extended family— of cracker sandwiches and sibling rivalry. And bourbon.

But just like Ezra and Kaleb, they were not here.

There was no Harper. No Ryker. No Lyra. No Soren.

. . . No Von.

I didn't know why, but *all of it* was hitting me hard. Maybe it was the loss of my old world—of the simplicity, of how things used to be. Maybe it was the building pressure I felt to get Kaleb home. Or maybe it was everything that happened tonight.

Maybe . . . it was all of those things.

A single tear slid down my cheek.

I brushed it away with the back of my hand, fighting to rein in the rest.

Something *tap-tap-tapped* on the window, the sound reminding me of a chicken pecking the ground. It sounded birdlike.

I rose from the worn stool, deflated and flat from too many years of use, and walked over to the window. My fingers did a poor job of convincing the brass latch to open. It was stiff, like it hadn't been used for quite some time. Adding a bit more pressure, finally, the latch complied. My hands went to the wooden handles on the window and opened them inward, into my room.

Fresh air filled my lungs, scented with the distant smell of rain.

There, on the lip of the weathered sill, a black feather teetered in the lullaby of the gentle wind.

I took it. Cradled it in my hands. Its color was like the blackest of nights, dusted with a shimmer that twinkled like stars. It was just like the others. Magical. Ethereal. How could such a lovely thing belong in my world? Perhaps it didn't.

Remember.

The word echoed, carried in on a phantom thought.

Closing my eyes, I leaned into its command, following it like a child would a mother. It took me to the part of my mind that I had never been able to connect with. It was like a vast canyon, where you could yell and yell and yell but nothing would ever reply. That part of me had always been vacant—a house without fixtures, furniture, or inhabitants. It was my void, lifeless and empty. My very own Endless Mist.

There came a loud knock at the door. Arkyn's voice called from the other side, "I brought you something to eat."

Although the feather looked delicate, it was far from it. It was sturdy. Strong. Impossible to break. Still, I carefully placed the feather in my bodice before I walked to the door.

My gait was a bit slow—Arkyn's presence determining my pace more than anything now that he knew I was Cursed. Considering who he served, that could not be a good thing.

Using my unwounded arm, I opened the door and stepped back, allowing Arkyn enough berth to walk inside. Like Von, he didn't just take up space—he dominated it.

I was reminded of the first time I saw him, of all those men surrounding him in the pool at the bathhouse, their serpent bellies up, basking in his light.

Arkyn slid the wooden tray on the end table, effectively pushing a few books to the side while he did it. He wore a long gray coat that looked brand new, and like the rest of his clothing, it was perfectly tailored. The coat was unbuttoned, exposing a crisp white tunic beneath. His red hair was slicked back, still wet. Any evidence of what happened earlier was now washed away.

He glanced briefly at the window, the sheer drapes gently mussed by the wind, and then to me. One brow shot up. "Is it not counterproductive to have the fire going and the window open?"

That curious brow of his seemed to ask, *Why is it open?* But I did not feel like talking to him about the feather. Besides, he sniffed out lies like a hound searching for an egg in a hen house, so making something up was pointless. Instead, I evaded the subject. "You can close it." I gestured to his coat, shifting the conversation just as I had done with Ezra half a million times. "A bit much for being inside, no? Why are you wearing a coat?"

"I had to go outside." He flipped one side open, searching for something. "There is an apothecary just down the street." He produced a small wooden box from an inside pocket and placed it on the end table beside the tray. "For your wound."

"Thanks," I replied, my senses somewhat occupied. The smell of carrots, potatoes, and some type of meat wafted towards me. I sauntered over to the tray, my mouth watering when I saw the bowl of steaming stew and the golden bun sitting beside it, a dollop of half-melted butter glistening on the delectably browned top. A silver goblet filled with something red—wine, I presumed—sat just to the left.

I plopped onto the bed and slid the tray onto my lap, oh so ready to dig in. But just before I took a bite, I paused.

"It's not poisoned, if that's what you are thinking. You are of no use to me dead," Arkyn said as he swung the window closed.

Arkyn's last statement did not bode well with me as I had no desire to be of any use to him, in any shape or form. I could ask him what he meant, but this seemed like one of those moments where it was better to let sleeping dogs lie.

My stomach grumbled, urging me to eat. I was a slave to food. So naturally, I complied. Savory broth greeted my tongue. I chewed the diced potato, a subtly sweet taste. When I got to a piece of meat, I melted.

Beef.

My toes curled—this was better than sex.

Arkyn removed his coat and placed it on the small wooden chair in the far corner of the room. He sat beside me, the bed dipping under his weight.

Silence drifted between us as I devoured my supper, my taste buds humming with each bite. When I got to the bottom of the once-heaping bowl, my stomach near bursting, I debated if I could polish off the last of it. But, like I said, *slave to food,* so I scooped it up and inhaled that too. I debated smooshing my finger against the remaining crumbs and eating them as well, but I refrained—for Arkyn's sake, not mine.

"Some things never change," Arkyn chided under his breath, his shoulders bowed in ease.

"What?" I asked, returning the tray to the end table, my attention still somewhat occupied.

"Nothing," Arkyn replied with a soft shake of his head.

I didn't need to turn and look to feel his gaze drift over me. I had spent enough time with men to know what such looks meant. And I knew, if I turned, if I connected our gazes, it could lead to something more. Arkyn was handsome—yes, divinely so—but it was who he served that bothered me.

Quite simply . . . he was not Von.

So, I stared at the coin-sized knot in the wooden floor, just beside my right foot, and let the moment pass.

"Your arm needs stitches," Arkyn finally said, his voice rougher than usual, like a foxtail barb was stuck in his throat.

I knew it did. I had seen cuts half as deep that Ezra stitched up before.

I leaned to the side and plucked the wine cup from the table, inspecting the few sips still left inside—now I knew why he brought it. I chugged the bitter-tasting wine and said, "Well, let's get it over with."

Arkyn nodded, his long arm stretching over top of me, reaching for the wood box. I could feel his heat caress my skin, a knock at a door that was closed to him.

I leaned back, granting him more room and myself some

needed space.

After he cleaned my wound—the alcohol chewing into my sore flesh—he sanitized the needle and scissors over top of the wash basin. He popped the cork back on the little brown bottle—the disinfectant. Turning around with the suture instruments on a white cloth, he brought them over to me. I spared a withered glance at the gaping flesh, and then what it was about to be met with, and took a deep breath, wishing for another glass of bitter wine.

Arkyn rolled up his sleeves and then he went to work. His strong fingers plunged the needle through my tattered flesh as he pulled the thread through, putting it back together.

The first stitch wasn't so bad. But it was the next one that had me ready to howl. I gritted my teeth and held it in. I decided that whoever dreamt of using stitches to sew up a wound was a sick bastard—I was a human, not a damn quilt. As if it weren't already sore enough.

Truth be told, I was a bit of a baby when it came to stitches. I had Ezra to blame for that. Kaleb and I were both accident-prone children, so Ezra developed a salve that allowed the skin to stitch itself back together. I still remember watching it as it worked. She would dab it on, and we would watch in awe as the skin started to generate little threads that would weave together and close any flesh wounds. It was marvelous stuff. Well, besides the fact it would cause the skin to keep growing little thread-like hairs for the next week or so. Otherwise, amazing stuff. I would take that side effect over stitches any—

I yowled like a cat that just had its tail lopped off as the needle sunk in.

It was loud enough for the patrons downstairs to hear. Loud enough for the whole city to hear. Probably.

Probably not—it wasn't that loud. Like I said, a big baby.

"Almost done," Arkyn said reassuringly, his fingers coated with my blood.

I nodded somberly, swallowed hard, and waited for it to be over with. It was taking longer than I had hoped, but my pain receptors were beginning to dull down—my shrieking more like a baby's just-waking-up cry now.

I turned to Arkyn, looking for a distraction. "You once spoke of a girl with hair similar to mine. What was her name?"

He stopped abruptly, as if the mention of her triggered an old memory. Continuing, he said, "Aurelia."

"Aurelia." I tested the name on my tongue, pausing to wince when he finished another stitch. "It is a beautiful name."

"As was she," he said, his gaze lifting to mine. "As are you."

I didn't know if it was the wine or the fire or the honey in those brown eyes—but my cheeks heated. I looked away. Damn it, it was the wine. I was more of a broody-male-with-obsidian-eyes kind of woman.

After the stiches were finished, Arkyn caught the housemaid in the hallway and asked her to bring another pitcher of water. While we waited for her, he emptied the wash basin and dropped the bloody needle and scissors inside. With his back turned to me, he said, "The tattoo on your arm, I do not recall seeing it before. Is it new?"

Instinctively, at the mention of the tattoo, I looked at it.

"It is," I said, not sure where this topic was going.

"*Why* did you get it?" he asked, turning to me. A thin cloth was slung over his shoulder, a light dusting of bloody fingerprints faintly visible on it.

I traced the vine as I answered his question, half mumbling to myself. "Same reason I'm here with you."

I regretted it as soon as I said it because his eyes narrowed and the room fell stagnant. Lukewarm at best.

"*Who* did you make a deal with?" he asked, calculating things faster than I thought possible. I was reminded of his age and that he was the one trusted to advise the king. Of course he could map out things faster than most.

My brain tossed the question over, inspecting it for sink holes. I decided there were plenty. "I don't think that's any of your business."

Arkyn slung the towel down on the floor, opening his mouth to speak—

He was cut off by a knock at the door.

Arkyn offered me a withering stare before he walked over and opened it, revealing a buxom maid. She looked up at him and batted her eyelashes, her chest thrust up suggestively. Immune, he offered her a dashing smile, took the pitcher, gave her a, "That will be all," and closed the door swiftly. He walked over to the basin, dumped the fresh water in, and continued to clean—vigorously, intensely. I was starting to feel sorry for the scissors. At that rate, all that would be left of them were nubs.

"Do you want me to do that?" I asked, feeling every bit of his soured mood dampening the air.

"No," he said firmly. His voice was not unkind, but it

wasn't exactly friendly either.

After he was finished, Arkyn stood at the door. He opened his mouth but then closed it. Whatever it was he wanted to say was snuffed out as he turned and shut the door behind him.

The sound of his bootheels faded as he walked down the length of the hallway, until the sound of them was completely gone.

I flopped onto the bed, my one foot on the floor, the other stretched out before me, my head swarming with what just happened. Why did he react like that?

I sighed, giving up the question to the gods, and pulled the feather from my bodice. "Tell me your secrets," I whispered as I studied its silky, black plumes.

But the feather did not answer. So, I turned to my dreams instead.

One push. That was all it took.
Down. Down. Down.
I was but a leaf destined to never hit the ground.
Forever falling.
Down. Down. Down.
A rustle of feathers.
I was saved.

Chapter 32

I tugged my cloak tighter; I had never been this close to the Endless Mist before.

It seemed alive, somehow. Like it was breathing. Pulsing.

The sound it made was low and steady, like hummingbird wings—a constant flutter of white noise. If I took two steps forward, I could touch it.

. . . I reached out.

I snatched my hand back.

Twirling, I glared at Arkyn, who stood a few feet behind me. "You woke me up at the crack of dawn and dragged me all this way . . . just to come see the Endless Mist?"

He nodded, his expression strained. He had been more distant than usual this morning, like something was eating at him. Whatever it was, I could not place it. I questioned if he was still upset about last night. He had been angry and irritated, there was no mistaking it. But this? This was different.

"Do you hear anything?" Arkyn broke his vow of silence.

"It sounds like hummingbirds' wings," I replied, confusion saddling my brow. When we went to the Temple of Light, he'd asked if I tasted anything. I'd found out that what I tasted was vastly different from what other people tasted. I had lived long enough in Edenvale to know that being different wasn't a good thing.

Unease began to slide into my gut, weighing it down heavier than last night's supper.

"Do *you* hear anything?" I asked.

He shook his head. "I hear nothing."

I regretted asking—unease slipped into my belly.

"Okay. We came. We saw. We heard. Shall we go now?" I took a step, ready to go back.

Quick as a viper, Arkyn's hand shot out, seizing my wrist. "We aren't finished yet."

"What are you doing?" I tried to pull away, but his strength was insurmountable—just as it had been when the leader of the raiders had his boot on Arkyn's back, pressing him into the mud. I remembered that triumphant look on his face when I used my Water Curse. How easily he had gotten up from the ground. How quickly he'd slayed them all. Not an ounce of remorse visible.

But where had such strength come from? And why hadn't he used it before when we first stepped out of the carriage? Questions by the dozens swirled around me, until two words cleared the static.

Deal's off—that was what the leader of the raiders had said. The way he'd said it . . . he wasn't talking to *his men*—it was directed to Arkyn.

"What deal did you make with them?" I hissed, my tone pure venom. Why hadn't I thought of it before? "Don't act like you don't know what I'm talking about."

"I needed to find out if you were Cursed or not and I knew you would never tell me on your own. I paid them to make it look like they were going to take my life. I knew you wouldn't risk losing the information about your brother and if you did have the Curse, you would use it to save my life, and therefore the information you needed. I thought they might go back on the deal, and when they did, it just added to the theatrics of it all."

All of that—it had just been for show. He'd paid them to rob us. The coachman had died because of it. Then Arkyn had taken their lives . . . He'd decapitated them.

Ice ran down my spine.

"Why . . . Why do all of that just to find out if I was Cursed?" Arkyn's hold slackened and I tore my wrist free. I stepped back, anger and confusion driving my body, as if I had to move or I might risk exploding into a million pissed-off little pieces.

"It was necessary. It was a test, just as the Temple of Light was."

"Have you finished your tests now?" I stared daggers at him. I was hurt by Arkyn's betrayal. Somewhere, deep down, I had thought that we were becoming friends. The thought was laughable now.

He shook his head. "I have one left."

And then he pushed me into the Endless Mist.

Chapter 33

I blinked. Not once, but twice—as if that were enough to clear the darkness from my sight.

It didn't work.

I moved my hand in front of my face. I couldn't see it—I couldn't see anything. I swallowed down my fear, trying not to panic.

I felt like I was floating. My hair lifted, moved by some foreign, buoyant force. Cool air kissed my neck. My feet were weightlessly suspended—nothing touched the soles.

Gravity had no dominion here—*wherever* here was.

Suddenly, a light, bright as the morning sun scattered across a still lake, blazed before me. I raised my hand over my face, sheltering my eyes.

"Who are you?" asked a plethora of voices in unison—they were all female. Young and effervescent. Sweet and sparkling with life, like the finest glass of bubbling wine. And even though I had never tasted bubbling wine before, I wanted more. I licked my lips. I craved hearing them speak again.

"Sage," I replied, my steady tone quickly chewed up by the void.

Slowly, I lowered my hand, wanting to see where the voices came from and if they were connected to that blinding, beaming light.

My eyes adjusted, or rather, the light dimmed, tucking itself neatly in, configuring itself into a glowing silhouette until standing before me was a woman, lean with gentle curves and bathed in soft gold. Her hair flowed behind her, adding to her allure. She wore a simple dress, but the way it hugged her slender frame made it look perfectly tailored—not one wrinkle or thread out of place. Everything was pristine. Perfect. The dress parted at her hips, revealing a peek of her long legs. Like her, her dress was also illuminated in a soft gold.

But it was her face that made my breath falter.

Because her face . . . it was my own. She had the same straight nose with the slight upturn at the end. The same almond-shaped eyes and narrow-angled jawline.

The glowing woman wore my face.

"Wrong," spoke the glowing silhouette, the voices no longer effervescent, no longer sweet. Now, they tasted bitter, full of contempt. I quivered at the sound, like a leaf shaken from a tree.

Her silhouette flickered, her light fading in and out in unsteady waves. With each flicker, she grew dimmer, like a memory fading away. She was disappearing.

"Wait," I called out to her, my hand outstretched, but it was too late. The woman who wore my face was gone, painting my world in darkness once again.

I bristled as the sound of crashing rocks and moving land started in the distance. It was the sound of a landslide, the sound of an approaching force, and it thundered my way. Something shook, and whatever kept me suspended and weightless suddenly gave way.

I thrashed from side to side, feeling for something to grab on to, anything. But in this void, this never-ending abyss, there was nothing.

I was falling and it was infinite.

The very stuff made of nightmares, the kind where one continuously falls but never hits the ground—the fear of their impending doom eating them alive. I could feel it gnaw at me now. The sanity I clutched onto was beginning to fracture and fray.

I screamed, or at least I thought I did, but no sound came.

I was stuck there, in an eternal struggle with gravity, never knowing when it would stop, *if* it would stop.

Panic gripped my throat, choking off my air. My lungs heaved, ached. Where had the oxygen gone? I couldn't breathe—I couldn't breathe! I clawed at my throat, my nails biting deep. There was a blockage—I had to get out.

My mind lit up with red flags, begging for relief, begging for life-giving air.

But there was none.

My panic faded, giving way to acceptance. My body was beginning to shut down, a sense of peace overcoming my panic.

This.

This is how I die.

Just as the thought occurred, power—immense and

divine—pulsed in heavy, undiluted waves, forcing the darkness to slink away, to bow, to hide.

There was only one thing that could shake a black void to its knees.

That was when I knew that Death had come for me.

But I did not fear him. I reached out, accepting my fate.

He wrapped his arms around me, pulling me in to his steely embrace, the kind that lays a claim, the kind that never lets you go. His hand drifted over my throat, healing the pain of my clawed flesh. When he kissed me, so deeply, so intently, I forgot if I was breathing my air or his own.

I didn't care.

I gulped it down, my greedy lungs yearning for more. In exchange . . . *would he demand my soul?*

I heard the rustling of wings, could feel the refreshing blast of wind against my heated skin.

Then I realized it—I was not falling anymore.

Chapter 34

With a surge of light, the darkness gave way, birthing a blue sky dolloped with lazy, fluffy clouds and a rocky autumn-painted ground, dusted with a light layer of fallen leaves.

I was standing close to the same spot where Arkyn pushed me in.

A thick, black fur mussed by the breeze blocked my view. I tipped my head up, peering over top of a broad shoulder, staring at the Endless Mist. I shivered, the chokehold of it all too fresh. But when I looked up and met the eyes of the male standing in front of me, all of it seemed like white noise, floating away on the wind.

A hand, large and warm, gingerly cupped my cheek, the rough pads gliding along my skin. I nestled into it. Into *his* touch. Von.

"You came for me." My voice cracked.

His onyx eyes held mine. "I will always come for you."

He said it like it was an oath, written in stone. I knew in that moment, he meant every word, sure and steady, like the setting sun bowing to the clutch of night.

I stared in awe at the male who made the void itself quiver and hide. His long black hair, tinged with an iridescent blue, was unbound, wild. It matched his eyes. The way they held mine.

I let out a withheld breath.

Everything about him pulsed with ancient power, unbridled, a warrior from another time, adorned in black, from his fighting leathers to his hair, cast in steel and shadows. Darkness divine.

For some time now, I had been looking away from what so plainly stared back at me—at a truth I did not want to see, not that I could explain why that was. But now, there was no denying it anymore. Von was not some mere Cursed mortal. He was . . . something much *more* than that. I was beginning to suspect that Von was a Demi God, a direct son of the Old Gods. Which would make him . . . I couldn't even fathom how old he must be. Hundreds of years, at least.

The wind wrestled with the leaves on the ground, swooping them up, reminding me of the sound I heard just before I stopped falling—the sound of rustling wings. Some of the Demi Gods were said to have wings, something they received from their divine forebearers. I glanced over Von's shoulder, searching for any remnant of what I had heard, but nothing was there. I wanted to reach out, to feel the air behind him and see if what I heard, what I expected to see, was invisible to the eye but not the hand.

"How did you find me?" I asked him.

His fingers drifted down the length of my arm, roaming over my tattoo, stroking it softly with the rough pad of his thumb. "This allows us to find one another."

"It's for tracking," I whispered to myself—realizing why he didn't tell me the other day. Yes, he would have sounded like a complete jackass then. I would have clawed his eyes out for it. But now. . .

That fierce part of me, the lioness that hated when a man thought he had a right to possess a woman—right now, she was purring like a kitten on his lap. I never thought she could be tamed by a man, but now, I was learning she could be . . . It just took the right one.

I looked up at him. "Can I use mine to find you as well?"

"Yes. It works both ways," he replied, that carnal mouth twisted ever so slightly at the corners, like the thought of me looking for him pleased him. His hand stilled, just above the bruising around my wrist. Gently, he raised it to his lips. The warmth of his mouth spread over my skin like the morning light stirring the cool, slumbering earth awake. I watched in awe, in silence, as the bruising began to dissipate, until it was completely gone.

"How did you do that?" I asked, confusion painting my brow low. I stared at my healed wrist, completely amazed.

"We are *bonded*."

The word felt secure, sure, like something I could bet on.

"Can you heal this one too?" I asked, lifting my arm so he could see the stitched gash, the wound itchy and raw.

There was no denying the way Von's mood darkened when he surveyed it. He wore that look that was tailored so perfectly to him, the signature look that stated he might just burn everything to the ground. Suddenly, the harsh lines in his beautiful face softened. Bending forward, he carefully lifted my arm, bringing the heat of his mouth to the cut, and suddenly, it healed, the stitches falling out, shoved away by the wind.

"Do you always have to kiss it to heal it?" I asked, a light smile playing at my lips. I watched as he rose back to his towering height, cloaking me in his shadow.

"No," he replied beneath a self-indulgent smile, the tip of a long canine peering out beneath his full top lip.

A memory surfaced of when my neck was bruised because of his sister and how quickly it had disappeared. I didn't need to ask because now I knew—that had been Von too.

I looked up at him inquisitively. "Can I heal you as well?"

He shook his head slightly, his voice soft but firm. "No, you cannot."

I didn't understand. "If we can both track each other through the tattoos, why can't we heal one another as well?"

"Because our bond does not come from our deal," he said, his eyes searching mine. Whatever he looked for . . . I didn't know.

Our bond—that was what the constant pull was, the consistent tethering that drew me to him.

Fate.

I nibbled on my bottom lip, releasing it as I asked, "So then if you can heal me, but I cannot heal you, then what can I do in return?"

His black lashes lifted slowly. "You can offer me something no one else can."

"And that is?" I asked, my voice breathless.

He tipped my chin upwards, his eyes holding mine. "The ability to feel alive."

And then he kissed me.

I fell into the feel of it—of him, his arms holding me, tethering me to his world. Our lips moved, his tongue darting into my mouth, taking and teasing and taunting. I melted into him. When I was certain my clothes would combust into a plume of cinders, he removed his lips from mine. Lightly, he pressed our foreheads together, his wide chest slowly rising, his breaths calm and certain. Unlike mine—quick and sporadic.

Slowly, he lifted his forehead from mine, looking over to a dense thicket about a stone's throw away from us—a Ryker-sized throw, definitely not Soren-sized. "Come out from your hiding spot," Von said, his tone an inescapable command.

Something stirred from there, rustled around, before a male figure stepped out—Arkyn.

I scowled.

My Water Curse begged to be set free, demanded to show him what it felt like to not be able to breathe.

He dusted off his coat, plucked a stray twig from his red hair, and then strode towards us, mindful to keep some distance. Arkyn's tone tasted as sour as the look on his face. "Ever the dutiful watchdog, are you not, Blood King?" He spat out the last two words like they were poison in his mouth.

Blood King?

Von's arm draped leisurely around my waist, protectively coiling there. "I could say the same for you, *king's advisor*."

I sputtered. They knew each other? My mind swirled, ransacked by a thousand and one questions.

"The cloaking spell you used to distort her features—to hide her from me. That was a clever trick. You nearly had me fooled. I wasn't aware you possessed that form of magic," Arkyn said, muscular arms crossing over his chest, his feet spread shoulder width apart, locking him to the ground. It was a laid back but ready for battle stance if I'd ever seen one.

Cloaking spell? Distorting my features? What in the Spirit Realm was Arkyn talking about?

"I possess a great deal of things you are unaware of," Von replied in his signature smooth bourbon tone.

"Yet, you will never possess the thing you want most." Arkyn's gaze shifted to me and then back to Von. "You know full well who she belongs to."

Who I *belong* to? I sneered. This was getting out of hand.

"How do you know each other?" I questioned, clutching at the few puzzle pieces I had, the rest of them scattered and missing.

"We go *way* back," Arkyn answered with a sneer before he stretched out his hand, offering it to me, the shining pin of the king's advisor reflecting in the sun. "Come, our king awaits us."

Instinctively, I clutched at Von. "You are insane if you think I would go anywhere with *you*. You tried to *kill* me."

"Not exactly," Arkyn replied, his arms relaxing, drifting to his sides. Still, he watched Von carefully.

"*Not exactly*? Do you know what it's like not to be able to breathe?" I took a step forward, water droplets building in my palm. I turned my head to the side, disgusted by the male that stood before me. "Why? Why did you do it?"

To his advantage, he looked remorseful, and my anger

winced just a hair. "Because I needed to know. I needed to know if you were *her*."

"*Her*? You tried to murder me to see if I was your dead lover?" I shook my head. What I was hearing was beyond logical reason. Anger welled, a teakettle left too long over the fire, red hot and ready to blow. I hit my boiling point.

Water came rushing out of my hand. I didn't care to give it shape, leaving it in its pure, raw form. I threw it at him with everything I had, echoing the force of my mounting frustration.

Arkyn raised his hand and a shield magically appeared in front of him, conjured from thin air.

I gasped . . . His shield was made from the same thing I attacked him with.

"You are *Water* Cursed?" I sputtered. My burst of water lost its form. It fell to the ground, shattering upon impact, drenching the dead prairie grass.

Arkyn dropped his shield, the water evaporating at the mere twist of his hand. "I can manipulate water, yes, among other things." His brow furrowed, his words spoken slowly, "So then . . . the Endless Mist did not return your memory."

Return my memory?

My mind spun amongst the chaotic amounts of information that were being dropped on me. Von and I were bonded beyond our tattoos. He could heal me, but I could not heal him and in exchange, I made him feel alive? Whatever that meant. Von and Arkyn knew one another, the origins of their acquaintance still a mystery to me, even though it apparently went way back. And Arkyn believed me to be his lost lover, which was why he threw me to my death, which made absolutely no sense. Not to mention the traumatic experience of what I just went through inside the Endless Mist. And now the connection that it was something to do with my lost memory?

My head pounded, a drum beating louder and louder. *Too much. Too much. Too much.*

Arkyn said something, but his voice was like a wave, coming and going, ebbing and flowing, the words out of reach.

I swayed, or maybe it was the sky. Regardless, something black licked at the edges of my vision.

"Enough." Von cut Arkyn off, his voice full of steel. His grip tightened around my waist, keeping me from falling. "She fulfilled her end of the bargain. Now you will tell her where her brother is."

There was no *asking* in his tone.

I held on to his words as tightly as I held on to him. Clarity slowly began to seep back in, the world no longer spinning.

"She needs to hear this," Arkyn said, daring a step forward. But he didn't take another. Instead, he sputtered, his eyes going wide as his hands darted to his throat. His tanned face turned an ashen white and he dropped to his knees . . . He couldn't breathe.

On the surface, I felt no remorse—he had done the same to me mere moments ago, whether it was intentional or not. And yet, deeper down in the crevice of some forgotten space, I wanted it to stop.

"Things are quite simple. I will restore your ability to breathe and you will answer," Von stated, his voice surprisingly patient. "If you choose not to comply, I will leave you as you are for the ravens to feast on."

That was when I noticed them, the sleek black ravens swirling above—ten of them.

Whatever Arkyn did to signal he would comply, I missed it, my attention stuck on the birds—in particular, their sleek, shining black feathers. They were like the one I had tucked in my bodice, but theirs were much, much smaller.

Slowly, Arkyn stood, his hand massaging his neck. "Very well," he said as he drew a long, much-needed breath. "The men conscripted from Meristone are stationed at the Arundal training barracks, a short ride northeast of Clearwell Castle." He handed over the information between heavy breaths.

Life had finally handed me a boon—that, or it had a strange sense of humor. Kaleb, who I had felt so incredibly far from, was not far at all. Clearwell Castle was just outside of Belamour.

All this time, he had been so close. And I'd had no idea.

I gave an odd little laugh, surprising myself. Another one bubbled up, as bad as an unannounced hiccup.

"Sage, I am sorry for all of this," Arkyn said, his expression stating as much.

But I did not want to hear anymore. Whether that was for my own sanity or something else, I didn't care. I turned to Von. "I want to leave."

"No, Sage, wait. There is so much you don't know. Please, give me a chance to explain. Do not go with him. You know not what he is, what he did to us," Arkyn pleaded.

But it was too late.

Von pulled me against him and the glades winked out of

existence.

A swirl of shadows and twinkling stars exploded around me, and suddenly, we were standing in Von's room back at the mansion in Belamour.

Chapter 35

I gaped—flat out gaped.

When I had asked Von to leave, I thought it would have been on foot. Not grab, poof, and here we were—miles away, in his room back at the mansion.

His room . . .

I had peeked my head through the door before, but I had never been *in it*, and usually it was dark, which meant I couldn't see much. But now, courtesy of the soft light that shone through the windows, I could see everything.

Judging by its ridiculous, sprawling size, his room was the master suite. From floor to ceiling to everything in between, all of it was black, with the lightest doses of dark, rich golds. The furniture was larger, bulkier, like it was crafted especially for him, for his size.

Directly to my right, a canopy bed crafted from a dark wood was wrapped in black silk, a large chest at the foot of it. To my left, two leather chairs sat beside the bay window and down from them sat an incredibly solid-looking desk, its top littered with papers and various books. Behind the desk was a private library, the shelves reaching to the ceiling. There was no ladder to reach the top shelves, and I wondered how one would get those books down, but knowing Von, he could probably just flick a finger and they would float down to him.

Speaking of Von and his mysterious abilities . . .

"How did you do that? How did we just poof here?" I asked, my palms against his chest, his arm hooked around my waist. "Is it part of your Wind Curse?"

"Something like that," he answered with a sinfully handsome grin. Thick black lashes naturally rimmed with kohl emphasized his midnight orbs as they lowered, snagging on my lips before he slowly pulled away.

I watched his steady fingers work as he unbuckled the black straps that secured his chest plate. While he did this, he walked over to the large, wooden chest painted with a dark stain and inlayed with gold strips of metal. When he stood in front of it, the lid spontaneously opened, but I scented no magic in the air.

"So, you two know each other," I said, more to myself than him, eyeing the chest where he stored his fighting leathers. "Why did he call you Blood King?"

"There are a variety of reasons I have been given that name." He folded the leather straps against the shining chest plate and set it inside the chest. "The main reason is because of who I become when I am on the battlefield."

I swallowed that bit of information. "Have you fought against Arkyn? In battle?"

"I have," Von replied as he gently tossed the fur into the chest. "He was lucky to walk away after."

There was no ego-stroking in his words. He was simply stating a fact. Arkyn served the king, a direct enemy of the Cursed rebels. Why would Von . . . My eyes shifted from the floor to him. "Why didn't you kill him?"

Von turned, obsidian eyes meeting mine. "I would have, if it weren't for a deal I made."

"A deal? What deal?"

Von began rolling up his sleeve. "I was in a position to take his life, but I spared it and made a deal instead." He rolled his forearm, and my gaze lowered to the golden spear trapped between lush, feminine lips.

"What did you get in return?" I asked, tempted to reach out, to touch it, to trace it.

Von grinned, the wicked twist of his lips enough to drive me feral. "I received *a lot* more than I bargained for."

I couldn't tell if I was turned on or jealous by the inclination in his words. The lips made me think of a kiss, but if he got more than he bargained for. . .

"Are you telling me you got laid in return?" I asked bluntly, warring between jealousy and my own arousal. Knowing full well that Von only had an appetite for women, I wondered what kind of woman would barter for Arkyn's life.

But my thoughts were scattered when his gaze captured mine. That sinful smile spread. "Many, many, many times, Little Goddess."

I sucked in a breath, an indecent heat rolling across my cheeks.

He chuckled softly, noting my reaction, before he turned back to the chest.

I watched him, my attention snagging on the way his

tunic stretched across his broad shoulders, a slight ripple in the middle, emphasizing just *how* stretched the fabric was. His muscular arms, corded with veins, contracted as he gathered his unbound hair and pulled it up into a topknot, exposing the one shaved side, a few strands falling out. He lolled his head back, glancing over his broad shoulder at me. "See something you like?"

I smirked coyly. "I see a few things."

"Like?" He turned, his gait a slow prowl as he moved towards me, his movement reminding me of a hunter tracking a deer on silent, deadly feet, like he was trying not to scare me away before he stole the very life from me.

He stopped when our bodies were but a breath away.

"Your lips, for one," I replied, my gaze drifting to that full, sensual mouth. Ever so kissable, with its demanding, claiming tongue.

"Hmm . . . ," he rumbled as he leaned forward, his mouth painfully close to mine, but not enough to touch.

I sucked in a breath.

He smirked—he knew what he was doing. And goddess above, was he ever good at it.

"And your shoulders," I said, my voice throatier, parched.

"Broad enough—" He draped my arms over his shoulders, one at a time. "—to rest your ankles on."

His words, his voice—it was a sinful combination. The image they stirred, of bare skin and panting, heavy breaths . . .

I nibbled my bottom lip, my arousal building.

"And your arms . . ." I looked up to him expectedly.

His hand gripped the fabric at my hip, bunching it. He pulled me into him in one swift move. "Strong enough to lift you up as I fuck you against the wall."

I swallowed—*damn*.

He chuckled softly, those dark eyes watching me, lapping at me.

A knock sounded from the door.

Annoyed, I shifted my gaze from the hottest male I had ever laid eyes upon to the ultimate cockblock, Soren, who poked his blond head through the cracked door.

"You're back!" he exclaimed loudly as he barged in, butchering the moment between Von and me.

Von looked even less pleased, although he didn't use his little choking party trick on Soren, to my surprise. Instead, he left me standing there and sat in an unoccupied leather chair. His long legs spread out, dominating the girth of the seat. It was impossible not to notice the evidence of his attraction to me pressing against the seam of his pants. Goddess divine. I reaffirmed my hopes that he had something stuffed in there because from this view, he looked . . . Cataclysmic.

I looked away, fighting the telltale red burning my cheeks. "Yes, I am," I said, straightening my skirts.

"Were you successful?" he asked, hands slipping into his pockets.

"I get the feeling that if you really wanted to know, you could easily find out," I replied honestly. I had not felt his presence for a while. Still, as small or as mouselike as he made his shadow seem, he was still there, hiding in the deep crevices.

"I try not to," he said sheepishly, his gaze dropping to the floor, still beating himself up over it.

I tapped him playfully on the arm as if to say, *Don't worry about it.* "Yes, I know where Kaleb is," I said, hardly able to believe it myself.

Soren grabbed my hands with excitement, beaming a vivid, white smile. And it dawned on me just then that he was a true friend, sharing in my triumph, just as the others would when I told them.

I sensed something scatter across my mind.

"Sorry," he said, frowning. "I let it slip."

"It's okay," I offered, noting that Von was silent—an unusual state for him. "I would like to talk to everyone together so I can tell them about Kaleb. Can you gather everyone in the sitting room?"

"I'll let them know. Give me ten minutes," he replied before he left the room, leaving me alone with the sinful, lascivious male.

I turned slowly.

His powerful body swallowed the chair beneath him. One tattooed arm draped over the curved arm of the chair, the other moved to his muscular thigh. He tapped it twice, silently commanding me to sit in his lap, his metal rings glinting in the light.

Willfully, I complied and seated myself in his lap, my rear supported by his one leg, my legs stretched out over his other. Like this, he still possessed a great deal of height over me.

"Did you hear that?" I asked, draping my arms over his shoulders, my fingers lacing at the back of his neck.

"Hmm?" he purred in that deep, bourbon tone. His hand

traced small circles against the small of my back, his fingers like a matchstick, lighting my nerves on fire wherever he touched.

I smiled mischievously. "We have ten minutes."

"That—" A single finger coiled under my chin as he gently tipped it up, his gaze locked with mine. "—is not nearly enough time."

I sputtered. "Not nearly enough time?"

A dark smile graced his lips and he nodded, his voice dropping an octave. "I intend to worship this body of yours for hours, Little Goddess."

"For hours?" I whispered breathlessly, picturing him wearing nothing but that carnal grin as he lowered his face between my legs.

"For hours," he confirmed, just before he brought his mouth down on mine.

Kissing Von was like taking a shot of bourbon—smooth, neat . . . addictive, and it always left me craving more.

His arms wrapped around my waist—the chair groaning in relief as we rose. He carried me over to the large desk, the papers and pens and candles suddenly gone. I wondered if my clothes were next—hoped they were—because I was going to combust.

Slowly, he slid me down the length of his torso, his body, especially his belt and *what* rested beneath, providing friction against my core as he set me on the bulky desk. Gently, he pushed me onto my back.

I shifted my hips as he took his dreadfully sweet time removing my skirts, revealing my moonlit skin beneath. His fingers drifted along the inside of my leg, a whisper of a touch, as he purred, "You are intoxicatingly beautiful, Little Goddess."

I inhaled the moment, taking in the mighty warrior standing over top of me, those otherworldly eyes exotic and wild. Right now, they looked more beast than man.

His hand gripped my leg as his hot, branding mouth kissed the inside of my knee. He nipped at it playfully, a carnal grin spreading across his lips. Slowly, he took his time, working his way up my leg, that heated gaze occasionally flicking back to mine. Every so often, he suckled my flesh, and I could feel the suggestive scratch of his sharp canines, causing the skin to sting in all the right ways. I moaned as his mouth moved closer to my throbbing core.

Goddess divine . . . he was so close now.

I reached for my underwear—they were in the way.

He caught my wrist. "So eager," he teased, clicking his tongue as if I were in trouble. He jerked my hand upwards, pinning it over my head. With his free hand, he dragged his knuckles over that sensitive spot at the apex of my quaking thighs, his eyes meeting mine. "So fucking wet."

I trembled, the cadence in his voice acting like a praising stroke.

He massaged me *there*, the pathetically thin barrier of my underwear adding to the erotic nature. I twisted, my body shaking as I lay back, losing myself in the sensation of him touching me, stroking and swirling. I moaned as the crescendo built, higher and higher, until . . .

His hand stopped. "Not yet, Little Goddess."

I glared at him—wondering what sort of treachery this was.

Swollen and throbbing, I was ready. My free hand darted down—if he wouldn't give it to me, I would take it for myself.

"Ah, ah, ah, Little Thief. I will not let you steal this from me," he scolded softly as he grabbed my hand and forcefully raised it over my head, pinning it there with the other.

A sprinkle of light flashed across his onyx eyes as he pulled his hand away, the pressure replaced with something else, something that snaked around my wrists, binding them tightly in place.

I looked up and gasped—my underwear. They wove around my joined wrists, the fabric nailed down to the desk. *What the—*

I tugged against them, but the more I did, the tighter they grew. My head jerked back to Von, his eyes firmly set on mine—darkness swirling within them. I caught the warning those eyes held. That once I let him inside, there would be no going back.

With his gaze firmly locked on mine, his hands slid to my legs. Slowly, he pressed them wider, testing me. Testing my understanding of what this meant. Oh, but I understood perfectly and even though a small part of me wanted to clamp my legs closed, to run from the devastatingly beautiful creature that loomed before me, the bigger part of me craved this—craved *him*.

Choosing him, choosing this, I let my legs fall open.

My offering brought a devilishly handsome grin to his lips as he murmured under his breath, "Good girl."

His fingers returned to that sensitive little bud, but this time, the cloth barrier was gone.

He slipped a finger between my folds before he dragged

my silky wetness upwards, spreading it over those electrified nerves, working them, his touch a sinister thing. I bucked my hips, wiggling under the intensity of it as his fingers skillfully worked that sensitive piece of me. With his other hand, he teased my entrance, testing the wetness there before he slipped one finger inside. A little breath of air escaped my lips.

His fingers were so much larger than mine, and just the one felt deliciously divine.

But when he put two in . . . I praised his name out loud.

I lolled my head back, riding his fingers as they moved in and out, my breasts bouncing with each thrust, the fabric on them suddenly all too scratchy. As if Von sensed my thoughts, suddenly my white tunic was gone, leaving me completely naked and him still fully clothed—marking us on uneven territory, establishing who was in control and who was not.

It felt both filthy and freeing. All at the same time.

Von swirled his fingers so his palm faced upward and with each stroke, he hit that sacred spot inside, all while his free hand worked the swollen bundle on the outside. I jerked my head up, watching the way his muscles moved as he pumped me, his prominent veins and his tattoos, especially the one that matched mine, adding to the erotic nature of it all.

When I realized that he hadn't taken his rings off, that they were still very much on his fingers as they glided in and out . . . something carnal howled inside of me. Filthy. Filthy male.

He drove me higher and higher. I fixated on his touch, my world cleaving apart as the swelling tidal wave forced me, step by step, closer to my crescendo.

"Come for me, Little Goddess," he commanded, dark

eyes watching me.

Driven by rapture, my breathy moans filled the room as I orgasmed for him. For me. My body shook in the afterquake of it as it rippled through me in heavy, rapturous waves. I panted, my chest heaving for breath. My legs had gone numb.

Slowly, he raised his fingers to his mouth. His eyes held mine as he licked a glistening finger from top to bottom with the tip of his long, thick tongue.

I trembled at the sight of him—my beautiful, dark conqueror tasting his newest conquest—easily won, easily given.

His irises, which had been as black as coal mere seconds ago, began to fill with color—a lush, indescribable color. It reminded me of the forest—of the freshly rained-upon grass in late spring, of the leaves on a tall, sturdy oak tree.

His eyes reminded me of home.

I sprung forward, my hands suddenly free. Cradling his face, I exclaimed softly, "Your eyes."

He smiled, and it was the most beautiful smile I had ever seen.

"How?" I asked, my voice but a whisper.

"It is part of our bond," he answered, pressing a kiss against my palm.

"Will my eyes change, too, if I—" My gaze dropped pointedly to the unattended bulge in his pants.

He chuckled, shaking his head softly. "No, Kitten, it doesn't work like that."

"How can you be so sure?" My hand drifted to his pants, pulling him closer. "Perhaps we should test it and see."

A black brow shot up, a grin slipping to the corners of his

mouth. He thumbed my bottom lip. "As much as I would love to feel this sexy little mouth wrapped around me, not right now, Little Goddess."

"Why not? Are our ten minutes already up?"

"Ten minutes be damned," he growled as he pressed me back down against the desk. He lowered to his knees, draping my thighs over his broad shoulders, one at a time. "I want to taste *you again.*"

"Von!" I screamed as his head dipped between my thighs. Powerful hands jerked me forward so that my core ran parallel with the edge of the desk.

"Yes, Kitten?" he purred, his hot breath fanning my sensitive folds. His tongue flattened, slowly sweeping along my slit, licking me from bottom to top, claiming my body and damning my soul in the process. He did it again. I had never been licked in such a primitive way before. His tongue dipped inside me, his fingers spreading me, allowing him deeper access as he drove his tongue in and out. His mouth was so wet, so hot, and that tongue was so incredibly powerful— relentless.

"Fuck," I gasped, my body rolling sensually. I gripped the edge of the desk, my nails biting into the wood.

His chuckle rumbled through me, vibrating into me, and my head rolled back, a moan escaping my lips. His fingers pressed on either side of that sensitive spot, swirling it better than I ever could.

"Von," I praised, his delightful ministrations working me at all the right angles, guiding me higher. And higher. I was so close now.

Just when I was about to come, he pulled his tongue from

me, cutting my pleasure off.

Pain sliced through me as he bit—*he bit*—that sensitive bundle of nerves.

"You bit me," I hissed in disbelief. It was both erotic and terrifying.

"I did," he purred, his dark eyes settling on me. "And I will do it again if you try to come without my blessing."

"What?" I huffed, my breathing sporadic.

"Like your lips, your orgasms belong to me, Kitten," he purred before he delved back between my thighs.

"That's—" His tongue swirled circles around that sensitive, swollen bud. "—oh." I lost track of my thoughts as two of his fingers slipped in, snatching the air from my lungs.

Hot, liquid heat pooled low in my belly as he used his tongue and fingers on me, the two of them working together, burning me in rapture and drowning me in pleasure—it was a wicked, tantalizing affair.

Two failed attempts at an orgasm and two dizzying bites later, I could not even begin to articulate how hard I had gotten off when he finally let me come. When I came down from that cataclysmic high, I realized that Von was going to ruin me.

The truth? I wanted him to.

Chapter 36

"I don't believe it." Harper shook her head.

"I know, right?" I said as I sat on the arm of the leather chair in the sitting room, my feet tucked between Von's legs. Von sat in the chair, his fingers drawing irregular shapes on the small of my back.

"What? You don't believe what?" Ryker asked as he entered the room. He dabbed a towel over his forehead, his skin glistening with a post-workout sheen.

"Come here," Harper instructed, waving her twin over.

I stifled a laugh as she moved his face inches from Von, like he needed to be that close to see the change in his irises. It was as drastic as night was to day.

Ryker whistled low as he leaned back, slinging the towel around his neck. He looked at me, then Harper, and then back at Von. "How?"

I shrugged nonchalantly, but I slipped in a warning look to Von not to say anything.

"He tasted Sage's sweet tang," Harper exclaimed, the

words hitting me as softly as a pillowcase stashed with bricks.

Von smirked. The bastard even nodded, to my complete and utter mortification.

I couldn't trust either of them to keep their big traps shut. Von and Harper were no better than a bunch of gossipy hens.

Ryker shot me an impressed nod.

"There you are!" Soren panted to Ryker as he rushed into the room. Bending over, he placed his hands on his legs, his shoulders heaving as he wrestled for breath. "I've been looking all over the place for you," he exclaimed.

"I was just outside training." Ryker's broad, muscular shoulder performed a careless shrug. "Harps told me there was a meeting." He walked over to the settee and flopped down, his head landing in Lyra's lap. She smiled at him, her small hands patting his head.

"Oh," Soren huffed between breaths as he flopped into a leather chair, his arms dangling over the arms, feet spread out limply before him. His face was tinged red, and I wondered just how much of the mansion he had covered in his search for Ryker and how quickly he had covered it—the poor guy looked like he ran a marathon. Clearly, he'd taken that ten-minute commitment seriously.

Von, on the other hand, certainly had not. Heat dusted across my cheeks as I recounted the past thirty minutes with him. Goddess divine . . . *that* tongue. It was sinister. Demanding. Branding. And utterly sinful. I would have to pray to the gods for the sake of my soul later.

Von's emerald eyes met mine, and satisfaction and pride stirred within me, like I had laid my own claim on him for all the world to see, the evidence written clearly in those breathtaking eyes.

Since we'd left his room, Von kept me close, always within reach, whether that be by the caress of his shadow or his touch. It felt primal, protective. Rooted in something I didn't quite understand, but I wanted to.

"Von. . . ," Soren started, his breath finally recovered. "Your eyes are . . . green."

I sighed and flopped my head into my hands, waiting for Harper to spill the beans.

But it was Von who spoke first. "They do that sometimes."

My brow shot up at his quick answer which was sorely lacking. He had no problem admitting to Ryker what had caused the change in his eyes—he even seemed proud about it—but for some reason, he was holding back from telling Soren . . . Why?

I searched Von's carefully masked face for answers but found none.

"So . . . about the meeting," Harper drawled as she settled onto the arm of the settee beside Lyra, her arm draping over the back.

Right. The meeting.

I stood up, the words ready to explode off the tip of my tongue. A smile sprawled across my lips as I said, "I know where Kaleb is and I'm going to need everyone's help."

My admission hooked their attention. Even Ryker shifted from his supine position and sat up.

For the next three hours, we delved into planning mode.

Somewhere in the middle of our talks, that *am I dreaming* feeling began to shift, giving way to reality. I realized that this was it . . .

We were going to get Kaleb back.

Chapter 37

Apart from the sound of horses' hooves thudding against freshly frosted ground, the world was quiet. Even the natural wind had toned down, as if it, too, were operating on bated breath.

Ryker, Harper, Lyra, Soren, and I rode through the rolling hills, the gentle curves of the land flattening like an outstretched palm the closer we got to the barracks. The landscape was dotted with massive boulders, smooth and worn, as if the bison that once roamed these lands had polished them with their backs.

I determined that life did, indeed, have a strange sense of humor.

Kaleb, who I had felt so incredibly far from, had never been far at all.

The men conscripted from Meristone were stationed at the training barracks a short ride west of Clearwell Castle. They were among a large group that would be trained, given piss poor armor and dull swords, and shipped off to the

Cursed Lands—to their deaths. Their blood would stain the hands of the Cursed, while the king's remained unmarred and clean—not that I could say the same thing about his soul, although I doubted he had one.

After our meeting, Von and Ryker had traveled to the training camp to do some early espionage. That was two days ago. Ryker returned yesterday, while Von stayed behind . . . Why he decided to stay behind was beyond me.

According to Ryker, it took less than a three-hour ride to get there, but as we rode towards the training camp, for me, it felt much longer than that. Everything I had done over the past weeks, all of it was for this moment. I was not leaving without my brother.

A grove of dense trees stood before us, their barren branches lulled to sleep by winter's sudden approach. The towering trees, the forest—they reminded me of home. I inhaled deeply, my lungs yearning for more.

When the rolling landscape was half a mile behind us, we tied our horses to the trees and walked the remainder on foot, the gentle nickering of our horses disappearing as we traveled farther north, into the dense bush. We walked in silence, all of us on high alert. We were in the chokehold of the enemy, and we all knew it.

Ryker led the group, Soren falling closely behind, with Harper and Lyra bringing up the rear. I was a few paces behind them, my sleep-deprived body dragging me down more than I cared to admit.

Something flashed behind me.

I grabbed my knife and turned to swing.

"Little Goddess," Von purred in my ear, his hand cuffing

my wrist, stopping my arm mid-swing. He wore a long black cloak, the hood pulled up, casting his face in shadow.

"Von," I said by way of greeting, my tongue at a loss for words. Damn him and his devilishly handsome face.

"Were you hoping it would be someone else?" he teased. His eyes were still tinged with green, but not nearly as vivid as before. I yearned to see the intense, satisfying color return.

Those lush lips of his turned into that signature, lazy, unperplexed grin, like he knew what I was thinking. He removed his ringed fingers from my wrist, arm disappearing under the black veil of his cloak. As he walked over to Ryker, he called out over his broad shoulder, his cape flowing behind him, carried on his wind, "Come, Little Minx."

I blew out a breath, my lips vibrating as I scuttled behind him, those impossibly long legs of his covering ground much quicker than mine.

After a brief exchange of words, and a rehashing of the plan, we followed Von and Ryker as they led us forward.

The land descended into a steep valley, a slender river vein snaking through the middle. It was a far cry from the water that once would have run through here, carving out the valley. Nestled in the belly of the valley, beside the river, was a barricaded camp—the Arundal training barracks.

Lookout towers stood at the four corners of the camp, keeping a watchful eye over the surrounding grounds. I didn't doubt they were fully equipped with archers, their bows held at the ready. My eyes traced the oval-shaped perimeter, the outer wall taller than a two-story house, tall enough that no one could get in and no one could get out. It was made of pine trunks, their tops carved into spikes and their bottoms buried deep within the ground. They were strapped together with thick rope that looked to be made of hemp, although it was worn and aged and hard to tell. Slumbering crimson banners were hung evenly around the perimeter, placed every ten feet or so.

Inside, there had to be close to a hundred tents, if not more. On the righthand side of the camp, placed in neat, organized rows, smaller tents made up the majority. Larger, extravagant tents were sectioned on the left side—I counted ten in total. Stretching down the middle was a sandy area lined with weapon racks, some wooden and some made of metal. One section consisted of long laneways and bullseye targets, used for training archers. Beside it were rows of cloth dummies, stuffed with straw and set on a rotating pole.

There were two guarded entrances into the camp. One was on the side of the larger tents and the other one was located on the opposite side from us, the side that faced the direction one would travel to go to Clearwell Castle—I recalled this bit of information from studying one of Lyra's hand-drawn maps.

I wondered how many times the king had traveled that road. I doubted his pompous ass cared to do so, although I imagined his advisor had—I clenched my fists.

"Alright, you filthy rebels, any last words?" Ryker said with a smirk, hands slinging off his cloak, revealing his carefully honed, heavily muscled body beneath wrapped in fighting leathers and adorned with a multitude of weaponry. I counted six weapons, but I bet he had more.

"I don't think so," Soren said, feigning courage, although his droopy posture suggested otherwise. As soon as the thought occurred, Soren quickly straightened his shoulders, his gaze darting to me.

Out! I hissed.

Sorry. His shadow mouse returned to its hole.

Great divine and Lord of Light on a Sunday, that was getting old.

Harper and Lyra stepped off to the side. Harper whispered something to her. Lyra's eyes were wide. She looked horrified, like she was on the verge of a breakdown.

"You should have stayed back at the manor." Harper's voice was no longer a whisper, worry written plainly in her doting gaze, her hands gently rubbing Lyra's arms comfortingly.

Lyra trembled, her knees wobbling.

Harper took her in her arms, her hand rhythmically stroking Lyra's hair. Lyra clutched on to her as if her very life depended on it, as if some horrible monster were lapping at her, threatening to drag her away.

"It's going to be okay," Harper reassured her as she gently tipped Lyra's chin up and sealed her promise with a kiss. Under the light of the moon, they looked like a painted picture, sealed in one another's embrace.

Ryker strolled to his sister's side. "Rock, paper, scissors?"

She smirked, a visibly much calmer Lyra still held in her arms. "You're on."

Harper's face was cast in a honey-soft glow as she nocked her arrow against the string of her bow. Her curved bow and arrow were both crafted of flame—simple and elegant, a testament to her craftsmanship. She kept the flame dull purposefully, so our location was not exposed. Elbow straight, her fingers drew the taut string back. The limbs flexed as the tension increased, and when she released the arrow, they vibrated with a sigh of relief. She didn't lower her bow, her gaze transfixed on her arrow as it launched into the night, soaring over the wooden barracks and embedding itself in one of the cloth tents.

Her lips curled in triumph. "Bullseye."

Lyra leapt up and down, sharing in Harper's victory.

A gentle breeze brushed my cheek, caressing the ends of my hair before it tugged reluctantly away. Seconds later, Harper's flame arrow burst into a monstrous, hungry flame, eagerly lapping at whatever it could taste—whatever it could burn. The fire leapt to another tent as if it had a mind of its own, but I knew, by the scent of his magic, the will of his power—it was all Von.

He did it all without moving a muscle.

The tents continued to catch fire, the flames jumping from one to the next, doubling in size by the second, until the air above was tinged with a smoky orange glow.

Men staggered out, screaming and shouting, alerting the others, telling them to get up. As the flames multiplied, so did the men. I was amazed how many poured out of one tent, wondered how they all fit in there—there would not be enough room for all of them to lie down. The training grounds buzzed with chaos, like a jar of upturned, shaken ants scrambling over one another, uncertain what to do next.

My eyes darted back and forth, trying to find Kaleb, but none of the men were him.

I tilted my face to the starry sky, a prayer on my breath. *Please, Lady Light, let me find him.*

One man grabbed as many buckets as he could carry. He shoved them into the hands of the others, rallying them to fill them with water from the well, to put out the flames.

My heart struck with such force it nearly fractured my chest in two—I knew that unyielding determination.

"Kaleb!" I screamed. I didn't think—I just moved. I ran.

An arm cinched around my torso, nearly sweeping me off the ground. "You cannot just charge in there," Von commanded, his voice firm in my ear, his grip constricting.

Imprisoned by my own sudden need to save Kaleb, I abandoned the plan and shoved against Von's arm. "I need to get him out."

"And we will. But we stick to the plan," he countered, his arm slipping from my waist when he felt my fight calm. His eyes met mine. "It is your turn now."

Clarity restored, I nodded and stepped forward. Concentrating, I reached within, my body mapping out every droplet of water that surrounded us. I focused on the well, whispering to the water within—coaxing it to seep into the veins in the ground, sucking it down, lower and lower, until it was no longer of use.

Until the well ran dry—not a single drop left.

And just as Von had planned, the soldiers were forced to abandon the well and go outside of the barracks, to the river north of the camp, making them farther scattered apart and harder for the soldiers to keep track of.

"We'll keep them busy," Ryker said as he raised his bow made of white flame.

Von's hand cupped my cheek tenderly. "Stick to the shadows."

My hand fell over his, determination knitting my brow. "I will."

Soren gave me a nod, signaling he was ready.

I inhaled a deep breath—this was it.

Chapter 38

Von

As I watched her descend into the valley, it took every ounce of willpower not to chase after her. Not to say *fuck* the rescue mission, toss her over my shoulder—surely kicking and screaming—and take her away from this place—away from everything.

When it came to her, everything felt primal. That part of me was relentless in its demands—to protect, to provide. All of it, for her. It was always for her.

At their core, they were basic needs traced back to the dawn of man. Although I was a far cry from a mere mortal, those needs burned tenfold in me. And then some.

"They are nearly down the side of the valley," Ryker stated, his flame bow still in hand.

Lyra nodded solemnly as she clutched Harper's side, her wide eyes glued on Sage and Soren. She understood the horrors of what happened in training barracks better than anyone. I had found her in one, much like this one, a few years back, her little body bloody and bruised and broken. I had not expected her to survive, had thought one of my ravens would come to collect her soul soon. And yet . . . she'd proven me wrong.

I turned to Ryker. "See the tent with the soldiers stationed out front?" I'd been watching that tent for well over a day now. It was why I had stayed while Ryker went back to collect the others—to make sure the rat inside didn't go anywhere.

His eyes shifted over the tents until he found it. He nodded, lifted his bow, and conjured an arrow. "On it." He nocked the arrow, drew the string back, and released. It launched into the air, soaring up and over the barracks before it bit into the top right corner of the tent.

"Nice shot," Harper said to her twin, her gaze constantly shifting between what was happening down below and Lyra—who she had tucked safely against her side.

That, right there, was why I had to make a last-minute change to the plan.

Originally, I was going to send Harper with Sage, instead of Soren, but after what happened with Lyra earlier on, I scrapped that idea. Harper would have worried about Lyra the entire time she was down there. It would have made her distracted, eligible for slip-ups—a risk I couldn't take . . . not that an attentive Soren was much of a better option. But it wasn't Soren I was betting on. It was Sage's need to protect him, someone she viewed as a little brother—a stand-in Kaleb. I hoped that factor would keep her from doing anything brash. Then again, this was *my* headstrong, impulsive Little Goddess we were talking about.

Fuck. I should have gone with her.

I knew all too well what it was like to lose her.

But I wouldn't lose her again—I'd shred apart all three realms before I let that happen.

That was why I had to stay here—why I couldn't go with her. Because even though there were multiple threats to her down there, none of them posed as big of a threat as *that* half-breed God of Truth.

Speaking of which . . . I glanced back at the expansive tent, the back of it aflame, encouraging some of the soldiers to come out first, blades held at the ready. The two soldiers that stood at the entrance reached for the tent flaps and pulled them open. The pompous little prick emerged, one gloved hand stroking his red hair.

"I'll be back in a moment," I told the others, not waiting for a reply as I let my shadows take me.

A few seconds later and my hand was wrapped around his throat.

With a great deal of force, I threw the rat right on back into the burning tent he'd just walked out of. I prowled inside, my bone-snapping wind at my back, ensuring none of his soldiers had access to our little reunion—well, unless they wanted their necks broken.

The half-breed slammed into the extra-long table, scattering the maps and papers and tiny wooden soldiers from their slumber. I glanced at one of the little toys these so-called *grown* men used to plan wars, one skeptical brow raising. Mortal men had fallen a long way from their grunting neanderthal forefathers. Creator above, how I missed those days—life was simple then: kill or be killed. Everyone had gotten soft.

"Blood King," Arkyn spat the title at me as he slowly peeled himself up off the table, a tendril of red hair falling over his forehead.

"Royal ass licker." I greeted him. Ignoring the heat that radiated towards me as the flames worked their way down the backside of the tent, I strolled leisurely over to a table, set just off to my right, filled with silver platters of meats, cheeses, breads, and various fruits and vegetables. I searched for an apple and grumbled when I didn't see one. "I'd fire your cook, if I were you." I shifted around the cheese platter, purposefully making a mess while not committing to anything. "They forgot the apples."

I was fucking with him. I would get to the point shortly, so I could get back to watching over *my* female.

"She's here, isn't she?" Arkyn demanded as he took a step towards me.

I ignored him as I rummaged through the cheese platter. Knowing full well that it was an ass clogger, I moved on to the fruit tray. I snapped a grape off the petrified vine, took a bite, and tossed the other half over my shoulder. I plucked another one, repeating the same action.

"Answer me," Arkyn growled with more bite than I thought he had in him. I would have congratulated him on finally finding his balls, but compliments weren't really my thing.

He took another few steps towards me, all while I continued to make a mess of his extravagant little food table. If the poor young trainees only knew what their superiors feasted on every night while they scrapped over moldy bread, surely it would have caused a riot. But as the old adage went, out of sight, out of mind.

"Answer me," Arkyn grated once more, his body within arm's reach.

Someone had forgotten their place and I felt compelled to remind him.

"Alright," I replied at the exact same moment I grabbed the large silver platter and sent it colliding into the side of his face. A firework of meats sprayed out every which direction, a round, thin slab of salami landing on my outstretched arm.

The blow knocked Arkyn to the ground, rendering his consciousness somewhere between this tent and the stars.

Briefly, I eyed the silver platter, slightly impressed at the clear imprint of Arkyn's face now forged into the light metal, before I tossed it to the side, a metal ting sounding when it hit the ground.

My brow darted up—the slice of meat was still stuck on my arm. Taking aim at Arkyn, I flicked it off and it landed on his chest.

Did I say he was somewhere between here and the stars? I took it back. He was beyond the stars.

Some Demi God he was.

I booted the side of his perfectly polished shoe. "Wake up."

He grumbled, but that was it for a response.

Well, fuck . . . I needed him awake for the next part.

Chapter 39

Sage

We merged with the shadows, sticking in their embrace as if our lives depended on it—and I suppose, in a way, they probably did. It took longer than I anticipated for us to descend into the valley, but after a good half an hour or so, under the watchful gaze of the moon, we finally made it. We weaved through the bush, making our way around the barracks, towards the glistening, rushing river.

The soldiers' voices were easier to make out now that we were so much closer to them. Some sounded younger, like they hadn't even hit puberty yet. I could hear the panic in their voices, could hear the barking higher-ups yelling at them to do more, to move faster while they called them names like "low-born dogs" and "bastards of a whore."

I wondered how many of these conscripted men would be alive by winter's end, but my gut knew that answer. Very few would make it that long, if any at all.

My jaw locked as my teeth ground together. I wished I could free them all.

We clutched to the side of the barracks before we moved to a dense grove of buffalo berry bushes. I pressed my hand against the slender, barren branch, careful of the thorns, and pulled it down slightly so I could get a better look.

The soldiers ran towards the rushing river with their empty wooden buckets. On their way back, their paces were slower, some struggling with the weight, water splashing over the sides.

Come on, Kaleb. Come on.

As if my heart had willed it, Kaleb emerged from the barracks.

He was thin—too thin. His hair was long and matted, and those once-vivid blue eyes were now dull and hollow.

My heartbeat jumped into my ears, pounding. *I'm going to get you home, Kaleb.*

He was too close to the other soldiers for me to get his attention without being noticed, without putting all three of us at risk. I needed to think of a way to let him know I was here. Something that only he would know. Something . . . I glanced at my hand and suddenly, I knew. I conjured my Water Curse and I filled his empty bucket to the brim. His arm sank with the unexpected weight.

His mouth fell open. Dumbfounded, he stared at the bucket, at the water sloshing from side to side. Instantly, he dropped it, water jumping out as the ground smacked the bottom. He twirled, his eyes searching for me—because he knew it was me.

Without thinking, I sprung from the shadows—he

needed to see me, know that I was here, and that we were going back home.

When he saw me . . . it felt surreal. A tangle of emotions—sadness and happiness and relief—slammed into me, knocking me two steps forward.

Kaleb sprinted, conquering the distance between us. He shouted at me, but I couldn't hear his words—all I could see was him. The horror written on his too-thin face. Gods, what had they done to him?

His body slammed into mine as he drew me into his arms and twirled me around—except he wasn't twirling me . . .

Before I could process what he had done, I heard it—the whirling, followed by an abrupt, sickening . . . *thunk*. The sound of an arrow meeting its target.

Kaleb dropped to his knees, his body slumping just enough that I could see the arrow protruding out of his back, directly over his heart.

"Kaleb!" I screamed as I dropped in front of him.

His eyes met mine, his hand reaching for my cheek, as he brushed away a single tear. He tried to smile, but blood dribbled out from his mouth and his legs gave out.

I caught him before he collapsed completely. Soren helped me guide him to the ground. We positioned him on his side, and I leapt over top of him so I was facing his back. My hands frantically clamped around the arrow, trying to apply pressure to his wound, trying to stop the blood.

Another arrow whirled past, nearly missing me as it bit into the ground a few feet away, causing a spray of tiny rocks and dirt. I didn't move when I heard another one whiz by because right now, the only thing that mattered was stopping

Kaleb from bleeding out.

Soren jumped up, twirling, trying to locate the archer, but the archer's arrow found him instead. He stumbled back. His hands wrapped around the shaft as he looked at me, white-eyed with horror.

My bloodstained hand shot out towards him, and a scream—my scream—shredded through my throat.

Cast in moonlight, soldiers—*real* soldiers—began to fill in around us. Everywhere I looked, the king's crest stared back at me. A soldier stalked up behind Soren, his sword raised.

"Look out!" I screamed, but it was too late. The soldier ran the pommel of his sword into the back of Soren's head, and he crumpled to the ground. He grabbed Soren's collar and dragged his unconscious body away from me.

I screamed something, I thought, but I could no longer hear sound—only a steady ringing in my ears followed by the frantic cleaving of my heart. This was not how it was supposed to go. I looked down at Kaleb. This wasn't it . . .

Ba-dump. Ba-dump. Ba-dump.

Tears fell down my cheeks.

Ba-dump. Ba-dump. Ba-dump.

Hands ripped at me, trying to pull me away from Kaleb.

Ba-dump. Ba-dump. Ba-dump.

No—not again. I would not let them take him again.

Sound suddenly came filtering back and I called upon my Water Curse, but a bluish-purple fire answered instead—the color itself a dead match for the gaze of the moon.

The soldiers that held my arms scrambled away from me, screaming as they tried to remove the red-hot metal gauntlets before my flame welded it to their skin. The smell of singed flesh permeated the air, clogging my nostrils.

"She's Cursed!" yelled one of them. I didn't know which one. They all looked the same—wearing the emblem of the king.

"I am." I embraced the word, reveling in this newfound power—in my Fire Curse.

The soldiers moved closer towards us slowly, cautiously.

My hand shot out, a trail of fire ripping through the ground, the flames spinning into monstrous waves, a serpent of flame that swallowed its tail. It birthed a ring of protection around Kaleb and me.

"Stay with me," I pleaded, my trembling fingers wrapped around that arrow.

Blood. There was so much blood. No matter how hard I pressed, it just kept coming. It felt like there was no end. No end to the blood that seeped out of him.

"Want . . . to . . . see your face." His voice was weak. "One . . . more time."

Kaleb knew. He knew the very thing that I was struggling to comprehend—that he was dying. And there was nothing either of us could do—not even my shaking hands could stop the blood pooling from his back. He had accepted it and asked to see my face because that was the image he wanted to have before . . .

I knew what I had to do—knew that it was going to be the hardest thing I had ever done. I turned my head to the side, wiped away my tears with the back of my sleeve, and left the wound, knowing full well what abandoning it meant. But I also knew what staying there meant too—it would rob me of these last moments with him. Rob him of his last request.

I lay down beside him and took his hand and pressed it over my heart. "I'm here, Kaleb. I'm here now."

And for a simple moment, we were little again—just two kids sitting by the window, waiting for Ezra to come home.

Chapter 40

Von

Figuring out how to wake him up was tougher than I had expected—who knew that no kicking was required and a vase of water would rectify the problem?

Okay, okay . . . I did—I just couldn't help myself. The little weasel had been a thorn in my side since the day I met him. If it weren't for one of my prior deals, I would end his immortal life tonight. I had the means to—thanks to this lovely fire.

When Arkyn *finally* woke up, he tried to use his magic to fight, but that was a waste of time. My power trumped his easily, and his magic bowed to its superior, leaving him with very little to defend himself with.

"Where is it?" I asked, my fist clenched around Arkyn's collar as I shoved his head closer to the hungry fire. The white-hot flames chewed up the back half of the tent, cloaking the air with thick, heavy smoke. The flames worked their way forward, nibbling on everything in their path. Even the crimson-colored rugs draped over the plank floors were starting to catch. It wouldn't take long for them to set the rest of the tent aflame.

"I'm the enforcer of truth. You know I have to answer you honestly, regardless of if I wish to or not. So why don't you give me a second to breathe? You know damn well that fire is my weakness," he choked, his hands wrapped around my wrist, trying to push me away.

"Oh, but I would rather make you squirm instead." I grinned wickedly as I forced him a hair closer. A glowing ember floated overtop. With a gentle nudge of my wind, I corrected its path and made it land right between his eyes.

He let out a hiss, wiggling under my grasp as it singed his skin, permeating the smoke-filled air with a light hint of burning flesh.

"Now, one more time, where is the crown?" I asked, eyeing another floating ember, this one larger than the last.

He squirmed, his teeth doing a piss-poor job of clamping down on his tongue. It slipped free and he answered my question unwillingly. "The *rightful* king has it."

"Fuck," I growled as I shoved him down. I strode over to the long table and grabbed the edge of it with my hand. Roaring, I tossed it over, paper and man toys scattering everywhere. I turned to Arkyn, my jaw set in steel. "How in the Spirit Realm did *he* get his hands on it?"

A grin spread across his swollen, bloody face. "Your sister."

My eyes flared, my shadows slithering around me, begging to rip his throat out—begging to rip *her* throat out. I knew her hatred for me ran deep, but this betrayal . . . it was unforgivable. I would deal with her later, but right now, my shadows ached for retribution, and Arkyn just happened to be the closest thing.

Sure, I had made a deal not to kill the God of Truth many, many years ago, but I was not above taking a blade to my skin, cutting that slab of meat and ink straight off and then taking that same bloody blade to his throat. I'd revel in slitting it.

But before I could do that, before I could do anything, my breath was snatched from my chest. Inside, something gripped at my heart, like a hand squeezing the juice out of a lemon before it took the husk to the shredder.

I stumbled backwards, my hand shooting to my chest as I grappled with the cataclysmic pain, wrestling it into submission.

I had felt this before, but this time, it was different.

It was not *my* heart breaking.

It was . . .

My head jerked up.

Sage.

Chapter 41

Sage

When I realized that his chest was no longer falling, no longer rising, I jerked upright, my hands darting to his face, to his shoulders, gently shaking him, trying to wake him up.

But that was just it, wasn't it? Kaleb wasn't sleeping.

My world cleaved, my glass heart struck by a mallet, shattering it into a thousand tiny pieces. I tipped my head to the starlit sky, cursing it for twinkling on a night such as this and I let out a guttural roar.

Appearing out of nowhere, a raven swooped, talons stretched out as it landed gracefully on the ground. I watched it bobbing as it side-hopped towards me cautiously. I blinked, trying to clear away the film on my eyes created by my tears. It might have been my blurry vision, but it almost seemed like a faint glow illuminated the silhouette of the beautiful bird. This one seemed smaller in size than the ones I had seen before.

It focused on Kaleb, cocking its head from side to side as if it were studying him. It tapped his shoulder with his beak, waiting for a response. By reflex, I swatted at it. It cawed at me. It ruffled its feathers as if I had insulted it, body shaking from side to side before it smoothed them out, each sleek, pristine feather falling dutifully back into place. The raven looked up, its eyes . . . squinting at me. The raven was squinting at me.

I was hallucinating. I had to be.

It cawed again, the sound transitioning into a woman's voice. "Do not interfere."

It turned back to Kaleb and tapped his shoulder again. A hole, burning with the brightness of the sun, was born from his chest. I gasped, sheltering my eyes from the bright, vivid light. I peeked between my spread fingers. A glass orb, a bit larger than a marble, raised from the hole. It was beautiful, the colors inside of it swirling together as if they were dancing, a vibrant yellow and a deep, rich brown—the colors of the sun, of tree bark and sunflowers.

The very colors I would choose to explain Kaleb's personality.

As the hole in his chest closed, the glass orb spun slowly, moving towards me. I cupped my hands beneath it. I did not dare to touch it, did not dare to taint this crisp, beautiful thing with my dirty hands. I could feel it reach out to me, feel a comforting weight fall on my shoulders, as if a blanket had been placed on them.

Just as Kaleb would do.

"You must say goodbye now," the raven said, her voice soft, kind. "The longer we stay in this realm, the harder it will make it for him in the next."

"Will you take care of him?" If I could ensure he would have someone, anyone, that he wouldn't be alone, then I wanted that for him.

"Yes," the raven answered after giving it some thought.

I could tell she meant it, but still—

"I don't think I can say goodbye," I said, wiping at my tears.

"Then don't," she suggested, as if it were that simple.

"Will I see him again?" I asked, my words sounding so very wrong, like they did not belong in my mouth. The thought of not seeing Kaleb again . . . My brain shut down, unable to process such a thought.

The raven did not answer for a long time. Finally, she said, "We all are reunited in the Spirit Realm."

Her answer was far from a yes or a no, but it sounded, well, hopeful. And that was something I could latch on to.

The marble moved away from me. I watched as it spun towards the raven. Gently, she caught it in her beak.

"Wait," I said, reaching towards her, my voice but a rasp, bound in thistles.

But she gave me little mind, drawing out her majestic wings and flying away, taking the blanket of warmth with her.

I looked down and stroked his cheek. He was so cold, so terribly cold. My gaze lowered, stopping abruptly when I saw the metal cuffs locked around his wrists. They were made of a thick, heavy metal, the sides so sharp they bit into his skin.

This was wrong—shackles had no place on my brother's wrists, no place on any of the innocents' wrists.

I took his hands in mine. I had no idea what I was doing,

but somehow, some way, I used my lilac-blue flame to disintegrate those shackles, reducing them to ash. I never let the fire touch his skin, but even when the shackles were gone, the evidence of them remained—the flesh raw and tattered beneath. I filled with anger.

I craved one thing—*vengeance*.

Standing, I let my protective wall of flame come down.

"Did you burn yourself out, Cursed Bitch?" sneered a soldier as his fingers wrapped around the hilt of his sheathed sword. Slowly, he pulled the blade out, moonlight glinting off the sharp edge.

I didn't answer. I merely watched as they unsheathed their swords, their glinting blades singing for blood. *Good.* My Curse was singing for it too. I could taste that insatiable need for vengeance on my tongue, feel it nestle within my bones, filling me with purpose. I would end them all for Kaleb.

This is wrong, said my inner voice.

But how could it be wrong? These soldiers deserved to die for what they had done—deserved to die because of who they fought for.

And yet, their minds have been warped so badly by the Crown, they do not know the monsters they have become. Have mercy on them.

Mercy . . .

Wrath's chokehold released, its fingers drifting from my throat. I crumpled to my knees, fisted my hands in the ground, and thought of every young boy and young man that had been forced to leave their families to come to this fucking camp— forced to wear those shackles. I thought of the little girl I had met at the Temple of Light and how she'd prayed for her brother so he could come home—what if he was here?

My need for revenge receded, caving to something else.

Just as I tracked the droplets of water, I searched for the metal cuffs scattered around the training barracks, each and every one of them lighting up like a star in the blank sky in my mind. I focused on them and conjured from that lava pit of flame that swelled inside, and when I let it out, a warrior's cry tore through me.

I pushed with everything I had, diving well past the limits of my powers. The harder I pushed, the more it felt like my magic was being torn from me, but I continued anyway. Sweat perspired from my skin, my teeth threatening to shatter as I bore down. My legs trembled, threatening to give out. No matter how hard I tried, the cuffs did not budge—there were *too many* of them.

Tears of flame rolled down my cheeks as I roared to the gods, *Help me!*

And just when my power threatened to cave, I felt *her*.

I am with you, she said, her ethereal voice echoing around me.

I trembled. It felt as if I were standing upon holy ground.

I felt her power fill my empty reservoirs. I felt her work through me. And when those shackles slipped from existence, when I heard the cries of victory, I fell to my knees, my mortal flesh humbled. Overcome.

My shoulders shook and I wept.

The king's soldiers closed in, but I had no fight in me left.

And so I took Kaleb's hand in mine and waited for my fate to come.

The light from the moon clouded over and the world was

cloaked in darkness. A star fell from the sky, landing in front of me, the ground cracking beneath his feet. A blast of unsurmountable wind slammed into the soldiers, sending the front row crashing into the others. Yet when it touched me, it caressed my skin—softly, affectionately. Lovingly.

The scent of amber and leather tinged the air, and that was when I realized the creature of the night was Von.

"I am sorry, Sage. It never should have come to this," he said, his voice thick with an emotion I could not place. I stared up at him, his back facing me. His long black hair whipped angrily in the wind. I wondered if the wrath I felt had passed on to him.

The soldiers scrambled back on their feet, a battle cry emitting from their lips as they charged at us. A tidal wave of wind pulsed from Von, and it didn't just knock them back this time—it scattered them like they were leaves. Before they had a chance to crawl to their swords, to stand on their feet, another wave hurtled at them, this one was stronger than the last. And when it hit them, it crumpled their armor, and I thought—no, I knew—I heard the sickening crunch as it broke their bones, saw the spray of blood as it misted the air.

Now I understood why he had been given the name Blood King.

The power he emitted was extraordinary. Ancient and brutal and unparalleled. And not of this world. This was no mere Curse. This was the power of the gods. I knew because I had just felt it. The only difference was that Von didn't need a god to grant him such immense power—it belonged to him.

"We have to get out of here." A voice said, but I couldn't look away from him—this dark creature of the night.

Hands fell on my shoulders, gently shaking me.

The soldiers scrambled away, a few of them helping their broken brethren up, but most of them just ran.

Harper's face fell in front of mine. I blinked and suddenly, I was released from my spellbound state.

"Kaleb," I choked, glancing down at him, my hands still holding his. Gods, they were cold.

Harper cupped my cheeks tenderly, her face solemn, her sadness for me ringing in my ears. "I know. I know. I am so sorry, Sage." She paused. "We have to get out of here." Her hands drifted to my arms. Gently, she rubbed them. "Ryker is going to take Kaleb's body now. Okay?"

Kaleb's body.

Those words repeated in my mind.

Harper said something as she looked at me, but all I heard was static. I focused, trying to understand, reading her lips as she repeated the words again. Slowly, I pieced them together.

Could I walk?

I looked down at my legs, but they no longer felt attached to me. It was the strangest feeling, like I was a bird without wings. Unable to fly.

And then, Von was in front of me, his voice cutting through the static. "I will carry you."

His arms, strong and steady, lifted me from the blood-soaked ground. He cradled me against his chest, his dark orbs drifting over my face, studying me. His hold on me lightened, as if he thought I were made of glass.

Von carried me.

Away from the training barracks.

Away from the place that had taken my brother's life.

Chapter 42

Lightning carried Kaleb's body, Von's black cloak draped over top. Ryker held Lightning's reins, leading her behind him, leading all of us back to the mansion, back to Belamour. I slumped against Von, his hard torso and strong arms keeping me from falling off his stallion. I had little strength. And as much as I craved to close my eyes, to escape, I couldn't do that either.

I didn't know how long we had been traveling because my mind was adrift, stuck in a world that ebbed with scattered thoughts and flowed with blame. In truth, all of this was my fault. I should have never leapt up from that bush. Should have waited for a better time, found some other way to get him out. Because of my impulsive actions, Kaleb was . . .

I couldn't say the word.

I was faintly aware that we made it back to the mansion, faintly aware of Von's hands slipping around my waist, of him pulling me down from his stallion, into his arms, my feet never hitting the ground. Lyra held the door open, her eyes filled with sadness . . . for me. I wanted to reach out, to tell her not to be sad for me, that I didn't deserve it. But words were hard for me to string together.

Because of me, not only was Kaleb gone, but Soren was too.

After the soldiers and the conscripted men scattered like a deck of cards thrown into the wind, Harper and Ryker had searched for Soren, but they were unsuccessful. I was ashamed to say I couldn't bring myself to look. I couldn't bring myself to do much of anything, let alone stand.

I feared that they might return with Soren's body, my mind playing out the final moments I saw him—the arrow chewing into his flesh, the hit to the back of his head. I felt a fraction of relief when they returned empty-handed, but it was quickly snuffed out when I imagined what awaited him wherever they were taking him. He had not done anything to show that he was Cursed, but because he was with me, because of what they would have seen, they would claim him guilty by association.

I reached out in my mind, calling for him, hoping to find any remnant of a shadow mouse, but like the twins, my search also turned up empty-handed. I made a note to myself to try again later. I could do that much for him. I owed him that. After what he had given for me. For Kaleb.

Von set me down, the soft bed sighing underneath me. I blinked, looked around, surveying familiar surroundings—we were in my room. I didn't recall the process of us getting from the front door to here.

Von looked at me, a hawk peering down from its lookout branch. He exhaled a long, steady breath as he sat on the bed beside me. "What do you need?"

What did I need? I didn't know. How could I need anything when Kaleb's body was out there, slung over a horse, waiting to be buried?

"What do I do with him?" I asked, looking up at Von, the rich green color of his irises now gone, an inky black settled in its place. His eyes roamed over my face, as if he were searching for physical wounds, something tangible that he could heal.

"What do you want to do with him?" He continued to study me carefully, as if I were porcelain, riddled with hairline cracks.

I thought about his question, an answer forming on my lips in unison with the thought. "I want to give him a proper burial." The words scarred my throat on the way out, causing a lump to build there. Weeks ago, when all of this started, I had vowed to bring Kaleb home. I swallowed the lump down, feeling my cells start to thrum, my purpose renewed.

"I need to take him home," I whispered to myself, needing to hear it out loud.

Later that day, when the too-bright, too-cheerful sun was positioned well into the clear blue sky, I stood outside with Harper, Ryker, and Lyra, exchanging goodbyes and hugs.

The three of them had decided to stay back, to see if they could find out anything about where Soren was. Déjà vu planted itself in my gut, anchoring it down with dread. I hoped, prayed to the gods, that they would be successful in their search, that it would not end how mine did with Kaleb. I warred with myself and my decision to leave. Part of me wanted to stay—to help them find Soren—but the other part that needed to take Kaleb home was stronger. Still, I would do what I could to try to help find him. It was becoming habitual to check internally for him, calling out for him. I even imagined a piece of cheese, like that was enough to coax his shadow mouse out. I had checked so many times over the past few hours, it was beginning to feel like an itch, one that constantly needed to be scratched.

Harper draped her arm over Lyra's shoulders. "We have things covered here, so don't worry, okay?"

I gave her a reassuring nod, noting the bags under her eyes courtesy of lack of sleep and too much stress. We all shared that same look. Well, everyone except for Von. I didn't know how he managed it—to always look like he had a full eight hours of rest every night when he so rarely slept . . . if he slept at all. I doubted it. The last time I remembered him sleeping was that night in Norwood, the image of dirty streets and poor, decrepit houses conjured in my mind. Now, Norwood felt like a lifetime ago. Perhaps it was.

The air crackled, hissed, and seethed, parting for the dark male as he appeared before us. Yet one more thing I was not used to—him appearing out of thin air.

"Do you ever get used to that?" I asked Ryker, who stood beside me.

Ryker glanced at me, a thick brown brow shooting up. "Von shadow walking?"

I had never heard that term before, but it made sense. Sort of.

I nodded.

Ryker smirked, large hands bracketing his hips, broad shoulders performing a slight shrug. "Not really."

Von slipped a hand into his pocket, his other hand hanging by his side, black and silver rings glinting in the sunlight. He tilted his chin up slightly, peering down at me in that big cat way of his. "Ready?"

"Yes," I said, without an ounce of hesitation. I moved to Von's side, his hand lazily drifting to the small of my back, guiding me closer to him. Instinctually, my hands moved, lying flat on his chest, the soft cotton fabric of his black tunic doing little to hide the hard muscles beneath.

I turned my head, took a good, hard look at the three people waving goodbye, the weary eyes mismatched with smiling faces. I realized just then how much they had all done for me—for Kaleb, for Ezra, for my little family. They had given up weeks to bring Kaleb home, someone they didn't even know. And if my frozen heart was capable of warming, I think it would have in that moment.

"Thank you," I mouthed to them before the mansion shifted out of view, my world suddenly twinkling with brilliant stars, sparkling and shimmering, as Von shadow walked us to the cottage.

"What is this place?" I asked, tempted to reach out to one of the stars, to touch it. They seemed so close and yet so far away, all at the same time. They were not static, either—no, they were constantly moving, swirling and dipping and dancing like they were alive. I looked down and my jaw fell slack . . . We were walking—*walking*—on clouds.

Von tipped his face down, those long black lashes

flickering as his eyes settled on me. "It is common ground." A smile hinted at the corners of his lips, like being here fished out some precious old memory.

"Common ground?"

"It is in-between, a place where life and death can meet."

"That makes no sense." I shook my head.

"Perhaps not right now, Little Goddess," Von countered, a playful grin touching his full lips, like he knew something I did not. A common theme. "But someday, it will."

Chapter 43

It was a bit strange how distance could change your opinion on things, bring about a different perspective. I was aware on some level that the cottage was small and yet, I hadn't really thought about it. If you asked me before, it was the perfect size for us three. Now, standing here in front of it, it just sort of hit me—it was small. Like teeny tiny small. Especially in comparison to the expansive mansion I had been living in for the past weeks.

But still, one thing would never change—it was home.

I walked to the front door, Von following, his long legs leisurely keeping up with my quick pace. There was a spare key under the terra-cotta flowerpot, the lifeless husk of a plant withered inside, crusty and brittle. I had no idea what the plant was—it was one of Ezra's, which should make even the bravest of souls steer clear of it. But this one seemed particularly bad because not even the locusts, which had come in droves this summer, would touch it. And those little suckers ate everything. No wonder she'd chosen that particular plant to hide the key.

Not that I needed a key. My hand turned the knob and the door sprung open—we didn't bother to lock the cottage.

There were two reasons why that was—the first being that the cottage was well off the beaten trail, nestled deep in the forest. It was well hidden—something drunk Kaleb would attest to when he returned after a wild night or the next morning, when he finally found his way home. The second reason was because the lock was broken—courtesy of Kaleb . . . and partly me. Although I was only ever willing to take a wee bit of the blame.

It had happened about five years ago, when Ezra was away and we were left without parental supervision—if that was what you could call what Ezra did. Kaleb had slept in that day. When he finally woke up, he headed outside to relieve himself. As he was only wearing his underwear, and it was a particularly frosty January morning, I'd thought it would be a good idea to lock him out.

Now, let me just say that I'd had full intentions of doing it for just a little bit, and then I was going to let him back in— after I had a good laugh. But it turned out Mr. Sunshine had woken up on the wrong side of the bed mat that day, and he'd reared up and booted the door in, breaking the lock as well as a bit of the trim around the door. He came tearing after me like a bull chasing a matador, and I ran for my life, howling with laughter.

I smiled, my hand drifting over the broken trim that never got replaced as I passed through. It was still there, reassuring me that Kaleb was once here.

After I gave Von the tour of our home—which didn't

take very long as he could see most of it from the front door—
we returned outside, searching for the right place to lay Kaleb
to rest. I wished Ezra were here. She would know what to
do—she always knew what to do. But judging by the
untouched state of the cottage, she had not been home for
some time, most likely since we departed in Norwood, which
meant she was probably still in the Cursed Lands—waiting
for word that Kaleb and I had returned. A visceral ache
stabbed at my heart. I shoved away from my feelings, coated
them in ice, and focused on the task at hand.

It took me awhile, but finally, I decided on the perfect
spot—beside the log shed, under the tall, watchful gaze of an
oak tree.

One of Kaleb's main jobs had been making sure the
cottage and log shed were stockpiled with split wood. Just as
training was my escape when I was a child, that was what
chopping wood was for Kaleb. It gave him a refuge, a place
for him to sort through his thoughts. It gave him purpose. And
it was just one of the many ways he looked after us.

"He always made sure the log shed was fully stocked," I
remarked, my hand drifting over the wood wall, my fingers
snagging on the remnants of cracked red paint. Like so many
things around here, it was losing its battle with time.

"He looked after you well," Von finally replied after a
passing of silence drifted between us. "And for that, I will
forever be indebted to him."

I turned and rested my back against the shed, propping
one leg up, my bootheel against it. I looked up at Von, my
knuckles tapping the shed. "We moved this once. It used to
be—" I nodded to the north. "—*way* over there." I pursed my

lips, swishing them to the side in thought. "It was my idea to move it. I went through a bit of a princess stage, believe it or not, when I was thirteen. I hated how far I had to walk in the winter to get the wood. So that spring, I wrangled Kaleb into helping me move it here, so it was closer."

I didn't know why I was telling Von this, couldn't imagine it meant much of anything to him. Still, I wanted to tell him all of my memories of Kaleb, so that Kaleb could live on in someone else too. And I didn't know why, but it just felt . . . good.

I needed good right now.

"I would expect nothing less from the thirteen-year-old version of you." Von smiled—really and truly. And it was breathtaking and familiar, like I had seen it a thousand times before—and yet I could not place where or when. Von was not exactly the smiling type. I didn't know why I felt this way, but the way he looked right now . . .

My body just reacted. Like it had a will of its own, suddenly, I was in front of him, my palm pressed against his face, my eyes darting between his obsidian eyes. "Sometimes . . ." I swallowed, looking down, reaching deep, trying to find the words. I fumbled with what I was about to say because it made no sense, and yet, it demanded to be said. My gaze returned to his. "It's like I knew you *before*."

That smile slipped, giving way to something I could only explain as . . . torn. His hand drifted over mine, blanketing it in his warmth. "Before what?"

At surface level, it seemed like a simple question, but the way he studied me, with such complete intensity, I knew it was much deeper than that.

I replayed his question in my head, searching for an answer. And when I came up with nothing, I searched again. Still, nothing.

Frustrated, I shook my head, whispering in defeat, "I don't know."

I looked at the ground, feeling emptier somehow. My hand slipped. He let it go.

Silence passed between us. The soft wind tugged at us both, wisping our hair to the side. The contrast between us had never been so prevalent. His hair, the color of obsidian stone, and mine, the color of soft snow. We stayed like that for some time, not speaking, just stuck in our private thoughts.

Von broke the silence. "I will return shortly."

I blinked, looking up at him. He wore the same look that I had seen before, but I had never been able to place a label on it because he always carefully covered it back up. But now, his façade faltered, and I could see what it was. It was written plainly in those black eyes, in the firm setting of his jaw, and I knew for him, that my answer was like I had taken salt and poured it into a deep wound. The look was raw. Visceral.

Tortured.

Just as I went to reach out for him, he slipped that mask back on, nodded his head in place of a goodbye, and then he was gone.

Digging through the topsoil was easy, but it was the compacted clay beneath that made it feel like I was digging into rock. I shifted my body weight from side to side, forcing the end of the shovel farther into the ground. Heaving it up, utilizing the long, wooden handle as leverage, I threw a shovelful to the pile I made on the side. I was about three feet down, maybe four on one end. I wiped the back of my sleeve against my slick brow before a bead of sweat rolled into my eye. I ignored the need to stretch my aching back, ignored the fire rasping my overworked lungs, and continued to dig. My body might crave a break, but my mind did not.

I whittled down what I was doing to a step-by-step process. One shovel after another. That was it. I didn't look at the grand picture of what I was doing—that part remained a protective blank. When I asked myself, *Why am I digging?* my brain would perform a mental shrug and say, *I don't know.* And so I just dug. And dug. And dug.

When the blisters on my hands popped, caused by the friction of the wood handle, I gritted my teeth and dug some more. I got lost in it, paying little heed to the fact that Von should have probably been back by now.

I grunted as my shovel refused to sink any lower. Had I thought the clay was hard? This—whatever it was—was far worse. I dug around the hard thing, working away the ground that cradled it as if it were some precious gemstone. Well, stone didn't cover the half of it. It was more like a boulder—a big, ugly, gray one. I glared at it—how dare it get in my way? Dropping to my knees, I clawed the ground with my fingers like some deranged hound digging out a buried bone. Dirt flew out behind me as I worked, uncovering more and more, revealing its increasingly growing size.

"Damn it," I seethed when I realized the rock went past the four-foot-wide perimeter I'd marked out earlier. I rolled over onto my butt and leaned against the side wall, bent one knee, and propped my arm on top. Frustrated, I slammed the back of my head against the dirt wall—why must a simple task be so hard? I inhaled a deep breath and stared at the gods-damned sky, particularly the sparkling, cheerful sun.

I glared at it.

How dare it shine today? It could shine on any other day, but today? Today, the sun should never have risen. It should have dipped its head in sorrow while the sky blanketed itself with heavy, dark-bottomed clouds and mourned.

I wiped a tear away, snorted, and got back up. I didn't need clouds to make the sky weep—I could do that all on my own. I raised my hands, feeling the moisture around me—in the ground, in the air. I forced it to move for me, to meld with other molecules like it, to grow and replicate. I let it build and build, and then I let it go, and the rain came crashing down, pelting the empty canopy of the trees, sailing right on past, to the ground, washing over me. It drenched my hair and clothes, mixing with the dirt on my face, on my hands, on my knees, turning it to mud.

"Do you see?" I screamed at the sun, tears streaming down my cheeks. "This is how it's done."

This time, I did not wipe them away.

I let the sun watch as I wept in my brother's grave.

"Sage?" called a voice through the light pitter-patter of rain. The voice sounded impeccably similar to Ezra's.

I must have been imagining things because that was

impossible—she was supposed to be in the Cursed Lands. Or gods only knew where else her wanderings had taken her.

Ezra's voice called out again.

"Go away," I said, dismissing the phantom. I lay in the hole I dug, flat on my back, saturated in mud. The rock beneath me had jammed a part of itself into my side, as if it weren't bothersome enough.

A head, gray-haired and white-eyed, peered over the edge, a hand-carved cane pointing down at me. "What a find!"

"Ezra!" I jerked upright, my eyes going wide. I shot to my feet, my head growing fuzzy with the sudden shift from latitude to longitude.

"Yes, yes, hello, hello. Now, scuttle to the side. This old bird would like to get a better feel for that marvelous specimen," she said by way of greeting, bending to her knees and scooting down, as limber as a twelve-year-old. It was funny how rocks had that effect on her. It was like they were her own personal fountain of youth, and even in her blindness, she could miraculously sense them. Rocks, for Pete's sake—whoever Pete was.

She shoved her cane into my dirty hands, her white orbs staring right on past me. She plopped onto her knees and cocked her head to the side. "Oh yes, very promising indeed. If I can just . . ." She tugged off her scarf and began to carefully rub some of the mud away, like she was polishing a diamond—exquisite and rare. She froze, her knobby, arthritic fingers flaring wide open, twitching in anticipation, like she was just about to dig into a nice, juicy steak. She leaned forward and pressed her ear against it. Suddenly, she jerked upright, the side of her face covered in mud. "Do you know what this is?"

"A rock?" I asked, her vast excitement making me question myself.

But this was Ezra asking, and I highly doubted it was a secret passageway to some forbidden world. It was—I glanced at it again, just in case—a bloody rock after all.

"Hush, child. You must not insult it," she scolded, pressing her hands over the rock as if it had ears, as if it could hear my thoughts—it was bad enough she could.

One would think after spending a lifetime with Ezra, that I would get used to her bizarre antics, and yet, here I was, still not used to them. I doubted I ever would be. Still, a small part of me was thankful for them.

Ezra leaned forward, pressing her ear against it again, listening for gods only knew what. "Mhm," she said to the rock before she turned her muddy face back to me, her milky white eyes narrowing as if she could see. "Why are you trying to dig it up?"

My mouth popped open. Quickly, I snapped it shut. "Because it's in my way."

"Funny. It says the same about you." Ezra cackled, patting it softly with her aged hands, like they were two gossiping old biddies.

I rolled my eyes. "How did you get here?"

"Von shadow walked me here," she muttered under her breath, a mechanical-sounding reply, her mind otherwise occupied.

I looked around, searching for him, but he was nowhere to be seen. I swallowed, knowing this next part was going to be hard. I dreaded the words, and my brain hadn't even formed them yet. I led with a question instead, looking down at the ground. "Do you know?"

Ezra stopped. Her hands went rigid, her curved shoulders sagging even more. "I know." She shifted slowly as she moved to her feet. She reached a muddy hand out to me. "Come, let us go inside. And you can tell me. All of it."

I took her hand and we walked towards the cottage.

After I started the fire and changed from my wet, muddy clothes, we nestled in on our old spot on the settee, steaming cups of tea in our hands and a hand-stitched quilt thrown over our laps.

I told her.

All of it.

Beginning to end.

And together, we wept.

Chapter 44

Later that night, Von returned with Kaleb's body. Ezra and I prepared Kaleb in the traditional way, washing away the blood and the dirt and wrapping him in a shroud—a white, winding sheet.

When the moon was set high and the crickets were singing, we laid him to rest beside the log shed, under the protective watch of the oak tree. Up above, on the oak's barren branch, two ravens sat side by side. One was small, like the one I had seen before, but the one beside it was larger, its feathers unusually light. It almost looked . . . sickly. Its head slunk down, like it was struggling to keep it up. I felt Von's eyes on me as I watched the ravens, his steady hand at the small of my back, his touch comforting.

Shifting, I turned back to look at Kaleb's grave, the fresh, brown dirt heaping over top, contrasting with the lighter ground surrounding it. Ezra spread seeds over the fresh dirt so that next spring it would be decorated with wildflowers.

Together, Ezra and I marked the head of his grave with

his trusty, old axe, his fingerprints worn into the wood. Von strapped a flat board across it, utilizing his magic to carve in his name, as well as the words: *Beloved Son and Brother*.

And it was the strangest thing because when the wording was complete, I could hear the faintest sound of metal striking wood. Ezra's knobby fingers squeezed mine, a great big smile warming her solemn face. I knew she could hear it, too, that distinctive sound of Kaleb chopping wood.

Finally, the three of us were home.

Together, at last.

Chapter 45

I awoke early the next morning, my hand slipping from underneath my cotton covers, reaching for Kaleb's empty bed. The sheets were thrown over, spewed about, the way he'd left it the last night he slept there. I made a solemn wish as I slipped from my padded down mattress that his sheets would always remain that way, just as he had always left them—unmade. The irony was not wasted that I used to get after him for not making his bed—Ezra did too—and now, here I was, cherishing those unmade sheets.

I scurried down from the loft, my stomach grumbling for the first time in two days.

The house was quiet. Ezra's door was closed, signaling she was still asleep. Von, of course, was nowhere to be seen. I wondered where he had slunk off to, although I had a feeling it was probably to do with his search for the Crown of Thorns. The fireplace had been recently stoked, and so I assumed he had not left that long ago. I warmed myself by the fire before I headed to the kitchen, a grueling ten steps away.

I tapped my chin in thought, my breakfast options limited. The potatoes had sprouted enough eyes I wondered if they were watching me. The onion bread—or rather, what was left of it—was a lump of green-blue mold. I threw it in the garbage then glanced at the small basket of eggs. There were six. That gave me a place to start—if they weren't rotten. I lifted one, sniffed the shell. I hissed—even through the shell, it smelled horrific. Sighing, I dumped those out too.

A thought—a dangerous thought—occurred. I dared a glance at Ezra's shelves, dared a few steps forward. I stopped abruptly, remembering what horrors she stowed inside and shook my head. I was hungry, but I wasn't *that* desperate.

It was too late in the season to visit nature's produce store, and I didn't have it in me to go hunting. Ezra would probably be asleep for a while anyway. I glanced at my wicker basket, hung in its usual spot just beside the door, and decided to head into town.

As I closed the protesting front door, the hinges a few swings away from calling it quits, I turned and bumped into something that felt like steel. Warm steel. Leather and amber enraptured me.

"Von," I said, looking up at him.

Gods, he was tall. Inappropriately tall. Doorways must be a bit of an issue—I imagined he did a lot of ducking. That would be annoying, wouldn't it? No wonder people stared at him. Well, there was his height, and then there was the way he looked—sinfully built, impeccably dressed, and his face, divinely made. Today, he sported a five o'clock shadow, which emphasized his chiseled cheekbones and masculine jawline.

Von raised one thick black brow—the one with the slit through it—and glanced at the empty wicker basket hooked on my forearm. "Going somewhere, Little Goddess?"

"Yes, to the village to get some food. Everything inside has gone rotten, moldy, or stale," I exclaimed, my stomach grumbling, furthering my claim.

We both looked to my protesting stomach.

Eager to retrieve something to eat, I stepped around Von and began to walk towards the village. When I didn't hear his footsteps behind me, I glanced over my shoulder and said, "Well, are you coming or what?" It wasn't a question, so I didn't ask it like one.

"So *very* bossy," Von chastised playfully, his words steeped in his rich, decadent baritone.

I made a point to roll my eyes just so he could see before I continued forward. In a few strides or less, he easily caught up with me.

"That looks heavy, let me take it for you," he purred, his voice coaxing a shiver down the length of my spine. His fingers, adorned in black and silver rings, slipped around the handle of the basket, brushing intimately against mine. I didn't need to look. I could *feel* his heated gaze sweeping over me slowly, sensually.

Lady Light, help me.

I heard him chuckle.

The jerk. He knew what he stoked in me—like wind feeding a flame.

A flame—that was one of the many things I had yet to process. On top of being Water Cursed and Dream Cursed, I now bore the Curse of Fire. Or at least, I thought I did.

What else could that have been?

My mind replayed the chopped-up memories from that night, of the shackles and how I'd disintegrated them to ash, off the wrists of the conscripted men—off Kaleb's wrists. Kaleb . . . I stumbled upon the image of him lying there, his lifeless eyes staring up at me, and I choked, my mind recoiling like a stepped-on snake.

I shoved the thought away and turned to Von. "Have you ever heard of someone having three Curses?" I asked, my voice breaking the steady hymn of our shoes crunching leaves.

He nodded. "Yes, many years ago, it was not uncommon to have more than one *Gift*. As you know, the Gifts came from the Old Gods. They were passed down to the Demi Gods. The Demi Gods then bred with humans and passed those gifts on to their children. But with each generation, the bloodlines became more diluted, and so the Curses did as well. That is why most people only have one Curse now."

I sat with that for a moment before I asked, "Why do you call them Gifts?"

"Because that's what they were always intended to be," Von replied, his elbow pointed to the sky, the basket slung behind his shoulder. Sunlight filtered through the swaying branches, dancing across his face. The dark-haired warrior looked so casual, so carefree—I liked seeing him like this.

"Did any of the Demi Gods have all six Curs—Gifts?" I inquired, banking on Mr. Know-it-all knowing it all.

He looked to the sky, returning the basket to his side. "There is no Demi God strong enough to possess all six." He turned to me. "However, there is one god that does."

"Really?!" I exclaimed, fascinated by this. I quickly realized that I sounded like a little kid. "Which one?"

When he didn't answer, I glanced his way, grinning.

My smile faltered—he wore that same pained expression as before—a hint of it—before it flashed away, that phantom mask slipping back into place. It was like a storm that came with a sudden onslaught of pounding rain and cracks of lightning and window-shaking thunder—visceral and real and raw, and gone as fast as it had come.

But I was tired of not knowing, so I threw that internal door open and chased after his storm. "Why do you do that? When I ask you certain things or our conversation goes a certain way, it's like . . ." I paused, trying to find the right words. There weren't any. No words in the English language could possibly describe *that* look. *Tortured* was as close as I could come, and even that seemed dimmed down. I licked my lips, trying again, without any idea what I was going to say. "It's like—"

He cut me off, his expression as bleak as his eyes. "It's you."

. . . What?

"I'm the reason you look like a steel blade slit you from hip to hip and your insides are being ripped out?" I half blurted, half seethed. My brow shot up as I repeated my words in my head. They weren't bad. I was getting closer, but still not quite there.

"Yes, it's because of you—vicious little creature," Von remarked coyly as he held a spindly, barren branch up, allowing me to pass underneath.

Misjudging how low to duck, I got a wisp of my hair

stuck. I tugged on it while the branch tugged back, snagging a few strands as a memento from its entanglement with me. The branch was as bad as Arkyn and his obsession with my hair, all because it reminded him of his dead lover. A ghost that haunted him, even in her death. And now, Von said *I* was the reason for his haunted expression? For his torture?

"Actually, you look much worse—it's a look akin to *death*." I paused, riding a wave of sudden emotion. "Also, I'm insulted."

Von smirked at that.

"I'm amusing to you now, am I?" I hissed as I tromped through a thick layer of leaves. The sound of crinkling destruction did wonders for my budding nerves.

Von caught my arm and spun me towards him, bringing our bodies a breath away from one another. Thick black lashes dipped slowly as his gaze raked over me, stoking my coals. His voice lowered, hitting that deep, decadent baritone. "I find you a *great* number of things."

My inner divine female stirred, awoken by the primal alpha male standing before her.

But as quickly as that fire was lit, guilt exhaled and blew it out.

I was a horrible person. My brother was dead, and I was here, living like it was just another day. But it wasn't. And it never would be again.

"I can't do this," I whispered under my breath.

I pulled away from Von and continued to the village.

Joe's bakery shop was closed according to the crooked sign hanging on the inside of the window.

But Joe's shop was closed on Mondays and Tuesdays, never Wednesdays. And I was fairly certain it was Wednesday—although the days had been a bit more blended lately. Also, it was early enough in the day that there was no way he would have run out of bread. Joe wasn't just like clockwork—he was the epitome of it. Unlike a lot of the vendors in this village, he was the one I could always count on. Always on time. Always there.

So, naturally, I concluded that Joe's shop was open and he'd simply forgotten to flip the sign. I slipped my hand into the brass handle, my thumb pushing down on the latch.

It didn't open.

"It's locked," Von stated, the basket thrown over his shoulder once again.

"It's just stuck," I exclaimed, jiggling the latch and the door. Neither of them budged. I turned to Von, gesturing to the door. "You try."

He sighed. Slipping his hand from his pocket, he wrapped his long fingers around the latch and gave it a go. Nothing happened. "Satisfied?" he asked, taking a step back, his gaze drifting lazily to a soldier standing at the end of the block.

"No," I said, moving to the window. I pressed my hands against the glass, filtering out the reflective sunlight. I peered in. The shelves were overflowing with bread—cinnamon rolls, buns, pastries, various loaves—onion included. My mouth watered. All of it was stocked and ready for a day of sales. I waited.

And waited some more.

But Joe never came out. A sickening feeling swarmed in my gut.

"Shadow walk me inside," I said, turning to Von, shoving myself into his side.

His brow darted up before his hand fell to the small of my back and he guided me around the corner of the building, where no one could see us, and shadow walked us inside.

The divine smell of yeast and flour and freshly baked dough hit me first, the interior of the building—the neat shelves and tiled floors—filled in next.

Von looked down at me, his lips twisting into a coy smile. "Shall I add bread thief to your growing list of titles?"

I squinted at him.

Turning my head and my attention, I called out, "Joe?"

Chapter 46

My search of the bakery turned up empty.

It occurred to me that after all of these years, I had no idea where Joe's actual home was. I decided I would ask Ezra when I returned. Looking for another missing male, I did a mental check for Soren, but still, there was nothing.

Sighing to myself, shoulders sagged in defeat, I glanced up at the sign gently swinging above. It read *Ferster's Food Shop,* the crisp white paint so fresh it still looked wet. The food shop used to belong to the Haymen family. I had never thought the owner, Rose—a woman who had been widowed in her younger years—would agree to sell it. She and her two sons had poured their heart and soul into this place, much like Joe had with his bakery. And yet, she'd sold her beloved shop.

I was reminded, in that moment, that time waited for no one and things continued to change. I cursed change under my tongue as I trotted up one lonely step and inside. The door, which looked brand new, was propped open, letting in the cool, autumn breeze. Von followed me inside, ducking under the too-short doorframe.

Years ago, the shop had been much smaller. When Rose and her husband—whose name I could not recall, as he'd died when I was young—purchased the shop, they also bought the building beside it. They knocked out the middle wall, joining the two, making it the largest food shop in Meristone—not that there was much for competition.

Not much had changed inside, other than the new door, a fresh coat of paint on the walls, and a few reorganized shelves. I supposed that was to be expected, as Rose had kept this place working like a well-oiled wheel. A few people waited in line at the front counter, while others drifted about. Some wandered aimlessly, pondering if they should buy this head of cabbage or that sack of potatoes, and others were more determined, grabbing what they needed before moving on to the next.

"Sage!" greeted a familiar male voice.

I smiled, recognizing it as soon as I heard it. There was no mistaking that accent anywhere, poised with clipped tones, spoken clearly and briskly and proper. It was almost melodic, like it had a ring to it.

"Thomas James Ferster," I said by way of greeting as I walked towards him, more excited to see him than I should be—considering how things ended between us last spring. Thomas was handsome, with his sandy-colored hair, deeply tanned skin, and sparkling, clear blue eyes. He looked like summer, or what I imagined a day at the beach must look like—not that I had ever been to a beach, unless the weedy bank of the lake counted as one. Thomas had a small gap between his two front teeth, and where most people couldn't pull a tooth gap off, he sure could. It added to his charm. He was dressed casually in brown trousers and a white tunic that hugged his lean, lightly muscled frame.

He flashed a grin, that space between his teeth making its debut. "Well, aren't you a sight for sore eyes." He looked me up and down for added emphasis.

I smiled warmly. "It's good to see you too." I raised my hands, gesturing to the shop. "This is all yours now, I take it?"

He grinned proudly, hands bracing on his hips as he took a look around, as if he were still walking in a dream and he had to survey it to make sure it was real. "Yes, she sure is. As of last week, actually."

"That's wonderful. Congratulations. I remember you talking about wanting to open up a food shop last spring. This is even better, really. It has everything you need," I said, feeling every ounce of my excitement for him. "How did you get Rose to agree to sell it?"

His smile shifted from daylight bright to a thin, downturned line. "You haven't heard then?"

"Heard what?" I asked, my brow lowered, hooked down by his solemn expression.

"Last month, Rose's two boys were conscripted under the order of the king. The wagon that was carrying them was involved in an accident. The boys managed to escape, along with some others. Charles and Danny came back to Meristone, rather than turning themselves in to the king, thus evading the draft—which, as you know, is a criminal offense." His accent thickened, and I thought he sounded a bit judgmental, like he disagreed with their choice to return. Like they should have handed themselves over to be slaughtered. It didn't sit well with me. "Rose hid them for two weeks in the cellar beneath." He tapped his foot on the wood plank, and my gaze drifted to the pristine floor.

I imagined her two wide-eyed sons hidden in the dark down there . . . how frightened they must have been, Rose included. I swallowed the lump forming in my throat.

Thomas's arms knitted loosely over his chest as he continued. "For two and a half weeks, Rose refused to open the shop. You know how this little town is—people started talking until finally the truth washed up, and it quickly spread. When the soldiers heard, they kicked the door in, searched the place, and dragged the boys and Rose out into the streets."

"What did they do with them?" I asked, glancing over my shoulder to the new door that was proudly swung open, allowing customers inside to shop—the evidence of what happened here so easily erased.

"Evading the draft of the king and aiding in the evasion are both punishable by death." There was no sympathy in his tone.

His reply hit me like a landslide, threatening to wash my feet out. If I had any tears left in me, I would have wept right there and then for Rose and her poor, poor boys.

Von moved behind me on soundless steps, his hand drifting to the small of my back, a gentle, steadying touch, like a tall, ancient tree, sturdy and sure, bracing me. Casually, he glanced around, his gaze pointedly wandering before it lazily drifted to the male standing before me.

"Hi there," Thomas said by way of greeting, his gaze darting between Von and me, trying to piece together what we were to one another.

As if Von noticed it, too, his hand shifted from the small of my back, his arm draping over my shoulders, intimately tugging me closely into him, staking his claim. Answering Thomas's question without so much as a word. "Hello, Tom," Von said flatly, using his name like he knew him. Judging by the off-kilter look on Thomas's face, he did not. Von, the predatory male, was playing his big cat, little mouse games.

Thomas's face turned ashen. "Sorry, Sage, it was nice chatting with you, but I have to get back to work." He scuttled back, raised his hands in defense, and then stumbled away, nearly tripping over the basket of granadilla—a fruit with an inviting, bright-orange exterior but filled with gray, slimy seeds on the inside. They tasted like frog eggs. I didn't know why the villagers ate them. Even Ezra wouldn't touch them.

"I look forward to seeing you *again*, Tom," Von called out as Thomas darted into the back. His words sounded like a promise, like it was inevitable that they would meet again.

I peered up at him accusingly. "What did you do to him?"

A careless, one-shoulder shrug. "Nothing he didn't deserve." Von walked over to a row of slanted wicker baskets. He inspected the fruit—apples, of course—discarding a few rotten ones on the sparkling, just swept floor—to my complete horror. Finally, he plucked a shiny, red apple from the pile. He brought it to his mouth and sunk his teeth into its flesh, eating it right there, in the middle of the store.

I made a disgruntled sound, muttering a few insults under my breath.

Von raised a black brow. "I'm sorry, Little Goddess." A sinful smile twisted the corners of his full, sensual mouth. He rolled his wrist towards me, offering the half-devoured apple.

"Would you like a bite?"

My stomach grumbled, begging me to partake. I almost reached out, almost pressed my lips against the decadent-looking fruit, but the way he said it, it sounded like one simple bite would cost me my life. And with Von, the king of inky deals, one could never be too sure.

"No, thank you," I declined before I briskly walked away.

I could hear him chuckle behind me, followed with a crunch as he took another bite.

I quickened my pace as if the hounds of the Spirit Realm were nipping at my ass.

Von and I returned to the footpath carved by my feet and Kaleb's, heading back towards the cottage.

I carried a sack of potatoes, while Von carried the rest—the basket and two heaped burlap sacks, a wispy leaf of cabbage sticking out on top, bobbing as he walked. Like this, my otherworldly, ancient warrior looked almost . . . mundane. I smiled softly, deciding I liked it. I paused, my mind backing up—*my*?

Since when did Von become *my*?

As if I had a right to stake a claim. And yet, when Thomas had looked at us, wondering what we were, Von had no problem staking his.

"The shopkeeper has feelings for you," Von stated flatly. It was the first thing he had said since we started our walk back.

Apparently, I wasn't the only one thinking about Thomas and relationships and claims.

"I'm aware," I said, watching Von, who looked less than pleased—annoyed, even. I gargled a thought, swishing it around—was this mighty, powerful male jealous? I smirked. Now *that* was a juicy one. I had to know. I decided to test my theory. "We courted last spring, a record three months. It was the longest relationship I have ever been in."

Von snorted at that.

I quirked a brow before I continued delving in. "Thomas's father was a shopkeeper, and his grandfather before him. He grew up in one. He dreamed of running his own, just like his father. I'm happy he was able to accomplish his goal." I paused, pivoting to the next part of my plan. "I'm sure you are wondering why we broke up." I doubted he was, doubted he wanted to hear anymore, yet this was too fun to give up now. I'd get him back for his apple antics, one way or another. I prattled on, "Kaleb didn't really like him. Also, he thought he was a bit old for me. I didn't see the problem with the nine-year gap between us. Many women marry older men. And . . ." Oh, this was going to get dirty. "He was pretty good in bed."

Von stopped dead.

"Goddess divine, you *are* jealous, aren't you?" I exclaimed, reveling in my victory.

It was short-lived.

Von dropped the basket and the sacks. His bootheel crunched a string bean as he strode towards me, rearing me back, like a helpless sheep driven through a chute. With my back firmly pressed against a tree, Von stood at my front, towering. His sleeves were rolled back, exposing his tattooed forearms. He gripped the trunk on either side of me, caging me in, the bark itself gasping under his grip.

"No." He bared his teeth. "I am territorial."

I eyed those sharp white canines—why did they seem longer than before? My throat bobbed—something felt stuck there. I wondered if I had forgotten and taken a bite of that apple and now it was lodged in my throat.

"What's the difference?" I asked, fixated by those incredible incisors. In the deepest crevices of my mind, the places filled with empty paper and cobwebs, there was something, a memory perhaps, that seemed to stretch and stir. Those teeth—I had felt them sink into me before. An indecent blush dusted my cheeks as liquid heat pooled low.

"Jealousy is when you covet something that is not yours," Von said, lowering his face, hovering his lips just over mine. His fingers weaved into my hair. "Territorial is protecting what is yours." He tipped my head back, exposing the length of my neck. "And you, sweet angel, are forever mine."

And that was when he *bit* me.

A flash of sharp pain seared into my neck, and just when I was about to scream, a moan escaped instead as pleasure swept over me. Rapturous. And fast.

He scattered my thoughts like ash on the wind, with his teeth embedded in my neck.

His free hand moved to my waist, and he pulled me against his hard, forceful edges. His other hand kept my head in place as he drank from me. I didn't fight him. No, freely, I let him.

In return, he took me higher, my body trembling at the tidal wave of oncoming climax. It was too much. Frightened by the height of it, I braced myself for impact as it dragged me under into a release of bliss so pure, so intense, my legs gave out underneath me.

I would have fallen if Von had not held me to him. His tongue slid across the throbbing wound, healing it in one sweep but allowing the tenderness of it to remain, a stinging sensation reminding me of his claim. *Mine.*

Slowly, he lifted his head. With my blood on his lips and the taste of me in his mouth, he peered down at me, those emerald-green eyes framed in heavy black lashes. I felt a sense of satisfaction seeing the deep, rich color return. His tongue swept over his lips, his eyes closing briefly, and when he opened them—there was nothing human about them. Only beast.

"Do you want a taste?" he asked, lowering his lips just over mine.

I didn't need to think about it.

My arms wrapped around his neck as my mouth clashed against his, our teeth clacking with the impact. His tongue tangled with mine, and the taste of copper bloomed inside my mouth. I didn't know if it was because Von was kissing me, but the taste of my blood was somehow sweeter, as if a droplet of honey had been added to it.

I reached for the hem of his shirt, pulling it up, breaking our kiss so I could lift it over his head. His lips came crashing down on mine as I tossed his black tunic carelessly to the ground. His hands moved to my pants, shoving them down while my hands worked on his belt. He snarled when I broke the kiss to get a better look at my fumbling fingers.

"Fuck this," he growled, and suddenly, my clothes were gone.

Just like that. Not even a snap of his fingers. Just gone. That was going to take some getting used to—then again, with Von, I doubted I would ever get used to these things.

Bark scratched against my skin, grating my already electrified nerves as the cool air drifted over me, stirring a shiver, pebbling my nipples. But it wasn't just the cool air that was to blame—it was the way Von was looking at me—like I was a juicy red apple, ripe for plucking. Replace the 'pl' with an 'f' and you get the idea.

Slowly, black lashes lowered, his gaze trailing down the length of my body, my skin catching in his inferno. "So fucking beautiful, Little Goddess," he murmured darkly.

My gaze snagged on those dangerously stacked abs—so chiselled, I could use them as a washboard. So chiselled, I wanted to rub up all over them. Skin upon skin. Flesh upon flesh.

My fingertips leisurely slid down his torso, exploring, learning—his muscles contracting under my touch. When I reached his pants, I looked up and asked, "Why am I the only one naked?"

Von gave me a sinful smirk, the kind that dropped my heartbeat all the way down to my core—electrifying it. His hand roamed down the length of my body, those ringed fingers slipping between my folds, spreading them, a finger teasing my entrance, testing the wetness, "Because, Little Goddess—" His finger dipped inside. "—you are not ready to have sex with me."

I gasped at the feel of him, at that intrusive large finger, pushing its way in, claiming and damning me all in one stroke. "What does that mean?" I asked, my voice as shaky as my inhale.

"It means . . ." He pressed a second finger in, stretching me, and I moaned. His were so much better than mine—they were so much bigger, longer. "I'm not like the men you fucked before." He twirled his fingers just right, working that sacred spot inside—the one that made it hard to stand.

"Von!" I cried out, his sinful ministrations causing my eyes to roll back. My hand grabbed hold of his forearm, and I felt those steely muscles work as he pumped his fingers. There was something about feeling that incredible strength in his arm and knowing what he was doing to me that painted me all shades of wild.

Cool metal bit into the bottom of my chin, forcing me to look up at him. "I'm no five incher, Kitten—" He pressed a third finger inside, stretching my walls beyond reason. "—and as much as I need to fuck you, to bury myself in you, to claim you, I have no intentions of doing so until your body is ready for mine."

I exhaled a shaky, shaky breath, and he inhaled it, his mouth capturing mine, consuming my moans—*consuming* me. His hand wrapped around the base of my neck, keeping me there as he kissed me so purposefully, so intently, I no longer knew where he began and I ended. He withdrew his fingers, not enough to slide out, but just enough to relieve the pressure, and then he began to work them in expert, soft strokes, gently breaking me in, thrust by thrust. Slowly, his tempo increased, until those three ruthless fingers were pounding pleasure into my sex, forcing me to accept what he was offering.

Von was an inescapable storm. He was going to consume me completely and I would let him.

My breathing turned erratic as my hips bucked against his hand, meeting his powerful thrusts. I weaved my fingers into his hair, securing myself to him, bringing his blazing inferno closer, and still it wasn't close enough. I wanted him in me. Everywhere. Touching and tasting and taking.

He tore his lips from mine, trailing passionate, scalding kisses over my jaw and down my neck, mapping out his lust. When he ran his thick tongue over the sensitive bitemark, hot, white rapture surged straight to my core. Coupled with his wicked, wicked fingers, my body exploded with an orgasm so strong that my breathing turned labored and my knees gave out. Von caught me before I could fall.

"That's it, Kitten, give it to me," he purred as I rode out those powerful tremors working their way throughout my body, each one starting where his fingers stroked me, drawing my climax out in length and intensity.

When I finished, he withdrew his fingers, leaving me empty and clenching at nothing—searching for him. A gush of arousal slipped out, coating my thighs. His hand slid between my legs, his fingertips tracking the extent of my pleasure.

"What a beautiful little mess you've made," he teased, clicking his tongue. "Shall I clean you up?"

Before I could ask what he meant, the towering warrior lowered to his knees. It was like watching a king relinquishing his throne, and it did inexplainable things to me. Adrenaline laced with power forged within my soul, and it was a potent combination.

"Spread for me." He wasn't asking. Nor did he need to.

Without a second thought, I widened my stance.

"Good girl," he praised. One large hand cuffed the back of my leg, holding me there as he brought his mouth to that sensitive part of my inner thigh, coated in my wetness. His heated breath skittered over my skin in warning before he ran his tongue upwards, lapping me up. Lick by incredible lick.

I held onto his sturdy shoulders, my jaw unhinged as his tongue laved my skin, cleaning me, all the while tasting me. Savouring me. I realized, in that moment, that I was forever fucked, because no male could ever compete to the one kneeling before me.

When he was done, but still positioned between my legs, he looked up, his incredible green eyes meeting mine. He purred in that throaty, sated tone, "On the contrary, Little Goddess, the victory is all mine."

And truly, it was.

After I regained sensation in my legs, and somewhat of a half functioning brain, I got dressed and then we gathered the food and continued onwards, leaving the squashed string bean behind.

Forget Von being a Demi God—he was something of his own design.

"I'm tempted to ask what you are—" I said ever so casually, like I hadn't just had my neck tapped into like a keg full of red wine and my nether regions roughly and thoroughly finger banged. "—but I have a feeling it rhymes with something that goes bump in the night."

Von tipped his head back and laughed, my blood and arousal now gone from his lips, although the deep green color of his eyes remained.

"Actually, I don't think I want to know what you are," I followed up, banking on the whole ignorance being bliss thing. Besides, my mind had been ransacked with things I had yet to process.

"Then we can revisit this topic another time. I will, however, tell you two truths," Von said, tipping his head to the side in that *I own all I survey* look, a look that only he could pull off.

I waited for him to continue, all the while taking him in. There were times when he looked dark and menacing and warrior-like, but right now, he looked ethereal. He had called me an angel moments ago, yet it was him that looked like one now, his sinfully handsome features framed by his black hair blowing freely in the wind.

"The first is that you have horrible taste in men." His black lashes flickered, eyes shifting pointedly to me.

I scowled, instantly retracting the angel tag. Bastard was more like it.

"The second truth is that *Tom* is the one who ratted to the soldiers that the original owner was hiding her sons."

My feet slowed. "Why would Thomas tell the soldiers about Rose?"

Von gave me a look as if to say, *Really?*

I shook my head. "I know he wanted a food shop, but he

wouldn't be *that* desperate. That low. No. He wouldn't do that," I denied, my words less than convincing.

"Wouldn't he?" Von asked over his shoulder as he continued to walk forward.

I didn't know.

If he had . . .

Something fierce filled my veins. If he *had* told on Rose, if he was the reason she and her sons were dead, just so that he could acquire her shop . . .

I felt murderous and sick with nausea . . . I'd slept with *that* prick.

I sped up my turtle speed and caught up to Von, all the while fighting the bile rising in my throat. My face probably looked as sour as the taste in my mouth.

Von glanced at me. "As I said, horrible taste in men."

"I like *you*," I jabbed.

He nodded, flashing those wickedly sharp teeth. "Exactly."

Chapter 47

I dried my hands on the corner of my apron while I leaned over the counter, trying to decipher the recipe written in Kaleb's chicken scratch. Kaleb never did much cooking—he had one signature dish, and this was it.

The stubborn drawer resisted when I tried to pull it open. Something was lodged inside, keeping it closed. I wedged my hand in, the top of the drawer biting against my wrist. I pushed down the wooden spatula inside and the drawer opened. I plucked out a knife and shoved the drawer shut with the side of my hip.

After I diced the red peppers and onions, I threw them into a sizzling pan over a dim fire—perfect for cooking over. I sautéed them in a thick layer of butter, scenting the kitchen in the smells of a homemade meal. I breathed them in, remembering when I would come home from training and Kaleb would be here, standing in this very spot, cooking this very dish.

My gut twisted.

I returned to the counter and grabbed a bowl from a top shelf, inspecting it to ensure it was clean, then moved on to cracking eggs.

Besides the crackling fire and sputtering frying pan, the cottage was quiet—Ezra's door still closed, despite it being around noon. Von had left shortly after we returned to the cottage. Wherever he shadow walked to, he didn't bother to say. When he was coming back, he also didn't bother to say. My fingers drifted to my neck, floating over the now-healed spot. As soon as I touched it, a droplet of a shiver grew in intensity, rippling throughout my body. I clutched the counter to steady myself, my eyes going wide.

What was that?

The smell of something burning wafted towards me. Cursing, I grabbed a towel, wrapped it around the handle of the pan, and took it off the fire. I eyed the sad, burnt crisps of peppers and onions and charcoaled butter. Sighing, I dumped them out and started all over again.

After lunch was done, I carried two heaping plates outside.

"I made your signature dish." I lowered the plate on top of his resting place, just beside his axe. I sat down on the lumpy ground, crossing my legs, and deep dived into a bit of sibling rivalry. "Looks like the competition is on now." I shifted to a cocky tone. "I'm not bragging, but I'm pretty sure I've got you beat."

I waited for Kaleb to reply, to make things interesting by raising the stakes, just as he usually did. When he didn't, I continued, "Loser does dishes for a week?" I nodded, confirming that was the deal, and cut into the ingredient-specific omelet with the side of my fork. I took my first bite. Tasting it, I let it sit on my tongue. But as I looked at my brother's untouched plate, it turned bland in my mouth.

My shoulders drooped. "It's not as good as yours."

After I was done eating, I returned inside and cleaned up my cooking-derived mess. When everything was clean and sparkling, I leaned against the counter, my hands spreading out behind me. I tilted my head to the side, eyeing Ezra's closed door. This was ridiculous. She had never slept in this long before. I took the dishcloth draped over my shoulder, flopped it over the sink, and trotted over to her door.

I knocked gently against it before I propped it open, sticking my head through the crack in the door. "Ezra?"

Clothes were strewn carelessly on the floor, creating a trail that led up to the bed. I eyed a suspicious pair of pants— they looked like a man's. My gaze shifted, moving to the carefully polished shoes that clearly also belonged to a man, one teetering on its side and the other sitting upright, like their owner had been in a hurry to get them off.

Ezra's head popped up from under the sheets, her gray hair wild, her milky white eyes even wilder.

A second head darted up just behind her.

I gasped.

Joe gasped.

Ezra flopped back down, her hand shooting out from the covers, dismissing me as if I were unwanted room service.

Joe sat at the table while Ezra bumbled around the kitchen, the hem of her robe dusting the floor. I stood by the dwindling fire, warming up lunch for the two apparent lovebirds.

Joe cleared his throat, his voice solemn. "I am sorry about Kaleb."

My breath caught, hooked in the back of my throat. It was strange hearing those words strung together.

"Thank you, Joe," I squeezed out, eyes locked on a dark knot in the floorboards, staring at nothing.

The cottage fell silent.

"Eureka!" Ezra suddenly cried out.

Joe and I both jumped, our heads swiveling towards her. She cradled a mason jar, filled with gods only knew what, against her cheek. She shuffled towards the table and then motioned for me to come sit down.

I took the sizzling cast-iron pan off the fire, dished up two plates, and served them. As soon as I set it down in front of Ezra, she shoved it to the side with the back of her hand. I debated pushing it back in front of her, just to mess with her, but decided not to, in case she shoved it onto the floor next.

"Come, child, sit down and let me show you," she said, petting the side of the jar as if it were a spoiled housecat.

I plopped into the wooden chair, watching skeptically as her wiry fingers began to unscrew the lid. When she opened it up, on reflex, I paused my breath and leaned back, eyes darting over to Joe, who didn't appear to smell anything foul. I tested the air, daring a delicate sniff. I scented nothing, just the leftover smells from lunch—a sweet harmony of onions and peppers and spices.

Ezra turned the jar over and dumped the contents out onto the table. Dirt came pouring out. I rolled my eyes, shifting to get up from the table.

"Patience, child," Ezra said, her head dipping close to the table as she shifted the dirt around, her finger hooking on a black string. Smiling, she yanked it up, revealing a dirty ring.

"Kaleb's mother wasn't a day over sixteen when she found out she was pregnant with him." She inspected the ring with her vacant eyes, turning it over in her aged hands, rubbing this spot and that. "She was the daughter of a noble house. And as you know, a child born out of wedlock, well, it would ruin her and her family name. Not wanting to face condemnation from the community, her mother sent her to see me for a tonic to end the pregnancy. But when I pressed my hand to her stomach, I felt the fate of the child being knitted beneath. I told her I could not make the tonic." Ezra shook her head as if she were saying no once again. "The poor thing sobbed. You see, she was afraid, afraid of what her father would do when she told him. Afraid no man would marry her because she was 'soiled goods.'" Ezra chuckled. "Those were her own words, not mine." She tipped her head thoughtfully to the side, chuckling some more. "What a strange notion. A woman . . . soiled goods."

"A silly one, indeed," Joe agreed as he worked on the last two bites of his food.

I blinked, watching him and then Ezra, noting how comfortable they were with one another. I wondered how long Joe had been sneaking into Ezra's room. Decided maybe I didn't want to know.

"So then, what happened to Kaleb's mom?" I asked, wanting to hear more.

"I agreed to help her, to raise Kaleb as my own. After a

bit of persuading, her mother agreed to it as well. She told her husband that her daughter was going to visit an aunt and sent her to live with me for the next eight months. After Kaleb was born, she returned to her family home, just in time to learn that her father had accepted a request for her hand in marriage—a duke from the west, if memory serves correct. Before she was due to travel to her new home, she came by and gave me this ring." Ezra handed it to me.

I took it, studied it in my palm. A thin gold band endorsed an intricate, scalloped bezel shaped like a flower. A sizable sapphire, oval in shape, was nestled in the bezel. I couldn't imagine what something like this must have cost.

"It was her engagement ring," Ezra added.

"Why did she give it to you?" I asked, shifting the ring, watching how the light caught the sapphire, making it dance and twinkle, even with a layer of dirt on it.

"She asked me to sell it and use the money to give Kaleb a good life. But I didn't need money to give Kaleb a good life. It was the only thing I had of his mother, so I decided to keep it. I had hoped to give it to him when he found love." She tapped her chin. "I'm giving it to you now, to keep for him."

I bit my bottom lip, staring down at the ring. It suddenly felt a lot heavier. "Why didn't you ever tell Kaleb the truth about his mom?"

"I intended to tell him on the day I gave him the ring," Ezra said, her shoulders slumped down. "But I never got the chance."

Joe reached over the table and patted her hand. "You did the best you could, Firecracker."

My eyes narrowed. *Firecracker?*

"Thank you, dear," Ezra said. It might have been the most mundane string of words I had ever heard come out of her. It was weird. All of this was weird.

I looked down at the ring. "What do I do with it?"
Ezra winked, her milky white orbs staring right on past me.
"You keep it safe until you can return it."

Chapter 48

One week had passed since I'd last seen the dark, brooding male. Von had said he was going to be away for a little while, following up on a lead in his search for the Crown of Thorns and checking up on the others who were still in Belamour, searching for Soren. I was tempted to ask him if I could go with him because I did miss Harper, Lyra and Ryker, but I felt like Ezra needed me more right now, so I decided to stay. Von also mentioned something about paying his sister a visit while he was in Belamour. I couldn't imagine that would be pleasant—for either of them.

I wasn't worried about Von. I had seen firsthand the type of power he wielded—felt it kiss the back of my neck at the same time it broke the bones of soldiers. If anyone could handle themselves, it was Von.

So why did his seven-day absence bother me?

Well, at the base of it—I missed him.

I missed him to the extent that I even tried talking to Ezra about it, but she was about as knowledgeable as the floorboards. In fact, the creaking slabs provided more conversation than her lately.

Ezra was in full-on Ezra mode. I thought the weight of Kaleb's death was starting to wear on her, even though when I prodded her about it, she insisted that wasn't it—that change was on the horizon, whatever that meant.

She kept herself busy, producing enough tonics and salves to fully stock an apothecary. They were everywhere— in the cupboards, on the floors, filling every nook and cranny, every ledge and every sill. Some of them even made their way up to the loft, infringing on my teeny tiny territory. The cottage was drowning in little glass vials and metal tins. Apart from them being everywhere, I also wondered how safe it was having that many inside, wondered what might happen if they spilled and their contents mixed.

Ka-boof! answered my mind.

My solution? Sell them. And so, every morning, I filled my basket carefully and headed into the village, to the market. Which was what I was doing now—working at the market.

Today was busy, more than usual. I eyed the scattered vials and salves. They were organized this morning, not that I could say the same for them now—who knew Ezra's tonic and salves would be in such hot demand? I certainly hadn't. I maneuvered a few, putting them back where they belonged, but gods, the table was a mess. The sporadic, colorful pattern of the tablecloth below wasn't helping with the chaos either. I decided I wouldn't use it again.

"I'll trade you six beets for the canker salve," said a blue-eyed woman who wore a bonnet on her head, her curly brown hair spilling out from underneath. She was a stocky woman, riddled with premature wrinkles—a telltale sign of a hard life. Two young children hovered closely by her side. She fisted the drooping stems, the large beets turned upside down, and thrust them in my face.

Gently, I pushed them and her hand to the side, out of my face. "Sorry." I gestured to the heaped bucket of beets behind the table—the common currency for the past few days. "I can only eat so much borscht. What else do you have to trade?"

The little girl who hung to her mother's leg looked up at me, offering me a big, toothy grin. She wore a matching bonnet, just like her mother's. She was a cute little thing, big blue eyes and blonde hair. Warmly, I smiled back. The other one, a boy, maybe a year older than the girl, wrapped his hands around the nook of his mother's elbow and gave a gallant tug. "Come on, Mama, I want to go home."

"Hush, child," the woman scolded, tugging her arm away. She flipped the cotton cover over her basket and began to rifle threw the variety of vegetables. She produced a stash of carrots, her gaze darting to me.

I sucked my teeth, motioning to the bucket sitting beside the beets—chock-full of carrots. I gave her an apologetic shrug.

She huffed at me, dug in her coin purse, and then slammed three coins down on the table. The force of it caused the vials and salves to chatter in response. Lifting her head, she glared at me. "Fine. But not a copper more."

I plucked the two coins, leaving the third. "Two coins is fine."

Her expression softened, like butter taken from the cellar and left out on the counter. "But I saw what the last lady paid for the same salve. She gave you four coins. And they were minted with the king's head."

I shrugged. "It's fine. Besides, you have more mouths to feed." My gaze roamed over the table as I looked for the canker salve. Finding the small golden tin, I plucked it and handed it to her.

"Thank you," she said as she took it. She placed it in her basket, bid me goodbye, and then stalked over to another vender a few tables down from mine. She tried to exchange her beets for something else, but the seller turned her down. Huffing, she trotted away, her little ducklings closely in tow.

I leaned forward, dropped my elbow on the table, and plopped my chin into my hand. The three reminded me of my younger years, when Ezra would bring Kaleb and me into the village to get groceries. That felt like a lifetime ago.

A dull ache formed in my chest.

Pulling away from the table, I took the two coins and dropped them into my coin pouch. I tested the weight in my palm, feeling a sense of satisfaction at the hefty, jiggling coin. Kaleb would have been proud.

"Hello, Sage," grunted Joe, his arms carrying a large bag of flour. He flopped it onto the ground, the force emitting a puff of white. His hands shot to his back as he stretched it out, blowing out a breath of air.

"Hi, Joe," I answered with a smile. I pointed to the bag. "Do you need some help with that?"

"No, no." He shook his hands and his head, emphasizing his response. "It's good for me. Keeps me in shape." His wiry brow dropped as he took in all the tonics and salves on the table before his eyes shifted back up to my face, his voice

386

sprinkled with concern. "How's she doing?"

I tilted my head from side to side, weighing my response. "She's doing alright. She seems to be slowing down a little. But that could be because she is running low on tins."

Ah yes, the treasured tin. Ezra had asked me to pick some more up in town today, but I decided not to—I wasn't sure if I wanted to feed her latest obsession. Then again, it was better than her just sitting around, not that she was the sitting around type—she was *always* doing something weird.

"I'm relieved to hear she is doing alright. I know how much Kaleb meant to her. How much you both mean to her," Joe said as he pulled out a handkerchief from his shirt pocket. He dabbed his slick brow with it before he neatly folded it and returned it to its designated spot.

"You mean a lot to her as well." I swished my lips to the side, pondering a thought before I voiced it. I decided to lead into it instead. "Can I ask you a question, Joe?"

He nodded once, a smile on his face. "Of course, what is it?"

"I know you proposed to Ezra a few times, many years ago. When she said no, why didn't you ever marry anyone else?" I asked, leaning in.

As bright as starlight, a twinkle blossomed in his eye. He shook his head, as if he, too, were still mystified by it. Finally, he said, "I guess the heart wants what the heart wants."

I smiled while releasing a breath of air through my nose. "I've heard that expression before. But still, I don't quite understand it."

"Ah, well, I hope someday, you are given the chance to experience it firsthand. There is no better feeling in the world than true love. It's the only thing that can stand the test of time." He sealed his words with a wink before he rubbed his hands together and heaved the flour sack over his shoulder. "Well, I better get this back to the bakery before the mice catch a whiff. It was good seeing you, Sage. Take care," he grunted before he turned and walked away.

"You as well, Joe. Take care," I called out, smiling to myself.

As the sun lowered in the sky, and the busy hustle and bustle of the market began to die down, Joe's words continued to repeat in my mind. I wondered what it would be like to feel that type of love for someone. One that was forgiving, sturdy, and certain. Something so deeply sowed, it lasted a lifetime—even longer than that.

My thoughts turned to Von and I wondered when he was coming back.

After the market, I returned to the cottage. Ezra was nowhere to be found. Knowing her hokey pokey patterns, I figured she must have gone out to collect more herbs or rocks or something.

I started a fire in the fireplace, utilizing the natural way and not my Fire Curse—an anomaly I had yet to practice with—not that I felt like training lately.

When the fire reached a steady, consistent flame, I brought in some more split logs. I didn't have it in me to chop any wood, even though that was a task that desperately needed to be done. Winter was well on her merry, frigid way.

But chopping wood, that had been Kaleb's job, not mine, and if I were to do it, it seemed like it would make things more . . . finalized. And I wasn't ready for that. So, I turned my sights on the heaping pile of beets and started the tedious process of making borscht.

When it was done and piping hot, I sat and ate and wondered what I was going to do with the rest of the beets. Deciding I'd make them tomorrow's problem, I put them in the cellar. After, I cleaned up my mess and then collapsed on the settee, my body tired from the length of the day.

The cottage was quiet.

And where I once would have taken solace in the quiet, now, I found it painful. Lonely. Suddenly, my bones were not so weary anymore, and sitting here alone was the last place I wanted to be.

Chapter 49

My toes squished into the muddy bottom of the lake as I padded along the bank, the water bathing my ankles. I traced the crisp blue outline as it stretched before me. It formed a stark silhouette against the autumn-painted ridge of the bank, covered with tall switchgrass, the wispy, seeded pods swaying under the command of the playful breeze. Their seeds would be scattered by the wind, ready to grow next spring.

Here, the world was quiet, other than the faintest whisper of hummingbird wings, reminding me of the first time I heard the sound, just before Arkyn threw me into the Endless Mist. How had I never heard it before?

My gaze shifted to the never-ending wall of black fog— the Endless Mist. I had never bothered to think much of it before. I had never seen the point in doing so. It was there, and I was here. We were two separate things. But that was then, before everything happened, and now, I found myself feeling . . . explorative.

Leaving the cusp of the cool waters with my shoes in one

hand, I walked on a steady incline, towards the Endless Mist. Rocks, polished by friction and time, dug into the soles of my feet as I padded over the rocky ground, through the sparse, crunchy grass.

I didn't realize how much I needed this, to be back here, in this familiar place. Second to the cottage, this lake was my home. During my younger years, when my Curse was unstable, this was where I would come. The lake safeguarded my deepest secret, embraced it when I needed to let it out. And now, with the loss of my brother, I needed it more than ever.

I breathed in deeply, filling my lungs with crisp lake air.

It took me about thirty, maybe thirty-five minutes to reach the Endless Mist, the metallic trill of fluttering wings growing louder the closer I got. I craned my neck, looking up and up and up. It reached to the sky, to the beyond. It was like a massive black axe had swung down and severed Edenvale from the outside world.

It hummed in my ears, a steady enchantment, calling me to it. Like a bee drawn to honey, my hesitant fingers uncurled, flexing straight as I reached out.

A hand, painted in shadow, formed from the Mist and reached for mine.

I did not know why, but I did not fear it.

When our hands touched, ethereal voices echoed, all of them speaking to me. "Who are you?" they asked.

"I don't know," I whispered back.

"Come back when you do," commanded the beautiful voices. It was the same sparkling-sweet tone I had heard before—the same voices that belonged to the woman who wore my face.

"Why?" I asked, my brows weighed down by a multitude of unanswered questions.

No answer came as the hand pulled back, returning to the Mist.

"Wait!" I tried to grab hold of the hand made of shadow, but my fingers sailed straight through, and the hand made of fog dissolved instantly.

I fidgeted with Kaleb's mother's ring. I felt lost, even more so than before.

Deciding I should head back to the cottage, I turned around, went to take my first step, but it was the immense heat that stopped me dead. The front of my body lit in an unnatural, orange-red glow.

My heart galloped in my chest, tears filling my eyes.

Below, the oaks stirred unnaturally from their slumber, jerked awake by the flames that licked and chewed their vacant branches. From here, they looked like giant torches, shoved into the ground. The blaze spread among them, jumping like a disease, from one to the next. The blue sky sputtered, choking on the heavy smoke as it clawed its way up, higher and higher. Hundreds of birds flocked to the sky, abandoning their homes, fleeing the inferno.

The forest—*my forest*—*my home*—it was on fire.

"Ezra!" I screamed, as I ran straight for the blaze.

Chapter 50

By the time I got past the lake, the fire had grown in intensity and size, spreading itself out, a blanket of flame thrown over the trees. The roar of it was loud, but the crackling, explosive sound the oak trees made as they fell was deafening. The way they combusted when they hit the ground, it sounded like they had been struck by lightning.

And when those ancient oaks fell, the earth trembled beneath my feet.

"Ezra!" I screamed her name over and over again. I was desperate to find her.

Another tree fell, landing just to the left of me, nearly bringing me down with it. Scrambling, I darted forward, towards the cottage, out of the reach of the flames chewing on the vacant branches of a red dogwood bush.

A widow-maker pine hung on another tree, then it came thundering down. I leapt backwards, narrowly missing it as it fell. It blocked my path. My hand shot forward, a blast of water emitting from my palm. The flames that ravaged that tree hissed in agony as I put them out. Steam and smoke weighed the air down, thick and heavy, riddling my lungs. I coughed and covered my mouth with the crook of my arm, my eyes burning as I peered over top.

I pressed on, but I wasn't so sure I knew where I was going anymore. The markings I had etched into the trees when I was a child to guide me back to the cottage were gone, and although I had outgrown them years ago, I no longer recognized the forest anymore.

When I was certain I was lost, that the inferno had swallowed me whole and I was now stuck inside this never-ending maze made of flame, when hope was about to give out, that was when I saw it—the cottage.

And by the grace of the gods, it was completely untouched.

I raced towards it, lungs working on borrowed time. My sleeve caught on a tree, pulling me back. I turned, eyes going wide—it was not a tree.

The raven was large, its feathers oddly light—just like the sickly one I saw the night we buried my brother. It looked healthy now, its massive wings flapping as it stayed suspended in the air, its beak tugging on my sleeve like it was trying to pull me back—away from the cottage.

I fought with it, surprised by its strength.

A scream—Ezra's scream—slammed into me.

Adrenaline coursed through my veins. I gave a final tug, and my sleeve sprung free. Twirling, my feet nearly tangled up in one another, I moved as fast as my legs would carry me.

The bird tailed me, dipping in front of me, trying to cut me off.

I threw a water ball at it, aiming just below it—not enough to hit it but enough to scare it off. It worked, granting me enough time to get ahead. Heart pounding, lungs hissing, I slipped my hand around the doorknob, not bothering to care if it scalded my fingers to the bone. But it wasn't hot. It was cool to the touch—an anomaly I had no time to think about. I swung the door open, my eyes darting around, falling, stumbling, when I saw Ezra standing there—a blade held to her throat.

My heart missed its beat.

"Soren?" I asked the boy I once thought of as a brother—the boy who now stood behind Ezra, his hand holding the dagger.

Ezra's eyes were even more vacant than usual. She stood there, her face impossibly blank, like she was a lifeless husk, her spirit gone. Something was very, very wrong.

"I am so sorry, Sage," Soren replied, his eyes wide, filled with horror. His hand shook, making me even more nervous.

I raised my hands slowly, gesturing defensively, as if I were no threat. "It's okay, Soren. Just please put the knife down and we can talk."

"They didn't give me a choice," Soren said, his voice raised, tears gathering in the corners of his eyes.

"*Who* didn't give you a choice?" I asked, trying to make him feel like he was being heard all the while stumbling to form a plan.

"The king's men!" Soren screamed, his hand shaking. The blade bit into Ezra's throat, drawing a droplet of blood to the surface. Her expression never changed, worrying me even more.

"Please, Sor, please, don't hurt her," I pleaded, my legs wobbling beneath me, and I was suddenly uncertain if they could bear my weight. I needed to keep him busy, to buy more time. "Tell me what happened." My voice was steeped in false warmth.

"I awoke in a cold, damp cell, the back of my head aching, an arrow embedded in my chest. I learned from the prisoner next to me that I was in Clearwell Castle. They didn't give me much for food or water—made me sit in my own filth, like I was a lowly, dying animal. I suppose to them, that's what I was. Then the guards came in and dragged me out. They took me to a room buried in the back of the dungeon—to a place that echoed with screams, the kind you never forget. There, they . . . they—" he stuttered. He held up his left hand, revealing the gruesome, leftover nubs, cauterized on the ends. Only two fingers were left. "They cut them off, Sage. They said they had two questions they needed answered—two questions and the pain would stop. They wanted to know who the Cursed girl was who freed the conscripted soldiers and where to find her." Soren paused briefly. "At first, I didn't tell them. Not for the first two fingers, but when they got to the middle one, when that blade bit in . . ." Soren turned ashen, the blood chased out of his skin. I wondered if he might pass out—prayed, he would—but a strange, disbelieving giggle slipped out of him instead. "I told them everything they wanted to know. I didn't have a choice. If I didn't agree, I would have died—whether that was directly because of them or the infected arrow wound in my chest." He shook his head, his voice a whisper, twined with a shaky breath. "I just . . . I don't want to end up like my parents."

"It's okay. I understand," I lied, my tone honey sweet. I didn't understand—I would have let them take every digit before I gave up my family and friends.

"You weren't there. You don't know what it was like," Soren seethed, defending himself.

I stiffened, remembering he had access to my thoughts. "We have time," I started, treading carefully. "The forest is on fire. They will have trouble navigating it right now. We can escape. You, me, and Ezra—we'll go to the Cursed Lands. Together. There is still time," I exclaimed, taking a daring step forward, testing his limits, as well as mine.

"No, there is no time." Soren performed a somber shake of his head. He didn't connect his gaze with mine, instead just staring, his eyes downcast to the floor. "They are waiting for you outside."

"No one is outside," I countered. "The forest is on fire."

"There is no fire."

"What?"

"When we showed up and you weren't here, I knew you must be close. I needed a way to draw you out, so I planted the image in your mind that the forest was on fire. I knew you would come looking for Ezra."

"But I saw the flames—" I sputtered, unable to form words. The heat of it. The smoke. All of it, it was real . . . Wasn't it?

"Turn around," Soren instructed, his voice sounding so incredibly unfamiliar. It was harder, older, and so unlike the boy I once knew.

"Please," I pleaded, my mind frantic. I couldn't do this

again. The three of us had just been reunited, and now . . .

"Turn around!" he screamed, angling the knife, threatening to make it bite.

"Okay, okay, I will. Just please don't hurt her." My eyes lingered, tracing Ezra's face, memorizing the laugh lines and all they represented, inhaling it all, as if it were my dying breath, before I complied and turned around.

"Walk out the door."

I did, my steps slow, uncertain. When I opened the door, when I stepped outside, it was hard to trust my eyes.

The oak trees stood, slumbering peacefully, untouched and whole. The sky was an azure blue, dotted with white, cottony clouds. They drifted leisurely, as if they had all the time in the world. The birds tweeted their songs as if it were just another day.

There were no flames. No fire.

What I was seeing warred with the blazing inferno replaying in my mind, the destruction, the chaos I had just witnessed. The two separate realities flickered back and forth, fighting—real or not real? One was a lie and the other was truth. And yet, I could not select which was which. My head started to throb as the battle continued, but what started as a dull ache quickly amplified. It built, an ice pick striking my mind, chipping and hammering the pieces away, one by one.

I gripped my head, slumping to my knees. A shrill scream tore through my mind, loud enough to chase the tiniest shadow mouse out of its hole.

My eyes flared wide, realization dawning.

"Enough!" I screamed at Soren, who stood behind me.

That was all it took to restore clarity, to end the internal war, as Soren relinquished his control, the shadow mouse returning to its hole.

"Why?" I panted, chest heaving. My hands fisted the dead grass, the strands anchoring me in place, keeping me from doing anything foolish, like turning around and blasting Soren, which would ultimately risk Ezra's life—something I was not willing to do.

"After everything that happened with Fallon and Ryker, the Elders forbid breaking the unconscious mind barrier, which meant I was never able to explore this part of my Curse, to test it limits, as I did with you just now. I was curious how deep my Curse went. Now, I know," Soren stated, his voice as blank as I presumed his face to be right now.

"What happened to you," I gritted. It wasn't a question, but rather a statement. The Soren speaking now was not the one I once knew.

"I told you. I refuse to end up like my parents." He paused. "No one wants to admit it, but we have been stuck on the losing side for years. With each battle, our numbers dwindle. The Cursed will never defeat the Crown. And now I know it is easier to submit than to fight."

"Just because it is easier does not make it right," I stated, my words sinking in. I was giving in right now, just as I had for so many years. I had been complacent, hiding my Curse because of fear—fear of what might happen to me if my secret was found out. Even now, I was still being complacent because I feared what might happen to Ezra if I did not obey Soren's demands.

I was sick of fear.

Sick of the power it held over me.

And yet, as much as I wanted to fracture its hold, as much I wanted to break free—I could not risk Ezra's life.

The steady rumble of armor-clad footsteps was birthed from the trees. Soldiers emerged, fully armored, from metal helmet to polished boot. Some carried their swords, more than ready to strike, while others carried crimson banners decorated with the Crown's royal emblem—staining *my forest* in the color of blood, in the colors of the king.

"Don't fight *him*," Soren said, his words tainted with magic.

I heard the steps come from behind, the screech of improperly fitted armor. I tried to move, tried to do something, but my arms and legs were anchored to the ground, my body feeling as though it did not belong to me. The weight of something cold and hard snapped around my neck, dozens of little spikes drilling themselves in.

My eyes widened as I winced in pain—the iron collar.

My Curse dried up, evaporated.

Blood trickled down my throat, staining my flesh in a river of crimson.

"I am sorry for this, Sage," said a familiar voice that came from behind me.

"Arkyn?" I gritted through the pain swelling in my neck.

My question was answered with a sudden whoosh of air, before something collided with the back of my head, a sickening whack, a splintering of pain.

And I was rendered unconscious.

Chapter 51

I awakened, immediately aware of four things—the consistent throbbing in the back of my head, the piercing pain in my neck, the hard thing poking its slivers down the length of my back. As for the fourth? It was the abrasive rope that chewed into my flesh and strapped me in place.

My eyelids sprung open, reality setting in. My head dropped as I peered at the pile of kindling spread beneath my feet—dry kindling, the kind that burned within seconds.

I was caught in my own nightmare.

I'm strapped to a pyre.

Quiet, I hissed at my frantic mind. I needed to get my shit together and form a plan of some sort—if I had any hopes of making it out of this alive. I jerked my head up, looking at my surroundings for help. I was in the downtown square of Meristone—the typical spot for Cleansings. But unlike the other Cleansings, there was no crowd. There was only a platoon of soldiers stationed around the perimeter of the square, their backs to me.

I wiggled, testing my stubborn restraints. They were relentless in their hold against my mortal strength—I needed my Curse. Desperate, I reached, burrowing into that well, not caring which one came forth—water or fire, it did not matter.

Neither answered my call.

My power had been tamped down, like a roaring beast caught under a weighted net. That was when I remembered what was forced around my neck—the iron collar. It was to blame for my sudden loss of power.

I threw my head back, an irritated scream erupting from my throat.

Bootheels sounded, cutting me off.

"That's it," Arkyn said as he strolled towards me, his clothing perfectly tailored. That fucking pin he wore, the one stating that he was the king's advisor, stared at me. "A bit louder next time so that *he* can hear your call."

"Why are you doing this?" I gritted out, staring daggers at him. I was a fool. Of course, he could do this—he had thrown me into the damned Endless Mist after all.

"In time, you will see that this was necessary," Arkyn said, his hand resting on the pommel of his sword.

"In time? Judging where I am, I don't have much time left," I said, struggling against my bonds, desperate to loosen their choking, restrictive hold. My wiggling stopped as I noticed what I was wearing—the official attire of the soon-to-be-Cleansed: the cheap white garb. I slammed my head back, half frustrated, half wild with fear.

Metal clanked upon metal, the improperly fitted armor screeching uncomfortably as a soldier stiffly walked up to Arkyn. I forgot about the awful sound as my attention locked onto what he carried in his metal gauntlet—a torch bursting with flame. He handed the torch to Arkyn.

Horrified, I watched the exchange.

Watched as Arkyn turned his sights on me.

Efficiently, he closed the distance between us, the torch lapping hungrily at the midnight air, prophesying my fate.

"Arkyn, listen, you don't have to do this," I pleaded, eyes wide as I stared at the torch. Every fiber of my being wished it would burn out, praying to the gods that it would.

"Unfortunately, I do," he said, his gaze settled on me, determination in the straight line of his shoulders. He was a good soldier, after all, the king's dog. No different from the rest of the cowards that wore the king's colors.

I cursed them all.

Arkyn reached forward, preparing to light the kindling.

"Please. Just wait," I begged, grappling with my reality. "I need to ask something first."

"Alright." His voice was remarkably calm. For the time, he paused what he was doing. I would have breathed a sigh of relief if the constricting rope granted me the ability to do so.

"The woman at the cottage. Where is she?" I asked, desperate to know where Ezra had ended up. If this was where my story ended, if this was the place I was destined to die, then I wanted to do so knowing that Ezra was safe.

"I don't know. She was not there when we arrived," Arkyn said, glancing over his shoulder. My gaze followed, landing on Soren. He didn't make eye contact with me, instead staring at the ground, his good hand rubbing his arm as if he were trying to comfort himself. Arkyn continued, "Like the fire, she was an illusion that Soren conjured. He got the image right but did a poor job of copying her mannerisms. It's something he will have to work on."

That was why she seemed off, unresponsive. I felt relieved. "So then . . . she is safe."

"I would imagine so," Arkyn answered. His gaze met mine once more before he lowered the torch to the kindling. As he lit the fire that would claim my life, he held my gaze. "Again, I am sorry for this, but it will be over soon."

"Wait!" I screamed, fighting against the ropes, fighting for my life. I felt more animal than woman. I was desperate. Caged.

Horrified, I watched as the fire lapped up the kindling, watched as it slowly chewed its way closer to me, as if it were an old lover of mine. Inch by inch, the flames grew, the heat increasing, my frantic, erratic state growing the closer it got.

When the fire reached my feet, when I felt that scalding-hot flame bury itself into my flesh, I tipped my head back and screamed—the same hair-raising sound I had heard repeated in my nightmares, now brought to life.

I wasn't ready to die. Not here. Not like this.

I screamed again, but this time my mouth formed a single word.

A name—Von—I called for *him*.

My arm tingled, the vine cast in a dull, pulsing glow. The sounds of the horrific crackling fire were replaced by a high-pitched ringing. The market, the village, all of it began to dissolve like bits of ash scattered on the wind, and in its place, a darkness grew, stretching and yawning before me, until there was only one thing I could see . . .

Massive, endlessly black wings kissed with star dust.

They spanned before me, their expanse encumbering my vision. I could not look away, not even with the flames at my feet. My eyes struggled to understand what I was seeing. I wanted to reach out, to touch them, to feel, as if that would help me process—real or not real? Those sleek, mesmerizing wings tucked in, the movement so simple, yet so incredibly . . .

Breathtaking.

And even though the wings were not familiar, the feathers were—they were the same feathers that came to me every once in a while, came to me in my hour of need.

All this time.

It had been him.

My dark guardian angel. Von.

Obsidian eyes met mine—a distinguishable anguish written clearly in their setting. Horrified and tortured and angry—the anger so visceral, so raw, it would bring an army to its knees, cause mountains to crumble . . . bring tears to my eyes.

Seeing Von like this would strike fear in another's heart—but it hurt mine.

I tracked those devastating eyes, framed by his thick black lashes, watching them drop to my feet—blistered and bloody and marred. His expression turned murderous.

The flames winked out—the supply of air they needed to burn severed, choked off. The heat of the flame was gone, and not even the charred wood beneath dared to smolder. My feet were healed, instantly made whole. The nerve endings destroyed by the fire came back to life, but I felt no pain. His gaze shifted to my bonds, and the ropes that bound me to the pyre dissolved, their existence erased. Even the markings stamped into my flesh were gone.

His eyes returned to mine, that invisible tether between us strung too tight.

That magnetic pull, it was unbreakable, unyielding. Eternal.

And it demanded that we collide.

He cupped my face tenderly as he brought his forehead against mine. I could feel him breathing me in, as if I were his air—the very thing he needed to survive.

You found me, my heart sang.

As I promised you I would.

I heard his reply, the words unspoken, yet so incredibly clear.

Something in me shattered, like a glass wall coming down.

That was when I knew.

Von and I had always belonged to one another—well past the bounds of a single lifetime. This was a truth I could feel in my bones, seated so deeply in my soul.

"Blood King," Arkyn sneered behind us—his voice like a dagger, unceremoniously slashing into our private world.

Von pulled his gaze from me but not his arms. When he set his sights on Arkyn, I understood why he had been given that title. The look he wore—it *promised* death.

"As much as I know you would like to end my immortal life for what I have done, I will give you one good reason not to," Arkyn said. "The cloaking trick you used to change her appearance so that I wouldn't know who she was, so your sister wouldn't know who she was . . . I took it upon myself to learn how to use it. Allow me to show you what I've hidden beneath." Arkyn snapped his fingers, looking towards me.

I didn't need to look up. I could feel it—like a punch to my gut, a hand wrapped around my throat. Something treacherous hovered above. My hair raised, like it was being pulled towards it. Fighting the waves of nausea, I looked up.

My eyes flashed wide—there was no mistaking what it was.

The Crown of Thorns.

White vines, adorned in needle-like thorns, twisted together. They almost appeared to be moving, as if they were snakes slithering overtop of one another. It was both breathtakingly beautiful and devastatingly sinister-looking.

"I advise you to tread carefully, Blood King. My power is the only thing keeping the crown from moving to its rightful place. I am sure you can feel it, but the crown has been altered . . . It no longer bows to your will."

"You said the king had it," Von snarled, the wind picking up around us.

"At the time you asked, it *was* in his possession," Arkyn answered with a shrug. "*Now* I have it."

Tears pricked my eyes as I fought another wave of nausea, this one so powerful, it dropped me to my knees.

Von was there, his hands and eyes swarming over my face before he drew me tightly into his chest. He growled at Arkyn, his voice so powerful, it echoed throughout the village like a crack of thunder. "Get rid of it. Now."

"For the sake of my own life, I can't do that."

Another wave came crashing over me, and I pushed away from Von as I scrambled onto all fours, vomiting on the worn cobblestones.

"I'm surprised you want me to," Arkyn stated, his voice sounding genuinely confused. "After all, you made it for her. I thought you would like to see *your bride* wear her gift."

His bride?

I spat out a string of bile and blood, bracing myself as another wave barreled into me. I vomited again, my body quaking with the force of it. The nausea ebbed once more. Before it could flow back, I turned to Von, my bloodshot eyes meeting his.

"What is he talking about?" I asked, choking on my confusion, on my nausea, on a river of oncoming memories that had been dammed up for so long.

"Now's your chance to tell her the truth," Arkyn said.

I was at a loss for words and judging by the way Von looked, he was at a loss too.

Arkyn sighed. "Very well, I can tell her for you."

"No," Von said firmly. "I will tell her. She deserves that much."

But he didn't get the chance. One of my memories sprung free, and the weight of it dragged me under.

I sank—a pebble dropped in a lake. Down, down, down, I spiraled.

Chapter 52

"*Shield wall!*" *I yelled at the top of my heaving lungs as I plunged the base of my long shield into the muddy ground. I was tired, exhausted, but I would not stand down.*

My soldiers answered as they fell in beside me, their shields biting down, the sides braced against one another, locking them into place. Another row of shields fell into place above us, creating a second layer. And then a third, forming a protective barrier over our heads. One shield alone was weak, but together, like this, they were as tough as a dragon's scales.

We held tight, a single breath falling from my lips as I braced for impact.

This battle was one of many taking place across Gaia, our beloved Living Realm. I could not speak for the other battles, but this one had been raging on for days, and now we were in our final moments.

My power reserves were fully tapped out, as were the rest of my comrades'. After a brief break in the fighting, we were able to reform our ranks. And now, we were down to the nitty-

gritty of battle—fighting with swords, with our fists, with whatever we had left.

The enemy charged with the wind at their backs. We held our position, our feet firmly rooted to the ground as the army who fought for the Old Gods collided into mine.

I tugged my shield to the side, rendering a fist-sized gap as I shoved my sword through it—feeling the iron blade sink deeply into my enemy's flesh. I pulled on my sword, utilizing my shield as leverage to tug it free. I closed the gap, took a breath, and then forced my sword through again. Wash, rinse, repeat.

"Forward!" I bellowed.

A mighty grunt arose from my army of five thousand, as we gained—the ground shifting from mud to mud mixed with blood to the corpses of our enemy.

The wall was holding. I took a deep, necessary breath. We might win this one . . . if he didn't show up.

But my thoughts of victory were short-lived.

I heard the phantom horses, monstrous beasts that had no place thinking they were horses at all. The galloping of their hooves grew louder. Louder. Until it was all I could hear, like thunder sprung from the clouds—coming to strike us down.

They barreled into our front line, throwing the soldier beside me flat on his back, running him over as they stampeded through, creating gaps in our otherwise impenetrable wall.

Before I could order someone to close the line, a boy— too young to be fighting in this war—grabbed a shield and jumped in beside me. He looked up at me, young eyes full of *fear and determination. I didn't have time to question what he was doing here, didn't have time to get him out. Not when we were in battle.*

The best I could do for him—for all of them—was to fight.

More horses stampeded into our wall, throwing my brethren back, leaving us exposed, allowing the enemy to penetrate through—the boy suddenly gone.

"Hold the wa—" yelled my general, his voice cut off. I looked behind me just in time to watch him fall to the enemy's blade, his head swiped clean from his neck in one final, fatal swoop.

"No!" I screamed, my gloved hand outstretched.

A horse barreled into me, its sinister red eyes burning into my mind.

I flew backwards, my head smashing into something that was far harder than my helmet. A sharp sound pierced my hearing, followed by a constant ringing—the sounds of battle muffled out. I could feel the warmth of my blood seep down my neck as I stared up at the swirling, cloudy sky. Massive white doves circled above—reinforcements, they were coming— Aurelius was coming. We just needed to hold on. A little longer.

I closed my eyes, willing them to clear. I needed to find my sword, to fight. When I opened them, they were no better than before, and the thrumming in my ears refused to ease. I grunted as I rolled onto my side, every bone in my body singing out in pain, begging me to stop, to rest. But I was relentless, and somehow, someway, I rolled onto my stomach. Saliva mixed with blood gobbed from my mouth. I spat it out.

Black combat boots entered my vision before a hand, ringed with black and silver metal, tipped my chin upwards, forcing me to look up, to look at him, the tips of his canines glinting in the daylight. "Your blood sings for me, Little Goddess."

"Blood King," I grated between clenched teeth, my hand aching for the hilt of my sword.

He grabbed my arm roughly as he hauled me to my feet, his body so much larger than mine. I was reminded of his ancient, unparalleled power—he was the original predator, from his towering height to his muscular build to those dark, obsidian eyes. And then there was his hair—black as a starless night. He wore it up, weaved back and tied, the sides shaved—battle ready.

"I've been searching for you." His finger stroked my dirty cheek. I recoiled from his touch. My movement caused him to tip his head back and laugh, revealing those infamous canines.

The bastard was enjoying this.

Powerful, black wings unfurled behind him, the height of them double his own. Like his hair, they possessed that same black-blue color, and their shape, the outlay of the feathers, reminded me of a raven's.

He pulled me against him, his hard edges as unyielding as his arm around my waist. I struggled, tried to shove him away, but his strength was insurmountable. His wings slammed upwards, and when they came back down, they severed the air as if they were a blade made of steel. The motion carried us off the ground and up towards the clouds.

The battlegrounds winked out of sight, and my

bloodstained world turned an azure blue. Reaching the peak of a mountainside, on the lip of a drastic cliff, he landed.

I peered over the edge, my heart aching as I surveyed the bloody battlefield below. From this vantage point, it was like watching a bunch of scrambling, warring ants, their colonies sorted by the color of their armor—the relentless, obsidian army slaughtering the army of snow.

From this vantage point, I realized . . . we were going to lose.

I glared up at him with the veracity of the God of Hatred. "Is this why you brought me up here? To gloat over your victory? To make me watch as my loyal men die?"

"Partly, yes. Although, your judgment paints you as a hypocrite." The Blood King pinched my chin, forcing me to look at him. "Tell me, when you murdered my men, when you bathed in the spray of their blood—" He flashed a wicked smile. "—how did that feel? Did it feel good, darling? Did you take joy when you ended their lives and delivered them back to me? Because I think that rather strange. I would think that would counter the very point of your existence." Darkness swirled in his sinister eyes. "Goddess of Life."

I spat in his face. "You bastard. I did not take joy in it. I am the keeper of life. The guardian of the living. When you declared this war, you forced my hand. With every life you forced me to take, it has served but one purpose—to build my hatred for you."

He clicked his tongue, and I wondered if I'd struck a nerve. Tipping his head, he brought his face closer to mine. "What a pity. I thought you were rather fond of me. After all, goddess, you swamp my realm with so many, many gifts.

Continuously, you send them to me—second after second, day after day, year after year. So many beautiful, departed lives."

My heart ached.

He continued, his smile as wicked as the black fighting leathers he wore. "You see, I was beginning to think you were in love with me. I mean, you take such excellent care of my apple trees."

In love with him? He stole everything from me. I hated him.

"You bastard, you know nothing of love," I seethed, glaring at him, my angry, unyielding gaze firmly meeting his.

"And you do?" he challenged, his smooth, deep tone turning irritated. "You have never loved him, and you know that, but you are too stubborn to admit it."

I gritted my teeth. "You are wrong. I love him. Deeply. Just as I love my people and they love me. It is because of them, because of their prayers, that I am made strong." That was when I felt it, the smallest trickle of my power slowly seeping into my depleted reservoir. It wasn't much, but it would have to be enough. "Strong enough to finally end this."

There, standing on the peak of a cliff, with his wind in my hair, I conjured my water blade—the molecules packed so tightly, it was almost like ice, except it was not cold. With a battle cry, I drove the blade through his leathers, twisting it into his stomach. I jolted back, my hands moving in front of me, conjuring another ten. They floated behind me, sharp and ready to hit their target, to force him right off the edge of the cliff. But when I looked at his face, when I saw his expression, I . . .

I couldn't do it.

The expression he wore . . . it was made of pure shock.

His ringed fingers dropped to his stomach, sweeping over the ichor staining my azure blade. He studied the crimson liquid as if it were the most mesmerizing thing he had ever seen. His eyes flashed to my face, but there was no anger in his voice, only curiosity. "What sort of illusion is this?"

"It is no illusion."

"Tell the truth. You spoke with the Goddess of Fate and learned of the prophecy. You thought to use it against me." He stated it more for himself than me, as if he were trying to piece together an answer.

"I have spoken to the goddess, but I do not know of whatever prophecy it is that you speak of," I answered, confusion weighing my brow, but then when I looked at the bloody wound, understanding lifted it. My voice softened, just a hair. "So, the rumors are true then."

"Yes, they are true. I do not bleed," he stated as his hand wrapped around the hilt of my sword. He gritted his teeth as he pulled it out. He let out a small, disbelieving laugh, tangled with an exhaled breath, as he inspected the blade coated in his thick, red blood. His eyes shifted, meeting mine. "Until now."

Blood came pooling out of the wound.

He threw the blade onto the rocky, barren ground with such force that it shattered into hundreds of tiny pieces, like it was made of glass. He strode towards me and the wound grew, the flow of blood increasing the closer he got. But he did not stop. He didn't seem to care that he was bleeding out.

I held my ground. I didn't move. I didn't unleash my swords, but I didn't disarm them either.

When he was but a breath away, he captured my gaze. "I

am calling the war off."

"And why would you do that?" I replied, my tone saturated in heavy disbelief.

He reached forward, his fingers caressing a wisp of my hair that was beaded with mud and streaked with blood. "Since the dawn of time, I have spent millennia searching for an answer to the empty void inside. And now, at last, I have it. How fitting that she should be the very thing that can kill me."

He let my hair fall to the side, and then the God of Death was gone.

In his place, a black feather remained.

Chapter 53

"Sage?"

Slowly, I came to, my hearing kicking in faster than my sight.

My eyelids parted, revealing a bit of blinding light and a stark silhouette. I fought with them until finally, they fluttered open. We were still in the village square, the cold cobblestones biting into my skin, but something strong and sturdy and warm chased the cold away.

A beautiful dark-haired male held me close to him. The wind gently teased the tips of his black hair, pulling it to the side, as if it were coaxing him, begging him to take flight. Because that was something he could do—he could stretch out those incredible wings and fly away if he wanted to.

Or, he could stretch out those incredible wings, whisk me off the battlefield, and fly me to the top of a sharp, drastic cliff—where it was just the two of us.

My breath hitched, caught somewhere between my throat and my lungs as I stared into those eyes that held no light—that were made entirely of darkness itself, older than time.

He wasn't just Von anymore. He was the God of Death.

And I . . . I was no longer just Sage. I was the Goddess of Life.

I had a decision to make—to decide what this was between us.

Seconds ago, I had been in a place where we were on opposing sides. Where we were enemies. Where I felt that intense hatred for him in my heart. But that feeling warred with what I felt now as I looked at him.

I could trip on my path of personal growth and fall back into old habits, I could assume the worst based on that single memory, but deep in my heart, I knew that it was just the beginning, and that in between then and now, we had made a hundred more memories.

Those memories, the good ones, were the ones I wished to see. And even though I couldn't remember them right now, I was not without good memories from this lifetime, because the memories where Von walked in the sun with a basket thrown over his shoulder as we headed into town, those ones came back to me.

No, I would not fall back into old habits—I had grown since then. And with time, I would regain those memories. But now, all I wanted was to follow the feeling in my heart.

And so, maybe there was a time where he was the God of Death, but right now, here in his arms, he would always be . . .

"Von," I said breathlessly, my fingers reaching for his freshly shaven cheek, but something was wrong. When I touched him, my fingers left a smear of blood in their wake. I stared at them. Where did it come from?

"I remember. Some of it. You are the God of Death," I said, my torso lifting, my bottom still firmly planted on the cobblestone road. "And I . . ."

Von waited, his hand cradling my face, his free arm around my torso, supporting my weight.

"I'm the Goddess of Life." I finally said it, taking a deep, much-needed breath. And it was strange because it felt like my first real breath, like I had been wearing a constricting corset my entire life and I had finally ripped it off.

"I am pleased to hear you have regained some of your memory. It is relieving to know you finally remember who you are," stated a voice to my left.

I grimaced . . . Arkyn.

I turned and glared at him, noticing that my movement was no longer riddled with nausea. The incessant, aggravating power that made me throw up was gone. I blinked and looked up . . . The Crown of Thorns was gone too.

But the iron collar was still around my throat.

Why hadn't Von removed it? Why were we still here?

Better yet, why was Arkyn still standing?

I looked to Von. "I want to get out of here."

His eyes traced my face as if he were committing it to memory. He held me in his strong, steady arms, my fingers woven into the black fur that poked out from underneath his chest plate. He leaned forward and pressed his lips against my forehead. "You will do one thing for me, Little Goddess." His request came with the saddest smile, and seeing it there was like someone had taken a dagger to my soul. He whispered, "*You* will live this time."

419

I had never heard his voice like this before because normally, it tasted of bourbon, but right now, it was more like whiskey—the kind you drank when you needed to smother your sorrow.

I shook my head—I didn't understand.

My gaze fell, and I stumbled when I saw it.

A large wound gaped near his stomach. Beside him, a shattered sword of glass drowned in his ichor.

I jerked up from his arms, my hands shooting to his stomach. "Did I do this?" I cried out.

"You had some help," Arkyn replied faster than Von could. He thumbed over his shoulder, directing my gaze to Soren.

Soren sat not far from us, rocking back and forth, his arms wrapped around his knees with his head dropped into them. Although it was faint, I could hear it—he was crying.

My head swirled with a dozen thoughts, like how had Soren been able to harness my power when I wore the iron collar? But the semantics of it didn't matter. Right now, only one thought mattered.

"You have to get away from me, Von," I said, trembling like a leaf caught in a windstorm. I pulled away from him, my movement awkward and weak, like a baby deer learning how to walk. If I could get far enough away, maybe the bleeding might stop.

He let out a withheld breath, that mask cemented in place, hiding the pain I knew he felt. "I'm sorry, Little Goddess, but I cannot."

"What are you talking about" I said, stumbling backwards, desperate to put some distance between us. I bumped into something hard.

Hands wrapped around my shoulders, steadying me. Arkyn's voice filled my ears. "The Blood King could not stand to see you suffer, and so we made a deal." Arkyn let me go.

I twirled, facing him, watching as he rolled up the sleeve of his crimson jacket, revealing the tattoo on his forearm—a skull wearing the Crown of Thorns.

"What is the deal?" I cried out, turning to Von.

"That the Crown of Thorns is given back to the Spirit Realm so it can be properly destroyed, so that it cannot hurt you anymore," Von answered as he slowly rose to his feet. The ice sword was nearly gone, melting from his heat. Even like this, he was still the epitome of a strong, mighty warrior. Proud as ever, even as he was bleeding to death.

"And in return?" I asked, my body aching to go to him. But I held firm, anchored my feet to the ground.

"He asked for your life." Arkyn paused. "So in return, he is giving me his death—his immortal death."

My world teetered, spinning as if it were off its axis. An immortal death—that meant Von would be gone—forever. Erased from existence.

"No," I whispered, panic constricting my breath.

"Come, Little Goddess." Von conquered the distance between us, unfazed by his gaping wound. He pulled me into his arms, his embrace instantly righting my off-kilter world. Obsidian eyes locked with mine. I had never realized how spellbinding they were, how easy it was to get lost in them.

That was, until now, and now . . . I couldn't look away.

He tipped my chin up, his deep, decadent voice burrowing into my soul. "And let me kiss you one last time."

Chapter 54

The irony was not lost on me that I was the Goddess of Life and it was my kiss that stole the last and final breath from the God of Death.

Chapter 55

I lost track of the days. They came and they went, just like the waves outside, lapping against the mountainside before they returned to the sea. Not that I had bothered to venture out to see said waves. Each morning, when the housemaids came in, they opened the balcony doors, allowing the sounds of outside to flow in.

From this, I derived that the private chambers that I stayed in overlooked a body of water. I learned from the gossipy housemaids that I was in Clearwell Castle, and it most definitely had a rat infestation problem. Luckily, the rats did not bother me a whole lot. They were better than snakes. I shivered at the thought of the unnatural, limbless creatures. Involuntarily, I pictured the one Von had tattooed on his beautiful, muscular bicep.

Von.

I sighed, sinking lower into my numbness, and rolled on my side. The movement reminded me of the unyielding iron collar wrapped around my neck, reminding me that I was a prisoner. This one was different than the one they used in the forest. Where that one was large and clunky and fit with nails, this one was thin and small—designed for the neck of a woman or a child. More importantly, the inside was smooth— no rusty incisors.

Despite their differences, they were both made of iron, and they both served one purpose—to tamp down my power . . . and my spirit.

Not that my spirit could get any lower.

On more than one occasion, I wondered if my eyes had lost their ability to see color because everything around me was gray. From the stone floor to the stone walls to the stone ceiling. All of it, gray. Even the thick, heavy wolf pelt I lay under was gray.

I nuzzled farther into the embrace of the too-plush bed. Peering over top of the soft-as-silk furs, I traced the vine carved into the bedpost pillar for the sixteenth time today.

Okay, I lied.

Not everything was gray—the pillar could almost be classified as an off-white. Was it made from white rosewood? I could probably tell if I got up and touched it.

The problem with that? It required getting up.

The arched wood door, inlaid with iron, swung open, birthing the last person I wanted to see. The deep red color of his jacket was jarring.

I turned over and tugged the fur over my head. I preferred my world to stay gray.

He walked over to my bedside, plucked something from the untouched food tray, and then tossed it back down. Judging by the sound, it sounded like metal striking a plate. It was probably a spoon—the only utensil they allowed in my room.

"I see you are still refusing to eat. You cannot die of starvation, goddess, but you will grow weak," Arkyn said, the fur blanket doing little to muffle his voice.

I didn't respond. I found that to be a foolproof policy. Over the past however many days it had been, we had done this quick meet and greet dozens of times. He strode in, said something about me getting up or eating or taking a bath, I didn't respond, and then he left. Wash. Rinse. Repeat.

So I hunkered down like the little bed flea I had become and waited for his departure, something I would confirm by the sounds of the door shutting and his bootheels fading down the hallway.

"Aurelia, we need to talk," Arkyn said, his voice soft.

I glowered under the dark of my sheets. I wanted to hear fading bootheels, damn it.

"We need to figure out why the Endless Mist refuses you."

Ah yes, The Endless Mist.

After Von's death, Arkyn marched me into the forest, straight to the Endless Mist—not that I went willingly. I did, however, willingly touch it when he demanded I do so, hoping it would take me away from him. But nothing out of the ordinary happened. The ethereal voices asked who I was, to which I replied, "The Goddess of Life." The voices then responded that I would need to return another time—like I had arrived one minute before they closed up shop for the day.

Arkyn was less than pleased that our trip to the Endless Mist had not been successful, muttering under his breath that *we* would try again later. The *we* bit was laughable—like when a man cut off his partner who was talking about the birth of her child and made it seem like he was the one who pushed it out of his dingle.

Following our trip to the Endless Mist, Arkyn allowed me to stop at the cottage to gather a few of my things. I found the offer odd, like he was trying to make amends for everything that happened earlier that day. Another laughable notion. Under his watchful gaze, I gathered a few of my things, but he didn't see the paper I found when I went up to the loft. There, on my bed, was a letter from Ezra—her print always surprisingly legible for someone who was blind. The letter explained that she would be away for a while, that she was returning to a place that filled her with hope. I knew what that meant—she was going to the Cursed Lands. A small portion of me felt a bit of relief—she would be out of harm's way for the time being.

Arkyn let out an audible sigh. "Oh, for the Creator's sake, this is getting ridiculous. You are mourning the loss of a god who attempted to murder you on more than one occasion."

Great divine, he was persistent today.

I didn't reply. Just a bit longer and he would leave.

The bed sighed, heaving as he sat down on the end.

This was new. I didn't like it.

"Look, I get that all of this is a lot. You are very much in the infancy stage of your goddesshood right now, and you have hundreds of years of memories stowed away—ones you haven't even started to tap into. I can help you go through them, help you sort them and make sense of them. If you would just open up to me."

I pursed my lips, steadfast in my vow of silence. Fuck him and the king's carriage he rode in.

"There is something I need to get off my chest." He stopped, took a deep breath.

I rolled my eyes. Oh goody.

"That day in the bathhouse—you thought I was speaking of an old lover. I should have corrected you back then." I could hear his fingers comb through his hair. "I realized I needed to tell you the truth when you said it again at the Endless Mist. Although I have felt moments of attraction towards you, you and I were never lovers. We were always just friends. We could have that again."

Be friends . . . with him? His not-so-little red head was delirious. He claimed it was ridiculous that I was mourning the loss of a god who apparently tried to murder me. What a hypocrite. Not only did he throw me in the Endless Mist, he also threatened my life with the Crown of Thorns and a hot, hungry pyre.

Currently, in the game of attempted murder, he was leading the score.

"I know we have gone over this many times, but I feel like I need to say it again. I never planned to take your life that day, but I had to make it look real. The God of Death was the king of our enemies. He could have taken the Living Realm back from us at any given moment. I couldn't let that happen, so my hand was forced, and I had to use the thing that weakened him—unfortunately, that was you. And I apologize for that, but like I said, when your memory returns, when you remember *what* he is—that he is the villain—then you will trust in what I did and understand why it had to be done."

We had gone over this many times, from many different angles.

It always fell on my purposefully deafened ears.

"Aurelia, please, you have to talk to me eventually."

That was where he was wrong. I didn't. And I really wished he would stop calling me *that* name—it might have belonged to me in other lifetimes, but right now, all I wanted to be was just plain old Sage.

"Fine," he stated bluntly. The bed groaned, telling me he was on his feet, on his way out.

Mentally, I waved a flag in victory.

"I have business in the countryside. I will return in a week's time. When I do, I hope we will finally be able to talk about things. The king is looking forward to seeing you." His bootheels sounded against the flagstone floor as he strode over to the door. "Goodbye, Aurelia. And please . . . just eat something."

Then I heard the sounds I had hoped to hear—the door shutting, followed by fading steps.

Good riddance.

I poked my head out from underneath the furs, thankful for the fresh air. Maybe I *did* need a bath.

Forget it—that was too much work.

Besides, I had more important things to do. I returned my gaze to the vine pillar and started the task of tracing it for the seventeenth time that day.

Chapter 56

"We'd be alright if the wind were in our sails. We'd be alright if the wind were in our sails. And we'll all hang on behind." The elderly housemaid sang the unfamiliar sea shanty as she bumbled around my room. She dusted the tall dresser, wiggling her hips from side to side. Despite her age, she was surprisingly agile.

I had never seen this housemaid before.

I didn't know if it was her age or the quirky way she conducted herself, but there was something about her that reminded me of Ezra. Perhaps it was the rat's nest of gray hair piled on top of her head. I wondered if that was where the castle's infestation problem had originated.

I watched her as she worked, imagining I was back at home at the cottage, watching Ezra make one of her tonics.

She put her duster down and walked over beside the bed, her arthritic fingers plucking the untouched tray from the night table.

She continued to sing as she took the tray over to her

wooden cart. "Oh, another shot of whiskey wouldn't do us any harm. Another shot of whiskey wouldn't do us any harm. Another shot of bourbon wouldn't do us any harm. And we'll all hang on behind."

I jerked up, my eyes flaring wide. "What did you just say?"

The right side of her lips twitched upwards, her gaze meeting mine as she sang the line in a questioning way. "Another shot of whiskey wouldn't do us any harm?"

"Yes, and then you said bourbon," I stated firmly.

"I don't think I did, my dear," she exclaimed in an exaggerated tone, shaking her head. "I don't even know what that word means." She continued over to the fire, throwing a few more logs in, her singing picking back up again.

I eyed her suspiciously.

After the fire was stoked, she went to the balcony doors, her hands grabbing hold of the handles as she carelessly tossed them open in time with the last note of her song, as if it were some big, grand ending. She stood there, peering out as if she were taking in her clapping audience, waiting for them to demand an encore.

As the cool night air blew through the open doors, I was reminded that we were on the cusp of winter. I nestled farther beneath my furs, wondering if she was attempting to freeze me to death—knowing that she worked for Arkyn, that sounded about right. Murder attempt number three: death by elderly housemaid.

Caught in the wind, the dusty rose curtains tugged to the sides of the balcony doors were suddenly brought to life. They reminded me of two cloth hands waving in an intricate, billowing dance, as if they were casting a spell.

"Can you close them? It's quite cold outside tonight and a bit too windy to have the doors open," I stated in my official *I'm not asking* tone.

She turned to me, oblivious. "It's a bit windy, yes—but us retired, sea-faring folk enjoy nights like this. They remind me of my younger days. Besides, can't you feel it?"

My brow shot up. "Feel what?"

"The Goddess of Fate is at work." She offered me a wink, her eyes a stormy gray-blue. She placed her hands on her hips and looked around with a satisfied "I just cleaned that" huff, and then waddled over to her cart, picking up the same sea shanty she had just sung from the top as she rolled the cart towards the door. "We'd be alright if the wind were in our sails. We'd be alright if the wind were in our sails." And just before the door closed, I heard her sing, "And we'll all hang on behind."

I sighed, flopped back onto the bed, and stared at the balcony doors. I realized that because I was an immortal, I *wouldn't* freeze to death. But that didn't mean I wouldn't freeze. I imagined myself as a Sage-sized ice cube. Huffing, I decided I would have to get up and close the doors . . . eventually.

My gaze shifted, returning to the vine carvings.

In a blur of gray and black, something shot through the balcony doors with the speed of a cannon ball. I jerked upright, eyes wide, wondering if we were under attack. Whatever it was collided against the wall, wings flapping hysterically as a poof of feathers blotted the air.

Wings? Feathers?

I peered over the side of the bed, looking at the large raven as it flapped on the ground—a spray of its feathers haloed around it.

Was it hurt?

It reminded me of the one I had seen on the day of Kaleb's burial, the same one that had tried to attack me when I thought the forest was on fire.

When it stopped flapping, I wondered if it was dead.

But then its head lifted and it jumped onto its feet. It cocked its head to the side as it peered up, its small, black eye shifting, focusing . . . on me.

Its chest heaved up and down, beating wildly. For a moment, we just stared at one another. A sensation began to well in my stomach, something I could only describe as a gut feeling—a feeling that this raven and I . . . that we knew each other. And I knew it sounded insane, but lately, what in my world was logical?

A flash of blinding light burst from the raven and I was forced to cover my eyes with my hands.

I heard its wings flapping.

Heard when the flapping stopped.

The brilliant light flashed once more with such power, such intensity, that even with my gaze blocked behind my hands, it was like a star was being born.

The hair on the back of my neck stood straight up, not because I was afraid—because there was an overwhelming feeling growing in my wildly beating heart.

Tears began to race down my cheeks, and then warm, soft hands gently touched my wrists, gently pulled them to the side.

"Sage," said a soft, familiar voice—a voice I'd never expected to hear again.

Slowly, I opened my eyes.

Bright blue eyes met mine, as bright as the summer sky. I whimpered. "Kaleb?"

Chapter 57

"In the flesh!" He beamed.

I took one good, hard look at him before throwing myself into him, tossing my arms around his neck and nearly knocking him back onto the floor. His sturdy arms folded around me. Our bodies trembled like two little leaves—the last ones standing just before the kiss of winter knocked us free.

How long we stayed like that, just hugging each other, I didn't know. Time simply slowed. And when we were ready, slowly, we pulled back at the same time. Our hands remained locked on each other's shoulders, both of us unwilling to let go.

He reached up, drying my tears. "Quit your crying, silly." His hand not so sneakily dabbed away his own.

"I can't," I said, staring at him. I didn't dare to blink, worried that a single blink might cause him to disappear. I shook my head. "How are you here?"

Kaleb swallowed. "Are you sure you want to have this

conversation right now?"

"I do," I answered without hesitation, smiling and shaking my head in disbelief.

He nodded and took a deep breath. "After I died, I awoke in the Spirit Realm. A woman was there, at my bedside. She cared for me as I transitioned. It was . . ." He paused, shaking his blonde head. ". . . not a fun process. I felt sick all the time. I couldn't keep anything down. She said it was because I had left loved ones in the Living Realm, that I was tethered to them and felt like I still needed to be around for them. She wasn't wrong. From the day the soldiers took me, all I could think about was getting back to you and Ezra." He stopped, squeezing my hand.

I understood that need deeply. It was the primary driving factor in everything I had done over the past weeks. All I wanted was our family to be restored. Of course, Kaleb yearned for the same thing. Even in death, his love remained intact—that bond stuck.

"One day, a man strode into my room, a bottle of something he called bourbon in his hand." His eyes flashed to mine. "He poured me a glass . . . said I was going to need it. And that's when he told me everything. That he was the God of Death, my new employer. And that you were the Goddess of Life." Kaleb smirked. "And you know, I wasn't incredibly surprised when he told me who you really were. You've always had a knack for bringing strays home." He chuckled.

Gods, how I had missed *that* sound—gods, how I had missed him.

And yet, this moment was bittersweet because behind-the-scenes, Von had been meeting with Kaleb, offering him friendship and a connection to me. I knew why he did it—he did it for me, and the knowledge of that made it feel that much harder to breathe now that he was gone.

"Whenever you went to the Cleansings, you'd get this expression on your face. It's one thing to watch someone die, but I could just tell, it hit you different. Where people would go home and forget the Cleansing in a few days, you carried them around with you—like a weight on your shoulders. Like each death was a burden you had to carry." Kaleb paused, his voice soft. "I think that's why I felt like I needed to look after you. Because, maybe, deep down, I sensed what you were." He moved from his kneeling position and sat down on the bed beside me, his shoulder touching mine. "Regardless of who you are, one thing will never change—you will always be my little sister."

His words were the finishing nail to my already bleeding heart.

I shoved him playfully to the side before I wiped away a few more tears. "Get out of here with that."

He laughed, nudging his shoulder against mine.

I chuckled softly, although the smile did not meet my eyes. Even though I wanted to revel in this moment, to feel the joy of being reunited with Kaleb, I could not, at least, not completely. I was broken inside, and it was all because of Von. He'd done as he said—he'd staked his claim on my flesh and left his brand upon my soul, and without him . . . well, nothing would ever feel right again.

Kaleb cleared his throat. "I'm a reaper now."

A what now?

"A reaper?" I repeated, tasting the word on my tongue.

"As in carries a scythe, wears a black robe, and collects souls, reaper? Like the one from those books we used to read?"

Kaleb snorted. "Not quite. Those books said there was only one reaper, but in fact, there are hundreds of us. Also, I don't carry a scythe. And I don't wear a black robe. But I do collect souls."

Putting two and two together, I asked, "Is that what the marbles are?"

"Sage, that's terrible. Those aren't marbles—those are people's freshly departed souls." Kaleb side-eyed me, reminding me he had been a bird not so long ago. Reminding me of the not-so-great landing he'd performed—his feathers were still scattered on the floor. Yet another reminder of Von. I pushed away the thought, focusing on Kaleb.

"I don't know how I would feel about you transporting my soul." I chuckled softly, taking a long overdue jab at him. "I saw how you flew in here." I clicked my tongue, shaking my head. "Feathers all over the place."

"I know," Kaleb drawled before he burst out laughing. "I'm terrible at it!"

I couldn't help but join in, the image of the cannon-ball bird crashing into the wall replaying in my mind. "Oh, I'm sure I'd do a much better job than you."

"I'm holding you to that." He grinned.

"Deal," I said, offering him the best smile I could muster.

A moment of silence passed between us.

"What did you think of my shift?"

"Your shift?"

He nodded, finger pointing to the floor, where he'd shifted from a bird to a man. *Oh!*

"It was . . ." I tapped my chin while I searched for an appropriate word. "Bright."

"I'm working on that. Early shifts are usually bright—it happens to all fledglings, or so I've been told." He slapped his thigh. "I'm just happy I shifted with clothes this time. You have no idea how many times I've shifted and found out I'm buck naked." He sighed. "Fal has been working with me on shifting, although. . ." He grinned mischievously. "She told me she didn't mind the view."

"I'm so happy you think I'm one of your male friends. Thanks for sharing that last bit of information," I said sarcastically.

"You're welcome," he teased, performing a single salute of a nod.

I rolled my eyes with extra emphasis, just so he could see. My brow darted up. "Who is Fal?"

"She is a reaper as well. She transported my soul to the Spirit Realm and helped me transition."

I nodded. "I met her briefly. When she took your little *marble* soul."

He squinted at my usage of the word. I grinned.

"Without her, I don't think I could have made it through the transition," he said, his tone almost . . . dreamy. I felt the sudden urge to flick him between the eyes, to knock him out of his spellbound state.

My mouth dropped slightly.

"You like her!"

"It's more than that, Sage." His hands shifted uncomfortably in his lap.

I gripped the sides of my face, feigning shock. "Could it

be? Could the so-called Meristone heartthrob be falling in love?"

He didn't respond—his answer telling me all that I needed to know.

"So when's the wedding?"

He grinned. "Mine or *yours*?"

I looked down, my eyes growing watery. It was impossible to fight the feeling bubbling up in me—the tremendous loss I felt. "So . . . you don't know then."

"Know what?" Kaleb asked, a blond brow lowering.

"Von—the God of Death is—" I choked on the bitter words, gagging on them. They were stuck in my throat, clogging it up, taking my ability to breathe away. I had not been able to put *those* words together. I feared that once I did, that once I spoke them aloud, there would be no coming back. It would be the final thread that led to my unraveling, so for now, I couldn't say them. All I could do was look to Kaleb and let the tears sliding down my cheeks, born from the remnants of my shattered heart, convey what my tongue could not.

The love of my immortal life was gone.

That's when it hit me—I loved Von—*I loved him*.

"No, Sage." Kaleb moved, kneeling in front of me. He took my hands in his, gently cradling them as he spoke the very words I had never expected to hear. "Von is alive."

. . . That sneaky bastard.

Acknowledgements

Let me just start off by saying that it takes a village, because really and truly it does. *Between Life and Death* would not be what it is today without the help of *so many* amazing people. I'm just going to dive right in and probably bawl my eyes out as I write this, but I've got my tissues ready so here we go. I cannot express enough gratitude and love to:

To my beta readers, thank you so much for all of the hours you put in reading my story and working with me to take it to the next level. Your input was invaluable, and it truly shaped this story for the better. I appreciate you all so much! Super shout out to: Michelle, Helyn and Jessica—my all stars.

To my ARC readers, when I put the call out, YOU GUYS answered! I'm so thankful for *all of you*! Thank you for applying, for supporting and reading *Between Life and Death*. Thank you for the reviews—to a small fry like me, they make a world of difference.

To my editor, Jessica McKelden, my MVP. As soon as we started talking, I knew I needed you on my team! You were so wonderful to work with and you brought the experience, patience, and friendship that I truly needed. Thank you so much for all the hard work you put into *Between Life and Death* and for *truly* taking it to the next level! Oh, and Von wants me to tell you: "Hey, *Kitten*."

To my proofreader, Norma Gambini. Norma! I hoped we would have the chance to work together, and here we are— just a dream come true. Thank you for sneaking me into your incredibly busy schedule and playing such a vital role in polishing *Between Life and Death* and making it truly shine.

To Amy Kessler at Imagine Ink Designs, it was such a delight to work with you! Thank you for answering my bajillion e-mails, for coming through on my very specific requests, and getting my debut novel ready to be shown to the world. I can't wait to work with you again in the future.

To Keylin Rivers at Fantasy Cover Design, my fairy godmother! When you sent me the cover for *Between Life and Death* I had to sit down because it was just that good. You did such a phenomenal job with it. You went above and beyond my expectations and I cannot wait to work with you on book two! You were heaven sent. Truly.

To Lucas Fortier, thank you so much for the time you put into working with me on the chapter art! You are so talented, Lu, and it was so dang cool working with you on this project. I can't wait to see where your love for art takes you.

To the Pin to my Pak, the yellow power ranger to my pink power ranger, the Yuki to my Ruka, the Jupiter to my Sailor Moon, the Anna to my Elsa, the Sylmeria to my Ace, the Crix to my Az, the Pook to my Zu, to my bestie who has been with me since our womb days, Helyn, I could never articulate how much your support means to me or how much

I appreciate those three-hour phone calls going over this story. Thank you for being you and cheering me on. In so many ways, this book is for you.

To my mama and papa, who raised me to be wild and free—a child who would rather bathe in the muddy water outside and howl at the moon until all hours of the night. You guys taught me that no goal was ever out of reach, and because of that, this book exists. Thank you for letting me grow up into the person I was meant to be. Mom, thank you for being my biggest cheerleader and for encouraging me to write this story the way my heart wanted to. And dad, thank you for teaching me that building something is as simple as putting Lego pieces together—you simply just have to do it.

To my brothers and sisters, in-laws and out-laws, nieces and nephews, I'd like to write a paragraph for each one of you, but I don't want to find myself in Guinness World Records for the longest acknowledgment, so, thank you, thank you, thank you. Bits and pieces of my memories with you all have gone into the creation of this story, and even into some of the characters. This story wouldn't be what it is without each and every one of you.

To my loved ones who are no longer here. I felt your guidance and cheers all the way through, especially in those quiet moments when I was alone doubting myself.

To my husband, who had to live with someone who was physically in the room but mentally in Edenvale. Tan, Woof, Woofka, Munch, Jeff, Donnie, your patience, understanding and genuine heart of gold got me through more than you will ever know. Thank you for showing me what a good man is, what it is to have unconditional love and thank you for coming along this crazy, amazing journey with me. I love you and I love our life together. Thank you for being the love of my mortal life.

And lastly, but most importantly, to my readers and my TikTok family. Without you guys, this dream of mine couldn't live on. There are some of you that jumped on board while I was writing this novel, and you became my ride-or-die. Your love is what got me through the tough times of being a writer, and without your support, I don't know if I ever would have finished this novel. And for those of you who are just joining in, thank you for taking a chance on me.

Thank you *all* for giving me the opportunity to tell Sage and Von's story.

<3 Jaclyn

About the Author

Jaclyn Kot is a prairie girl, an avid reader, occasional Netflix binger and a total foodie. She is a proud mama of many chickens, two fabulous kitties and a good doggo. She lives on a farm in Saskatchewan, Canada with her husband.

She writes high fantasy fiction and likes her fantasy served with plot twists, a side of spice and morally grey males with a palate for strong-willed females.

It is her hope that readers will fall in love with Sage and Von's story just as much as she has.

Looking for the latest information on the Between Life and Death Series or wanting to connect with Jaclyn? You can here:

www.instagram.com/jaclyn.kot/

www.tiktok.com/@jaclyn.kot

www.jaclynkotbooks.com